The Gathering

of the seven stars

by Andrew James Graham

"Life is like a game of chess

you win some,

you lose some.

Always in coexistence.

Chess is like a journey through life

pressing forward,

moving backward,

a game of life and death.

An engrossed player and an all knowing onlooker."

CHAPTER ONE

After all the planning and effort, his time had finally come.

Twenty minutes had passed since the glare from another car's headlights had lit up his rear view mirror.

As the moon slipped in and out from a cloud the trees were dark and losing their shape as his headlights scored soft channels through the mist.

He sped along through mile after mile of bleak open road, he knew he didn't have much time. His captive would soon begin to wake up, even though he'd given him a good needle full.

It needed to be done, the sooner the better. He must get to the river bank and finish what he'd started.

He'd gone through this process in his head many times during the past few days. He knew he had one chance.

He could feel sweat slithering down his face and wiped it away with the back of his hand. As he opened his car window, the cool damp autumn breeze refreshed him.

He was about to do something terrible, something so bad he wondered if he was going mad, but then again, he had no choice, get a fucking grip, it wasn't the first time and wouldn't be the last.

In darkness close by the river he drove past disused factory buildings, pebble dashed garages with corrugated iron doors, metal shipping containers and deserted warehouses.

The shadows pressed in quietly around him, he was now way out of the sight and sound of the busy City Centre.

With Industrial landscapes disappearing in the mist, the trees, bushes and shrubs appeared to step forward when the edge of his car headlight beams touched them as he drove down under bridges and finally around onto a grass verge.

When he was sure that nobody was in sight he opened the door and got out, the cold air was so refreshing after the stuffiness of his car. He double checked, looking around to see who might be watching. He was OK, he hadn't been followed.

Gravel crunched underfoot as he moved around to the rear of his vehicle. He opened the boot, was he still conscious? Poking him hard in the leg he felt him flinch, heard him moan, just a slight mumble, at least he was still alive, just, but not for much longer.

He groaned as he was dragged out, checking that his hands and feet were still firmly tethered, he laboured as he pulled him towards the water's edge. The river looked dark, water lapped gently close by as he laid him down on the grass damp with dew and waited for his eyes to open for one final time.

His voice was merciless and chilling as he looked gravely into his eyes. "Now let's see if Pork floats." The smile began to form on his face. Dank earth accumulated under his fingernails as he pulled him through the marshy mud, and dropped him over the edge of the bank into the foreboding bone-chilling water. He watched, he waited, and he smiled, got back into his car and drove off.

After an abnormal humid morning on Tyneside, rain was now bouncing off the window panes. Detective Sergeant Oscar Smiles sat alone at a table in the Chinese restaurant. Waiting for his dinner guest to arrive, he took another incurious sip from his half empty glass of merlot un-hunched his shoulders and let out a deep sigh as he checked his watch. He was late as usual. His boss was always late.

This was supposed to be a catch up session. He was due back at work in the next few days; he knew that his boss would want to end the evening with his usual excessive drinking session, if he hadn't already started without him, that is.

Reaching into his waistcoat pocket he checked his mobile phone. No messages or missed calls. *There's a surprise. That was so typical of the man.*

He rubbed his eyes and willed himself to keep them open. It had been a long and difficult couple of weeks. He considered ringing, see where he was, was he going to be much longer?. Shaking his head he shoved the phone back into his pocket. His weary eyes wandered to the large oriental clock on the back wall. *Ten more minutes then I am ordering.*

He wiped the condensation from the window as the sight and sound of a transient ambulance blared passed echoing through the empty restaurant and bringing a waiter's face to a part glass kitchen door. As the room briefly filled with the flicker of the flashing blue lights, his thoughts meandered to his Grandfather, their own race to the Hospital and the previous two weeks of concern and uncertainty.

Staring down at the table he again straightened the menu and organised cutlery so that it was all symmetrical. Knife's, forks, spoons and chopsticks each the exact distance from the edge as the other.

As the moments went by vacant tables reduced, workers began to think about their evening's entertainment and forget about their drab habitual nine to five jobs.

His stomach rumbled in a low continuous resonance. He hadn't eaten since breakfast. He was engulfed by a delicious combination of Red fried pork wontons and crispy noodles, an aroma that aroused his taste-buds, drifting in from the kitchen.

He'd already decided what he was going to have, whether McGovern chose to show his ugly bearded face or not. The All you can eat buffet menu for only £13.50. It was well worth it. Plate after plate. A great variety of items. Help yourself to pan fried pacific saury, Yangzhou beer fish, duck wings with coriander, oil braised King prawns, fried Pork, chicken with sweet and sour sauce, winter melon and spare rib soup, with Pavlova and ice cream or more for desert, and lots more.

Under previous owners on entering there used to be an overwhelming smell of damp, so musty it caught your breath. Faded gold and red Lion patterned wallpaper had not been replaced for decades and lighting dim and dingy from forty watt light bulbs.

A single unisex toilet, used to always be in a horrendous condition, even if you had been first person to go in. There was never any justification for its predicament and couldn't be blamed on a previous customer using it earlier.

This newly refurbished establishment had been open for quite some time, with proprietors came lots of improvements.

The new owners were always a bit of a mystery. They were new to the Dragon Gate and had appeared to have put a lot of money into the business, which was now thriving, the best, and by far most popular Chinese restaurant in the City.

Oscar gave his watch yet another monotonous stare, McGovern was now almost half an hour late. Draining the remainder of his drink he lethargically headed for the toilet.

As he laboured to push open the heavy toilet door he was alerted straight away to the blood stains on the floor, they looked quite fresh; his eyes following them to an empty cubicle. He could see muddy footprints on a toilet seat. He moved to the next cubicle, it was clean.

He exhaled loudly as he emptied his bladder; a relieving spurt first splashed then trickled into the still water at the bottom of the shining ceramic toilet, sound echoed around the empty room. A noise disturbed only by raised voices coming from the kitchen.

He washed his hands as he listened, moving closer to the door. His ears throbbed straining to hear but couldn't understand the voices. Chinese. Talking soon became shouting. They were becoming louder, angrier and more animated.

CHAPTER TWO

Detective Inspector Jim McGovern needed another complaint from the public like a hole in the head.

The continued absence of a DCI, empty desks and bulging in trays of trivial cases pending told their own story. Not since Don Waterman's gangland assassination had he felt there had been a difficult case worthy enough for him and his team.

Chief Superintendent Crammond *had* promised to press for more manpower, 'should the need arise', but all his superiors seemed to be interested in was harassing him about targets and budgets. So far the only pressure put on had been heaped on *his* broad and tired shoulders.

DCI Alan Hart had been on long term sick for six months, rumours were he wasn't coming back and would be taking early retirement. There seemed to be no hurry in replacing him either. God forbid if a big case came in. McGovern was doing his best, acting up. He knew he would never be a DCI, and wouldn't want to be.

Paperwork that he'd been putting off for weeks could wait no longer. He sat and stared at the ever growing mound of files on the desks. He'd tried to get this incident report filled out three times, each time trying in vain not to incriminate himself further.

It was one of those days when it was difficult to just try and spell his own name.

Scrunched up forms crumpled into balls filled his wastepaper basket. He couldn't recall how long it had been since he'd had a good night's sleep. This wasn't real police work; this work was for pen pushers not detectives.

Checking his watch he knew he was late for his meeting with Oscar. But he couldn't really afford to put this report off no longer.

The complaint involved a well known troublesome Tyneside family who were threatening to make an official complaint and take legal action. There was a chance, of course, no accusation would be forthcoming, but he wasn't going to kid himself, or hold his breath. McGovern had always thought it strange that these types of people who despised the Police so much, always seem to be queuing at the station door like shoppers on black Friday to report even the slightest of misdemeanour from a police officer. When real crimes committed against them and their family would be overlooked, for fear as being labelled as grasses.

He'd survived plenty of accusations in the past, disciplinary hearings, grievances and written warnings, Christ, the DPS had a substantial enough file with his name on it. They wouldn't need much of an excuse, to get shot of him once and for all, to finally put the dinosaur into extinction. McGovern physically assaulting a thirteen year old boy would be enough for them to masturbate over; literally, *they were probably all nonces anyway.*

It wasn't even a punch, more like a clip around the ear, but the little bastard *had* deserved it. It was only that he had cried like a two year old child and thrown himself to the floor with all the cunning, and deviousness of a Premier league footballer that made the incident appear a lot worse than it was. He was just a mouthy, uneducated little fucker who, although so young, had been done for practically every petty crime you could think of. Unfortunately just hours before the alleged incident McGovern had been to McCaffrey's bar and overindulged. He had also gone to the property alone, with no back up or anyone to accept, reluctantly the little white lie that may just save his skin, again.

The parents were to blame. Had they been better in disciplining said little bastard when he was younger this teenage tearaway, this thirteen year old crime wave, would have been given at least half a chance of becoming something resembling a model citizen. Not that the kids parents, and especially his absent father had been the ideal role model.

The whole episode had made McGovern think about the kind of role model he'd been to his own two daughters, not a particularly good one either, but at least they had turned out OK, no thanks to him. They certainly hadn't been one of those families that you saw in TV ads.

Lifting his portly frame out of the chair and brushing crumbs from his suit, his varicose veins were still giving him gyp. His knees cracked as he made his way towards the office door. Cleaners were already in the building but for a couple of young career hungry officers the place was almost deserted. He patted his pockets, found and lit a cigarette.

Better hurry myself up and see how Oscar's shaping up, that's if he's still there.

Oscar could hear that a heated conversation was rapidly turning into a fully blown argument. As he tiptoed along the short corridor, his fingers groped over the stubbly pattern of the wallpaper. He headed towards the kitchen door, it was open. He peeked his head around it.

A young Chinese man, holding a meat cleaver with a bloody nose was now shouting, at two other men. His fists clenched his face purple with rage. The two other men were both also Chinese, one a chef, the other a large man in a smart suit.

He observed for a few seconds; his heart began to beat faster, he needed to feel in control of the situation as much as he could. Screams of rage scraped the young man's throat raw, his cheeks burned with anger as he raised the meat cleaver. There was a heavy thud as the chef was hit in the head with it? The chef crumpled to the floor.

Oscar knew he had to act quickly. He didn't have long to gather his thoughts, as fragile as China, his body blazed with fear. He shouted "Police Officer, calm down," his breathing in time with his thumping heart.

The young man with the meat cleaver stopped and stared directly into Oscars eyes. He was shaking and mumbling. His voice quivering with anger.

The man in the suit watched carefully from a safe distance. The chef was sitting on the floor, his face was ashen, and his breathing came in ragged gasps, shifting about, restless his mouth wide open with shock, holding his head, trying in vain to stop the bleeding.

Oscar tried to remain calm, although he was as frightened as he had ever been before; the voices in his head were telling him to run. Another problem, he didn't even know if any of the men spoke English. Oscar's heart was thundering in his chest, so loud he wondered if anyone else could hear it.

"Why don't you put that down and we can sort this out." His heart was in his mouth now, pumping fiercely as he swallowed with awkwardness.

It all happened in a flash. The large man in the suit lunged at the youngster who swung the meat cleaver catching him on the forearm, cutting deep through the flesh.

The large man yelled out in pain and took a step back holding his injured arm. Oscar dived across at full stretch pushing himself and the young man to the floor.

The meat cleaver was swung; Oscar winced at the metal on metal sound as sparks flew when the sharp metal blade scraped the leg of the kitchen bench inches from Oscar's face. Turning fast Oscar grabbed him by both arms and threw him forward, cracking his head against the wall. He brought his knee up fast into his stomach and hit his head against the wall a second time, but the young man was full of hate, fear and fury.

They rolled over, and over and in a split second his young assailant had the momentum and Oscar by the throat, sitting on top of him, his face red with rage, the vein in his temple throbbing, staring down at Oscar his eyes burned with rage.

As he raised the meat cleaver, Oscar noticed the Chinese symbols tattooed on the lad's neck. Oscar closed his eyes, was this the last thing he was ever going to see?, He didn't want his eyes to open and leave this darkness. He froze, not daring to even breath, every last nerve tingling. He expected any second to feel the meat cleaver cutting through his skin into his body, the crunch of bone, the blood.

He didn't even see, or expect the saving boot to the throat which sent his young assailant rolling over into the corner, falling backward choking as he sprawled on the floor, a kick with an abundant amount of force. That fucker was not getting up in a hurry. He did however hear the all too familiar dulcet Glaswegian tones.

"I leave you alone for half an hour and see what trouble you get into." Oscar had never been happier to see DI Jim McGovern.

Oscar lifted himself up off the floor and rubbed his throat, as he stared despairingly at his scuffed new shoes "Better late than never, I suppose, sir"!

He'd only been out of prison for six months, but now, free from licence and probation involvement, Mick Western, contemplated his next business venture.

He drunkenly staggered down past McCaffrey's Irish bar, through the indiscriminate rain, trying, in vain, to avoid the pools of sullied water that had gathered in the cobble stones and potholes of the old Tyneside Street.

He was headed towards the Dragon Gate area in ChinaTown of Newcastle upon Tyne.

The fatal shooting of Tyneside hard man, Don Waterman, outside a City nightclub had meant there was a gap in the market, a vacancy he wanted to fill. He revelled in his growing notoriety. Western had a business to build and he saw this as his opportunity.

Dragon Gate was a district of ChinaTown, located to the west of the city on the edge of the shopping and commercial centre. It lay within the historic heart of Newcastle's Grainger Town; Buildings were a mixture of contemporary and antiquated. The central street of the ChinaTown area, Stowell Street was narrow, with its tall buildings and its gold, green and red street lamps in the form of ancient Chinese lanterns hanging from the lamp posts.

Steam and smoke from the Chinese market, cafes and restaurants engulfed his senses with an alluring aroma as he zig zagged through the busy crowds and along past the glossed red and gold painted litter bins.

At the far end of China Town, on St Andrew's Street he could see, through the misty rain, the famous colourful Chinese arch, facing St James' Park, home of Newcastle United Football Club.

The murder of Waterman, almost two years previous, was still fresh in people's minds and had given an opportunity to every wannabe gangster or hard man, to come from out of the shadows and claim a piece of the action. A power struggle was expected.

Don Waterman was a former doorman, cage fighter and martial arts champion who had coordinated the security of a chain of Newcastle nightclubs and bars keeping a tight control on the locals. He had respect from the Tyneside underworld and ensured that the places he controlled remained free from extortion, drug dealing and racketeering.

Mick Western was never his biggest fan, and the one time friends had a mutual dislike of each other. In fact he hated Waterman with a vengeance. Even though he was in prison at the time of the shooting and because of his many underworld contacts he was still interviewed at the time but as ever the underworld closed ranks and no-one spoke about the murder, especially to the police.

Mick Western's three years of incarceration had stripped the weight off him. His time had been put to good use, making him stronger and preparing for life back on the outside prison, training in the gym. Sit ups, push ups, stretches and curls. Forty five years old with a shaved head, six feet in height and very stocky in build, This one time nightclub doorman had been jailed for his part in a football riot between Newcastle and Chelsea fans.

Call him unlucky if you like but his previous record for assault and with him being well known to the Police he was never going to get away with anything. The fact that when the Police arrived he was caught red handed kicking fuck out of one of Chelsea's top boys didn't help either.

He was charged and convicted of causing GBH with intent. Served three years, he was, as the Judge had described him, and always would be, a nasty piece of work.

He was so different from Waterman in many ways. Where Waterman was often seen as a 'protector of the innocent and vulnerable' Mick Western was a bully who prayed on these types, taking protection money from the small family run businesses, corner shops, and loaning money to the poor and needy with horrific interest rates and punishments for non and late payment. A clout across the face or the beating of a lifetime was the minimum you would get if you declined to cough up on time.

Western was vicious and uncompromising, had a bad attitude, and a fondness for kicking's that made him a legend in his own time.

He began in his late teens, collecting money for a local loan shark, and one day discovered that all he had to do to take over the business was keep all the money he collected.

His growing reputation and willingness for violence soon put the loan shark out of business. He knew he could make a small fortune from the most vulnerable people of society.

In the early days he would 'buy' peoples benefit books for £100, knowing full well the true worth of each weekly slip would add up to much more. He was once reported to the Police but statements were withdrawn, and witnesses scared off when one witness was tied by the legs, to the back of his BMW car and dragged through the streets of the nearby Meadow Well Estate.

Western was on his way to see sixty three year old Chinese businessman Mr Walter Chang, at Chang's main and largest establishment The SnapDragon Casino complex.

The snapDragon Casino was, as the advert stated, more than just a Casino, it was the perfect day and night leisure destination with a fantastic restaurant, amazing bar, sports & entertainment lounge, great poker, conference room and much, much more. It was the biggest building by far, in the centre of the Dragon Gate area of Chinatown.

Inside they had numerous Roulette, Blackjack and Poker tables with popular slot games to make your gaming experience the best in town.

Chang was well respected. He owned several businesses within the City Centre and in particular the Dragon Gate district. He was a second generation Chinese immigrant, his parents coming to Newcastle when he was young. He was hard working and had made his money from various establishments, mainly the SnapDragon. To the Chinese population he was a bit of a legend, with his own hard earned cash and a young trophy wife to boot.

Western saw Chang as an easy target. The several drinks he'd had over the last few hours had fuelled his ego and given him ideas above his station but, since his release from prison, things had already begun to change in Newcastle. The role he'd expected to take advantage of had already been filled.

Once he had reached the snapdragon Casino he walked straight through the heavy, impressive doors and headed towards Mr Chang's office.

CHAPTER THREE

In his role as match day Chief security Steward, Alex Brennan stood in front of volunteers gathered in the main stand of St James' Park, home of Newcastle United Football Club. He liked to get his staff in early for a pre match briefing. Tonight's game was no exception. Newcastle United v West Ham United a match that, over the years, had not been short of trouble and always had potential for crowd unrest.

No-one could forget the shock and horror following a petrol bomb throwing incident in the eighties, when West Ham fans were trapped and penned in the away section, unable to escape. Luckily, on that occasion only one person was seriously injured. There was also an incident where the West Ham ICF hooligan firm infamously attacked a Newcastle social club, both incidents never forgotten, or forgiven in some respect.

Alex Brennan was a tall man, his hair slightly greying at the temples. As usual he wore his customary long padded navy blue Stewards Jacket, smart trousers and nicely polished shoes. He'd been in this role for several years, mostly part-time supplementing his main income.

It had been a very difficult few years for him. He'd been made redundant from his well paid job, working as a manager for the City Council and now the role at the football ground was his only source of income. His wife had been forced to give up her job as a teacher due to ill health as a dramatic reduction in income began to take its toll on the family finances. Due to his new found financial troubles he always seemed preoccupied.

They had nearly lost their home. The building society eventually losing patience with months of missed mortgage payments, took them to court in an attempt to repossess. They somehow, due to a loophole, had managed to hang onto the roof over their heads, which was now in a desperate need of refurbishment due to lack of money. It had forced them to neglect minor repairs which had now grown into major ones. It had become a high maintenance house that needed money to be spent on it and money was one thing he didn't have.

Brennan cleared his throat with a cough before giving his instructions. "Now then everyone, we know what to expect tonight. Two and a half hours till kick off and the gates open in half an hour. This is always a high risk game, especially as it's mid week and some fans have been drinking in the city centre since lunch time. You must always remember to keep in control, if you lose your temper and react then you're no better than they are. Police *have* reported some minor scuffles already in and around the central station area but, hopefully, it won't carry on into the ground; it's approximately an hour before the West Ham supporter's coaches arrive so, I want an extra few of you up at the Leazes end to make sure they all get in without any fuss. Newcastle have started the season well and we're second top of the league," there were a few distant cheers from the Stewards, "But, this is a game we *should* win, however, we are all aware what Newcastle United are like, we're due a bad result. So, try to make allowances for supporters being anxious, frustrated or angry but I stress, *do not* stand for any anti social behaviour that would spoil the match for the majority. Clamp down quickly on any foul mouth chanting, especially racist abuse and throwing missiles which, I remind you are punishable by immediate ejection. Please make sure you report these to the Police control centre straight away, and don't wait too long, don't let things get out of hand, try, if you can, to nip things in the bud."

He pointed towards Hugh Grey, senior Safety Steward. "If you're not too sure where you're going to be stationed this evening, check with Hugh, he will direct you to your spots for tonight, now remember you lose your temper, you lose control. Off you go and get sorted for the masses coming in, any problems speak to Hugh, if he's too busy or it's urgent you can contact me via your walkie talkies. Thanks for listening and here's to a trouble free evening."

The stewards all clapped and rose to their feet, as one, then, individually headed off to their various turnstiles, entrances and staircases where they will be stationed.

Brennan and Hugh Grey climbed the steep metal staircase to the Police crowd control centre to have a quick meeting and if they were lucky, a quick cup of coffee before the turnstiles opened for business.

The Police control centre was state of the art. With 52,000 thousand people expected to attend the game tonight, officers patrolled inside and outside the ground and used the control centre room to check CCTV and share information with officers and security staff. Inside four officers each sat at desks facing the pitch and seating areas.

The control centre had once been an executive box; it was fully glass fronted and gave full panoramic views of the pitch. On each desk were three small screens, one of which was linked to a central computer and the other two screens displayed various CCTV images of both the inside and the outside of the stadium.

Sat at one of the desks was Gary Shannon, a Police Officer linked to the football intelligence unit. His job was to keep an eye out for known hooligans and people on banning orders. He scanned the images on the screens, his weary eyes searched every corner as he sipped at his cup of coffee, and what a coffee it was, his favourite, a single espresso. His face told it all. It was made with precisely two ounces of great black coffee, with creamy brownish foam on top. The flavour had thumped him like a hammer, as the after taste radiated like sunshine.

As the Police control centre had formerly been used for companies to entertain guests it backed onto one of the many restaurants in the ground. The coffee served was from a different planet to the brown slop served up by vending machines in the local stations. Another perk, it was free of charge, and unlimited.

Shannon wore a police uniform but no tie. He had a small set of headphones that kept him in contact with various turnstiles and stewards. He lifted his head and smiled as Brennan and Grey came into the room. "Nothing to report yet, let's hope, it stays that way."

Hugh Grey was looking forward to the match, and his taste buds were aroused by the glorious aroma of freshly ground Arabica beans. "Should be a good game tonight, they are unbeaten in their last four games and we're still unbeaten here', you want a coffee, Alex, while we still can"?

Brennan pulled out a chair and settled himself down at the table. "Of course that goes without saying, I'll have one of those that Gary's drinking."

Hugh Grey left the room for the drinks and returned in minutes. He handed Alex his coffee and lifted his own, a large creamy Caramel Latte Macchiato off the tray.

Alex Brennan was smiling as he rubbed his hands together in anticipation. "I love games like this, they really test us, we have to be organised, which we are."

Hugh Grey took a sip from his coffee, the first big gulp seared his throat and he nodded his head, the taste was orgasmic. "Got us down for a 3-1 home win tonight could win me £100 if it comes in, what about you"?

Brennan blew on the top of his scalding hot cup "Betting's a mug's game mate; you should keep your money in your pocket."

He turned to Gary Shannon, spooning the froth off the top of his drink "let me know if you see anyone of interest Gary."

Shannon stood and saluted sarcastically "Yes Sir."

After finishing their coffees, Hugh and Alex left the comfort and warmth of the Police control centre and climbed back down the steep metal staircase that led to the main concourse. Brennan pulled his coat tightly around him, as a cold blast of air hit them.

Hugh Grey had known Alex Brennan for many years, they didn't socialise at all but they were good friends at work, "you got any plans for Christmas then Alex" ?

Before Brennan could answer he was distracted by the beep signalling of a message coming from his mobile phone. He closed his eyes in distress. His hands were shaking and he was trying to act normal. It read...

As soon as the second half kicks off.

From glittering crystal chandeliers to dapper tuxedoed waiters, Walter Chang's SnapDragon Casino had become the grandest in Newcastle.

Mick Western walked past the many state-of-the-art slot machines and the numerous table games which were housed in the lower floor. He knew it well. He'd been in there enough times, and been forcibly removed on many occasions.

He reached Chang's office in what seemed like no time at all and walked straight through the door without knocking.

His unwelcome visitor made Chang shift uneasily in his chair. *Just how had this uninvited guest managed to breach his security measures?*

Walter Chang had a small round face and a receding hairline making the top of his head completely bald. He had small grey tufts of hair, each side above his ears. He wore a dark suit, dark shirt with the grandad collar fastened right up to the top button, giving the impression it was almost choking him.

Western approached Chang's desk, his eyes fixed firmly on him, he wanted to see awkwardness in Chang's face, the sweat on his brow, and fear in his eyes.

"Hello Walter just thought I'd pop and see you, it's been a while." He looked into his face directly, holding his gaze.

Walter Chang felt a churning in his stomach, although his heart was racing. He scrutinized Western over the top of his half lens tortoise shell glasses, wrinkling his nose to stop them from sliding and hoping help would not be too far away. He greeted his visitor with a congenial false smile and offered him a seat.

"Yes Mr Western, It's been a while, I'm glad to see you and look forward to your business once more."

Western with his slurred speech and bloodshot eyes came straight to the point. "This time it's going to be *me* who makes money outta *you*."

Chang pressed the silent panic button under his desk. The old man appeared to be growing in boldness as he locked eyes with Western "And how, my dear friend, do you intend to do that. Have you suddenly found some new magical gambling system then"?

Western pushed his face closer to the old man, and spoke through gritted teeth. "Stop the wise cracks Walter, I can make sure that nobody bothers you, and that none of the local vermin come in here causing trouble, a business agreement between you and me, you know what I'm getting at"?

Walter Chang shrugged his shoulders wishing his guest a million miles away. "That is very noble and thoughtful of you Mr Western, a business agreement. I am a very good businessman, but I need to know what's in it for me"?

Western sat forward in his chair. He picked up a photograph on Chang's desk, a photograph of his wife, Sara. "Your wife is beautiful Walter. As part of the service I am offering you, I can ensure that she remains beautiful, and safe."

Now the conversation *was* going the way that the old man *had* expected. He reached under his desk and again pushed the panic button that would alert security to his assistance.

MickWestern didn't notice, and continued. "I will also make sure your lovely house and all your businesses are fully protected twenty four hours a day, after all, it would be terrible if something bad was to happen, wouldn't it? Walter, you get my drift."

Chang fidgeted in his seat, sweat began to run down his back, *where were the security men;* he took a deep breath and regained his composure. "So, Mr Western, exactly how much is this going to cost me"?

Western was a large man and threatening. He knew his worth down to the last penny. He lent forward in his seat, as he stared into the eyes of Walter Chang, "I'm not a greedy man Walter, I was looking for two grand a week, cheap at the price, you must agree."

Walter Chang didn't have time to answer as the door opened and two identical and intimidating, oriental men entered the room wearing suits and ties. As they moved towards Western Walter Chang let out a huge breath and held up his right hand.

"Thank you my friends, but violence won't be necessary, Mr Western is just about to leave, isn't that right Mick"? Western shook his head and raised his voice, Walter Chang wasn't taking him seriously enough.

Western opened his arms expansively to thrust home his message. "Now look here Walter, I'm trying to arrange a nice little business agreement I don't think you are aware of what I'm fucking capable of."

Chang sat back in his chair, smiled and folded his arms across his chest almost as if he was holding a burden there. "I think you better leave now Mr Western before you insult my intelligence further. You sit here, in *my* office making threats to me, my family and businesses. You want *me* to pay protection money to *you* and even bring my home and wife into this, I don't do business with ex-cons, and especially ones who are fond of a drink or two." Chang laughed as he gave instructions to his security men by pointing to Western with his index finger and then the door with is thumb.

Western was forcibly grabbed by the two men and lifted from the chair. He pushed his head backwards as he tried to lift his arms, but the men had a firm hold. Walter Chang gloated "As you can see, Mr Western, I already have adequate protection."

Western regretted having had so much booze. On better days he was pretty sure he could have taken both men out, but he'd have to be top of his game to stand a decent chance. He knew he *was* the worse for drink. He remembered what Don Waterman once told him; *never start a war you can't win*. Western could see the whole picture; this was a battle worth losing, so as he could eventually win the war, a war that *he had* started.

Walter Chang continued to laugh, he spoke with a confidence and cockiness that made him sound untouchable "I think it's time for you to leave Mr Western, you don't mind if my boys show you out, do you"?

As Western's arms were held firmly he tried to kick out with his legs. His head was pushed forward. His fists and adrenaline pumped and nowhere to go, wincing as he tried to raise his head "You'll regret this you Chinky cunt, I'm telling you, you will." The two security men frog-marched Western along through the main body of the SnapDragon, the heavy emergency fire door was kicked open and Western was thrown into the back alley, into the gutter, like a piece of rubbish, as the metal door behind him slammed shut.

He got up from the cold wet cobbled street and dusted himself down. He wasn't going to give up without a fight but that war was for another day. He had a football match to get to tonight. The fact he had a football banning order over him was something that, hopefully wouldn't stop him.

A few more drinks in the pubs and clubs in the City Centre before he headed off towards St James' Park, stopping every few yards to spit phlegm noisily onto the street, he was prepared for a fight and he would make sure he got one if needed.

Alex Brennan looked at his text, and then deleted it immediately.

"Bad news Alex"? Hugh Grey softened his voice, concerned to see how his face changed and how one text message could make him instantly become so secretive, cagey and look somewhat sorrowful.

Brennan made a show of checking his watch and wrinkled his nose before trying to regain his composure, lying to his colleague.

"No, No, it's just my wife reminding me to book a taxi, we're flying to Jersey tonight, got to go straight from here, straight to the airport for a couple of weeks in the sun."

Hugh Grey saw a definite change in Brennan's mood, almost immediately following the text. In a twenty minute period Brennan received a further five messages and Hugh noticed sweat appear on Brennan's brow, his darkening eyes, the look of a guilty man.

For the first time he'd known him Brennan was changing right there in front of him. This confident, pleasant colleague had become secretive, nervous and culpable, quite agitated, with haunted eyes. Brennan clearly distracted as he checked another text.

As soon as the second half kicks off, please confirm.

Hugh Grey shifted from his earlier casual conversation to a more pointed question "Are you sure every thing's ok Alex"?

Brennan snapped back at his colleague, tilting his head upwards "Look, I'm ok, right. Now get on with your fucking job, punters will be coming in any minute, and stop fucking asking me if I'm all right will you."

Brennan, his face solemn, and without further comment left the room. He made the short journey to his small office at the back of the Gallowgate stand, while a concerned Hugh Grey took up his usual position by turnstile 24A.

Once in his office Brennan took out the mobile phone from his pocket, he dropped it as his hands began to shake. He felt his head was going to burst at any moment. He picked it up off the cold concrete floor, sent a quick text then opened it up, removed the battery and sim card and threw the empty phone carcass out of the window. It landed, hardly without a sound in the long grass verge that the football ground over hung.

He took the sim card and using a pair of scissors from his office draw carefully cut it up into several pieces, his hands still trembling as pearls of sweat began to appear on his brow.

He fastidiously wrapped the sim card pieces up in a tissue and took the package to the small bathroom across the way. Tossing the tissue paper down the toilet he flushed.

Standing at the sink, he sniffed and then rubbed his hand across his nose as he looked in the mirror; he noticed how his eyes were sunken, his brow was furrowed.

He placed his hands over his eyes. He could barely look at his own face, his own reflection without thinking, would it all go to plan.

He turned on the tap and splashed his face with cold water, washing his hands and turning back to dry them. He wiped his face dry with a paper towel, scrunched it up and threw it in the waste bin.

Brennan glanced at his watch again, as he walked back towards his office. A young steward jogged passed him, his eyes sparkling "Not long to the kick off now sir, it's nearly time to go."

Alex Brennan nervously checked his watch again, nodded to the youngster and thought to himself, *yes, definitely, nearly time to go indeed.*

Heading back into his office he opened his locker and took out a blue hold all, opening the side pocket he took out, and checked another mobile phone; there was one message from his wife, the usual trivial stuff and a missed call from his father. Alex dialled the number of Polaris cabs and booked his taxi for the airport. He placed this mobile phone in his pocket, his palms cold, clammy and wet with perspiration as he wiped them on his trousers.

This was a night that would change his life forever. He was nervous but he knew exactly what he was going to do. He sat for a few moments going over and over in his head the plan that had been several weeks in the making. Could he get away with it? of course he could, and this time tomorrow he'd be starting his new life in Jersey. Goodbye to Tyneside, goodbye to debt, and goodbye to the run of the mill boring life that he had become accustomed to.

His eyes bright with emotion, he sent a quick text to his wife, telling her he loved her and would meet her at the airport later. Hoping the text reassured her that he had ordered his taxi and hadn't forgotten.

He contacted the lead Steward at the Leazes end, the West Ham fans were all in safe and sound, and a buzz of anticipation went around the stadium that was gradually filling bit by bit with each moment that passed. There was now only half an hour to kick off.

Brennan got to his feet and walked over towards the window; he looked out at the Tyneside skyline and could see the Sage, the Millennium and Tyne Bridge from his vantage point at the highest part of the ground. The River Tyne glistened in the moonlight, as his mind began to wander.

His chain of thought interrupted by the crackling of his walkie talkie, it was Hugh Grey.

"Shannon's spotted something, you better get down here."

Brennan took a deep breath and shrugged his broad shoulders. He closed his eyes and let a thousand emotions pinball around him. *That's all I need* "I'll be there in a minute."

He pushed open the blinds and peered out through droplets of rain on the glass. Gazing out of his small office window, the clouds hung weighing down the night. Down below the pre match hustle and bustle continuing to build. Thousands of supporters dressed in black and white shirts were beginning to swarm as they queued at turnstiles like herds of Zebra waiting their turn at an African watering hole.

He could hear the muffled sound of the fans inside the ground as mist drifted across the busy streets into the headlights. Sirens and horns blaring from gridlocked traffic on the wet roads outside.

Young children grasped the hands of their fathers, as they approached, looking up in awe at the massive Cathedral that was St James' Park, their hearts full of hopes, dreams and memories that would last them a lifetime.

The floodlights alone shone like a beacon, lighting up the Newcastle skyline, visible from almost everywhere for miles around, a fabulous sight, drawing, beckoning the believers to come, more often than not, in hope rather than expectation.

There were Police vans at bus stops, programme sellers touting their wares, friends meeting up, shaking hands and man hugs.

People queued at mobile refreshment stands as the smell of fried glistening onions added to that unmistakable aroma of hot dogs, hamburgers and horse shit.

An atmosphere and build up to a big midweek match night at St James's Park was something Alex Brennan *was* going to miss.

His walkie talkie crackled again. He needed time to clear his head, give him time to think. He felt a cold shiver somewhere deep inside him. He recognised what it was. Doubt and fear. *Better go and sort this out.*

CHAPTER FOUR

How dare he try and double cross me. He looked at the naked man suspended by his arms before him. The offering, the sacrifice.

His face darkening with anger, he knew he could understand everything he was telling him, and would feel everything he was about to do.

Fear was in his narrowing eyes, this man must pay for his wrong doing and the syndicate demanded it had to be of a barbarous nature.

He drew a large sharp knife several times along his chest and torso, legs and arms. He cut out his tongue so he couldn't scream for help.

He slashed him again, blood spreading from a chopped artery. His victim's mouth was full of blood and sick as the smell of vomit and blood was heavy in the air.

He wiped blood from his own face and smiled. He enjoyed this all too much.

His heart was beating faster now "No-one fucks with me. If only you'd done what you'd been asked."

Slowly he walked around his victim, proudly surveying his work like the old master artist admiring his canvas.

He cut another large chunk of flesh from his buttocks, and stabbing the knife deep into the back of his thigh with so much force, he chipped the bone, bending the blade.

The man let out a tongue less scream like some kind of alien animal. The feel of a sharp blade as it sliced through the skin and jarred on the bone was nothing he hadn't experienced before.

He cut slices of flesh from him, making sure he was still very much alive. This poor man would very soon look like a lump of blooded meat, just like an animal's corpse, hanging in a butcher's shop window, but the thieving shit had to be sorted. The punishment had to fit the crime and this was a crime of extreme magnitude.

"Sorry, did that hurt." He laughed at his own words and smiled a lopsided, nasty grin as he continued his work.

A Lakeland terrier dog panted as it excitedly scurried up a large winding staircase and reaching the top, headed through an open bedroom door and without breaking stride jumped onto Oscar's bed. It was seven AM, and it's time for his walk.

It nudged at the cream coloured duvet and eagerly licked at his owner's face. Oscar turned to avoid unwanted attention, but the determined little dog immediately leapt over to the other side to once again begin a relentless pursuit, his small wet nose nudging and pushing at his master's face.

"Buster man!, in a minute."Oscar sighed loudly and pulled the duvet back over his head, which a relentless Buster pulled back with his teeth as he enunciated plan B with an animated bark.

"Alright, alright, I'm getting up. Happy now? You little swine."As Oscar sat up in bed, his little companion gazed at him from the bottom of the bed, his small curly tail wagging in satisfactory triumph.

The TV was still on. Sky News had been on all night, *again*, Oscar was always falling asleep with the T.V on, he couldn't sleep unless it was on, too quiet, the lights needed to be on too. Most times he hated being alone, the dark and the fear of the memories of those nights enveloping him too much time to think. If only these nightmares would stop him going all the way back there, he might stop remembering at least for a little while longer. He puffed out his cheeks as his eyes welled with tears.

As well as his recent dramas with his Grandfather, it had been ten years since a road accident which killed both of his parents, on a well known accident black spot on a notorious stretch of the A69.

His sister, Gemma, had just moved to Canada, on what North Americans called a 'Soccer Scholarship'. She had returned for a couple of months as they helped each other, and their grandfather through the ordeal. It was a very difficult time for them all.

After his parents died their bedroom had felt like a wound in the home that had taken many years to heal. He still had nightmares when he'd wake gasping in the middle of the night, when every painful beat of his racing heart had felt like his last.

They had mulled over the idea of selling the family home, but Oscar decided he wanted to stay in a house where he had grown up in, and felt safe, as despite everything this was a place he loved, his house, his home.

Another initial plan was that his Grandfather, Alfie, would move in with him, but this turned out to be nothing more than a knee jerk reaction. It wouldn't have been practical in the long term.

His grandfather only lived only a mile from his house, which was close enough for emergencies, in a two bedroom bungalow in the Heaton area of Newcastle. He had a lot of friends, an active social life, and was within walking distance of his local post office, newsagents and social club. It was also felt that a large winding staircase would have a detrimental effect on his grandfather's seventy eight year old arthritic hips, knees and dodgy heart.

His Grandad did stay over on Sundays. The untimely death of his parents had brought Oscar and his Grandfather even closer together than they were before. They tried to see each other at least a couple of times per week and had phone calls to each other most days.

Younger sister, Gemma lived in Toronto, Canada playing semi-pro football or 'Soccer', as the natives called it, for the Toronto Ladies Lynx team in the

National Women's League. She had two children, Rudy and Abigail. Her husband, Don Carrington worked for Canadian Border Services Agency, it was a very good job, well paid, and Oscar and he got on well.

In just six weeks time, they would all be together for Christmas. Gemma and her family were due to fly into Newcastle airport from Toronto on 20th December and would be staying for a couple of weeks.

Grandad was especially looking forward to seeing them and spending Christmas with his whole family once again.

Oscar picked up a TV remote control from his bedside table and increased the volume. "I'll just catch the headlines then I'll get up, OK?", Buster yelped out a short bark again and rolled over towards his owner, inviting him to tickle his belly, victory was his.

As Oscar ran his fingers through the thick grizzle coloured curly coat of his dog's back. The sports news was just about to begin, the reporter spoke...

"Wins for both Manchester United and Arsenal in last night's Premier League matches, and a fabulous night for Newcastle United as their 1-0 victory at home to West Ham took them up to the top of the Premiership table, the goal coming shortly after halftime.

And *Now, breaking news from down under and it's not good. England have just lost the first Ashes Test match at the Gabber by 184 runs, mainly due to the brilliance of the Aussie bowling attack, just in the thoughts of the England captain..... "*

England's Cricket Captain did not get a chance to spout his feeble excuses as Oscar leant forward and switched off the TV.

"Bloody useless at Cricket and to think we gave it to the world wouldn't have been like that in Botham's day." Buster, still on the bed cocked his head to one side, left ear inside out, as if fully understanding what his master was saying.

Oscar had been particularly upset at the demise of English cricket. As a youngster he had been a fine cricketer, opening batsman, could have signed for the Northumberland minor counties and probably should have made it into the professional game. Opportunities were limited back then as Durham were still several years away from being a first class County side and a whole generation of very gifted north east cricketers were lost to the sport forever.

He was never going to be a footballer, like his sister. Oscar was way too puny and lacked that aggressive competitiveness that you somehow need to succeed in a career in the so called beautiful game.

Cricket was *his* game, slow, gentle and much more dignified, and of course snooker. He liked nothing better than a game of snooker, and not just because it gave him the opportunity to wear one of his many waistcoats. Enjoying the chess like tactical safety battles, crisp clean angles and really admired the skill involved snooker players needed to think three or more shots ahead when potting balls, and break building. Snooker was a detective's sport, lots of problems to solve, and answers to find.

Reaching down for his slippers he headed off downstairs to the kitchen. Walking down the stairs, counting to himself as he went, *thirteen steps, unlucky for some, but not for me because I count them*, and trying to not to tread or fall over as his curly coated companion, as Buster charged past him and headed off, leading the way.

"Suppose you want feeding now, as well"? as he reached into a Kitchen cupboard for a tin of dog food. The tins were all arranged in order, perfectly organised to a level of perfection, alphabetically in flavours, all facing the same way, neatly stacked in columns of two, never three. He opened one it and scraped it into the dog bowl with a fork from the cutlery drawer.

As Buster tucked into his breakfast he headed back upstairs to get ready for the day ahead, again the urge to count them defied logic and sanity but it was something he always needed to do, and as long as there were thirteen, he knew it would be a good day. Thankfully there were, and always would be.

The Shower, certainly did the trick, it was so refreshing. He stood and let the cascading steaming hot water engulf him, from head to toe, energising, and preparing him for what trials and tribulations were sure to be awaiting him in his first working day back for a few weeks in the Tyneside Police Force.

He'd never planned on joining the Police force. As a boy he was a gifted student, a child genius. He entered Durham University to study criminology, Physiology and law with a career goal of becoming a criminal solicitor. He had gained a placement with a local Solicitors firm following his graduation, but fairly soon concluded this wasn't going to be the job for him. It took the untimely death of his father, a DCI, to be motivation for him to follow in his footsteps and become a detective.

He joined at the age of twenty five and soon made a name for himself, showing lots of promise and ability he was fast tracked to CID and within three years the rank of Detective sergeant.

He was now thirty five years old and was well respected with lots of high profile arrests to his name. Oscar Smiles was definitely the man Tyneside Police Force could rely on, and turn to. He was renowned for looking at each case from a different perspective, often thinking outside the box, was very intelligent and never gave in.

He stepped out from his shower,and wrapping himself in a warm terry towelling dressing gown he walked back into the bedroom.

As he opened his wardrobe door, the array of expensive designer clothes, in immaculate order, all neatly pressed, ironed and ready to wear were all hung up and very systematically colour co-ordinated. He picked a plain white shirt and a navy blue waistcoat, trousers and tie, then placed them carefully on the bed.

He always was a snappy dresser. He always needed to look his best, even though he's only taking Buster for the usual early morning walk in the nearby Dene. Unlike McGovern who only seemed to wear clothes so as not to appear naked.

Outfit chosen, and on with his coat. Buster almost keeled over with excitement jumping up and squealing with delight at the prospect of his walk through the Dene

Before they headed off, he went through his usual checks, *oven off, TV, off, windows closed and lights off*. They went out through a big solid wooden front door of Oscar's Jesmond home, he pulled out his keys and rattled them into the lock. Shivering as he stepped out of the house he walked down a couple of steps and along the garden path. Just as the gate clunked behind them, he went back to check he'd locked the front door, which he had. *Always good to check*. And off they walked towards the Dene.

His house was what his father had described as a hidden Gem. It was a Georgian grade two listed period property in the heart of the Jesmond area of Newcastle. The detached property was bursting with character and incorporated an outhouse to the back. It had been lovingly restored by his parents. It had been the only home Oscar had ever known. It had many original features such as a stone flagged fireplace and solid wood flooring with sash windows. It was a large old detached house, with four bedrooms.

It was a cold and crisp morning. Doughy clouds rose over the horizon as autumn had finally given up the ghost and made way for winter. The house was warm but outside the frost was still white on the rooftops, garden sheds and outhouses.

Walking through the Dene, The calls of birds pierced the falling leaves. He slipped on one of them that the frost had plastered to the path and felt his feet skid. They passed Pets' Corner. Oscar was relieved to see it was closed with the gates bolted. There had been a rather unsavoury incident a few weeks previously involving Buster and a baby pot bellied pig. Buster hurdling the small fence and giving chase. Thankfully it all ended amicably, well kind of.

As their route took them up alongside the Ouseburn. '*Oh shit*', Oscar muttered to himself. Buster was still supposed to be on lead following a letter he'd received from the City Council with regard to the fallout from the incident he now referred to as 'Buster gate'. *Fancy that, a Detective sergeant who has a dog with an anti social behaviour order!.*

Anyway, Buster never had a lead on, he'd given that up years ago, far too stressful, let him run free, yes he could be naughty but not usually nasty.

A few leaves remained on frostbitten trees but this was, after all, Newcastle in the North East of England, and was well into November.

He treaded carefully trying not to slip on numerous wet frosty leaves littering the sheltered crisp pathways. His furry companion scurrying from tree to tree, bush to bush, his hot panting breath steaming in cold frosty air as they strolled towards the first of a series of small waterfalls. there was a loud splash as Buster leaped into the water, his attempt to catch a grey wagtail, an unsuccessful one, as shoals of sticklebacks swimming in the water scattered.

Parallel with the roadway Oscar could see the dip marking the Old Mill Leat and in places, the large rhubarb-like leaves of the Gunnera Plant and a trampled grassy path. This part of the walk was always tinged in sadness for him. He took a deep breath and glanced at the sunless sky. For it was here that he remembered his first murder case.

A young boy, Bobby Rafferty, had gone missing during a family picnic. His body was found three days later, partly hidden. He had been strangled. The search for him had been a difficult one. Lots of people from the community had helped including the man who was eventually arrested, and charged, with his murder. David Blacker. Unfortunately for Bobby's family they were never to see him convicted as he took a coward's way out and hung himself in Durham jail while on remand.

Young Bobby Rafferty would have been almost sixteen years old, had he still been alive today and probably studying for his GCSE's. Oscar had remained in contact with Bobby's family. He still received Christmas cards from them. He would never forget little Bobby. His photograph, his little smiling face which was all over both local and national press and TV. A face everyone would probably recognise but not many would remember his name.

As Buster disturbed the deep undergrowth a strong scent of wild garlic filled the air. It was a smell Oscar would always associate with the search, and sad discovery of a body of that little boy.

There weren't many people about that cold, crisp morning, just a solitary jogger that went by. Buster, for a split second, thought about giving chase, often bemused, this time distracted by a large fallen branch that had been felled by the recent high winds, a branch that was almost as big as he was. The jogger's footsteps faded, sounding thin and prim. A lucky escape.

They reached the point where two bridges crossed the burn together. Over either of the bridges and into the open space was the picnic field, an area of managed grass intended to stand up to considerable wear.

The picnic field was another favourite of Buster's, especially during the summer months, as sunbathers unguarded packed lunches and dopey Labradors tennis balls were there for the taking.

You could say that Buster was a typical 'Lakey' friendly, bold, and confident. Shyness is very atypical, as was aggressiveness. He was extremely intelligent and independent minded, quick to learn and easy to train though often exhibiting selective deafness' when his interest level was aroused. As with most terriers, Buster was energetic, daily exercise and play times were a must, or he would seek out other outlets for his energy, with undesirable results for his owner, as Oscar knew only too well

As they walked on past the pavilion and turned right over the Ouseburn once again,   he stopped for a moment on the bridge and looked left to see the largest of the waterfalls in the Dene, at its base, a deep pool sometimes used by energetic swimmers. This area brought back a lot of happy childhood memories for him. He'd spent many of the summer months splashing about in the pools with his friends, walking barefoot between mossy stones, hot sunny days, lemonade and ice cream.

Oscar had lost sight of Buster. He gave a loud whistle and in a couple of seconds he appeared from under a large holly bush.

He'd had Buster for five years. He was a stray brought into the station one night by a late patrol who found him limping around a Newcastle backstreet, hungry, tired and cold. Although Buster appeared to have a bit of a limp (which he still displayed at times), and extremely tired, he was still running amok in the station and the highlight of the evening shift was when he jumped onto McGovern's desk and stole his cheeseburger. *He was supposed to be losing weight, did the fat bastard a favour anyway.* Buster stole it from right under his nose just as he was about to take a bite to the amusement of all who saw it.

Buster was not officially a Police dog but still accompanied Oscar most days, sometimes just to the station but had been known to be his unofficial partner at times. Buster loved to just sit in the front seat of Oscar's car. Nobody else was allowed in that passenger seat as McGovern again once found to his cost when Buster bit him on his big fat backside when he dared to sit in the front seat, his front seat.

The path bought him out overlooking the quarry. He paused here a moment, looking back up the Dene, it really was a beautiful example of an original natural woodland with a mixture of oak, hazel and holly trees.

He enjoyed the companionship of his little dog. Initially the plan was to take Buster to a cat and dog shelter, but he immediately fell in love with him and offered to take him home, to look after him, at least overnight. The rest, as they say, was history.

Continuing on up to higher ground, were several horse chestnut trees which gave a splendid display of colour in the autumn. Oscar had fond memories of collecting the fallen conkers as a child. Mature trees grew on the top of rocks with little or no soil as their roots went down into cracks.

Here too, when the morning broke a few bats could be seen flitting among trees in their search for insects, before heading for darkness, and safety of the nearby caves.

The Dene was always changing and there were different things to see at different times in the year. It was a walk that both Oscar *and* Buster loved.

Mick Western drove his dark blue BMW through the refurbished, but already decaying streets of the Meadow Well Estate in North Shields. It had been several years since the infamous riots which sparked regeneration in the most deprived area of North Tyneside.

The Riots were a series of violent protests that took place in the early nineties. The bulk of the Estate was built in the thirties to accommodate low income residents from the slums in nearby North Shields.

Originally called The Ridges in the sixties the local authority changed its name to Meadow Well in an attempt to improve the image of the already dilapidated estate, which was already in decline just thirty years after being built. The estate was considered a no go area for many non-residents and police alike even long before the riots occurred.

The riots themselves were triggered by the deaths of two local youths, who were killed when a stolen car they were fleeing from police in crashed. Friends asserted on local news broadcasts that their deaths were caused by police forcing their vehicle from the road. Seemingly in response to such reports of police brutality, locals began looting shops and setting cars and buildings on fire and extensive vandalism and damage to numerous buildings and vehicles.

Police and fire crews which attended were pelted with bricks. It was estimated that at its height four hundred people were involved. Thirty seven people were arrested, including one who was jailed for four and a half years.

Since the riots, millions of pounds had been spent on regeneration. Hundreds of properties had been demolished and new houses had been built. A new community centre, health centre, and police station had also been established.

But the Estate still had a bit of a reputation, and once again quickly became a dumping ground for the local Council to put troublesome tenants. Meadow Well had more than its fair share of Drug users and dealers, alcoholics, paedophiles, and people you just wouldn't want as neighbours as Jeremy Kyle would want on his daytime TV show.

The vast majority of the residents of the estate, however, were decent, law abiding people, some of which were quite vulnerable. Some of the most vulnerable people of society. The elderly, disabled, people on low incomes and single parents.

This was Western's manor, his Kingdom. He ruled these streets with fear and intimidation. People looked into his eyes and saw menace. Everyone was afraid of him. Just raising his voice was often enough to get what he wanted. These people provided him with his living. He was no more than a vicious parasite, a thug, who preyed on defenceless people.

Still angry with what had happened at Chang's Casino Western thought of how he could gain the upper hand on Chang, how to get back at him, get money from him and become feared. He knew if he could intimidate Chang, then the rest of Dragon Gate would be easy for him to control. Meanwhile he still had a business to run and money to collect, with interest. *But where did those two Chinese gorillas, at the Casino, come from?, who were they working for?, Fuck knows, and who the fuck cared anyway.*

Trying his luck with somebody like Walter Chang was a massive step up for Western, maybe even a step too far. The Dragon Gate was a big area. Chang was only one of several successful Chinese businessmen who after initially working very hard for a living now were reaping the fruits of their labour.

Western parked erratically pulling his BMW in at the side of a road two streets from his intended 'client' so as to not give away his presence.

He lit a cigarette and blew the smoke out in a hazy stream, settling back into his car seat. He let his eyes and mind drift out of focus as he took another large drag and blew the smoke out slowly.

He sat for a moment before reaching for the door handle. *Well, time is money,* he thought, finishing his cigarette. *Better get this show on the fucking road.*

Lifting his large muscular frame out of the driver's seat, he locked the car and stretched his legs and back, his shirt pulling out of his trousers exposing his navel.

Walking a short distance down the road he couldn't help but notice every other house was empty with metal council embossed shutters on the windows and doors.

The gardens were all un-kept and strewn with rubbish. A happy birthday banner and balloons affixed to the door with the slogan *Happy 30th birthday nana.* It made him shake his head, *should all be fucking sterilised, the lot of them.*

He walked carefully trying to avoid the dog defecation that had been irresponsibly left on the pavement as a teenager raced blatantly by on a motorbike, the sound of the engine deafening and ear splitting and not surprisingly wearing no helmet. The teenager was closely followed by a police car with its blue light and siren going. Just an ordinary day in the ghetto, had anything really changed since the riots?

A cat with one eye and a stump of a tail sprang at the sound of his footsteps onto a crumbling wall covered in graffiti and pigeon shit, and darted across the road to watch him from a safe distance.

It may only have been a few short miles away, but this place was no Jesmond Dene.

He was soon standing at the address of his unlucky customer. Johnny Murray.

CHAPTER FIVE

As Oscar and Buster walked through the Dene towards Heaton, he saw that his Grandad's landing light was on.

What had begun as a light drizzle had now gotten heavier. Rain began to fall in swathes, seeping through his coat to his shoulders, he should call and see him, see if he needed anything, it would be shelter from the rain too, and not to mention the nice hot cup of tea which will undoubtedly be offered.

He knocked on the door, bent over and shouted through the letterbox, while scraping his muddy walking shoes on a cast iron grate.

"Only me Grandad."

His Grandfather, as always appeared pleased to see him. "Howay son, come in, come in, I'll put the kettle on."

Oscar removed his muddy shoes and headed along the thick carpeted passageway, his Grandfather meeting him halfway along with a friendly smile. "Fancy some toast Son"?

He'd had no breakfast. "Yeah, go on then, might as well. You just got up"?

His Grandad spoke as he walked away towards the kitchen, his voice getting less audible "No, no son, been up for ages, couldn't sleep for a bloody dog barking in next door's garden. Had a cat trapped on the top of the garden shed for over an hour. If I'd had a gun, I'd have bloody well shot it"!

Oscar made his way along a short passageway towards the living room. A blast of red hot air slapped him full in the face as the door opened, as if had just walked into a blast furnace. The gas fire was on full, as were the radiators.

"Bloody hell, I would hate to be paying your gas bill"!

"What do you mean?, winter now man, bloody cold you know, besides that Mr Ingram at the Hospital said I needed to keep warm in winter months, good for my breathing he said."

Buster wasn't complaining. He was curled up on the rug in front of the fire. His granddad handed Oscar a piping hot cup filled to the brim with strong sweet tea. He had to move quickly, his fingers burning, as he felt he would drop the cup that was as hot as if it had been heated with a welding torch. He tried to steady his mug with both hands, winced at the heat as he searched with his eyes for a safe place to put it down.

Grandad made his way to the lounge, still talking, "I see The Toon won again last night, top of the league now we are, you want some Custard Creams son, I'm sure I've got some somewhere"? Grandad half turned, as if expecting a yes.

"No, no, thanks anyway for the tea and toast just fine. Yeah, I heard on the news this morning, good result, they're doing well."

Their conversation was abruptly interrupted by the shrill of a smoke alarm. Buster jumping up with shock and barking manically as the smell of burning bread wafted in from the kitchen. Grandad shook his head "Bastard useless toaster, I'll make you some more."

Oscar held up his hand "No, No its ok I'm not really that hungry anyway."

Grandad Alfie laboured to get to his feet and headed back into the kitchen. Oscar placed his drink down onto a coaster on a small mahogany coffee table and followed his granddad through into the smoke. He quickly opened a back door as his granddad frantically wafted the smoke detector with a tea towel. Reaching up to open the kitchen window, Oscar's ears at last comforted as the shrieking noise of the smoke alarm eventually ceased.

"You sure you don't want some more toast, you got to eat more son, you need building up, you're far too skinny."

Grandad Alfie opened the freezer and began to rifle through the draws having used the last two slices of bread.

"No I'm sure, I'll get something to eat when I get home."

"Just as well son, I've run out of bloody bread, could have sworn I had a loaf in the freezer, that's old age for you. Never mind."

As Oscar and granddad made their way back to the lounge, the old fashioned red telephone on top of an antique China Cabinet began to ring. His Grandfather gave a short cough to clear his throat and answered.

"Hello, Alfred Smiles speaking." He listened intently for a few seconds then responded. His eyes narrowed. "Yes, yes, he's here. I'll just put him on for you, It's McGovern, and he doesn't sound happy."Grandad explained, holding out the phone, "Wants to talk to you."

Oscar gingerly placed it to his ear, expecting an onslaught of obscenities.

"Yes Sir"? The gruff Glaswegian voice articulated down the phone. "I thought you must be there, been trying your place for fucking ages, and why is your bastard mobile phone switched off again"? He fumbled around in his pockets as he tried to locate his phone. "Sorry sir, must have left it behind, think the battery must be dead anyway, what's up"? Oscar heard the click and hiss of a cigarette being lit.

McGovern elaborated "Were needed down the Quayside, the disused factory building between the Homeless hostel and the Old Barley Mow pub. There's been a body found, bit messy, by all accounts, meet you there soon as."

"Ok, on my way, see you in about half an hour." Oscar slurped down the remainder of his tea, and handing his granddad the empty but still warm cup, he headed for the door.

"Got to go granddad, thanks for the tea. Come on Bust."

Grandad poured himself another cup of tea from the pot and settled into his easy chair, reading the previous night's chronicle "Ok son, See you later, take care now, and thanks for calling in."

Putting on his shoes Oscar opened the front door as Buster scooted past him into the rain. He heard his granddad shouting from the living room as they headed down the path walking past his Grandad's rose bushes that needed pruning.

"You want a brolly son"?

"No, granddad, it's stopping now anyway, do you want me to drop you a loaf of bread in later, save you going out"?

"That would be great son, and the Chronicle, I'll make you something for tea if you like, what would you fancy"?

"Sorry Grandad I've really got to go, anything will do, but don't put yourself out, mind OK."

The rain was still sheeting down as Oscar walked Buster briskly back towards the Dene. On some mornings it was quiet enough to hear the kids singing to the teachers piano in the nearby infants school, but today all he could hear was the thickening traffic entering the city from the north and east, his mind ticking over, he loved a new case.

Johnny Murray rolled up his sleeve and tightly tied a rotten old handkerchief to his upper arm. Heroin had been his drug of choice for several years. His mere existence always seemed to be a cycle of plight and disaster. That's why he needed the smack. A nice bulky lush vein was swelling nicely and the high he was about to inject was causing his heart to race.

He loved it's feeling, it was fantastic, no cares or worries, just this big cuddle of safety and warmth in a big fluffy duvet. He'd longed for that feeling he'd had the first few times but it was never as good. He had to keep trying though.

Johnny was dressed only in a pair of boxer shorts; he wore a baseball cap that was far too big for his tiny little head and pale face. His rotten mustard coloured teeth, coated with scum were in a terrible state and a tell tale sign of numerous unsuccessful methadone intervention programmes he'd been on over the years. Only in his early twenties he looked a lot older, his appearance aged by his self abusive lifestyle.

His shabby wooden door had seen better days and already had several holes in it. The Yale lock had been smashed in and was covered over with makeshift plywood, as was one of the several broken glass panels. Mick Western tapped gently and stood to one side so as to not be seen through the spy hole.

" W-W-W-Who is it"? stammered a frightened voice.

"Royal mail, got a brown envelope here you need to sign for it." Western answered.

On hearing that, and hoping it may be a benefit cheque, the chain inside was removed as the door began to open slowly.

Western booted the door with all his might, enough to splinter the hinges clean away, his hand moved fast. Grabbing a shell-shocked Johnny's jaw, his fingers pressing hard against bone as he threw him down onto a bare dirty floor bruising his knees.

The dingy dwelling stank of skunk, heavy and sweet as it battled the smell of mildew and other not so pleasant odours. A dim light of a forty-watt bulb tried in vain to defeat darkness. Western looked around the scruffy flat and was in turn disgusted and fascinated by what he was seeing. It was like something from a television play; something you knew went on but never believed you would see for yourself.

As Johnny crawled towards his threadbare sofa bed Western helped him on his way with a violent kick in the buttocks. dragging himself along the floor and gingerly climbing onto the bed Johnny cried out in pain, skin and bone crumpled under the force, as Western punched him full in the face. Grabbing him by the hair and pulling him up close to his face. Western spoke into his ear. "You're late with your payments

Johnny, two weeks now. Fifty quid just turned into a hundred."

Johnny shook with fear. He knew only too well what Mick western was capable of. "But, Mr Western, I've got nowt. My money has stopped, honest."

Western scanned the room and spotted a table with drug paraphernalia on it. Grabbing him by the throat he pointed to it. "Well how were you able to buy that shit then? You're lying to me Johnny, I don't like being lied to, and you know what happens to liars."

Western threw him with excessive force onto the floorboards and held him down by the throat. He moved his mouth towards the boy's face, spitting with anger, close enough to smell the methadone on his breath. Turning Johnny's face to one side he bared his teeth ripping a fleshy chunk from the terrified boy's ear.

Johnny screamed in pain as blood gushed from his wound.

Western stood spitting his earlobe out onto the floor, as he connected with a vicious kick into his stomach. Walking over to some crudely drawn torn net curtains covering a tiny window while he wiped the dripping blood from his chin with the back of his hand.

Johnny sat curled up in the corner. The hurt was in his voice "I owe money for smack as well, and other stuff, please Mr Western, please, I'll get you your money, no more, please, please."

Western nodded his head "Yeah, well any tin pot, Mickey Mouse drug dealer will have to wait his turn, who is it, anyway, your dealer"?

Johnny didn't want to give too much away, "Just some bloke down the pub, don't know his full name."

"Liar", Western shouted and prepared for another kick at his helpless victim."

"No Mr Western, please no", Johnny held up his arms in supplication "its Sammy....Sammy Greenwood."

Western sat down on the sofa bed; He'd have laughed if he'd had a laugh left in him. He smiled lazily enjoying his fear "Now there's a good boy, always nice to tell the truth isn't it. I know dear old Sammy very well. We go back a long way. I might just pay dear old Sammy a visit, can't have your debts to him getting in the way of *my* business now, can we"?

Johnny spoke quietly through chattering teeth "No, Mr Western."

"Does Sammy still live above the garage"?

Johnny Murray didn't speak but just nodded.

"Well, when you see him, tell him I was asking after him. Tell him I'd like to discuss your debt with him."

Johnny pulled himself onto a chair, his body still aching from the beating.

"I will, Mr Western, I will, I promise you."

Western studied the lad as he sat terrified on the rickety old wooden chair. He could see the swollen veins in his ankles and the blotchy skin between his toes where he had been injecting himself "Good lad." Western picked up a scruffy sweatshirt from the floor and threw it in the boy's direction. "Right son, get some clothes on. We're going to get you a crisis loan! And if you drop any of your blood on my lovely car interior you'll owe me for the price of the valet as well."

Meadow Well Social Security office was a fucking depressing place. Johnny took ticket number 454 from the machine, as Western patted a hard plastic seat next to him and Johnny sat awkwardly frightened to make a noise, an old sock held up against his ear soaking up the blood, and looking up at a newly installed digital screen saw that as ticket 440 was currently being served they could be in for a lengthy wait.

A young lad in a Burberry cap, Nike tracksuit trousers, and River Island polo shirt was shouting obscenities and spitting at a young woman serving him through a protective Perspex screen, his benefit hadn't gone into his bank account and he'd been all weekend without any money.

In the foyer his tethered vicious Staffordshire bull terrier barked ferociously at anyone who came within two feet.

An ugly tango faced pregnant teenage girl, wearing large hoop earrings, hair scrunchy and pony tail sat opposite them. Gently, with one hand, rocking an expensive silver cross buggy inside of which sat a very young boy complete with a snotty nose and Greggs sausage roll. There was a constant annoying beeping noise as her expensive newly manicured fingers frantically tapped out one of numerous facebook text messages to one of her cronies. The incessant beeping that told young people of the world they were attached in some way to the rest of their peer group. She was so engrossed in her phone that she was totally oblivious that her other child, a girl, of four years old was marauding around the waiting area climbing on chairs. There for the taking, talking to any drunk, paedophile, or junkie who'd show her the remotest bit of interest, while picking and showing them the discarded paper tickets from the floor of the previously 'satisfied' customers.

Every few minutes her mother would lift her head from the wonderful world of her new expensive mobile phone and call out affectionately at her beautiful little cherub, "Savannah, Fucking get here now." Western thought *Some poor unfortunate bastard must have the unenviable pleasure of putting a paper bag over her head, and fucking it on a regular basis. Better him than me.*

An overweight thirty something woman, with peroxide blonde hair wearing leopard skin leggings, was overheard complaining to her friend sitting beside her "That's the last time I get a blokes name tattooed on my fucking arm," while bouncing a young baby girl on her knee, smiling at her, as she affectionately told it in a silly baby voice, in charming dulcet tones "*Who's a little fat cunt? you are, Who's* a little fat cunt"?

A happy drunk sat singing in a corner, wearing dirty stained clothes and in need of a good bath. The smell coming from his direction was all sweaty socks and crack plaque. The room was already stifling and smelling of perspiration, and he didn't help the aroma one bit.

There was a gentleman in his late fifties sat dressed in a Greenwoods suit and carrying a folder. A once proud shipyard worker now on the employment scrap heap and looking totally bemused.

A man of Eastern European descent argued down the phone demanding money to pay his rent, while in the booth next to him a woman in her forties with a rash of auburn hair and cheekbones that threatened to pierce the skin where they touched shouted was trying to make herself heard amongst the din.

There were two young Smack rats discussing the best way to cheat their pending piss tests, knowing full well what repercussions that a positive result might mean, the withdrawal of their valuable methadone prescription top up.

Western, desperate for a cigarette, looked around at the diversity of people who were sitting around him. He didn't feel the slightest bit sorry for *any* of them. Even for people who had fallen on hard times and were in between jobs. *Tough shit.* As for the rest of them, He despised them all; he thought *they were just scum, wasters, and a drain on society. It would be much more financially viable, and better for the country's long term economic state to just to put the bastards to sleep and be done with it, but on the other hand, what would the likes of Jeremy Kyle do for guests on his popular morning freak show, and, more to the point, how would that then effect his own business.*

He relied on these people to make his living, but not for much longer. He could do so much better for himself, a brutal loan shark earning a few hundred pounds.

He needed to find an assistant, an apprentice, if you like, somebody who would do whatever he told them to do, whenever he told them to do it. It was simple. He needed someone to collect his money for him. Western turned his head towards Johnny. "Have you *ever* had a job son"?

Johnny, bemused with the question, seemed quite offended "Job, Mr Western, me? Who'd give me a job"?

"Yes Johnny, you. What was your last job"?

Johnny's blank expression told its own story. He thought deep and hard he nodded dreading the answer he was about to give "School milk monitor"?

"Are you trying to be funny"?

Johnny didn't speak. He just shook his head.

Western took a deep breath. "What if I offered you a job Johnny? Would you accept it"?

"Would it affect my dole money"?

Western laughed, "Probably not."

Johnny knew what was coming next. "Do I have a choice"?

Western laughed again, "like I said earlier, Probably not."

"What is it Mr Western? The job - that is."

Western smiled without humour, and then moistened the corners of his mouth with his tongue. "I've got a big project coming up. I'm not going to have time to collect on the estate. I need somebody I can trust, somebody who will respect me and not try to rip me off, are you interested"?

Johnny turned to check the numbers board "Like I said Mr Western, do I have a choice"?

Western was serious, it was an offer he couldn't refuse "Well, let me explain something to you. That money you owe me. If you do this for me I'm prepared to write it all off and any money you owe Sammy, he can kiss goodbye to as well. You could be debt free son."

"But I owe Sammy Greenwood five hundred quid"?

Western smiled as he nodded, "But ask yourself how much does that slimy little shite owe me? Just imagine his face when you go to him and demand my money. Are you interested now"?

The look of amazement Johnny's face told Western that he didn't quite believe this.

"Why me Mr Western"?

Western moved in close, his mouth so close that Johnny could smell his own blood in Western's mouth, whispering to him menacingly, "Because I know I can trust you to do a good job. You know what I'm capable of Johnny. You want to impress me, don't you? You respect me, don't you? You're afraid of me aren't you"? Before Johnny could answer Western began to laugh and patted Johnny quite forcefully on the back of his head. "I knew I could rely on you Johnny boy."

Elsewhere in the room there was a bit of an altercation as the happy drunk asked one of the young smack rats for a light, and was answered with "Fuck off dosser."

The young boy in the pushchair, startled by loud shouting began to cry, as he dropped his sausage roll, puff pastry, snot and crumbs onto the dirty floor, his mother placing a dummy into his mouth in one swift movement without lifting her head or taking her eyes from her mobile phone.

The drunk stood to his feet before vomiting and falling clumsily to the floor, a bottle of white lightning cider he was trying to hide inside his coat spilled out all over.

A young girl tried to help him heedfully to a nearby chair as he began to shout back at the two young lads.

It wasn't long before the Police arrived. *Interfering Bastards,* Western, like all criminals hated them.

As the abusive lad in the Burberry Cap was asked to leave the building, he spat full in the face of one of the attending officers and was immediately thrown unceremoniously onto the floor restrained and handcuffed. The Police Officers warned everyone to quieten down and this seemed to do the trick, *at least till they were long gone.* Just another day in paradise.

Western didn't flinch, but sighed deeply and loudly, the insured palaver was sure to be putting back his pending payment even further. He shouldn't really still need to do this; He needed Johnny for jobs like this. Seeing that the Police had arrived, Johnny began to twitch awkwardly in his chair.

"Sit still, calm it, there not here for us,",Western placed his large tattooed hand firmly on Johnny's knee.

In what seemed no time at all a dog warden had turned up with more Police to take the vicious bull terrier away. Another extremely slim, pale, gaunt young man with the hollow eyes of an addict pleaded with them not to take 'his mates' dog away. A plea to fall on deaf ears as the vicious mutt was cautiously lassoed and carefully put into the back of the wardens van, *one more poor dog for the cat and dog shelter.*

Some poor, unfortunate, young Social Security employee came out of a side office, mop and paper towels in hand, cleaning up puke, spilt cider and the semi trod in dog mess that was in danger of being trodden through the whole building. Not part of his job description but one of those his work contract would describe as, *Any reasonable request as directed by your line manager,* a necessary evil of a role, along with zero hour contracts commonplace with many poor employers.

At last Johnny's name was called. He got his crisis loan. A total of £110.45. Western eagerly made him sign the giro cheque, giving him permission to cash it on his behalf and handed him a crisp £10 note. There you go son, don't say I haven't got a heart, that'll get you a bag of that shit you need to keep you straight, and I would get that ear looked at, if I was you. Your Job starts from now, that was your last payment, congratulations, your debt free. I'll be in touch."

CHAPTER SIX

Oscar reached his house in double quick time. Removing his muddy shoes in the hallway and replacing them with a pair of his hand made black Italian leather ones, he grabbed his car keys and put his dead mobile phone in his trouser pocket. He went into the kitchen to go through his usual routine, *oven off, TV, off, windows closed and lights off,* then headed out of the back door where his red Ford Capri XR2 Ghia stood sparkling bright in morning sunshine.

He opened the driver's side door and Buster jumped through into the passenger seat. Before he got in he had to go back and checked he'd locked up. He had, *always good to check*. He put on his seatbelt and turned on the ignition.

As the radio started up, the hush of the early autumn morning was disturbed only by the sound of his car engine as they headed towards the ever increasing traffic noise and horns that signalled the beginning of the City Centre rush hour.

His car crawled through an ever increasing build up of traffic in a part of town which always seemed to be busy, the Cradle Well area of Jesmond. *This new bypass has hardly made a difference just moved the bottle neck further up the road.*

He turned down past the Corner House pub and headed down towards Byker. He had driven round this area many times, he knew a few shortcuts. Turning right onto Shields road led him down past the cafes, pubs and boarded up shops, another area in desperate need of funding and investment.

In no time at all Oscar's car was heading along City Road towards the quayside. As he drove on past the old TV Studios he could see a sky filled with the plush blue glow of the numerous emergency vehicles that gathered at the scene, the outer buildings transformed by the flashing blue lights. He headed for the Police cordon around the old warehouse building, the proverbial x marking the spot.

He pulled his car alongside McGovern's grey Volvo and could see McGovern, standing up, leaning on the offside of his car, smoking the customary cigarette, although he was supposed to be giving up.

Detective Inspector Jim McGovern was a large man with his generous mass of Grey hair, curly and unkempt. He had a large bushy, mostly grey beard and a stomach big enough to house triplets hanging over his poor fitting trousers, He wore a jacket, which didn't match and a creased shirt from the collar of which hung a threadbare tie. McGovern had the look of, to contradict the phrase, a *hedge* that had been dragged through a *man* backwards.

As Oscar brought his Capri to a halt, he switched off the engine. Buster was up on his hind legs looking out of the passenger side window, tail wagging with excitement, he loved a new case as much as Oscar did.

As McGovern walked over towards him he took a final drag of his cigarette, released the smoke through his nose, threw the butt end to the floor and extinguished it with his foot. "Our victim's a male, they think late forties, no ID as yet, we'll have to start by checking missing persons. He's had his stomach slashed open, his guts are hanging out all over the shop, throats been cut, totally mutilated, the body has I'm told more cuts on it than a Tory Chancellor's budget and not a pretty sight or so i'm told."

"Any initial thoughts yet then sir"?

McGovern picked another cigarette from the packet he had just taken out of his trouser pocket and put it in his mouth. It jerked up and down as he spoke "Well, I think we can safely rule out suicide, son."

Oscar rolled his eyes as McGovern turned down wind taking five attempts to light his cigarette.

The two detectives walked towards the old derelict building and limbo danced under the police crime tape that was snapping loudly in the crisp breeze. At the entrance to the warehouse they became aware of the shouts of panic and commotion coming from inside.

They gazed at each other with puzzled looks; Oscar knew what was happening, as he got that awful feeling, the feeling that he was being dragged through his own arse backwards. He instinctively looked, and noticed the empty front seat of his Ford Capri, the door open. He had a pretty good idea as to what, or who had caused the insuring palaver. McGovern had also guessed, as he was tapping ash away impatiently with his finger. Looking into each other's eyes they spoke out loud at the same time "BUSTER."

An irate forensics officer was doing his nut as he came charging out of the building. "Can someone get that fucking dog out of here? This is a fucking crime scene, not bastard Crufts."

Forensic Officer Peter Devon, a thin pale, awkward man in his forties, was not happy. Oscar ran into the building to find Buster scurrying around trying to evade capture with the life or death determination of a Gisele being chased by a lion on the African savannah. Managing to grab him by the scruff of his neck as Buster attempted yet another quick sidestep, he took him out of the building, walked over to his car, carefully put him on the passenger seat, making sure this time the car door is not only shut but securely locked.

Oscar approached Peter Devon apologetically "I'm really sorry about that, he, erm, likes to get involved." Peter Devon dragged his chapped fingers through his greying hair, and put his latex gloves back on. He shook his head dismissing the thought. McGovern was waving his arms about and shouting as again Buster had caused some embarrassment to the department. "Who brings a dog to a fucking murder scene"?, cigarette still jerking in his mouth "I don't know why you do it; anyway that mutt stinks, and needs a bath."

The tension in Oscar's eyes relaxed a little "So do you sir, but you don't hear me complaining all the time."

McGovern nodded as if he needed telling,dropped and trod on his cigarette end and peered at him "Cheeky bastard".

They laughed as they re-entered the crime scene At the entrance Peter Devon handed them each a set of disposable overalls, shoe covers, and a pair of latex gloves. He was shaking his head "In all my years I have never seen such horrific injuries."

"Anything else you can tell us"? Oscar quizzed him.

Peter Devon shook his head, "I'll know more when we get the body back to the lab."

There was a growing number of disposable suited forensics milling around. Police gathering outside, as hoards of reporters and TV crews hungry for updates began to mingle outside the perimeter of the Police cordon.

An mostly empty room, derelict and cold, the sound of water dripping was only masked by the echoing clicks and flashes of the Police forensic Cameras as every angle of the scene was photographed. Other Forensic officers picked up every little fragment of rubbish, glass and paper knowing that anyone of those insignificant items could become a vital clue.

McGovern, as ever was having a moan, "This place smells like a wrestler's kecks"!

In the centre of the room a man's badly mutilated body hung by the arms from a large metal pipe, the pool of blood underneath him, had begun to dry. Oscar stood open mouthed; he could smell the dry blood. He had never seen anything on this scale before, well, maybe in some gory horror film but never in real life.

The two officers stood to one side to allow one of the forensics team to take some more photographs of the body.

Oscar blinked as the flash bulbs went off. "What sort of lunatic would do this"?

McGovern stared at the body, "One we need to catch and quick."

Oscar looked around the crime scene and saw a jacket in a crumpled heap behind an empty oil drum. Alerting a forensic officer to his discovery who carefully began to place the jacket into a large evidence bag. Oscar stopped him, gently grabbing him by the arm.

"No, wait a minute, there's something moving in the pocket."

Oscar put on his latex gloves and removed a buzzing mobile phone from the jacket pocket, just as the phone stopped.

"Missed call, one of six, all from the same number."He placed it into a separate evidence bag and headed back over to McGovern.

"Anything of interest son"?

"Yes a mobile ringing in the jacket pocket, several missed calls I think I recognise the number, Polaris Cabs. We'll need to check it out and contact them."

Oscar and McGovern studied the body hanging in front of them. They were horrified at the scale and number of injuries it had. Even McGovern, who began his career in the tough Glasgow streets during the time of the infamous razor gangs in the late seventies, was a little taken aback.

"The sick bastard, whatever happened to just killing someone, whoever did this wanted him to suffer, he must have really pissed somebody off."

Oscar noticed needle marks on the victim's arm and neck.

"Looks like he could have been drugged, definitely not an addict, not many marks, we'll have to wait for the forensic report, I wonder what this was all about then."

"Ling chi, death by a thousand cuts." A muscular Chinese man, approximately six feet tall, in his early forties, walked toward them. He spoke in good but broken English

McGovern turned quickly, demanding to know who he was "Hey sonny, you can't just walk into here, this is a major crime scene, who the fuck are you anyway"?

The oriental stranger continued "Yes, DI McGovern, I am well aware that this is a major crime scene, and it's strange that a dog appears to be more welcome here than a fellow detective." He held out his hand. "DC Daniel Lee, Manchester CID."

McGovern reluctantly shook, as did Oscar. McGovern was intrigued by Lee's initial comments "Sorry son, you were saying something about Ling fucking Ching or something"?

Lee laughed, "Yes Inspector McGovern, Ling Chi, is death by a thousand cuts. Gentleman it's just what we feared. Newcastle has finally got itself a Triad problem, and I've been sent here to help you sort it out."

McGovern looked again at the body hanging in front of him. "Well, I don't know about you two but I haven't eaten breakfast yet and something in here puts me in the mind for a bacon and tomato sandwich."

Oscar quickly turned his head and vomited up bile as McGovern and Lee laughed. McGovern patted Oscar on the back as he made a choking sound."Come on, I'll buy you breakfast, we can't do much more round here until they've finished so let's go leave the forensic guys to do what they do best, we'll head back down to the station and prepare the incident room."

The two officers declined McGovern's kind offer of breakfast and headed to their respective vehicles.

Oscar climbed into his car and patted Buster on the head. "Good boy" He securely put on his seatbelt and checked his rear view mirror. He could see McGovern being surrounded by reporters and photographers as he pushed his way through them towards his car, they were as usual, a formidable pack looking for any scrap or morsel of any news.

"Detective Inspector, any comment for the press"? McGovern held his hands up as he tried to get to his car through the media scrum.

"A body of a male has been discovered, that's all I can say at the moment, so thank you very much ladies and gentleman I need to go now."

There were a few muffled voices as several reporters shouted more questions at McGovern, who did his best to listen to but couldn't decipher.

"This is an ongoing investigation, we will let you know any more information as soon as we can, but I can't answer any specific questions at this stage, thank you, now please, please, get out of the fucking way."

Oscar laughed and shook his head, he'd always admired how Chief Superintendent Crammond handled the press, fending off every question like a master swordsman, McGovern, on the other hand was a different proposition, but having said that he'd done quite well there, till the last comment, good old McGovern. Oscar had no inkling to be a DI, far too much talking to the press, and he knew how much McGovern detested that part of his job.

Oscar was the first one back to the station, opening the passenger side door Buster shot out across the car park and through the doors.

The station was bustling with activity with the ringing of the desk phones and the blur of voices.

Three uniformed officers were attempting in vain to haul an irate eighteen stone African woman up a set of steps, following an alleged assault on a metro Inspector in an invalid ticket row.

Oscar climbed the steps and counted them as he went *the usual thirteen* to the first floor.

The incident room was buzzing with the news of the murder case. He was quickly joined by Daniel Lee, who pulled over a chair and sat close beside him. He began to explain his involvement and the reasons why he had been sent up to Newcastle.

"I've been in Newcastle for six weeks, working undercover. I'm one of the team that Manchester CID and the Met put together to try and infiltrate a Criminal Chinese Syndicate called the Gan-Yin. They are a Triad group, who control a lot of betting houses that are based in South East Asia, mainly Hong Kong, Malaysia and Singapore. We know that they are behind recent floodlight failures involving Premiership Clubs, and have made a fortune from illegal betting. We heard from a very good source that Newcastle United were the next target, and this, I'm afraid, has proven to be the case. The murder, shows all the hall marks of a Gan-Yin execution, and now confirms that they *are* now active in Newcastle."

Oscar poured himself a cup of tea, milk, and three sugars. Daniel Lee made black coffee and drank it as hot as he could.

McGovern, lumbered through the door brushing some of the remains of his bacon sandwich down the front of his jacket a freshly acquired tomato sauce stained dinner medal half way down his creased white shirt "You two have really missed out; this sandwich is the best one I've had in ages."

Buster appeared from under Oscar's desk, his senses roused by the aroma of McGovern's bacon sandwich. McGovern took a large bite, his voice barely audible as he pointed at the cheeky little dog "Not this time, you greedy little sandwich thief", then pointing at Oscar "You need to feed that dog more, it's always fucking hungry."

Oscar replied without lifting his head. "Should be *your* dog then shouldn't he," they all chortled but McGovern, for once, got serious, as he addressed the incident room.

"Right, our Victim's name is Alex Brennan, he was forty two years old, married, two kids, and but for a few money problems clean as a whistle, no previous and no criminal record. He worked for a security agency that has a contract with Newcastle United. He is, or should I say was, the clubs main chief security officer on match days, responsible for ground and spectator safety and security. We need to find out more about him, what kind of person he was? We need to check his house, his laptop, his car, I want all his friends and associates listed and statements taken. The taxi firm that had been trying to contact him on his mobile was indeed Polaris Cabs," he turned to his young colleague, "Well spotted son. They say he left a holdall on the back seat which contained wire cutters, rubber gloves, a torch, his wallet, passport, and a one way air ticket to Jersey. We have also found out that a Chinese man paid two hundred and fifty grand cash into his bank account yesterday morning. We'll need to find out who that was, and why. We tried to go and see his wife but she was already in Jersey, she had no idea about what was going on, he had told her that he'd been delayed and that he would catch the next flight out but didn't show up, she just thought they were just going on a family holiday. Looked like Brennan had planned this for a while as his wife said the holiday was booked two months ago. What's your initial thoughts gentlemen"?

Oscar got to his feet and walked over to the evidence board on the wall where, had already been attached, various photos of the crime scene and other miscellaneous information connected to the case. Oscar turned to address the other detectives.

"Detective Lee has filled me in on his involvement. The CCTV from the bank showing the transaction, do we have that yet sir"? McGovern shook his head.

Oscar continued "Well seeing that there was no floodlight failure at the last Newcastle match, and the fact that Brennan appeared to have been paid to kill the lights, had the means and equipment to do it, and was in a position to carry it out, but didn't is obviously would I guess be the reason he was killed. We could do with speaking to the taxi driver, has he been traced yet"?

McGovern was now licking ketchup off his fingers "Yes, he's on his way in, Lee, can you tell us any more about this Gan-Yin syndicate"?

Lee got to his feet. "They operate all over Europe; we think that in total there have been approximately four hundred or so games targeted right across the continent. We know they've made a fortune; estimation is around the seven Million mark. It's too easy for them. There is no will to regulate gambling in South East Asia. There is a lack of commitment betting is different across there. A single Premier League football match is worth millions of pounds to one of these syndicates. The main problem being, in their betting rules, as soon as the game passes the halfway stage the result stands even if the game is prematurely ended. We know that this has happened in two games already this season , Newcastle United should have been the third, as Oscar said, It looks like Brennan was bribed to cut the lights, didn't do it and paid the ultimate penalty."

Oscar listened with interest "Brennan was unlucky. If Newcastle hadn't scored in the second half he'd have been in the clear, typical Newcastle United, when you *Don't* want them to score they bloody well do"!

McGovern was more interested in the source of Daniel Lee's knowledge "You seem to know a lot about these Asian crime syndicates, so how long have you been investigating them then?"

Lee took a deep breath and gave a sigh; they could see the emotion in his eyes, the sadness in his voice.

"Simple fact is, I used to be in one! I was what they call a Blue Lantern."

Lee could see the puzzled look on their faces, and he looked up to the ceiling "I'll start from the beginning. I grew up in Hong Kong, when I was thirteen I got in with the wrong crowd. The crime syndicates used to recruit new members from the slum areas, 'Blue Lantern's' as we were called, weren't fully associated members, mainly just kids, like me, mostly older though, informants, wannabees if you like, and with the hope of fame, respect, and lots of money young boys were seduced by the idea of being in the safety, security and protection of the syndicate. I began running errands for the gangs 'White Paper'. He was a kind of an administrator, well how it continues is, I witnessed his murder several years later by a rival gang's young, up and coming enforcer or 'Red Pole' named Kong Hao, and foolishly agreed to give evidence in the pending trail. When Hao was sprung by the Gan-Yin on his way to court I was immediately put into Police protection. One of the officers who were supposed to be protecting me was found to be on the Gan-Yin's payroll, the other was killed. Kong Hao disappeared. My mum and dad were both dead, but I had relatives living in the UK and it was agreed that for my own safety I would be moved to England. New start, new life, if you like. I studied hard, went to college and decided that I wanted to become a police officer. I guess I was lucky as at the time the recruitment of ethnic minority police officers was a big thing, especially in the Met. I was eventually transferred to Manchester CID, where I have been ever since, trying to infiltrate these south east Asian crime syndicates who are rapidly spreading all over the UK."

McGovern and Oscar listened intently, they could see he knew what he was talking about, he was definitely an expert on the subject, Lee continued.

"The Gan-Yin are now the largest of these groups operating in the UK. They are mainly based in the Manchester area but are spreading and now have groups in Birmingham, Glasgow, and of course London, with smaller groups in Bristol, Stoke and Cardiff, although the members are recruited in the traditional manner, many members include prominent business men who either ally with the organisation for their own protection or as full associated participants in their own criminal activities. Because of its useful location it was only going to be a matter of time before they would come to the forefront into Newcastle."

McGovern interrupted him "Thank you Detective Lee, but we've had a Large Chinese population in Newcastle for years now, and we've never had any problems from any of them."

"Times are changing Inspector, perhaps one of the reasons you'd had no problems is the probability that the controlling syndicate that had always been present, in Newcastle, has kept it that way. Now they have decided to, shall we say, 'branch out' a little"?

CHAPTER SEVEN

Mick Western, drawing on his cigarette until the end glowed through the ash, laughed as he drove home; real laughing tinged with hysteria. Heading for his flat to begin toasting his new found 'business partner' in a heavy drinking session.

Calling at a local off- licence he bought some strong lager. So chuffed with himself he came close to colliding with the door on the way out.

Once home he drank himself to oblivion and fell asleep. Waking several hours later he sat in his rented one bed roomed flat and contemplated his next move. His wallet and pockets now empty after more cans of special brew and indefinite lines of heavily cut cocaine.

His head pounding, as he'd snorted the equal of Escobar's pension, he headed to the bathroom and looked at his reflection. Stubble, heavy red jowls and bloodshot eyes. He shook his head and smiled to himself as he made his way back into his living room and sat. Leaning back in his chair to stretch his back. He had to make more money, to fund his preferred lifestyle, and he would. With Johnny 'agreeing' to do shitty stuff for him, now to make real money. He just needed a better plan.

His antics at the SnapDragon Casino had not gone down too well, He had tread on some bodies toes, and he was about to get a visit, but not one he would have either wanted or expected. This wasn't a private war any longer. Someone else was in charge now.

Forensic officer Peter Devon entered the office, with a cup of tea in one hand, clipboard in the other and gave Oscar the autopsy report on Alex Brennan.

McGovern was eager for an update. "Anything of interest then"?

Oscar opened the folder and spread out sheets of information on the desk in front of him. He took a piece of A4 paper and began to read. "One or two things sir, he *was* drugged, large traces of opiate, maybe heroin in his system, there were traces of skin under his fingernails, just waiting for forensics to run it through the DNA database, cross check with criminal records, etc, etc. Time of death a little later than we first thought; it looks like Heroin was given to keep him from passing out, to make sure he remained conscious throughout the torture, although he must have gone through untold agony .Multiple lacerations some more than an inch deep, several lacerations severing the intestines and soft tissue of the abdomen, multiple lacerations on both sides of the torso and legs and the laryngotracheal passage being cut the final act which eventually killed him. From the initial cut in his chest forensics tests show he lasted well over an hour before he died."

The conversation was interrupted by the shrill of the desk phone, making McGovern wince, He answered it. "Oscar, that taxi driver who picked up Brennan is downstairs, care to do the honours"?

"No problem sir." Oscar handed the forensic report over to Daniel Lee. Leaving the incident room he made his way along passing the many small offices and then down the wide open plan staircase, counting them as he went, the usual thirteen, *unlucky for some, but not for me because I count them.*

A small man with a severe crew cut, several tattoos and a small gold hooped earring was sitting in the reception area downstairs. Oscar approached him in his usual friendly manner.

"Hello sir, are you the taxi driver"?

"Yes, Barry Dunbar, I work for Polaris Cabs, is this gonna take long, time is money you know."

Oscar joked to try and put him at ease. "Well, as long as you're metres not running" he held out his hand, "I'm Detective Sergeant Oscar Smiles, this way please."

He led Barry Dunbar to a small interview room, a room without view, no windows or natural light. Clinically white painted, just three chairs and a temporary plastic table with aluminium folding legs. The table was bare apart from several circular tea stains and a half empty plastic cup which had the remains of a brown liquid that was barely recognisable as coffee.

"Would you like a drink Mr Dunbar"?

The taxi driver smiled politely and shook his head, as Oscar sat and shimmied along towards the table the room filled with the noise of the chair being dragged across the bare floor boards. "Tell me what you can remember then"?

The taxi driver leant forward in his seat, placed his elbows on the table, hands together and began."I got a call about eight twenty, a fare, from St James' Park Football Ground to Newcastle International airport."

"What time did you have to be at the ground for"?

Dunbar ran a hand over his close cropped hair "The pickup time was eight thirty five; I'd just dropped someone off in the Dragon Gate and was quite near so I took the job on."

"So that would have been half time, did you not think that a little odd"?

"Not really, no, we often get calls to the ground while the games are still on but it's mostly when people have to be somewhere quick, like an emergency or something like that, you know, ill relative, child, wife locked herself out, or gone into labour, that sort of thing."

"So what happened next then"?

"The customer, Mr Brennan, I believe he was called, came down the stairs, followed by two men , both big one was definitely Chinese, the other couldn't say as he had a hoodie on and didn't speak, might have been

Chinese though. They all got into the back seats of the cab."

"How did Brennan appear"?

"Well, he didn't speak at all, one of the blokes, a Chinese bloke did all the talking, and Brennan looked a little shocked, surprised, a bit agitated."

"So you say Brennan didn't speak at all"?

"No the Chinese bloke seemed to be in control of the situation, he told me to drop them outside the Casino in the Dragon Gate, I asked about the airport, but he said there had been a change of plan."

"So, you dropped them off outside the Casino, what then"?

"The Chinese bloke handed me a twenty and told me to keep the change, the fare was only four fifty so I was well pleased."

"What about Brennan's bag"?

Barry Dunbar wriggled himself up to his full height. "The holdall, you mean, I didn't notice that until the next fare got in, a young lass, told me there was a bag on the floor. Once I'd dropped her off I contacted the office and they said they would try and contact the owner, and for me to drop it in."

"Now tell me what you remember about these two men"?

Barry Dunbar picked at his fingers removing some hard skin from just under his thumbnail. No matter how hard he tried he couldn't conjure up either of the two faces in any great or useful detail. "Not a lot, to be honest, didn't get a great look at the faces, it was dark, and they both sat in the back, either side of Mr Brennan. Sorry."

"Did they speak to each other at all, any conversation you can remember."

"No, total silence, apart from the instructions, I got the impression they weren't friends."

"Well thanks for coming in Mr Dunbar", Oscar took a business card out of his waistcoat pocket and handed it to the taxi driver. "If you think of anything else, my numbers on there."

Oscar headed back up the stairs, counting to himself as he went, *the usual thirteen, unlucky for some but not for me because I count them*, back to the main office.

McGovern was devouring the last of another bacon sandwich and Lee was busily working away on the computer.

"Brennan got in the cab with two guys, could have both been Chinese. But he's not sure."

"Is he sure of that"? McGovern shook his head in disgust, unfolded his arms, and attempted in vain to cross his short dumpy legs under the table.

"Yes sir, definitely, why do you ask"?

McGovern for once was smiling. It was midway through the morning, they had a breakthrough, holding up a piece of A4 paper. "The skin under our victim's fingernails, the DNA profilers have a match, Mick Western."

Oscar looked up from the file he was reading at his desk "You mean Mick Western Newcastle's friendly neighbourhood loan shark."

"That's the boy, we will need to contact him, bring him in for questioning. Murder is not his usual M.O but we need to find out how his skin is found under Brennan's finger nails. We're going up to the ground soon; see if we can find out more about Alex Brennan."

Oscar nodded and picked a cluster of files from his desk "I'll get sorting through these when we get back then."

CHAPTER EIGHT

The three detectives drove up a short hill towards an impressive towering structure which was St James' Park, home of Newcastle United Football Club.

They pulled in through the gates, driving past the towering West Stand and parked in the visitor's car park.

They entered the ground through a revolving door and into the impressive reception area, which smelt of polish and windolene.

As the three detectives approached the main desk. A Pretty girl in her mid twenties with long dark hair, slightly orange complexion and perfect eyebrows greeted them with a corporate smile. "Welcome to Newcastle United Football Club, can I help you gentlemen?"

McGovern stepped forward, hands in pockets. "We need to speak to some-one in charge"!

The young receptionist picked up the phone. "That'll be Kim Deehan; I'll see if she's available, do you have an appointment? and I'll need a name"?

McGovern took out his badge "Here's my appointment card love, DI McGovern Tyneside CID."

She smiled back at him this time raising those perfectly plucked eyebrows and made several frantic phone calls, then wrote down their names, time of arrival and who they were there to see.

Within a few moments a very attractive woman with long dark hair in a trouser suit, was hurriedly and carefully making her way down the most precarious of staircases, her high heels clacking on the marble steps. She approached the three officers solemnly but sleek with an air of elegance as she greeted them, before introducing herself. "Kim Deehan, Operations manager, how can I help you"? She spoke with the assertiveness and confidence you'd expect from a woman with an important role in such a male dominated business.

McGovern introduced himself, "I'm Detective Inspector McGovern Tyneside CID, this is Detective Sergeant Smiles and Detective Constable Lee, we want to ask you about Alex Brennan"?

She offered the men a seat, sat down beside them and moved a rouge strand of her long dark hair behind her left ear with her fingers. She smiled. "Oh he's worked here for about five years, lovely man; he's our chief security Officer."

McGovern loved being the bearer of bad tidings, and this was no exception, "Well not anymore he's not, because he's been murdered."

The news appeared to take several seconds to sink in. Her eyes were wide, shocked as she struggled to take it in.

McGovern continued "How well did you know him"?

"Fairly well, I suppose, murdered, oh that's awful, shocking news, what about his poor wife, and his kids. What happened to him? when ?, where"?

McGovern was about as diplomatic as always, ignoring her obvious concern, and shock "You were telling us how well you knew him"?

Kim tried to recapture her thoughts, obviously elsewhere as she came to terms with the bad news, "We... Erm... did a lot of interviews together, mainly match day staff, stewards especially, he was in charge of the security and safety of the stadium and the spectators, Sorry, Oh this is dreadful news, how's his family, his wife, kids"?

Oscar stepped in "He was murdered two nights ago, shortly after the West Ham match, his family have been informed, his wife and kids are on the way back from holiday, other family are meeting them, it's going to be difficult for them but hopefully they will be able to get lots of support to help them through it."

Kim smiled in a show of a sincere thank you.

McGovern, as always, got back to the point.

"Did you notice anything strange about him recently, any changes in behaviour"?

Kim thought for a moment, "We'll he did seem a little distant at times, like he had something on his mind, but nothing major, no, he tended to keep himself to himself anyway, a very private man."

Kim was becoming a little more distressed, her eyes were reddening and the tears were welling up inside her.

Oscar felt that it was maybe time to change the level of questioning. "Do you employ many workers from ethnic minorities"?

"Yes, we do", Kim appeared pleased that the level, direction, and focus of the questions have changed and saw the question as a chance to promote club policies "We have several employees from ethnic minority backgrounds, the club prides itself on opportunity for all. We welcome applications from all of society, all groups, we have a fantastic equality and diversity policy and remain true to it."

Taking out his pen and notepad, Oscar scribbled a few sentences down, as they spoke. "Were particularly interested in employees from the south East Asian area."

Oscar's attempts to remain diplomatic and politically correct were quickly shot down by McGovern's impatience, and moral principles."Chinkies, you got many Chinkies working here"?

Kim appeared a little puzzled by the question "Chinese workers? what has that got to do with Alex's murder"?

Oscar elaborated "We understand that Alex Brennan was paid by a Hong Kong based, Chinese syndicate to turn off the power to the floodlights during the West Ham game, a witness seen him get into a taxi with two people, at least one of which was Chinese, possibly both, all three came from the *inside* of the ground."

Kim listened intently nodding her head. "Oh, I see, we did have a dozen workers of oriental descent or maybe ten."

McGovern, thinking of impending extra work abruptly informed her "Well, love we're gonna need names, addresses, telephone numbers for them all."

Daniel Lee pulled out a mugshot picture of Mick Western and held it up for Kim to have a good look at "Have you ever seen this man, his name is Mick Western"?

Again Kim paused for a second in consideration, gave a quick shake of her head and bit her bottom lip as she thought "Wait a minute I don't know his face but I remember the name. He tried to get into the ground for the West ham game, I'm sure. He's on some banned list, a known Hooligan I think. I'm sure there was some kind of incident at one of the turnstiles, Alex would have been called, and there should be an incident report."

"Any CCTV"? Oscar, as ever, one step ahead.

"Yes, there will be. Each turnstile has its own camera, I can get you the recordings but it might take a while."

McGovern heaved himself to his feet his eyes less patient than his words "We'll love, any information you can give us would be most useful, we need lists of any stewards on duty, any Chinese workers, the security DVD's from the turnstiles, that incident report and whatever you can get us, Oscar you stay here and help gather that information, I'm going to take Detective Lee to McCaffrey's for some lunch, meet us there son, when your done here."

As McGovern and Lee headed through reception and out of the ground, Oscar apologised to Kim for the abruptness and insensitivity of his senior.

"I'm really sorry about the way you found out about Mr Brennan, Inspector McGovern is a bit of a dinosaur, tact, diplomacy, and sensitivity are not really any of his traits I'm afraid."

Kim laughed in his face "Unlike you eh"?

Oscar's face reddened, uncomfortable at her attempt at flirting.

She got out of her chair and walked over to the stairs, then turned back, "Can I get you a coffee, tea or something, and I'll be as quick as I can but it could be a while."

"No I'm fine, I'll just wait here and admire the view." Oscar's face again reddened, as he quickly pointed to the window overlooking the river. He instantly realised that Kim had her back to him, and may have thought him admiring the view had meant him watching *her* back side as she walked away and back up the stairs.

His face burned with self consciousness and guilt, hoping she wouldn't notice.

Kim grasped it immediately, and it amused her greatly. He was trying to avoid her thinking the worst of him, admiring the view of her back side. In other circumstances she might have wanted that as much as she sensed he did. *Cute* she thought as she walked back up the stairs to collect the required information.

As Oscar sat in the reception area, he was amazed to see the place so busy. The young receptionist fielding telephone call after telephone call, switching from English to French to Spanish, Oscar was well impressed.

It continued, no sooner than one phone was put down than other line would ring, From what he could hear listening to the one sided conversation there were many different types of enquiries from reporters wanting exclusive stories, agents wanting to speak to the manager, and companies booking corporate events.

St James Park was not just a football ground any more like it used to be years ago, it was now in place for conferences and functions, seven days a week. A Hub of activity.

An open mouthed doe eyed young fan dressed in full Newcastle strip came into the reception area with his father, an obvious competition winner there to claim his prize of what-ever it might be. They were closely followed by a woman in her twenties accompanied by an older woman, Oscar guest her mother, wanting to confirm and pay a deposit on her wedding booking. He picked up a glossy brochure from the smoky dark glass coffee table in front of him. He thumbed through it, and thought that his sister Gemma would have loved to have had her wedding here, *bet it was expensive though, well out of the reach of everyday working class people, us mere mortals.*

He read the first page of the wedding brochure, 'Whether you're planning a small, intimate gathering or a grand spectacle, our team at Newcastle United have the expertise to make your special day a treasured memory'.

Oscar looked around once more, *the money that this club must be raking in, it's staggering.* He thought

After twenty minutes, Kim returned with a large brown envelope and a stack of DVDs."Sorry for the delay, there you go detective, I hope your wait wasn't too long."

"No, thank you so much." Oscar reached into his waistcoat pocket. He produced a business card, handing it to her "Just in case you can think of anything else, you can call me, it's my direct line."

As Kim looked at Oscar she couldn't help but notice his bright blue eyes, his slim elegant frame, his shoulder length wavy dark hair and his expensive suit, she couldn't help but think how attractive he was. "What if I can't think of anything? Can I still call you then"? She laughed, as once again Oscar began to feel the red flush rise from his neck, and onto his cheeks. He didn't answer, he just smiled awkwardly and thanked her for the information she had given him.

Clumsily he got to his feet, dropping several DVD's and bending to pick them up and once again apologising for his clumsiness and offering her his hand and went to join McGovern and Lee in McCaffrey's bar.

CHAPTER NINE

McCaffrey's bar was situated at the beginning of the Dragon Gate. Oscar could hear live Irish music and laughter coming from inside as he pulled his car into the pubs small but secure car Park.

McCaffrey's, was an excellent example of a typical Irish pub, somewhat cluttered, and messy. Walking in through the doors he instantly became aware of heat from the coal fire inside, and felt like he had been transported back to a different time.

It hadn't changed one bit since it had first opened. Atmosphere was always fantastic, with its low lighting and dark decor; so relaxing compared to the hustle and bustle of other city watering holes. A big favourite of all the Police Officers and also reasonably close to the station. They had become permanent fixtures at the bar and they wouldn't remember a time when they didn't have a good night out there.

Today the pub was crammed with medical students from the nearby RVI Hospital with their laughter, large Brandy's and well spoken accents that sliced through the atmospheric din like scalpels.

Most of the people present seemed to have strayed in for a drink at lunchtime and stayed. From an adjoining room came sounds of breaking glass and ironic cheers and shouts of 'sack the juggler'.

McCaffrey's had a very Intriguing Irish menu with cheerful, helpful and friendly bar staff.

It was exactly what you want in a pub, no bandits, video machines or jukebox. There was no TV, except for special football matches and sporting events when a large pull down screen was specially installed. A great feel to the place, good beer and good food.

There was a busy section and a noisier side of the pub but there was a quieter side for those who enjoy conversation with their food and drink. Also, they had an outdoor fireplace with casual seating behind the pub with plenty of choices for everyone.

The food was good, very good - McGovern normally insisted on Irish stew with soda bread. McCaffrey's was very comfortable.

It had three bars in it. They only opened the basement bar for special occasions so there was always a place to get a drink. No long lines, lots of leather furniture and even a roaring fireplace.

Outside there was a fire pit, fountain and tiki bar. The basement was the place to hang if you were a fan of live authentic Irish music, most typically at weekends.

All and all it was the most easy going place around to just hang out and chill, perfect in fact to wind down after a hard day, or often in McGovern's case morning's detective work.

In contrast, the dining room area evoked an Irish peasant cottage. Bonding on the wall also from Ireland resembled render. Along shelves near the ceiling were antique jugs and other items of rural life, imported from the home country. Walls were decorated with old-time ads for cigarettes, beer and whiskey as well as calls to arms for Irish independence. The exposed wooden beams were old Irish railroad sleepers and ties, the hum of contented conversation, the flickering glow of flames in the two stone fireplaces, as a homey feeling enveloped you.

Landlord was the ever witty and Jolly Michael McLaughlin, with a deep pitched Irish accent, and curly ginger hair, who welcomed everyone as if they were indeed his own relatives.

McCaffrey's bar had been part of the Newcastle social scene for many years and, having taken over from his father, truly a family run business.

Because of its close proximity to the centre of town it was always busy, vibrant and normally the best place to begin, or end, your evenings out. Equally many people chose to stay there listen to the bands and have some good old Irish craic.

Squeezing himself past a large group of office workers on their lunch break, Oscar made his way to the quieter side where McGovern and Lee sat. McGovern washed down his second cheese and onion bap with his third pint of Guinness not noticing that some mayonnaise had slid from the edge of the bread onto his welcoming tie. He was already well into one of his stories, wiping foam from his lip.

"You remember him, don't you? That loan shark that Mick Western put out of business."

"Vaguely, sir, what was his name again"?

"His name was Billy the slasher."

"Yes I remember him, have you been filling Lee in about how Western got started"?

"No, son, Billy the slasher is sitting right over there." McGovern looked away gesturing with his head, sitting over by the door, drinking all on his own sat a shortish old man wearing a bulky jumper with a flat cap, grey hair and a weepy right eye.

Lee was inquisitive, his tone hopeful of hearing the story in full, "I don't think I would have wanted to owe money to somebody called Billy the slasher"!

McGovern continued to explain in greater detail, as he lifted his quickly emptying pint of Guinness once more to his mouth. "Yes, he was some boy, Billy the slasher, always got his money in the end."

Lee was hungry for more information, "So I suppose he got his name from the punishments he dished out to people who didn't pay."

"Yes son, spot on with that". McGovern placed his pint onto a beer mat in the middle of the table."

Sitting himself down Oscar handed the DVD's to McGovern, "Any incident with Western and Alex Brennan should be among this lot."

McGovern immediately handed the DVD's to Lee. "There you go son, there's your job for the rest of the day."

Lee took the DVD's and got to his feet but with curiosity getting the better of him sat back down.

"Tell me more about this Billy the Slasher character then"?

Oscar continued with the story. "How he got his nickname you mean"?

"*Obviously*", Lee made no attempt to suppress the sigh, his eyes locked on the little old man sitting in the corner.

Looking to both his left and right Oscar lent in nearer towards Lee and lowered his voice, almost to a whisper, "There was this family that borrowed a few hundred pounds from Billy to buy a three piece suite."

Lee was open mouthed with shock, "A few hundred!, he slashed them up for that"?

"No, no, there's more, listen carefully."

Oscar looked towards where Billy was sitting, he stopped in mid sentence as Billy got up from his chair and walked over towards them.

McGovern was a little concerned, "Do you think he's fucking heard us."

"Don't think so sir, the toilets are just behind us."

Sure enough Billy walked past their table and nodded his head at them on his way to the gent's toilet.

Daniel Lee was keen to hear the rest of the story, "*So*"?

Oscar checked to see that Billy had gone into the toilets before continuing. "So, like I was saying this family owed for this three piece they had bought with Billy's money. They had missed a couple of payments and Billy wasn't happy, he was very angry."

McGovern joined in "Fucking raging more like, face as sour as last week's milk."

Lee knew that Billy may be coming out of the toilet any second and wanted to get to the main part of the story, time was of the essence *"And"*?

Oscar looked over towards the toilets, the coast was still clear, "Billy called to see the family and as it had been a couple of weeks since his last visit he caught them off guard. The young son, seven years old, I think he was, opened the front door and Billy just barged in past him. The whole family were there just sitting there watching TV, nationwide, some shit show like that sitting on the lovely new three piece suite when he did it."

Lee was still sitting open mouthed "Did what? what did he do to them"?

"Something so grotesque, that it couldn't be believed."

Oscar put his finger to his lips and made a silencing motion as he craned his neck, the three detectives all looked in opposite directions as Billy the slasher returned from the toilet and walked passed them back towards his chair.

Oscar continued in a quiet whispering voice. "He took out his...." Oscar shook his head as he urged McGovern to continue.

"Big Chopper and pissed all over the sofa and chairs, fucking ruined them all, and so was born the legend of Billy the slasher." Oscar and McGovern could not contain their laughter.

"You bastards," Lee smiled at them, slurped down his pint, laughed at his own thoughts and grinned at them both; he'd fell for it hook line and sinker. "So who is that old bloke over there then"?

McGovern continued to laugh "Not a fucking clue son, never seen him before in my life."

Looking at the pile of DVD's Lee shook his head."I'll see you back in the incident room then sir."

"No, not today son, I'm gonna stay here a while longer, both of you meet me here about six, we'll have a catch up then."

Oscar ordered some Irish stew with soda bread, landlord Michael McLaughlin plucked the menu from his hands and insisted on bringing out 'only the best'.

It arrived within minutes. McGovern was right; it tasted delicious, always steaming hot.

Oscar had had a brief look through the football club personnel records and incident report involving Mick Western.

"I've got the report here sir According to Hugh Grey, Senior Safety Steward; he wrote the report, that stewards, Himself and a man named Rod Appleby, were called to turnstile 24A by Brennan for assistance. A call had come in from football intelligence Officer Gary Shannon, that a known football thug, Mick Western, had been spotted on CCTV and was heading up towards the ground, and looking like he would be attempting to gain entry to the stadium. He was intercepted at the turnstile and things got a bit heated. Western threatened him and Brennan apparently grabbed his face in an altercation which ended in Western being ejected from the vicinity. It all seems pretty straight forward, we just have to tie up a few loose ends, Lee needs to find the incident and I will need to contact the two stewards on duty at the gate, and speak with Gary Shannon to see if everything matches up."

McGovern, almost finished eating was, getting through a last mouthful and now starting back on the ale, he gulped at his pint before wiping his mouth noisily then put it down on the table, "Get your dinner in you first then get back to the incident room, you can go through those personnel records in more detail."

"Yes, sir, I've still got a fair bit to do, there's all those Chinese staff to contact and I'll need to arrange interviews with those two stewards as well. Gary Shannon should be easier to find, I'll try to catch up with him in the station."

Finishing his stew and soda bread Oscar pushed away the half empty plate and watched as McGovern put his hands on his thighs and shoved himself painfully to his feet.

Oscar also thought of heading back to the incident room to pick the bones out of the mound of potential evidence he had at his fingertips, as his mind ticked over.

Gary Shannon was sitting in the station canteen eating an all day breakfast and fussing around with a ketchup bottle, jinking little drops onto his plate. He recognised Oscar immediately.

They were of similar age, but although both did their initial training together Gary Shannon had remained at the rank of Police Constable. He enjoyed his role in the Football intelligence unit and didn't feel that promotion would be something he would consider short term.

Oscar drew out an aluminium chair and sat midway down the table, scraping it along the floor, to sit opposite.

Shannon took such a huge mouthful he couldn't speak for a few moments "You not having anything, Oscar"?

"No, had some of that famous Irish Stew at McCaffrey's, you know what McGovern keeps raving on about, home cooked it's better for you than that shortcut to a heart attack that you're eating."

Shannon spoke between mouthfuls of sausage , egg, and bacon "Maybe so, but this tastes *so* good, especially if you've had no breakfast."

Waiting for Gary to take a large forkful of food, chew it and swallow Oscar asked a question."Tell me about the incident with Mick Western, at the ground."

Shannon spoke as he began to cut his sausage and bacon into smaller, more manageable sizes. "I spotted him straight away. He's probably the most recognisable of all the hooligans that have attached themselves to the Toon. CCTV cameras picked him up just beside St James' Metro station. At first I thought he was heading towards the Strawberry pub but he turned and headed up towards the Milburn stand."

"What next then" ?

"I followed him using the various cameras as he went, it was just a matter of seeing which turnstile he was going to try and get through. He joined a small queue outside turnstile 24A, so I contacted Hugh Grey, who then let Alex Brennan know what was going on."

"So what normally happens in that sort of incident"?

Shannon used his fork to pick up a small piece of bacon, a mushroom and a cut up piece of sausage with his knife and dunked them into the yolk of his fried egg. "I normally contact Alex Brennan and ask him to see if he wants any Police officers present, he normally said yes, but on this occasion he said he would deal with it personally."

"So why do you think he did that"?

"Dunno, maybe didn't fancy it dragging on, or the paperwork involved, perhaps he felt he could defuse the situation." He shrugged his shoulders as he put the fork full of food into his mouth.

"Does seem a bit odd though, especially somebody like Mick Western."

"Yes, fucking nutter like him, you'd expect at least four officers would be needed, minimum."

"So did you watch the incident then"?

Shannon just shook his head with a mouth full of breakfast as he tried to quickly swallow, but coughed slightly and cleared his throat with a lukewarm cup of tea. "It's sometimes a ploy to get other hooligans in the ground. Send a well known face to a turnstile all the attention is taken away from other areas, I watched other areas of the ground but it appeared he was a lone wolf, when I went back to the camera beside 24A, it was all over. Western was walking back towards the Metro Station."

"Thanks, I'll let you get on with your dinner, try not to choke will you."

Shannon smiled, folding a slice of thick buttered bread in half as he began to slowly wipe it around his plate.

Oscar headed back to the incident room, through the main station doors and up the stairs, counting in his head as he went, *thirteen steps.*

He placed the file on his desk. He had a few names to check up on, it hopefully wouldn't take him too long.

It wasn't long before six pm arrived and Oscar and Lee headed back to McCaffrey's to give McGovern an update.

By this time McGovern was slightly intoxicated. Beckoning his two detectives over to where he sat, he ordered them both a drink and asked "Well boys, what you got for me then"?

Lee spoke first. He gave brief details of the mass CCTV footage that he had been checking over."Can't find anything on the CCTV yet but there's hours of it, I'll keep going with it."

"What about you then Oscar"?

"I've spoken with Gary Shannon; he didn't actually see the incident but identified Western", then thumbing through his notebook to find his shorthand notes he continued. "He also said that Brennan didn't follow the usual procedure and decided to deal with the incident himself. I've also arranged to meet those two stewards involved in the incident who were on duty, at the ground tomorrow morning, I've contacted all but two of the Chinese workers, one seems very interesting, fake ID, and fake address, basically Michael Yin doesn't exist. The other one, David Leung, I've left messages for him to contact me but nothing as yet. It's also strange that apart from that there are a number of coincidences with those two, they both started at the ground a week ago, both on the same day, they were both interviewed by Kim Deehan *and* Alex Brennan, and they are the only two on the list without a criminal records check.

Another interesting thing is that they both state Walter Chang, the Casino owner, as a previous employer, and he has given both of them a glowing reference. We need to speak to Chang on another matter as well. We've had the CCTV back from the bank, and it was Chang who paid the two hundred and fifty thousand pounds into Brennan's bank account the day he was murdered."

McGovern was pleased with the work so far. He stood up heavily taking hold of both their arms for balance "Well we can't spend all evening sitting drinking in here; we've got work to do."

Having just got there, Oscar and Lee looked at each other and then both stared at the untouched pints of Guinness standing in front of them on the table.

"Lee, you head back to the incident room, get through the rest of that CCTV stuff, get a couple of uniforms to help if you can. Oscar, you and I are going to see Mr Chang."

CHAPTER TEN

Outside it was dark and cold and the rain was coming down heavily. Oscar pulled up his collar as they quickly made their way to McGovern's Volvo which was parked in a nearby side street.

McGovern beeped his car open as he huffed and puffed, patting his pockets, then taking out his glasses he staggered clumsily forward

"Maybe it's better if I drive sir"?

"Yeah, go on then son, I might as well have another tab then."

As Oscar drove he watched the rain streaming down the windscreen.

McGovern's mind was ticking over as the two detectives headed for Walter Chang's Casino in the Dragon Gate.

McGovern lit his cigarette, inhaled and let the smoke drift from his mouth. "We'll see what old Walter has to say for himself, but we'll need to speak to Crammond as I think Chang's phone should be tapped and I want a surveillance team in place round the clock for as long as this takes. I'm sure he'll agree, Chang's involved in this right up to his slinty little eyes."

As McGovern and Oscar stood in the foyer of the SnapDragon Casino, their eyes were captivated by bright lights, their ears to the noise of a gushing waterfall, and glittering antique Chinese artifacts.

In front of them, the main casino door enticed them. Inside the ceiling lights soothed allowing an enchantment of a thousand flashing slot machines to fill the room. As they moved in the direction of the entrance sounds of gambling drew them in.

Two brawny Chinese doormen were keeping their eyes peeled, whatever their eyes should miss, the eyes in the skies captured. Most customers never look up, but Oscar did, the snapDragon these days had over fifty camera domes on every side of them. The foyer alone was protected by even more surveillance cameras. Since Mick Western's uninvited intrusion Walter Chang had improved security systems greatly.

Domes were hiding all sorts of cameras looking at them, between them, and maybe even inside them, using highly developed facial recognition software to look for those who were excluded and other software searched for dubious actions and patterns. The snapDragon casino was just about the most rigorously watched place a normal person could go.

As the two detectives walked through the central body of the Casino, they saw a collection of flashing colours and some absorbing individuals. From the foyer into the guts of the gambling engine, de-lux carpet and craftsmanship gave way to dense fluorescent light, shiny polished floors, and more solem oriental men in suits.

They were met by Jimmy Mei, security chief, who, McGovern felt reminded him of the Bond villain odd job, with his roundish face and serious eyes, a big man and bulky, the kind who could do with all the exercise he didn't get.

They showed their badges, were signed in and headed onto the main body of the Casino floor. Jimmy Mei called the casino owner, who after speaking to his security chief first then turned to them, and held out a bony clammy hand.

"Good day to you gentleman, I am Walter Chang, owner of this wonderful establishment. Now what can I do for you"?

McGovern introduced them. "Detective Inspector McGovern, and this is DS Smiles, is there anywhere where we could have a quiet word"?

Walter Chang was eager to impress "Certainly gentleman, please follow me."

The casino was brimming with colour, and a continuous murmur of slot machines. The noise was bizarre, it wasn't melodic yet it wasn't sound either. It was more of a mechanical environment, clanks, chimes and the infrequent bleep or short sound of musical harmonies. It was the resonance of a thousand slot machines in operation.

No one spoke. Players were resolute, their faces held intolerable impartial expressions concentrating fully on their machines.

Most of the gamblers were of oriental descent, and a surprising amount were elderly. They sat back, leaned forward, and drew deeply on cigarettes. Some pressed buttons. Others pull a lever. The days of the old one arm bandit machines were over. Everything in this modern casino was electronic. All of it glowed, sparkled and sometimes bleeped or cheeped. It was fascinating.

In the middle of the casino, flanked by rows and rows of slots, they could see the games. Card tables, roulette, poker and blackjack.

It was reasonably early but they still saw a hundred people in the time they walked the floor. Not one of them looked particularly happy. Some looked annoyed, but the rest looked determined. Indeed gambling was an important business.

Whatever occurred, there was forever another bet. The buttons sat there in front of you, gleaming gently, quietly mocking you to take your pick. To place your bet.

For some, gambling was a fresh and enjoyable experience. They walked in smiling as they threw pounds into a slot machine. Putting coins into the machine as if feeding a hungry infant. There's always the likelihood of a thousand pound jackpot, but they almost always know better. When their pockets were empty, they just laughed and walked away.

Those are the ones who can let it go. Oscar had seen them previously, on other days in other casinos. Some of the people he saw here were not enjoying it. They were carrying out what they had to do.

As he looked he could see how the games became addictive he was so glad he was never tempted to be a serious gambler.

Chang led the two detectives down a narrow carpeted staircase and into what he called his VIP Lounge, extravagantly furnished with antiques with Chinese vases sat on a walnut bombe chest painted with gold roses, expensive Chinese silk throws were scattered about the room, de-lux lounge furniture in designer Fendi material, and plush carpeting.

Chang's special VIP guests could enjoy exclusivity similar to that experienced in a private members club. Whether the aim was to relax and take in behind the velvet rope in the VIP lounge, with chandelier lighting, plush carpet and luxurious couches.

Sprawled on one of the couches lay Chang's young wife, Sara, Blonde ex-pole dancer and glamour model. She wore a short black skirt, black stockings, ridiculous high heels and a blouse that hung open over the top of her silicon enhanced breasts.

Chang did a kind of introduction. "Drinks for our guests, Sara."

She reluctantly wriggled to her feet, wiping some suspicious looking white powder from the tip of her nose and removed her shoes, her nostrils flared wide with fragile fury as she padded barefoot across the thick carpeted floor, trying hard not to look annoyed.

Sara Chang was a woman in a man's world- she had to use whatever weapons were to hand so she fluttered her eyelashes at McGovern and blew him a kiss, but he knew it was all part of her game and besides he was not feeling very hospitable "No drinks, thanks anyway Mr Chang, but we've got a lot to get through."

Oscar was somewhat surprised at McGovern's refusal of liquid refreshment.

Chang asked Sara to leave the room, which she did without any further reluctance, just a look of silent objection that could turn a man to stone.

McGovern got down to business. He didn't try to conceal his impatience. "Right, Walter, we want to ask you about Michael Yin and David Leung."

Walter remained, ironically, poker faced "Sorry gentleman I've not heard of either of those men."

McGovern knew he was lying, his over enthusiastic response gave him away. "You sure? Mr Chang, you better think again, because .." McGovern gestured to Oscar who took out a piece of A4 paper from his jacket pocket and passed it to his superior. McGovern triumphantly continued with a nasty smile, "Why do I think you're lying? Well, this is what *you* wrote in a reference *you* provided for them, Great timekeepers, exceptional employees, and an asset to any company, you remember now"? a jubilant McGovern pointing his finger at his temple. "And, Alex Brennan, how do you know him?, pretty well?, huh, obviously, as you were seen on CCTV paying a quarter of a million quid into his bank account a day before he was murdered, now you better start talking Mr Chang."

Walter Chang remained calm and nodded his head. He looked taken aback by McGovern's sudden bitterness "Alex Brennan was a regular here. He won that money on roulette, fair and square. We couldn't pay him straight away so I made him a promise that I would personally see to it that the money was paid the next day. I was just keeping my word. I am an honest businessman. As for the other two gentlemen I can't remember writing any references for any one, but may have done, do you have any idea how many people I employ"?

McGovern shrugged his shoulders in disbelief and folded his arms.

Oscar looked at his notes, and spoke "Okay Mr Chang, but I'm sure you can understand us needing to clarify what the money was for, as it's a substantial amount, and as he, Mr Brennan, is now dead, murdered, surely you can understand why we would need to question you about this."

"Yes, I would expect you to, but ask yourself this...If I were planning to kill somebody, wouldn't I kill them *before* I paid them and not after"?

McGovern wasn't impressed. He was obviously not taking any shit today "What *we* think or do Mr Chang is not the issue here. A man has been murdered, and *you* paid him a lot of money, maybe we should take this conversation down to the station, it was, after all, your signature on those references, and you who paid him the money, What kind of idiots do you think we are, enough of your bullshit."

McGovern moved a little closer to Chang, leaning forward drawing his attention. He was beginning to lose his already limited patience. The time had come to force the issue, hopefully get a reaction "Okay then, we need to look into this, a little deeper, so, just suppose we ask to look at all your employment personnel records as we need to find this Yin and Leung, or whatever their called and, just suppose it may come to light that you may, or may not, have an illegal or two working for you, and just suppose we were to report this. That would be a bit of an inconvenience for you wouldn't it, having several officers from the immigration enforcement unit turning this place upside down, Oh and not to mention how good it would be for business, the Police turning up at peak time, but, as we're getting nowhere fast I think we should sort this out down at the station, and make that call to immigration enforcement, you'll need to be arrested of course, just for good measure."

Chang appeared a little more cooperative, McGovern's bluff had done the trick. He swivelled his chair back round towards his desk "Okay, okay, I did write those references, and I don't know the two gentlemen, but I had no choice. I was ordered to do it."

McGovern smiled. He leaned forward in his chair and fixed his eyes on him "Ordered? by who"?

Oscar took out his notebook following McGovern's question. "Was it Mick Western"?

A quick smile, almost colluding, crossed Walter Chang's face as he laughed, finding that comment highly amusing, "Hell no, not that prick, it was the Red Pole."

McGovern rolled his eyes as he felt that Walter Chang was somewhat taking the piss, "A Fucking red what?"

Oscar enlightened him, cocking his head to one side "You know sir, What Lee told us about, a Red Pole in one of these Triad Criminal syndicates."

McGovern nodded, pretending to fully understand but still not sure, and still needing answers continued to question Chang. "Go on then, I'm intrigued."

Walter shook his head. His face creased with disappointment, he gave a deep sigh "This Red Pole is connected to the Gan-Yin Syndicate. He informed me it would be in my best interests to do this favour, know what I'm saying gentleman."

Oscar asked "What's his name? this Red Pole then, who is he"?

Chang shook his head and held up his hands, his voice already again set in defensive grimace. "I don't know, I only spoke to him on the telephone, never saw him, didn't really know much, or indeed, anything about him, but he was definitely Gan-Yin. I have a beautiful wife, and a lot of legitimate businesses to think about, and keep safe, and I would like to keep it that way."

McGovern for once, sounded a little sympathetic "Are this Gan-Yin group taking protection money from you? or taking a share of your profits?, you want to report anything Walter"?

Chang was beginning to become increasingly uneasy. He raised his eyebrows and tried to look shocked "Gentlemen, You expect me to admit to that? surely you can't expect me to answer that question, listen to me, the Gan-Yin insist that they look after security of me, my family and my businesses, and do a bloody good job, I have no trouble here, and wish to keep it that way, arrest me if you wish, but I won't be much use to you, as I have told you everything I know." Chang stood up from the chair he was sitting on, it rocked backwards fast and he was on his feet walking towards the door to open it. But he still didn't want to make an enemy of the Police. Walter Chang stopped and turned and smiled at the officers, a smile as wide as the Tyne Bridge as he paced slowly up and down. He had an idea.

"I am speaking the truth, please stay gentlemen, play my tables and machines, accept my hospitality, I'll even give you one hundred pounds credit on the house to start you off."

McGovern studied his face seriously before becoming quite excited at the prospect of a night's gambling, especially with somebody else's money. The tiniest smile appeared. It broadened to show the edges of his teeth. "Good man Mr Chang, prepare you to lose a fucking fortune."

Oscar was a little concerned at McGovern's lack of professionalism and apparent lack of continued interest in Walter Chang, or if indeed, if he *was* telling the truth.

"Sir, this hundred pounds, could be looked upon as a bribe, do you think we really should be doing this?, we need to get him down to the station, get him arrested, he's heavily involved in all this, I also think there's more to this quarter of a million betting win than meets the eye."

"Look son, just chill out for once will you, Chang is obviously telling the truth he's got far too much to lose, there's always tomorrow anyway, sometimes we have to let these communities police themselves, best not interfere with the politics of it. We need to find this Red Pole *and* Mick Western, there the *real* villains here, not Chang. Let's just enjoy the rest of the night, at Walter Chang's expense."

Sara Chang returned to the VIP lounge and took the two detectives up a narrow staircase and over to a roulette table, trying as she could to impress them with her exaggerated wiggle of her hips walking over to the bar. She returned with a couple of drinks, sat between them and crossed her endless legs. Her extremely short skirt did not leave much to the imagination. As the roulette wheel began to spin she took a cherry from a cocktail stick in her drink and put it suggestively into her mouth, moving her tongue around the cherry, then exaggeratedly leaning across the table,in the hope her enhanced cleavage would distract them, helped herself to two red chips from the pile in front of the dealer and placed them on black.

Oscar watched for several spins of the roulette wheel, McGovern in deep thought was chewing the corners of his moustache. Both hadn't noticed what Sara was doing, they were busy looking carefully at the dealer, the wheel;

While visiting his sister in Canada Oscar had spent many hours in a casino with his brother in law Don, watching and learning, he had spent a lot of time researching and knew it was all about physics and less about probability.

It was probably the result of the excess alcohol but McGovern was feeling lucky, for once, a smile was curling from one corner of his mouth, rubbing his hands in excitement. "Just stick with Red son and keep doubling up, you can't fail."

Oscar, however, was somewhat pessimistic about McGovern's system."You're trying a system called Betting progression sir, when you increase bets to cover losses. It doesn't work because every spin is independent, and when you change bet size you are only changing the amount you bet on an individual spin. At first it's hard to understand this concept because you may be stuck thinking a good win will get back losses, and thinking numbers are due, nothing is ever due to happen. Even after ten reds in a row, the odds of red or black spinning next are no different. If you don't believe me, watch a few spins first, and look for instances where ten reds spin in a row, check the amount of times red or black spins next. You'll find the odds haven't changed. There are many other common misconceptions and ineffective approaches. Ultimately you can only beat roulette by increasing the accuracy of your predictions. How accurate do you need to be? . . . I would say keep in mind the house edge is always a small two point seven percent so you only need to have slightly better than random accuracy. And this is quite easy to do."

McGovern shook his head and gave him a look that warned him there was such a thing as having too much to say, which could then be translated to boring the fucking pants of somebody. Sometimes he needn't wonder how Oscar was still single "Wish I'd kept me fucking mouth shut now."

The wheel spun, bets were placed, wheel stopped, McGovern lost. Oscar won. McGovern wasn't happy. "How did you manage that clever shite"?

Oscar gave a sigh, as he knew McGovern wasn't really interested in the method but tried to explain anyway "It's all about a thing called bias analysis which is basically exploiting wheel imperfections, and that's what this wheel has, a slight imperfection. I noticed this after the third spin. Most Roulette wheels have slight imperfections that make some numbers win more than others. This is, I believe, called a biased wheel, and all wheels are biased to some degree. You may have heard of the man who broke the bank at Monte Carlo"?

"I've heard the song"; McGovern became a little more interested.

"They called him Joseph Jagger, and he won a fortune after discovering roulette wheels were biased. This approach to beating roulette has cost casinos many millions."

The wheel spun, bets were placed, wheel stopped, McGovern lost, Oscar won.

McGovern was getting increasingly frustrated, "Bugger this bias analysis bollocks, I call it beginners luck."

Oscar leaned in and whispered some advice to his DI, "Look at the dealer, been watching four or five times now. This dealer tends to spin the wheel and ball at a consistent speed. This can lead to predictable patterns called dealer signature, which is why dealers are usually changed every twenty or thirty minutes."

McGovern was struggling to summon up any interest as Oscar continued. "I've seen some change on the other tables already. However, dealer signature can't work on every wheel. You need the right combination of dealer and wheel. The principles are very simple. Firstly, consider that on most wheels, the ball will tend to hit the metal diamonds more often than others. These are called dominant diamonds. If you drew a chart showing which diamonds the ball hits, it would look....",

McGovern interrupted and lowered his face into his hands "Draw a fucking chart, I just want to win some fucking money, for Christ sake!, Oscar this drivel is all bollocks man, it's pure luck and you have to have a system to have any chance of winning big money."

Oscar shook his head, and was growing increasingly frustrated at his superior's lack of understanding.

"No, I have to correct you sir, look and listen for once. Consider that the ball bounce is never completely unpredictable. For example, if you see where the ball hits the wheel, you can guess approximately where said ball will land. You won't have perfect accuracy, but you don't need perfect accuracy. Now say the wheel was always much the same speed, and the ball always did around ten revolutions before hitting the dominant diamond. This means that the ball would be travelling a predictable distance, be falling in a predictable area, then, and bouncing a predictable distance. Putting this all together, dealer signature requires you to first find suitable wheels. Then you need to find a suitable dealer for that wheel. There's nothing difficult about it, and although it works, it has limitations."

At last he'd noticed and McGovern was now too preoccupied looking down Sara Chang's massive cleavage to hear what was being said. The wheel spun, bets were placed, wheel stopped, McGovern lost, Oscar won again.

McGovern banged his fat, hairy sweaty fist on the table, so hard that even people on other tables looked over "Bastard."

McGovern's gaze left Oscars and Sara Chang's cleavage, meeting her eyes instead. "So how come a twenty something ex porn star ends up marrying a bloke like Walter Chang, his charm and good looks I suppose."McGovern laughed.

Sara Chang smiled, clearly and coolly amused by his interest stared back into his eyes for a moment, as if probing for weaknesses in him "Actually Inspector he is a lovely man, the gold credit card, swimming pool in our back garden, Mercedes car and as many clothes and shoes as I can possibly buy are just what I consider to be added bonuses, besides he's besotted with me, what more could a girl ask for, the stupid old fucker."

"Hey, Chang treats you very well; you should watch your mouth."

Sara couldn't help herself at what she saw as a chance to try and embarrass her guests. She leaned back in her chair with a broad grin "I've got a much better idea, Inspector, why don't I take that young detective of yours back down to the VIP lounge and *you* can watch *my* mouth, I can show you how I got my porn star name."

"And I suppose that's going to be just as predictable as well is it."

She sensed Oscars interest and felt his stare immediately flicking a few strands of her blonde hair behind her ear as she turned to match it. "Oh yes detective, you guess well, my porn name was Cindy Swallows"!

Oscar felt his face redden, and almost choked on his drink as he coughed it out onto the plush blue carpet and then continued to pretend not to watch her with a disinterested curiosity.

McGovern tried in vain to come up with some clever remark but was also a little flustered as he tried to focus his eyes on her "Behave yourself girl."

Sara laughed and held up her hands in a baffled apology and spotting a couple of Newcastle United footballers sitting down at another table, one of which just happened to be the maverick, Darren Harrison, she was off, the hostess with the most est. She walked away absurdly beautiful and somewhat frightening for any mere red blooded mortal male.

Within minutes she would be all but shoving her silicon enhanced breasts into their faces, and he, Harrison, like all men, would be lapping up the attention. Oscar feared Darren Harrison would require rescuing very soon because if he continued to stare into her cleavage there was a chance he could well fall in never to be seen again.

McGovern regained some composure. "Narrow escape there son, anyway wouldn't dare go there, Chang would have your balls chopped off, he knows full well what she's like, I suppose she's good for business, what she gets up to is okay with him, as long as he doesn't find out all that goes on. She's been around the turf more times than a Grand national winner that one."

The two detectives were joined by Daniel Lee, back from the incident room with some information. "I found the altercation between Western and Brennan on the CCTV, and Brennan did grab Western around the neck.

McGovern glanced towards him, and gave him a quick almost imperceptible nod, beckoning him to sit down beside them in the seat that Sara Chang had just vacated.

The wheel about to spin again, McGovern interrupted him, he had a determined look on his face, he once again tapped on the stool for Daniel Lee to sit down and winked, as he turned to Oscar, "Well, clever shite what you going for now"?

Rolling his eyes to the ceiling Oscar took a deep breath before answering. "Well sir, think I'll try visual ballistics this time, which is using eyesight to predict winning numbers. This technique uses your plain eyesight to estimate where the ball will fall. It's not as difficult as you may think. In fact it's quite easy. Visual ballistics is very similar to dealer signature, except you predict the winning number near the end of the spin instead. For example, you make your prediction when there are about five ball revolutions remaining."

The wheel spun, bets were placed, wheel stopped, McGovern lost, Oscar won and Lee collapsed on the floor almost choking with laughter.

Oscar finished the remainder of his drink, "We should still bring Chang in and Western, when we find him, and try and find out about this altercation with Brennan."

McGovern shook his head. "Be a waste of time, though son, he wouldn't give us much, but he's our only definite lead in Brennan's murder at the moment. Western's type never tell you anything, but he does need an alibi, see if you can find him, it should be easy, just hang around outside the nearest social security office, food bank or charity shop."

Getting up from the table, his winnings to cash in Oscar glanced up with a quick uncertain smile, "I've got an early start tomorrow guy's, think I'll head off home, and leave you trying to win your money back sir"!

As Oscar headed back through the Casino, stuffing notes deep into his pockets Sara spotted him, blew him a kiss and waved, "Goodnight pretty boy."

Despite the odd minor win, McGovern and Lee continued to lose money. When McGovern realised that he was beginning to use his *own* money, he called a halt. His speech slurring "Well Daniel, that's enough for me, son, think I'll head off home now."

McGovern took a final long swallow of his beer emptying all but some froth down his grateful neck, rolled off his stool, stumbled, and knocked it over as the numerous drinks he'd had that day were finally beginning to take effect.

A large doorman had been alerted by McGovern's loud behaviour, his head popping up like a meerkat, as he slowly approached.

Lee, keen to avoid a scene, held up McGovern's jacket for him, but he missed the sleeve and staggered against him. Lee continued to assist him with his jacket as if he was a child holding one arm out then the other.

The burly doorman pointed to the exit, "I think your friend needs to leave now, he's had enough," Lee chewed at his lip and nodded.

McGovern held up his hands, slurring his words in a loud sarcastic stage whisper. "Sorry, going home, yes....too much drink." Lee locked eyes with the doorman, smiled and shook his head as he helped McGovern to the exit.

It was well after midnight. McGovern staggered his way out of the Casino. He walked through the main exit doors and felt the freezing December winds cut into his face as he clumsily and slowly negotiated the small concrete steps out of the SnapDragon.

The pavement felt unsteady beneath his feet. He checked around and found a quiet spot, urinating onto the uneven cobbles and his own shoes. He could hear distant footsteps behind him, getting closer. The steps grew heavier, following him. He turned into a back alley leading away from Stowell Street when he heard a demand that turned him instantly sober.

"Give me your wallet"!

CHAPTER ELEVEN

McGovern turned to see a nervous looking young oriental man who in his late teens holding a large knife.

As McGovern turned fully to face his would be assailant, his eyes focused sharply "Pardon you slinty eyed bastard"!

The young boy was shaking, his eyes were vacant. Much of the colour seemed to have left his face. "Your wallet, Mr, give me your wallet."

McGovern let out a deep sigh and shook his head. He glanced down at his clenched fists. "Get out of my way you Chinky Git."

But the young man was unmoved and gestured with the knife "Your Wallet"?

Remaining as calm as he could McGovern glanced up quickly, keeping his gaze firmly on the large sharp blade. He felt he had an obligation to mock this little boy who with the aid of a large kitchen knife was trying to act the hard man.

This was not the first time he'd been in this kind of predicament. "Listen sonny, I'm too old, too drunk and too fucking fat to run, so if you want to fight me for my wallet it will have to be to the death." The drunken thought stopped his breath for a moment.

The young lad, his face sallow, lines curved from his mouth, his cheeks sunken lunged the knife towards McGovern's stomach area, but despite being quite the worse for drink McGovern grabbed him in a head lock and easily disarmed him; taking the knife and pushing it within an inch of his young would be assailants face. "You're in luck son. If I wasn't a copper I'd shove this knife right up your tight little yellow arse."

"YOU OK SIR"? Lee had spotted the commotion, from the top of the steps at the Casino entrance and before McGovern could answer was running towards him.

McGovern loosened his just grip slightly enough for his young assailant to wriggle free and taking his chance made a run for it. He ran, stumbling, almost falling. He knew that had it come down to it he would have been in for a battering from the fat Scotchman with the mad eyes and the clenched fists. McGovern made a move to give chase, then decided it would be far better if Lee did.

Lee grabbed McGovern by the top of his arm, his grip was brief but firm "Just leave it sir, it's not worth it, he's just another poor Chinese kid trying to subsidise his mediocre income, I think you taught him a lesson anyway."McGovern seemed annoyed by that but let it pass.

"Yeah, you're right son, I'm going home now, need to get my head down, I thought i'd recognised him at first, that young lad but then again you lot all luck the fucking same don't you ?, take care Daniel lad, you're a good copper you are, one of the best."

McGovern, rifled through his pockets for his cigarettes, lit and pulled hard on his regal king size.His eyes were heavier now, grin a little less refined, his back was slouched and his brain was running a few grades south of perfect.

He shrugged his heavy shoulders and wandered off down the back lane heading for the taxi rank, singing as he went. *"Oh flower of Scotland, when will we see,"* he threw the knife to one side and it hit the ground with a metallic echoing clang, *"You're like again, to live and die for,"* his song got quieter and quieter as he moved further down the lane and into the distance. Lee shook his head as both detectives' went their separate ways into the dark, damp, and cold December Tyneside night.

6:20am and Buster was sitting on the bottom of Oscar's bed barking loudly. TV had been on all night, as usual.

His eyes flicked towards the TV news report which had caught his attention *"Strange goings on in Belgium as the match between struggling Antwerp and run away league leaders Anderlecht was abandoned just after half time with the scores surprisingly still level."* Oscar shook his head, *got to be a connection.* He struggled out of bed and stumbled towards the bathroom.

In his High Heaton home McGovern, sleeping off the previous night's merriment was woken by his radio alarm clock. He could barely remember what had happened, even what day it was but knew he needed to be in the station in just over an hour's time.

He woke with a sore back and a stiff neck. He coughed as he reached for his cigarettes on the bedside cabinet. Labouring out of bed he lit one and again coughed severely as he took his first drag of the day. Bending down to pick his jacket and trousers off the floor, he vowed never to drink that much again. The shirt he has been sleeping in and wearing all night would have to do, oh the joys of being divorced three times over.

Armpit area of the shirt sniffed he, grabbed some deodorant and gave himself a quick spray then putting on his trousers which were straining under the pressure of his growing stomach.

In the bathroom he stood at the sink squinted at his reflection through the smoke of his cigarette and thought, *what a fucking state*. At nearly sixty years old you got the face you deserved. His head throbbing and his mouth dry, he rubbed sleep from the corner of his eye, turning on the cold tap he splashed water on his face as his attention was turned to the radio news reporter's voice.

And another match ends prematurely, this time in Italy as the Napoli, Roma match ends in farcical conditions after fifty minutes with the score 1-1.

Fuck me, its happening everywhere, he thought.

McGovern saw a pile of letters that had begun to stack up beside his front door. Walking over he picked them up beginning to work his way through them and attempting to prioritise by the way they looked. He opened a brown one with an NHS franked postage mark.

Dear Mr McGovern, blah , blah, blah, could you please ring to arrange a suitable time and date for your Cystoscopy, whatever the fuck that is, I'll ask Oscar, he'll know. He sighed and rubbed his chin.

Daniel Lee was up early, and out running through the deserted streets of Newcastle City Centre. Improving his cardiovascular fitness was always going to be useful in his chosen line of work. He had his healthy breakfast, didn't have time for the gym this morning and got to get in the station for 7:30.

He jogged down by the quayside and over towards Gateshead via the millennium bridge, he ran passed a newsagents shop, a bill board headline outside caught his attention *Brutal City Murder latest,* he Stopped and began to thumb through it. Four page special, and under the headline was a large mugshot of Mick Western. He didn't have any money with him, *one newspaper won't harm,* He had a quick look right and left and being pretty confident nobody had seen him run off with the paper, *I'll drop the money in later.* He headed off towards the station

The atmosphere in the CID room was tense, simmering, waiting. More than its usual hive of activity; Chief Superintendent George Crammond, his few strands of grey combed over his skull in memory of his hair, blinking through his precarious spectacles didn't normally like to spend a great deal of time in the main office.

Although good at his job he would always make one of his excuses and leave knowing full well the men were glad to see the back of him, free to talk, and free to call him names behind his back. He addressed the officers present, and handed proceedings over to the senior investigating officer for the case.

After sighing and putting down his bacon sandwich McGovern got to his feet. He looked dreadful, everything about him was crumpled. "I'm sure you're all aware of the news last night. Two football matches, one in Belgium and another in Italy both ended early in the second half in suspicious circumstances, both floodlight failures. I've got officers contacting the respective forces in both Italy and Belgium, see if there's any links, also the chief Super is in talks right now with the powers that be over there, we all need to liaise with any info and get to the bottom of all this, it looks like this Gan-Yin group are after European domination. Right, let's see where we're up to here then .Oscar."

Oscar was standing by the doorway, feet apart, hands in pockets. "I've got a meeting at St James' Park for ten O'clock, I've got those two Stewards coming in to speak to them about the Western and Brennan altercation, and I also need to ask Kim Deehan for some more info on those Chinese workers, who also both still need to be contacted."

Daniel Lee was still reading the stolen newspaper; a half cup of cold black coffee sat close by him, popping his head around from the paper, and spoke up next "What area do you want me to focus on next then sir"?

McGovern thought hard and long, pushing papers back into files in front of him as he looked at the evidence wall in front of him "Well, we don't seem to be getting anywhere fast, it might pay for you to go back undercover, see what you can find out, keep an eye on the casino and especially Chang, I can't believe that £250,000 was Roulette winnings. Keep your ear close to the ground for news on Mick Western, he seems to have gone off radar somewhat , and if he's *has* got nothing to hide, I want to know why."

Lee nodded over his mug of now undrinkable cold black coffee, neither as strong or as dark as he would have liked. "Okay sir will do." He shuffled through meaningless pieces of paper, took the more relevant items from his desk drawer and headed towards the door.

"Just a second son," McGovern opened his drawer and took out a spiral notebook, his voice stopped Lee in his tracks, "I'll need that mobile number, the one you're using for your undercover work. I need to keep in touch with you."

Lee shook his head and pushed his hands down into his pockets. "No offence sir, but I'll be in regular touch with my handler in Manchester."

McGovern began to raise his voice "This is *my* investigation sunshine and *I* want to know what's going on, not some dopey twat sat hundreds of miles away in Manchester."

"OK sir, I totally understand that but It's better you let me contact you, no phone calls, it could compromise my position and blow my cover, I'll keep *you* updated."

McGovern wasn't convinced it wasn't the way he'd been used to working. "I need to know what's happening, what if I need to call you"?

Daniel Lee locked eyes with McGovern. "Trust me sir, you're a detective, I'm an undercover detective, the rules are different".

"Okay son, I suppose you know best, keep safe, and I want daily updates."

As Lee left the room Oscar got up from his chair and headed down the stairs, followed closely, as ever by Buster. *Thirteen unlucky for some.*

Oscar got into his car to drive the short distance to the football ground. He parked in the club visitor's car park and headed up the stairs towards the revolving door.

Once inside he could see two men sitting awkwardly in the plush reception area. Kim Deehan was talking on her mobile phone. Her black hair piled above her long white neck emphasizing her dark eyes and delicate cheekbones. He caught sight of her, he smiled broadly, his face and large dark eyes relaxed.

As she spotted Oscar she waved, smiled, and quickly brought her conversation to a close with a legitimate excuse to hang up."Detective Smiles, it's a pleasure to see you again."

Oscar sensed the red flush of a blush beginning. Kim firstly introduced Oscar to the two men, and then turned to him. "This is Hugh Grey, Senior safety Steward, he filled in the original report, and this is Rod Appleby, crowd control Stewart. They were both on duty at turnstile 24A."

Oscar thanked them for coming in. Hugh Grey was the older of the two men, looked more senior, leaning back in his chair, one leg tucked under the other, and as he had filed the report Oscar thought its best to level the first question his way.

"Now then, Hugh can you talk me through the events of the incident prior to the West Ham match"?

"Yeah, certainly', Hugh began. "I was stationed in my usual position turnstile 24A with Rod Appleby. When we received a call from the Police Football Intelligence Unit officer, Gary Shannon. He had spotted on the CCTV surveillance cameras a well known and banned football hooligan, was tracking him and felt he was heading towards our turnstile and would try to gain entry into the football ground."

"And did you know his name"?

"Yes, I believed his name to be Mick Western."

Oscar then turned to the younger of the two men, Rod Appleby. "When did your supervisor, Alex Brennan appear"?

"Hugh called him, to let him know Western was in the queue and called him for assistance."

Oscar was carefully writing down quickly as he could, as Hugh Grey continued. "I didn't expect to see Alex come down. He would normally get the Police down to sort things out, for some reason he decided to deal with this himself."

Oscar turned to both men, "How did he behave"? Rod Appleby was first to answer.

"I felt he was a little jumpy, slightly anxious, you know distracted and distant..."

Remembering and interrupting his young colleague Hugh is quick to point out "And not anywhere near as patient and calm as he normally was."

Oscar was interested in their comments and probed for more expansion "What do you mean exactly"?

Hugh took up the story, "I think he overreacted far too much when Western challenged his authority, and obviously tried to press his buttons."

"More than usual"?

"Yeah, much more. In our line of work, lose your temper; lose control of the situation, that's what Alex used to drum into all of us."

"So Brennan did the opposite of what he should have, and didn't do what he insists his security stewards do"!

Both men nodded in agreement, Rod explained further. "Definitely yes, it was just not like him at all, so out of character. Western went to enter the turnstile and quick as a flash Alex had him by the throat and literally threw him to the ground."

"How did the situation end then"?

Rod Appleby sat forward in his chair. "Western was not happy about not getting in and , for want of a better word, being assaulted, he said he was going to stab him up, he threatened him."

"Then what"?

"Then Western staggered off in the direction of the Metro Station."

Oscar ensured that he had everything written down, took the men's contact details and just as they were about to leave remembered another question he wanted to ask them. "One more thing gentlemen, before I go, do either of you know either a Michael Yin or a David Leung"?

Both men thought for a few seconds and then Rod answered "I know David Leung, or washy as he's commonly known, he only started here last week, just match days, but his main job is in Walter Chang's laundry in the Dragon Gate, hence the knick name."

"What about Michael Yin"?

Both men agreed, shook their heads and raised their eyebrows sceptically "Never heard of him."

Oscar thanked the two men for their time and handed each of them his card "If you remember anything else, please give me a call."

Kim Deehan waltzed back into the reception area, Oscar noticed that she had appeared to have fixed her makeup and brushed her hair, possibly for his benefit he thought or even distantly hoped. She approached him in her usual confident manner "I Believe you needed to ask me some more questions Detective Smiles, people will be thinking you're just here to see me"!

"Yes, Kim, I do need to ask you something else, and please, just call me Oscar."

Kim laughed, "Okay then, Detective Oscar, what can I do for you"? she ran her hand through her raven black hair turning several strands behind her right ear.

Oscar, slightly nervously began "It's about these two Chinese workers, Yin and Leung. Were having trouble contacting them both, and, according to the personnel file you interviewed them both with Alex Brennan"!

Kim was somewhat taken aback, and gave a theatrical impression of being shocked"Well, I can assure you that's definitely not true, it must be a mistake, I've never heard of either gentlemen."

"Is that usual for Brennan to Interview people on his own then, and you just sign the paperwork, that is your signature, is it not? Oscar handed Kim both interview forms for her to inspect, which she did with furrowed brow and disbelieving eyes "That's definitely not my signature either, what on earth has been going on here"?

"That's what I'm here to find out, another thing, there's no CRB check for either man, and can't seem to find any background checks, just a reference from the Casino owner, Walter Chang."

Kim closed her lips tightly as she listened and nodded her head "Well, I'll certainly look into that as all our employees must be CRB Checked, especially the security stewards."

"That would be a great help, hopefully we will get this whole case solved by Christmas."

Kim looked at her watch, Oscar taking this as her hinting she had better things to do than speak to him but nothing could have been further from the truth. She still seemed to have the time to want to engage him in conversation. "You looking forward to Christmas then"?

"Yeah, my sister Gemma and her family are coming over from Canada; she's actually a semi-pro footballer, and a mad keen Newcastle supporter. She would have loved to have had her wedding reception, here."

"Well if you like I can get you some tickets for the Liverpool game on boxing day, in the Platinum Club if you think she would like that"?

"That would be great, are you going to join us as well"? Oscar asked in hope.

"No, sorry, I'm in charge of the corporate areas on match days, got to make sure it all runs smoothly, I'll pop up and see you all though, it will be nice to meet your sister."

Not wanting to keep her much longer Oscar nodded as he bid Kim farewell "Well, thanks for that; you *have* got my number haven't you, in case you think of something else? about the case of course."

"Yeah, sure I've got it; it's programmed into my mobile phone, under Detective Smiles"! Kim laughed as she held up her mobile phone.

"Well. Make sure you change that to Oscar then"!

"If you insist...Oscar." She watched him as he left, she smiled as she liked him, really liked him, was she falling in love with him? She found him to be very sexy, but not in a smooth movie star kind of way but there was something else, a tenderness that was insanely elusive

******

Sara Chang relaxed in the knowledge of thought that her husband truly adored her. Her cronies, (as Walter called them) had stressed their great worry keeping their husbands content. She had trouble getting hers to leave the house. He was glad just to come home, put on his slippers, and watch reruns of UK Gold, only fools and horses and open all hours on his sixty inch plasma screen. He never left the house unless it was to oversee his latest business venture that would earn him even more money. Not that she was too bothered by that. Only she knew the true price she paid for her lifestyle, and the longing she had for true sexually gratification.

The truth was, alas, poor Walter Chang physically couldn't give her what she needed and it was that very thing that kept her in the lifestyle she had been accustomed to. He preferred to keep her as his trophy wife, like an unplayed with doll that had never been taken out of the box and he would do anything for her.

This gave her the freedom to do whatever she wanted, with whoever she wanted, whenever she wanted, but she would never let on about their lack of passion to anyone.

She felt sexually abandoned by her husband, lonely but living in a lovely house with every luxury and nothing much to do all day but eat salad and soup and spend a fortune on blonde highlights and cocaine.

Until she'd met Walter, she'd never stayed with the same man for more than a week but now she had become an despondent woman who again hunted aimless, empty sexual liaisons and she knew she would never be short of offers .

She was sure that men were always gazing at her, making her even more confident about her looks, her racehorse physique, slim with long legs and those breasts. Her biggest fear was that Walter would fall in love with someone else, get bored with her, especially when she started losing her drum tight looks and figure so he'll upgrade she'd be traded in for a younger model and she would become surplus to his requirements. Is that what she had to look forward to?, not her.

She had already worked out an attractive little reward for herself should the unthinkable happen. She made a point of knowing all there was to know about his business interests. She knew what he was worth down to his Chinese yuan.

She couldn't help thinking what her friends really thought of her, her hunger for their good judgement. Their jealousy distressed her even more than their mockery, just a pack of envious bitches all of them, caught in a repulsive rotation of jealousy.

At least with men she knew exactly where she stood. They all wanted to fuck her whether they would admit to it or not, that was the weapon she used to get her own way, to manipulate them, they were all guided by their bollocks and dicks anyway.

She'd been on her usual shopping spree, to Gateshead metro Centre. Surrounded by the swell of people going about their ordinary lives, she looked good and she knew it. She was wearing clothes that cost enough to fund a year's missionary work, a pair of five inch heels, which crippled her but looked fantastic with her Birkin bag and eyeball sized diamonds.

Back in Newcastle, she'd called at her favourite hairdressers, topped up her tan and now fancied a drink.

She checked her watch, she would be early, for once. She made her way into one of the many trendy wine bars on Newcastle quayside. Finding herself a table she ordered champagne. When it arrived, poured two generous glasses and pushed one to the opposite side of the table.

He came through the doors and headed straight over to her. He kissed the top of her head, smelling her lavish shampoo and costly perfume. Sitting opposite her he caressed her hand as he took a sip of champagne. Grinning again and smiling at his luck he wiped a small trace of cocaine from under her nose. His face was quite different when he smiled, cheeky rather than fretful.

She looked so alluring and so tender that his heart missed a beat.

Taking a goodly swig from his glass he looked at her attractive faultless face with those long black eyelashes that never seemed to blink and stared into her shimmering blue eyes. There was something about her twinkling eyes that would always appeal to him.

CHAPTER TWELVE

For once things were reasonably quiet in Tyneside CID.

McGovern sat at his desk reading his NHS letter and muttering angrily to himself and Oscar was trying to track down information on the two missing Chinese men and staring angrily at a blank computer screen, mug of tea by his side, which now was so cold it formed an icy film on top of it.

McGovern looked up from the letter, he had a question for Oscar, "What's a Cystoscopy, son"? his face like one of those frozen dinners before it sees the inside of the microwave.

Oscar didn't look away from his computer screen but McGovern was right, Oscar *did* know what a Cystoscopy was. "A cystoscopy, is a medical procedure used to examine the bladder using an instrument called a cystoscope."

McGovern nodded pretending to fully understand. "Oh OK, you remember, ages ago I told you about my bladder problems."

"Vaguely sir."

"Well it's taken those lazy bastards five fucking months to get me an appointment, I'll let them know I'm not happy when I phone them up."

"Erm... I wouldn't be so aggressive with them if I was you sir."

"Why the fuck not ? lazy bastards."

"Do you know what the procedure involves"?

McGovern hadn't a clue but pretended he did. "Yes, they do some sort of ultrasound thing on my bladder, don't they, how does an appointment for that take five months to arrange."

Oscar smiled and shook his head, "Actually, it's a little more delicate than that."

"What do you mean delicate"? For once McGovern listened without interruption.

Oscar sighed, allowing himself the beginning of a smile "Well, a procedure involves inserting a tube into the urethra through the penis opening. It allows the doctor to visually examine the complete length of the urethra and the bladder for polyps, strictures narrowing, abnormal growths, and other problems, that sort of thing; it's a thin, fibre optic tube that has a light and a camera at one end. It's inserted and moved up into the bladder. The camera relays images to a screen, where they can be seen by a urologist, that's the specialist in treating bladder conditions."

McGovern had gone a little pale. He fidgeted in his chair. There wasn't a patch of colour anywhere on his face.

"You're not *scared* sir, are you"?

"Me, no son, just don't like the idea of someone poking about down there."

"Well, you better make the appointment; they must think you need one."

McGovern was trying to make excuses, "I'll do it later."

"Do it *now* sir, while it's quiet, here give me the letter, I'll dial the number for you."

McGovern handed the letter to Oscar who called and got through straight away. He handed the phone back to McGovern. After the usual date of birth, name address etc McGovern was put through to the correct department. A woman's voice answered.

McGovern spoke. "Yes, pet, yes, I've had a letter and need to make an appointment for one of those erm... Cysto... Cystos... you know love where they stick the camera up ya cock"! Oscar could only sit and shake his head . McGovern just gave a bad tempered grunt.

As the morning grew on Oscar continued to work through a couple of files and McGovern was doing his best to devour another large bacon sandwich. The hub of activity was enhanced by a shrill tone of the desk phone, which Oscar answered. "Good morning, Tyneside CID, DS Smiles speaking." The voice on the other end a somewhat stressed and emotional Walter Chang.

"It's Western, he's got Sara. Mick Western has kidnapped my wife."

Oscar tried to reassure him. "Calm down Mr Chang, now, nice and slowly, deep breaths, how do you know Western's got her"?

Walter Chang's voice was quickening and getting higher in pitch."I recognised his voice on the phone; he said he'll kill her unless I give him two hundred and fifty thousand pounds. He doesn't want you lot involved either, no Police, he said, but I just didn't know where to turn, or what to do."

Taking another sip from the freezing cold mug of tea beside him Oscar gathered his thoughts "Just stay put Mr Chang, we'll be there as soon as we can."

McGovern took another massive bite out of his bacon and mayo sub sandwich, his voice barely audible as he spoke with his mouth full, spraying crumbs fully over a ten foot radius.

"What's going on"? McGovern sat forward and clasped his hands

"That was Walter Chang, Western's kidnapped his wife, there's a ransom demand, and we need to go and see him, work out some kind of plan."

McGovern took another bite as Oscar got from his chair and headed for the door, holding it open for a uniformed officer to leave before following him out. McGovern looked despairingly at the sandwich in his hand, shook his head and placed it on his office desk. "Hang on a minute son; fuck me it's not a race."

McGovern chased behind, as Oscar made his way out the door. "Maybe now we'll get the truth from Walter Chang."

"Who knows sir, who knows"?

As the office door closed, the sound and general chatter from the other rooms, and other detectives was somewhat muted and could just be heard.

There was a sound though, a sound of a small tippy tap of scratching claws on the wooden laminate floor. Buster appeared from under McGovern's desk, jumped onto his chair and then onto his desk, the remains of the bacon and Mayo sub gone in a matter of a couple of seconds. A sandwich now a distant memory, Buster curled up on McGovern's big chair and closed his eyes to have a triumphant nap.

The two detectives were outside the SnapDragon Casino in no time at all.

McGovern had removed his glasses so he could give them a quick clean while rubbing the reddened skin on either side of his nose. "Let's see what this is all about then. Chang is holding something back, we both know it."

They went through the impressive Casino entrance, to be met by an agitated Walter Chang who was pacing up and down. "I've sent one of my security guards to the bank to get the money. I'm waiting for another call, at eight," he said.

"So you're actually going to *pay*"? McGovern sounded somewhat surprised.

Chang laughed a strange hollow sound, devoid of humour. "I don't have any choice."

Offering a reassuring smile, Oscar could see the tears in Walter Chang's eyes, *surely this was genuine?* he thought. Oscar looked at McGovern, he shook his head slowly, his eyes firmly focused on Walter Chang.

"I need to have my beautiful wife back; I'll do whatever it takes to get her back, anything."

Oscar checked his watch "Well, it's almost eight, I guess we've just got to wait. So, Walter, why do you think Western has done this"?

Walter Chang sat down on a bar stool in front of a high round table nearby, and placed his head in his hands, He looked both shameful and secretive "Well, he came to see me a few days ago, trying to offer me protection, at a cost, of course. He made a few threats, but I told him to fuck off, I guess this is his way of getting me to part with some money."

Oscar sat down opposite him, elbows on the table. "It's pretty drastic action though, isn't it"? He turned to McGovern "And not Western's usual MO, he must be getting desperate, there's a lot going on here."

McGovern chimed in, in his usual thoughtless manner "Yes son, far too many turds for one toilet."

Oscar felt it was time to ask Walter Chang if he'd been totally honest with them. There were so many missing parts to this puzzle. He had his doubts, as did McGovern that a quarter of a million had actually been won by Alex Brennan, who to the outside world was an upstanding, squeaky clean, family man, albeit one with financial problems. But as he contemplated his next move, he felt his heart jump as the phone began to ring.

Chang looked at the two detectives as if awaiting instructions, McGovern gave him a sidelong glance and nodded his head the sign of reassurance that Chang was looking for.

Chang, feeling his nerves could snap at any moment, hesitantly picked up the phone, which he'd put onto loud speak, his heart thumping loudly.

The detective's immediately recognised the voice of Mick Western, and so they should. Both Oscar and McGovern had interviewed him enough times over the years.

Western's tone was forceful and threatening. His voice colder than a Siberian gust of wind "You've got an hour to get the money to me, room 36 Royal Station Hotel. I want cash in a hold all. Your wife will be in the room, money must be left behind there, and *no* Police."

That was it, the line went dead. Chang didn't get the chance to ask anything further.

McGovern was in a determined mood "Well Chang if you're sure you're going to pay up we need to find someone to take Western the cash."

Oscar let out a long breath and immediately volunteered his services. "I'll go, I'll take Western the money."

Chang gave him a concerned look. "He said no Police, besides he knows both of you."

McGovern had a thought "What about Odd Job there", pointing to the man who had just entered the room. Chang's security man, or Odd Job, as affectionately named by McGovern had just returned with the money, two hundred and fifty thousand pounds neatly packed into a blue hold all.

Chang thought for a moment. "Perhaps it would be better if the young detective took it."

McGovern looked at Oscar who nodded his head, and he felt they were both thinking the same thing. *Chang just doesn't trust Odd Job enough.*

McGovern needed to clarify a couple of things. "You're gonna need back up son, I can't send you in there on your own, Western sounds desperate, and he's got nothing to lose. There's no telling what he's capable of now."

Walter Chang angrily interrupted him his eyes bright and fierce "No way, the less people involved in this, the quicker it can be sorted out, *I'll* take the money myself *I* want Sara back safe, you have to do as *I* say, nobody else needs to be involved, we just need a better plan."

McGovern agreed, they *did* need a plan. "But we are involved, Mr Chang. You can't take the money, son, duty to public safety and all that shit."

Walter Chang had held it together well but he caved: he leaned forward clutching his head as if it would break open with his hands covering his face he wept, gut wrenching snorts.

The three men sat together at the small round table as they discussed the options open to them. They finally agreed. Oscar would take the money to Western.

Pausing for a few seconds, McGovern was still in deep thought, "Okay Chang, I suppose this is your money and your wife, we do however, need to keep our superiors updated though, just to cover our arses if nothing else, I'll come along as well, stay a street away in the car, you ring me before you go in, son, and leave the call connected so I can hear exactly what is going on."

McGovern made a few calls, one to Chief Super George Crammond, and one to Daniel Lee, who didn't check in with him last night, or answer his phone, McGovern left no message.

Oscar gave McGovern a despairing glance. "You're not phoning Lee are you sir? you know what he said" ?

McGovern looked irritated. "He missed his check in last night, just want to know if he's okay or heard anything with regard to this."

Everything was Okayed with Crammond who agreed that it was best that the fewer people knew the better. He was also; however, quick to point out that if anything went wrong it was McGovern's hairy Scottish bollocks, and not his on the guillotine.

McGovern drove Oscar into the town centre. Ahead of them traffic slowed to a standstill. In a car opposite a thirty something executive in a shirt and tie wound down his window and added another cigarette to pollution levels, which were already high due to fumes from the idling buses.

McGovern pulled his car into a parking bay approximately four hundred metres from the Hotel entrance. He eased a finger inside his mouth, and scraped away at some bacon lodged between his teeth with a nail, as Oscar gazed out of the passenger side window towards the soft glow of lights that hung over the City.

There was something on Oscar's mind. "Do you think it's just a coincidence that the ransom demand is A quarter of a million quid."

McGovern lit a cigarette, took a long drag and nodded blowing out smoke "I don't know son, does seem a bit of a coincidence though, come to think of it, what's your thoughts, that Chang has staged the whole thing? Or some kind of smokescreen"?

"No sir, more like the original two hundred and fifty thousand wasn't Chang's to give in the first place, and wasn't actually won by Brennan. Maybe the person it belongs to may well want it back."

"*Mick Western*? surely it's not *his* money. Loan Sharking can't be *that* financially beneficial."

"Dunno sir. We *do* need to find Western as he's in this up to his ears, and I don't think Walter Chang is being totally honest with us either."

"What else are you thinking then, son"?

"Walter Chang sent his security officer to collect the cash, but didn't trust him enough to take Brennan's supposed winnings in, or take the ransom money, why do you think that"?

"I understand what you're getting at son. Walter Chang knows something that he aint telling us." His tone was light but his dark eyes were serious. "We'll speak to Chang later, after you've made the drop. Good luck son, and remember what Chang said. Don't try to be a hero."

"I know sir, I know."

Climbing out of the passenger seat of McGovern's Volvo, Oscar closed the door and walked around to the boot and took out a large blue holdall containing the ransom cash. His blood feeling like glue he walked slowly toward the Royal Station Hotel.

As Patchy clouds lumbered across the sky Newcastle town centre was bustling as expected. Oscar walked faster hugging himself, wondering why the chill should make him more nervous.

People were going about their business. Hustle and bustle on the crowded city streets. The fumes of the gridlocked traffic mingled with fresh tarmac. People were heading off to work, getting in some Christmas shopping, or just meeting friends for coffee, voices clanging and hurrying footsteps.

Oscar wondered what all those people would think if they knew what he was carrying a hold all with so much money in it. He became very conscious of what he was carrying and felt he was wearing a sandwich board advertising the fact and why all of a sudden was every person he saw a potential mugger?.But, with all crowds moving around, no-one was paying him the slightest bit of attention. He just blended in among the shoppers.

Feeling a spot of rain he turned his collar up as he crossed the road and walked past a bus stop, his breath steaming in the cold crisp air.

He stopped to tie his shoe lace startling a scattering of scraggy pigeons, who had previously been huddled on the sills of broken nearby windows.

A scruffy, skinny, un-kept man with a missing front tooth was sitting on plastic chairs in an adjacent bus shelter; he got up from his seat and approached and spoke in a mild Scottish accent, "Could you spare some change, pal? I haven't eaten for five days"?

Oscar was knocked out with the combined smell of his bad breath and his clothes that smelt like they had been steeped in stale urine and alcohol., "Sorry, only got my bus fare mate." *A bit ironic, but couldn't really ask him if he had change for a fifty pound note, could he, plus couldn't think of what else to say. Didn't think he'd actually have to interact with anyone.*

The man's face showed no understanding, his skin the colour of putty, his eyes glazed over like a drunken zombie, one of Newcastle's many infamous legion of the damned.

Oscar decided to stand at the bus stop for a while to compose himself, refocus, the hotel a matter of metres away and time to spare.

The vagrant approached someone else standing at the bus stop, a man, on his way to work. He was quite tall and stocky with a shaved head wearing a high visibility jacket, overalls and dirty steel capped work boots.

As the vagrant approached him, and before he could ask the man held up his hand and shook his head, his face tightened, his eyes tense and dark. He gazed at him until he'd wish he hadn't asked. "Sorry mate, can't help you," then he took a large draw of his cigarette.

The vagrant then changed tactics somewhat, "could you spare me a fag then, sir,"? the workman rolled his eyes, and raising a brow reached into his pocket, took out a packet of cigarettes and handed them to him, "There's only one left in there, you might as well have it, now piss off and stop bothering people."

The vagrant stood for a second and apologetically asked "Could you give me a light, sir, please"?

"Fucking Hell, do you want me to smoke the bastard for you as well? no, fuck off, you lot are nothing but fucking pests."

The vagrant, with a cigarette behind his ear, crushed the empty packet and dropped it, the crumpled packet floated down the street on a puddle in the gutter. He wandered off towards the town centre. Oscar watched him closely as he walked down the cold, damp Tyneside Street, still stopping people as they passed him.

Oscar looked at the workman at the bus stop, yes, he did agree the vagrant was indeed a pest, but if he gave him a cigarette he could have at least given him a light before telling him where to go. He then remembered. He had a quarter of a million quid in a hold all and he had a very important job to do.

By this time the bus had been and gone from the stop, the bus shelter was now empty. A young girl, dressed for winter, wearing some latest large head phones, walked into the shelter, checked the timetable and then her watch.

Oscar smiled at her as he made his way along the street towards the hotel. Looking back he saw the vagrant heading back to the bus stop. Another woman was standing there, an older one, surely one of them would spare him some change.

A smile played at his lips as he saw the young girl reaching into her handbag for her purse, or it may have been her lighter. He then saw him approach a young lad who was heading for the bus stop, hands in pockets, coat collar pulled up whistling Take that's could it be magic, as a few late stragglers hurried along the high street on their way to work.

Oscar checked his phone, and decided to call McGovern. "Almost there sir."

McGovern's somewhat inaudible response confirmed to Oscar he was eating again. Oscar shook his head. Nice *to know you've got my back and ready to leap into action at the first sign of any trouble!, not.* He thought

"Okay son, be careful now, and remember, nowt daft."

Oscar, his pulse quickening, walked through a main door of the impressive Hotel and looked in awe at what was inside.

The Royal Station Hotel was a Grade one and two Victorian listed building which was superbly located in the heart of the city centre, located adjacent to Newcastle Train Station. Inside the hotel it had its own leisure club, which consisted of a ten metre swimming pool, sauna, steam room, plunge pool and fitness suite. The many bedroom types would offer even the most difficult customer a relaxing and comfortable stay. Guests could enjoy a meal in the Empire Bar and Restaurant. Furnished with dark wood tables and with a contemporary feel, it offered a menu supported by a large selection of wines, beers and spirits. The jalou bar offered a lively alternative to enjoy evening drinks whilst watching live sport or listening to music from the DJ until late, *this is a different world*, Oscar thought

Oscar refocused so he could see in front of him a long marble staircase, wide enough to have easily allowed four people to ascend it side by side without touching. Needing reassurance he nervously spoke to McGovern again. "I'm in the Hotel reception sir."Oscar, as requested, left his phone connected and placed it carefully in his right waistcoat pocket.

McGovern did not speak; he just listened intently from his car, while stuffing the rather large remainder of his big Mac into his mouth in one go.

Oscar flashed his badge to the receptionist as he walked through the hotel lobby and headed for the staircase. *Not going to use the lift, what if it got stuck!*

He began to climb marble stairs, he counted as he went up the first flight, *and there were only ten*. He walked up the next flight, *another ten*. He had reached the correct floor and made his way along a wide heavily carpeted passageway. An olive skinned Latino chamber maid walked past him giving him a wary glance. Oscar was nervous but tried to keep focused, keep professional.

He could feel sweat cloying on his back. He realised he must look suspicious, like he's up to no good. Following the signs on the wall odd numbers to the left, even on the right, he looked at each door as he headed along the corridor, thirty, and thirty two, thirty four, and finally there it was number thirty six.

Wiping his clammy hands on his trousers and before he was just about to knock he took a few seconds to compose himself. Taking his phone out of his waistcoat pocket he checked he was still connected to McGovern, which he was. He took a deep breath, wiped the beads of sweat from his brow and knocked on the door. *Just stay calm, take deep breaths.*

There was no answer, *he'd hardly expected a 'Come In', had he.* He felt in danger if he didn't keep tight control of himself. His chest was tight, his heart was jumping as he tried the handle. The door was unlocked.

The door felt incredibly lighter than he'd imagined it would be and as a result he stumbled into the room more quickly than he meant to, there was no sound apart from his own fevered breathing as his heart pumped against his ribs.

The room was in total darkness. Heavy black out curtains drawn, blocked out the morning sun. Making his way carefully through blackness he forced his eyes to peer into the dark picking out a figure deep in shadows sitting in a wooden chair at the far side of the room.

It was too dark for him to be able to clearly see a face. Only light from the hotel corridor lengthened their faint shadow. He shivered as if he might never stop. Moving closer he could make out the light coloured contrast of Sara Chang's long blonde hair, she was tied to the chair, by her wrists and ankles, her mouth covered in gaffer tape.

Turning he placed the holdall carefully on the floor behind him. Walking slowly over to Sara, she suddenly became a little more animated, as if trying to warn him. In the dark was something to be afraid of. He felt a sudden pain and was hit from behind on the back of his head.

*****

He woke to find McGovern trying to lift him up, "There's an ambulance on route son, just take it easy, you okay"?

"I think so sir, got a hell of a headache though."

He looked around a now lightened, but ominously empty room, the hold all had gone and so too had Sara Chang. His head was throbbing so much he could barely see. He was breathless, annoyed at himself for having been so vulnerable.

"He's still got her son, it's not your fault though, he double crossed us, never mind quarter of a million gone in the time it takes to wipe your arse." Once again one of McGovern's not particularly helpful comments with Oscar feeling so bad about things.

The paramedics were there in a moment or two, the old Officer *down'* call always made them get there that bit quicker. After a quick check over a young paramedic advised Oscar to go to Hospital, he declined, despite McGovern's insistence.

Oscar wanted to see Chang first, to explain, to console, to reassure everything would continue to be done to get his wife back. McGovern gestured for the Paramedic crew to follow them, just in case.

Arriving back at the Casino; Chang was awaiting the arrival of his precious cargo. He was already feeling flutters of despair but when he discovered that neither the ambulance or car with the two detectives' in had his wife inside, a river of sadness ran through him.

What colour he had drained from his face. Letting the fraught emotion drain from his body, Chang broke down in tears and headed back inside. The look of confusion and devastation on his face was clear to be seen and no words were needed to explain the debacle of what has just happened.

McGovern could see that Oscar had gone a little pale, concerned for his younger colleague he pointed to an egg sized lump on the back of his head. "Do you feel dizzy at all?, Christ, you need to get that fuck awful bump on the back of your head checked out, again son, it's starting to bleed a bit. I'll speak to Chang, you go to the Hospital, and that's an order."

McGovern made sure that Oscar, reluctantly got into the ambulance that had followed them and then went into the Casino to speak to Walter Chang.

He found him sitting in his VIP lounge head in hands a broken man on the edge.

"Sorry Walter, Western double crossed us, nothing the laddie could do, he was hit from behind."

Chang sat in shock, listening intently and shook his head. Tears were forming in the corners of his eyes as his face contorted with the emotional pain.

"What happens now Detective McGovern"?

"To be honest with you Walter, I just don't know, we've just got to wait and see what Western does next."

McGovern decided time was now right for Chang to tell him everything he knew. He leant forward and placed a reassuring hand on Walter Chang's arm.

"Walter, we've been up front with you, if you want us to help you to get your wife back you need to start telling us everything you know. It's time to be honest."

Chang gave a deep sigh. He rested his head against the upturned fingers of his hand "I know Inspector, I'm sorry. I will tell you everything I know. The money I paid wasn't Brennan's winnings."

McGovern rolled his eyes "Walter, tell me something I don't know, will you"?

Chang was feeling totally wretched, tears began to spill down his cheeks "OK, sorry Inspector. I was ordered to pay the money into Brennan's account, by the same man who demanded I write those references."

"This Red Pole man who you've never met," stated McGovern trying not to sound sarcastic or patronising, while raising his eyebrows sceptically.

"That is correct inspector, yes."

"Weren't you curious what the money was for, and where it came from"?

"Of course I was."

"But you didn't think to ask"?

"I was scared, Inspector. When the Gan-Yin ask you to do something, you don't ask why, but I now guess it has a lot to do with betting scams across Europe. "

"You don't say, so where did it come from"?

It was obvious that Walter Chang did not want to tell him anymore, it became obvious to McGovern that the Gan-Yin had a very strong hold on Walter Chang, and he still may have had something to do with the alleged kidnapping.

"Come on Walter, you have to tell me everything you know"?

"OK inspector. The money came in a cash transfer from a Hong Kong based bank; it appeared to come from a legitimate business."

"Probably laundered though, through a bag man, collecting dirty money and cleaning it up, that you Walter, the bag man"?

"No, no, nothing like that. Like I said inspector, I wouldn't ask, I just did as I was told."

"Another thing Walter, if these Gan-Yin people have such a hold on the Dragon Gate, why didn't you ask *them* to get your wife back"?

"My security men, they are Gan-Yin, and to be honest I *did* think about getting them to help me get Sara back."

McGovern moved closer, "So why didn't you then"?

"Because I stupidly thought that you, the Police, might do the job with less fuss. You would do it how *I* wanted it done. If the Gan-Yin had helped me, I feared they would have gone in heavy handed, causing more problems, I now accept that I was probably wrong. For years the Dragon Gate has policed itself, sorted its own problems. I have made a big mistake involving you Inspector. I won't make the same mistake again."

McGovern kept his head bowed speaking softly "Well Walter, for what it's worth, I feel quite proud that you *did* ask us to help you, you don't trust that Gan-Yin lot though do you"?

Chang didn't answer the question directly "I feared that they would either keep the money or demand a large chunk of it."

McGovern leant forward, meeting Walter's eye "Always knew it came down to money Chang, Western knew that too, hit the old chinky bastard where it really hurts, in his pocket eh, Walter."

Walter Chang with his sad, heavy eyelids didn't answer. He just stared forlornly at the photograph of his wife on his desk. Distraught, duped, angry and humiliated. And as for the Police, the fact their prime suspect was still on the loose fuelled an undercurrent of frustration.

CHAPTER THIRTEEN

Once again McGovern wasn't happy, his booming voice dripping with disgust down the telephone. The least he'd been expecting was extensive footage from the main foyer from the interior security cameras "What do you mean, no CCTV images, what sort of a Hotel is that you're running"?

McGovern's anger aimed solely at the manager of the Royal Station Hotel.

"I'm sorry Inspector but the CCTV wasn't working, it was turned off for some reason."

"What time"?

"Just after midnight last night, and it went back on again at lunch time."

"By who"?

"The night porter's don't know."

"What do you mean, *they don't fucking know*? Have you not got security in there at night"?

"The night porters *are* the security."

"What about the room then, who booked it out"?

"Sorry Inspector but it was supposed to be empty, I guarantee we will hold a full enquiry as to what went on here, I know, it isn't good enough, we had a similar problem a while ago."

"Too right it isn't fucking well good enough; well thanks for your... erm... 'help'. "

McGovern slammed down the phone while the manager was still talking, he didn't say goodbye.

*****

Oscar sat at home nursing his sore head, Buster on his knee, watching Sky news, another football match, this time in Holland had ended prematurely, this time a security guard was arrested and Dutch Police were looking for a man of oriental descent in connection with the incident.

Oscar shook his head in disbelief *this definitely a world-wide problem.*

His chain of thought soon shattered by the insistent ring of his mobile phone. He recognised the number, McGovern.

"We need to get to Chang's Casino." He gave a weary smile. He should have known better thinking he was ringing to enquire as to his state of health Oscar was just about to explain that he was okay and been given the all clear when McGovern spoke again seemingly he'd forgotten about his head injury.

"There's been developments."

"What kind of developments, sir"?

"Just wait till we get there, apparently Odd Job has some interesting CCTV for us to see."

Oscar was dressed and out of the door in five minutes, grabbing his jacket from the back of a chair and munching on a piece of toast. Only to return seconds later. *Need to do my checks again.*

Oscar got to the station and jumped into the passenger side of McGovern's Volvo. McGovern drove as fast as the rush hour traffic would allow. During the short journey McGovern was still incensed about the CCTV at the Hotel. Oscar could feel the fury coming from him "So some fucker switched it off on purpose, and nobody knows who did it."

Oscar had a thought and remembered an incident several months earlier that he'd heard about from a colleague in the vice squad."I remember a while back this gang were supplying prostitutes to various hotels and giving night porters back hander's to turn a blind eye. The gang would also pay bribes to hotel staff to open up empty rooms. It only came to light as there was an incident where one of the prostitutes ripped a punter off. He reported it to the hotel manager, and involved police. Strangely there was no CCTV there either as the Night Porters had turned it off, so that there was no visual record of the girls entering and leaving various rooms."

"So somebody paid the porters to switch the CCTV off, it could be connected, but then again maybe not."

"Yes, sir, it only came to light because there was an incident, but I hear it's a regular thing."

"Must pay well, to risk your job for."

"Yes it must sir, so tell me again, what exactly we are going to the SnapDragon for."

"I got a call from Odd Job."

"Chang's head security man you mean, Jimmy Mei."

"Yes, him. He said he'd found something of interest on camera, let's hope *this* CCTV that *he* has is some bloody good."

The SnapDragon Casino was forever being targeted by fraudsters and people on the make trying to cheat Chang out of his money. Chang's head of security Jimmy Mei had called them. He had initially been asked to find evidence, or lack of that Alex Brennan was a regular on the Roulette tables, as well as doing his usual weekly forage through the CCTV DVD's and had found something of interest.

He appeared quite excited and rather proud of his discovery "I want you to have a look at this footage."

Having just been told about the Gan-Yin's involvement in the Snap Dragon McGovern didn't trust him one bit, but it was all they had.

Jimmy Mei, sat down in a small office surrounded by TV screens, each screen showed a different area of the Casino. He reached into a draw and put on his thin round spectacles; he sniffed and rubbed his hand across his nose.

McGovern thought he had an idea what the news was going to be. "I know that Alex Brennan's never been near the place, has he"?

McGovern and Oscar gathered round Mei's chair in a small rather cramped office deep within the basement of the SnapDragon.

"Right gentlemen, you ready for this,"? Jimmy Mei said, picking up the remote. They studied the screen as Mei fast forwarded pictures frame by frame until the image stopped.

They could see several people sitting at a roulette wheel playing and two people in particular were familiar to the two detectives. Oscar was the first to spot one of them tapping his finger against the screen "Isn't that Western,"? McGovern took his glasses out of his case in his pocket, and almost dropped them in his haste to put them on. He moved nearer to the screen for a closer look.

"And, look who's sitting beside him, stroking his leg"?

McGovern excitedly shouted at the screen, "It's Sara, Chang's wife, when was this"?

Jimmy Mei pointed to the top of the screen. The time code in the corner "Time and date are displayed there, look"! *23/11/ 20:35 pm*

Oscar could see that even with his glasses on McGovern was straining his eyes and couldn't make it out properly. "Twenty third of November, eight thirty five pm, that's the night of the Newcastle, West ham match, the night Brennan was murdered."

"Doesn't that put Western in the clear then"?

Oscar wasn't so sure "We'll as his time of death was around the ten fifteen mark there is still over an hour and a half before the murder but it's looking unlikely that he's our man sir, and how did he manage to get back in, didn't Chang tell us he was thrown out earlier that night"?

McGovern was more interested in the body language between Sara and Western. "If I didn't know any other I'd say those two looked just like love's young dream wouldn't you say Oscar"?

"They certainly look to be quite intimate, and familiar with each other."

Jimmy Mei smiled in excitement crinkles spreading from his face under his balding forehead "We'll you're going to love the next bit it's very interesting indeed."

He had another DVD in his hand and quickly replaced it with the previous one and pressed play.

McGovern forever impatient glared from beneath his bristling grey eyebrows "But that's just an empty room, where is that"?

Oscar recognised the room as Chang's VIP lounge.

Mei confirmed it "It's the VIP lounge, Chang wanted a hidden camera in there, thought his wife was up to no good, with drugs and stuff."

After a couple of minutes in which McGovern complained several times about the wait, the door was opened and Sara Chang and Mick Western came into the room, they kissed passionately as Sara slid down Western's body until she was kneeling in front of him, loosening the belt from his trousers.

The three men were sitting glued to the screen watching as the action moved on quickly, and more intimately. They watched as Western unhooked her bra. Sara Chang crawling onto the large sofa, Western behind her peeling down her panties and slipping them off her long slim legs.

Oscar had one eye on the timecode in the corner at the top of the screen "Look at the time sir"?

"Look at the fucking time! I canny see anything at the moment ma fucking glasses are steaming up"!

"It's ten twenty sir, there's no way Western could have had the time to kill Alex Brennan."

"Yes, son, your right. Western certainly has an alibi alright,that Sara Chang eh, wouldn't you think she gets her leg over enough times without having to shit in her own doorstep."

McGovern pointed to the entanglement of bodies on the screen as they moved in perfect flow until Western collapsed on top of her "As we can clearly and graphically see, he's definitely guilty of stabbing, with his pork sword but it looks like he's in the clear for Brennan's murder"!

"Another question then sir. Why would Western kidnap her then? and demand a ransom"?

"I don't know, Revenge, possibly, maybe it was just a one night stand thing between them, then she gave him the heave-hoe, you know what Sara Chang's like, total slapper."

"Yes, sir but the body language between them earlier, the way they look at each other, it just doesn't add up to a one night fling."

"Your right son, were going to need copies of those two DVD's, watch them closely, and a box of fucking tissues as well! can you get that sorted for us Jimmy"?

Jimmy Mei nodded his head, while chewing his nails to clean them "No problem detective."

Getting up from his chair McGovern headed for the door "Oscar I want you to try and find out as much as you can about Western and Sara Chang, build up a bigger picture. See if there's any other connection, don't leave any stone unturned, phone records, social media, bank statements, any people who link the two of them and whatever else you can think of "

In the past Walter Chang had always shut his eyes to Sara's amorous affairs, but they both knew he wouldn't be able to shut his eyes to this. As ever Oscar could see the bigger picture and was thinking about poor old Mr Chang. "Can I make a suggestion, sir"?

"Go on then, what"?

"I think with all he's been through today it's probably best we keep this from him."

"Yeah, your right son, he doesn't need to know. Yet,"McGovern patted Jimmy Mei on his bald head, not unlike Benny Hill used to do to his small straight man stooge in his seventies TV series.

McGovern smiled and the corners of his eyes creased into lines "Be a good boy and keep this quiet for now son, eh, and no making any copies for your very own little wank bank eh, or worse selling it to one of those internet porn sites, there's a good boy."

Again, Jimmy Mei nodded and gave a weary laugh.

Oscar and McGovern chatted as they headed back out of the snapdragon, McGovern, as usual had a story. "The thought of Odd Job putting that DVD of Western and Sara Chang on the internet reminds me of a stag do I once went to. *That* ended up on the internet. You remember Stanley Scott don't you, three stone overweight and a first class bull shitter"?

"Yes, I remember him, miserable bugger, hated the job even more than you do sir."

"No, he was a good copper Scotty was, it was a shame that he moved to Middlesbrough."

"You were just sad to lose the only drinking buddy who could keep up with you."

McGovern laughed, "Oh yes, he could drink alright, anyway this stag do we went on, Thailand, of all places, it was Stan Scott's birthday as well, and he was well gone, and I mean absolutely off his face. He'd been chatting up a couple of lady boys in a late night bar and we decided to set him up, thought it would be a laugh. We paid these two ladyboys to take him in the back of this seedy little night club. They got him all aroused and they told him that they both had a fetish for roller skates, and if he wore them they would give him a free tag-team style blow job. So Scotty puts them on doesn't he and one of these lady boy starts to play with his dick, the other one licking his balls and just when he'd reached the maximum of his hard on they both pushed him through this fucking paper wall and right onto the stage in front of two hundred people, fucking hilarious. Well, poor old Stan, he can't cover up the family jewels, due to trying to balance on the roller skates and his massive stonker, he's there trying to keep his feet on the stage. That was put on the internet somewhere."

"Christ what did his wife say"?

"What do you mean wife"?

"You said it was a stag do."

"It was, but it wasn't his, Christ, he wasn't even married then man, it was fucking years back. We picked on him because he was the most intoxicated and it was his birthday."

"I suppose he wasn't happy about it being put on the internet then."

 "He was more upset by nearly going with a couple of those ladyboy blokes"!

Oscar just shook his head. "Remind me never to go on holiday with you sir," *Not that I ever would*, he thought.

By the time the two men had reached the exit door of the Casino McGovern had come to a decision. "It's getting late, we'll drop those DVD copies from jimmy off at the station and we'll make an early start in the morning."

****

He'd had a good time and boy, the rumours had been true about her. He didn't care that he was about to kill one of his best clients; there was an abundance of others, always eager for his wears. He drove towards the business park. The sounds of the City had already fallen behind as the windscreen wipers thumped and squeaked repetitively. Hoping the shadows would hide him he knew it was too early to be noticed.

The traffic was getting quieter and less frequent. The Tyne Bridge silhouetted against the sunrise. The river glinted like black ice from the lights on the bank. He hadn't seen a car or a headlight in miles. The woman in question, in his boot was off her face, as usual, this time on cocaine and booze. She wouldn't put up much of a fight.

As rain speckled the pavements and showered his face, he got out of his car, took a cool breath of early morning air and stretched. Lifting her out of the boot he put his ear to her mouth. She was still breathing. Good. He needed her to be alive

He glanced up as the early sunrise snatched at the steep roof tops through a gap in the clouds. A dustbin clattered over, which set off a dog barking. He looked around, through force of habit. Coast was clear. He jemmied the gates then carried her over to the far side of the timber yard.

CHAPTER FOURTEEN

It was just gone eight AM when McGovern got into the lift in the Tyneside Police HQ and pressed the button for the first floor, nothing. "*BASTARDS.*" The lift was out of order, again.

Reluctantly he began to climb the stairs. He could feel his heart pounding and was out of breath by the time he reached the top, puffing and panting his face red and sweating. He wasn't surprised to see Oscar already busy at his desk, Buster lying in his basket under and sleeping soundly.

"They'll.... need to.... get that bloody... lift fixed, how long has.... it been out of action"?

"Dunno sir, I always use the stairs."

"You shit the bed again son"?

"You know me sir, been in over an hour, been busy too."

"Anything interesting then"?

"Definitely yes, I had a look at who Western came into contact with during his three year stretch in Durham, cell mates, visitors, known associates, that type of thing and guess what"?

McGovern sat down opposite him, took out his spectacles, put them on and looked towards Oscar's computer monitor, leaning forward intently, "Too early for guessing games son, let's see what you got."

Oscar turned his screen in McGovern's direction.

"We'll sir for his three years in prison he was visited monthly by a woman, her name Sara White, or to give her, her married name Mrs Sara Chang."

McGovern sat and nodded his head "So they must have been together before Chang married her then; they have obviously planned the whole thing, take Chang for a mug and get a quarter of a million to set themselves up somewhere else. Looks like they've stitched Chang up big time. Poor bloke, I suppose we better let him know"?

As they were contemplating there next move the phone rang, and Oscar answered it. "Sir, there's been a woman's body found in the timber yard, description matches that of Sara Chang."

McGovern,without fastening his seatbelt, drove down the road like a lunatic. The car carrying the two detectives, drove past two white forensic vans being loaded with equipment. The flapping police cordon looked a little tattered. The murder team had taken over the DIY car park.

McGovern pulled his Volvo into one of the many spaces. An area lit with flashing blue bulbs of numerous Police vehicles. Many officers both uniformed and forensic were each busy doing their respective duties. Uniforms providing extra back up, sealing an area with the infamous blue and white tape, while several officers stood in silence outside the police tape encircling the body.

A white forensic tent was being erected underneath there was sure to be something he knew would be somewhat unsavoury.

They were met once again by the cheerful tones of Chief Forensic Officer Peter Devon. Who had been co-ordinating the forensic teams and listing their findings as they were sent to the lab "No Mutt with you today, Oscar"?

Oscar shook his head and gestured over to McGovern, "Just him."

Devon began his update on the latest findings as he walked them through the crime scene results "Forklift drivers in a right state, he was putting a pallet of old railway sleepers down over there when an arm popped out from underneath, he's waiting by the back door for when you need to speak to him."

McGovern nodded "Will you do the honours son"?

Making his way over to the far end of the yard Oscar saw two men, obviously staff, both wearing yellow high visibility vests and hard hats, one of them quite obviously a manager of some description, tall with an obvious greater than thou persona, wearing a suit underneath the another a large man in DIY store uniform, his ale gut drooping over his waistband and a full sleeve tattoos on both arms, he was sitting on a bag of cement smoking. Both looked to be in shock, the larger man's hands shaking with each drag.

Oscar decided that he would speak to the manager first. "Hello gentleman, I'm DS Smiles, and you are.."?

The manager spoke for both of them "I'm Barry Davids, store manager and this is Michael Anderson."

"Thank you Mr David's, could you tell me what time the woman's body was found"?

Barry Davids checked his watch, "Approximately seven forty five this morning, we opened at eight, the back gates had been forced, not sure what time, we presumed just petty criminals after some wood or gravel stolen to order, but nothing had appeared to have been taken."

"Do you have any CCTV"?

"Yes but not at the back there, we figured that it would be too obvious to have one there, most thief's would just climb over the fence, there is some further along, you might get something from that."

"If you could get me a copy, that would be a great help, thanks."

Turning his attention to an obviously traumatised, chain smoking, fork lift truck driver, Oscar crouched down so as he was in direct eye contact, "Listen, Michael, I know this is going to be hard for you, but believe me, it's better you get this out of the way now, while it's still fresh in your memory, can you tell me what happened this morning"?

The forklift driver took another long drag on his cigarette and exhaled the smoke slowly as he gathered his thoughts trying to compose himself. "I began my shift at seven thirty, just getting ready for the public coming in at eight. We needed some railway sleepers moved from delivery to that point over there", his voice instantly becoming a little shakier as he pointed to the area where the dark blue tarpaulin covered the body. "I picked up the first pallet and placed it over there, it was only after I placed the third pallet down that I noticed what a assumed in the darkness was oil or something dripping down, and then I saw this...arm just flop out from underneath one of the pallets, they say it's a young woman, she's dead isn't she"?

"It certainly looks that way sir, sorry."

Both men bowed their heads, Michael Anderson still shaking.

"Could you tell me Michael, did you see anything suspicious on your way in this morning, strange vehicles, someone running away, anything odd"?

"No, not really, just that the back gate had been forced."

"What about you Barry, anything out of the ordinary"?

"No I was just in the process of reporting the break in, trying to confirm nothing had been taken, and it just seemed like any other day, nothing out of the ordinary."

"Thank you, I really appreciate your time, if there's anything else you can recall I would be most grateful if you would contact me." Oscar took two business cards from out of his waist coat pocket and handed them one each.

Oscar turned looking for McGovern, who had made his way over to where the body of Sara Chang lay; the covering tarpaulin sheet now removed as forensic officers gathered evidence and took their gory photos.

As usual McGovern was shouting at somebody, as he rifled through his pockets looking for his cigarettes. This time it was two young uniformed constables, obviously at their first murder scene.

"Will you two stop staring at her tits and do something useful, this is supposed to be a crime scene not one of these fucking shit love Island TV reality shows."

Oscar joined McGovern as the two young officers were deployed back to the Police cordon; they were needed there as the media scrum had begun to converge on the car park.

McGovern, for once, had a concerning serious look on his face. "It's definitely Mrs Chang, a few initial stab wounds but that's not what killed her forensics reckon she's only been dead an hour."

"Christ almighty, that means she was still alive when the pallets were put on top of her."

"Yes, son, that looks to have been what, killed her."

"Well, we better not tell the forklift driver, he's traumatised as it is, poor bugger, anything else sir"?

"Yeah, she may have been sexually assaulted, but can't be one hundred percent sure, definite recent sexual activity, quite rough, lots of bruising, but knowing her reputation may well have been consensual, we'll need to wait for further reports to be sure, and there's DNA evidence."

Oscar shook his head as he looked at Sara Chang's lifeless body, her dead eyes wide and open, there was so much pain in them "God, what a way to go."

McGovern attempted to sound Shakespearian "Yep, fucked, forked and flattened. Look yonder Is that a burger van I see before me? For I be fucking starving."

Oscar, did not have the energy to respond as not for the first time was deep in thought. McGovern's attempt at black humour as usual going straight over his head "So, I can't help wondering why would Mick Western kill her then, or at least stab her and leave her for dead"?

McGovern dug his hands deep into his pockets searching for more cigarettes "I know exactly why he did it...."

"Why then, sir, you figured it out"?

"He did it because he's a fucking lunatic son, that's why no rational thinking in him, they could have argued, you know what a temper he has, maybe he was just using her all this time, he didn't need her anymore, he's got his money. He screwed Chang's wife and his bank account. Maybe she was getting second thoughts, going to slow him down, that bonnie lad is what we're here to find out."

"I don't know sir, there's definitely something odd about all this, Western was always our prime suspect for the Brennan murder, but he couldn't have done that and again now, but this time for a different murder, we've got two dead bodies and were still nowhere near finding out what it's all about, there is a chance it might not even be Western, we don't seem to be making any headway."

McGovern squinted at him as the smoke from his now lit cigarette trailed from his lips. "Well one thing is certain son, we have a twisted killer out there with a sadistic mind and someone, somewhere knows who he is."

McGovern's stomach rumbled as if he'd not eaten in days (unlikely). The smell of a burger van wafted through the cold December air. "Come on sunshine, burger van's open, breakfasts on me."

Leading Oscar over to a burger van which was a hundred yards away at the far corner of the DIY car Park, McGovern broke the bad news to the dirty looking unshaven patron "You're not going to sell much today pal, the stores closed till further notice, it's a crime scene."

Burger van man gave a cold dismissive look "What am I going to do with all this then? pointing to the mounting pile of cholesterol filled sausages, bacon and burgers."

"Well for a start you can give me two of them breakfast sandwiches, both easy on the ketchup, we've seen enough of that already this morning." *So had his shirt*, thought Oscar.

As the two waited for their pending fix of the tasty high cholesterol greasy breakfasts, McGovern began to think about the coming festive season. "So son, your family is coming over for Christmas then"?

"Yes, they fly into Newcastle International at the end of next week, Christmas day, just two weeks tomorrow."

"Bloody Hell; better get my presents and turkey in then."

McGovern's phone began to ring. Oscar could tell by his facial expression that it was Crammond on the other end.

Oscar turned back towards the Burger Van, and clicked his fingers as a thought had come into his head. Maybe *the* vendor could have seen something. The man was beginning to pack up, it was still early and not too late for him to still sell his wares at another location.

"Do you mind if I ask you a couple of quick questions"?

Burger van man jangled his keys making it obvious that he was an impatient man eager to get on with what was left of his day. "Not really mate, I need to make a living and have only got half an hour to catch the morning rush."

"Well, OK but here's my card if there's anything you can think of that might help." Oscar passed over his card. Burger van man took it and ran his thumb over the edge. "Hang on, there was something this morning, a car driving quite fast, quite dangerously in fact coming the other way as I drove here a couple of hours ago."

"Don't suppose you got the reg number"?

"Your kidding me aren't you, it was a black or navy colour, maybe a corsa, definitely a Vauxhall though, sorry may not even be connected and no I didn't get the number."

"Well it could be connected, so thanks very much for that," Oscar turned to walk back towards McGovern who had now gone. Summoned back to the station by Chief Superintendent Crammond, leaving Oscar to try and scrounge a lift back in a squad car.

Oscar was keen to get back to the incident room. It felt like the killer was looking over their shoulders and laughing at the lack of results.

McGovern sighed heavily, wishing the day was over and was pacing up and down in the office when Oscar arrived back at the station.

"Lee's not checked in for two days now, I'm gonna have to ring him, we need him back here, double murder enquiry and were not making any headway. Crammond has told me he's looking to bring in some help so we better get him back here because we're gonna need him. I'm sure Crammond will be getting us a couple of muppets."

Oscar quickly remembered what Lee had said about not contacting him in case his cover was blown. "Leave it sir, he must be onto something, you know what he told you. He would contact you."

McGovern was beginning to look increasingly frustrated."Yes, but this just seems to get more and more complicated by the day, a murder that looked like gangland revenge, a kidnapping, another murder, this Gan-Yin connection, Chang probably knowing more than he's letting on and why the fuck can't thirty odd uniformed officers going door to door not find that waste of space Mick Western?, he's heavily involved in all this, we've got to find that bastard, and he's not making things any easier for himself by disappearing."

Oscar was upbeat as he reminded McGovern of the work that *was* being done. "All of Western's usual haunts are under surveillance; He's got to show up somewhere soon, people like Western can't just disappear. We just need to put more energy into tracking him down .Extra help would be a bonus sir, muppets or not."

The two detectives looked at the increasing amount of photo's, evidence and writing on the ever growing murder board in front of them.

Oscar tapped, thoughtfully on the board."We know It's all connected somehow, definitely, these football matches, the gambling syndicates, Walter Chang, Mick Western, Sara Chang, what's the latest from Europe"?

McGovern walked over to his desk, sat down, picked up some paper from his desk and began to read out loud, pausing for a second to take his glasses out of his top drawer and put them back on. "We've got news this morning about Football matches in France, Germany and Spain all being targeted, that's Seven countries in all have had reported problems with supposed match fixing, all the same set up, the floodlights being turned off or attempts to turn them off, a few arrests and some of them Chinese or Orientals, others football employees, but we've got or own problems here We've now got a double murder enquiry and MickWestern is still nowhere to be seen."

"And that's why that miserable old bugger Crammond has brought in reinforcements."DS Stan Scott's voice boomed as he poked his sharp chinned face into the room. He had seemed the ideal man, under the circumstances as he'd helped to put Mick Western away before.

"Good to see you, Jim."

"Likewise Stan. How's Middlesbrough these days?"

"Quiet."

McGovern gripped his hand firmly and they held each other's forearm as they shook hands.

So nothing like Thailand, eh, Stan. Oscar remembering McGovern's sordid tale of the stag do.

Chief Super George Crammond had, unbeknown to Stanley Scott, followed him into the room, and wasn't impressed at being referred to as *that miserable old bugger*, he Cleared his throat. "I see you have reintroduced yourself, DS Scott. Is Felicity here yet"?

McGovern was somewhat taken aback,"Felicity"?

Crammond removed his cap stroking his own sweaty forehead and flattened down what little hair he had left on the top of his head. "Yes, Detective Constable Felicity Somerton. Is she here yet"?

Oscar inquisitively stuck his head out of the office door and looked up and down, scrutinizing the corridor. He gave a very good impression of a sailor looking out to sea, his hand on his brow over his eyes. "Doesn't look like it yet, sir."

"Well, let me know when she arrives, she's late. Not a good start. DS Scott, a word, in my office please."

Stanley Scott, looked at the two detectives and raised his eyebrows as he followed Crammond out of the room and into the corridor, the naughty school boy had been summoned to the headmaster's office.

Oscar waited until Crammond's door was safely and softly shut behind them "Not a good first impression, there sir."

But McGovern wasn't happy, a female officer. His dislike of female officers was deep rooted and historic. "I asked for a couple of extra pairs of hands and we end up with an extra pair of tits"!

"That's you and Scott accounted for then."

 "Funny bugger."

McGovern, had a longstanding distrust of women, mainly born from previous failed marriages, and a couple of run ins with female senior officers, notably, DCI Ann Gatsby.

It had, however, been McGovern's first marriage to Edith that had really warped his opinion of women.

He had been a hard working young detective. As always the job had meant long nights and, as many officers had found that was often to the detriment of family life. McGovern's heavy drinking had also played a large part in the marital problems. McGovern had, on his way home from work, called to get some cash out of the bank. Finding the bank account, not only empty but overdrawn he returned home. Once in the house he'd quickly noticed that most of the furniture had gone, as had all the kitchen appliances and TV. There was no sign of either his wife, or his baby daughter Susan. There was a note on the fireplace. Edith had gone.

McGovern was angered that the only furniture that had been left behind was the stuff that still hadn't been paid for. Edith had also left Susan's small single bed, that was the only thing left in her room, complete with the pussy cat stencils on the homemade headboard that he had taken hours to perfect.

The story continued, as McGovern, at the time was a mad keen supporter of Clydebank Football Club. Clydebank were playing at home the following day and McGovern had originally planned to go to the game. He didn't feel like going, after all, his wife had just left him, cleaned out his bank account and taken away his newborn daughter. His friends, and in particular his mother had felt it would be good for him to still go to the game. They thought that it would help take his mind off things. Reluctantly McGovern decided to go.

Things were going well, Clydebank were 3-0 up at half time, the game was fantastic and McGovern was, at least for forty five minutes anyway, back in the land of the living. Things changed, however and the second half was in stark contrast to the first. He could not remember the opponents that day but slowly but surely they began to claw their way back into the game. With the score at 3-3, McGovern thoughts once again went to his empty house, his cleared bank account, his life in tatters. The last minute came and went, injury time beckoned, what had seemed to be a certain win was now looking like only a draw, but in a cruel twist of fate the opposition scored a winning goal with the final kick of the game, from 3-0 up Clydebank, his team, had lost 4-3.

Coming out of the ground McGovern was a broken man. An elderly gentleman who McGovern had never seen before, or since chatted on to him as they left the ground and headed for the bus stop. "You know what it is son, no matter how bad you feel when you come into this ground, you can always guarantee on these bastards making you feel ten times fucking worse."

McGovern had neither the energy, nor effort to respond.

He'd had bad luck with women. The only woman he'd truly loved was his second wife Elizabeth.

McGovern became slightly misty eyed when he remembered her, cruelly taken from him by cancer after fifteen happy years together. "Yes, my dearest Lizzy. Not a day goes by that I don't think of her. The woman couldn't cook for shit, but she was certainly a good one."

Oscar took McGovern's comments on Lizzy as a chance to put a positive spin on things. "Look sir, we *do* need help here, and who knows, this Felicity, she *may* be able to look at the evidence slightly differently. Give us a woman's perspective on things. It can't do any harm, surely."

"Well, where is she? as Crammond said bloody well late on her first day. Not a good first impression."

"Well she isn't going to be another Ann Gatsby sir that's for sure."

McGovern picked up and began to crush an almost empty plastic cup of coffee on his desk "I hated that fucking woman."

"Did you sir?, I'd never have guessed"! said Oscar flashing a sarcastic smile.

The very sound of her name made veins on his temple enlarge. Some coffee from the crushed cup began to drip out as it began to pool and then to run towards the edge of the table. McGovern wiped it up with his hands, and rubbed them on his trousers to dry them.

Oscar began to laugh. "I still remember the day she left; I remember that leaving present you bought her."

McGovern gave a smile and chuckled "Who could forget, I was quite proud of myself."

"Yes, her face when she opened the card and present, what was it again? and she still didn't know who it was from."

"Oh yes she fucking did, but she couldn't prove it." McGovern still giggling away to himself, his lovely warm chuckle altered his whole being, making him almost boyish.

"At first I thought you were a bit mean, refusing to put in for her leaving present and card."

"As I said son, I hated that bitch. I was just being honest. I wasn't like you fucking hypocrites, everyone of you hated her but you all put money in for her card and flowers."

"And all along you had planned your own special gift, eh sir, from the Anne Summers shop, of all places."

McGovern boomed out the verse he'd written on his very own leaving card. "Ah yes, Here's a vibrator. Now you can go and fuck yoursel___"

"___Inspector McGovern, sorry I'm late. Detective Constable Felicity Somerton." A young woman stood just inside the office doorway, and tried not to laugh, as he held out her outstretched hand.

Oscar noticed McGovern's face begin to redden. His mouth gave the impression he'd swallowed super glue.

Felicity, to her credit, remained diplomatic swiftly changing the subject. "The... erm... coffee machine? is it in the corridor, "? she fumbled for a tissue in her hand bag, blew her nose, dabbed her eyes.

McGovern was quick to answer, trying his utmost to appear friendly. The last thing he needed would be another complaint from a female officer about inappropriate language. He grabbed the edge of the table with both his redknuckled hands and hitched himself forward and up. "It's just out there, love, turn right..., my shout, and err... sorry about that."

As McGovern and Felicity headed over towards the drinks machine, Oscar sat, looking at the evidence board, as he thought, to himself, not *a good first impression.*

He saw out of the corner of his eye that McGovern had been called back into Crammonds Office and didn't look happy. He stood shaking his head, his constant requests for more officers to be drafted in had eventually been granted, and you'd think he'd be pleased about that but now as it had become a double murder enquiry Crammond had decided to bring in a DCI to oversee things.

CHAPTER FIFTEEN

The first day in a new job was always going to be stressful enough. She had taken more time and care over her hair and make-up than usual and looked at herself in the mirror, decked out in her new white cashmere pullover, black trousers, boots and wearing a string of pearls.

This was no ordinary job, especially when it was a job she'd previously had. To make matters worse the job had not been without its fair share of run-ins with colleagues, and one colleague in particular.

To say she wasn't happy would have been an understatement, A temporary placement it would be, Crammond had promised her that much at least, but she knew from past experience how things rarely appeared as they were in the brochure when it came to the force. Her first question to Crammond being "Is HE still here"? He being Detective Inspector Jim McGovern and she being his old adversary DCI Ann Gatsby.

With the wind whipping her coat, she headed out to her car and beeped it open. Her mind was going through the case that she'd been brought in to lead up on, as far as she could see it had been one step forward and two back.

As she pulled her car into the Police yard she could see McGovern's old beat up Volvo taking up two spaces, so typically ignorant and inconsiderate of the man.

Come on Ann you'll be OK just make sure you don't take any shit from anyone today, especially him.

Crammond had called them all into the incident room. He was immaculately turned out, as usual, in full uniform. He stood before them, removed his cap and, as was now customary, flattened a couple of Bobby Charlton style strands of hair that had strayed out of position. "Right, I want to formally introduce three new members of the team. Detective Chief Inspector Ann Gatsby, has been brought in temporarily to head the enquiry and lead the team. I would personally like to thank DI Jim McGovern for his hard work and efforts in the absence of a DCI. Detective Sergeant Stanley Scott, who most of you will know, has been brought back from Teesside CID. He has had a few previous run ins with Mick Western so his experience and contacts will be of great use."

Crammond turned to Felicity, "Detective Constable Felicity Somerton, first day as a detective, so go easy on her, okay guys. I trust you will make them *all.......*" (Staring at McGovern) ".......very welcome, and fill them in on the case so far." With that he put his cap back on and left the room, a press briefing beckoned.

DCI Ann Gatsby stood, a little nervous, before her new team, like a new teacher on her first day in a tough comprehensive School, looking at her watch, impatiently waiting for silence, her Cheekbones high and her hooded eyes unfathomable, "Right folks, if you could all listen up."

There were still some mumbles of conversation, despite her request. "PLEASE," she raised her voice and at last silence. "There's been enough time wasted on this case with visits to casino's and pubs, and while this has been going on, as you're all aware there has been another murder, the latest victim Mrs Sara Chang. I want you to go through her life with a fine tooth comb, her husband, her friends, associates, lovers, in fact anyone that can give us more information or clues about her or might have seen her last. I want you to hit the clubs she used to go to the coffee shops, hair salons, basically talk to anyone who might have recently seen her."

McGovern, somewhat narked about the derogatory remarks that she had already come out with about the way they had been handling the case to date, rocked back and forth in his chair flipping a pen up and down. He felt it was his time to pipe up "With respect, Ann, should we not be putting all our efforts into finding Mick Western?, he is after all, our only suspect."

Smiling at McGovern, Ann Gatsby was clearly not amused, giving him that all too familiar stare and but continuing on her own track, she paced around the incident room like a caged tiger her voice remained as neutral as always "Also any suspect could have used a vehicle, more than likely stole one, can we use any extra officers to check for reports of stolen vehicles on or around the day in question, I'm well aware that Western is our main person of interest but we must be thorough."

Gatsby noticed McGovern shaking his head and mouthing the words waste of time. His eyes bore into her with such hostility that she had to look away, but knew she needed to put an end to this, or at least agree a truce "Erm DI McGovern a word in my office please."

McGovern knew Gatsby was under pressure to get results and he knew he would be on the receiving end. He held open the door into the corridor, standing to one side to allow her to pass in front of him, pulling a face as she passed. Gatsby heard a few giggles and knew exactly what he'd done.

"If the wind changes direction Inspector you'll stay like that, and some of us might say it would be a mighty good improvement."

McGovern grunted as he slammed the door and made the short journey to McGovern's old office, now belonging to DCI Ann Gatsby.

Gatsby slowly walked behind her desk, sat down and gestured with her hand for McGovern to do likewise. He stared angrily over her head at a picture of the Tyne Bridge on the wall, his picture.

She was blunt and to the point "Just answer this question", her voice was patronisingly patient "I want to solve this case. Lets draw a line under our past disagreements and see if we can work together on this, I know you don't like me but I've already got the big boys breathing down my neck for results and the sooner we get this sorted the sooner I'll be out of your hair and vice versa, so what do you say Jim?, we need each other pulling together on this."

McGovern was pleasantly surprised. He'd expected a big power play, a bollocking, the old *I am the boss* speech and was for once, lost for words. There was even a slight apologetic smile.

Gatsby could almost see his brain ticking over, the tiny muscles moving around his eyes. The heat in the room was overpowering. McGovern ran his hand back over his bushy afro hair so that it stood up making it look twice the size. He knew how thorough she was. She had probably spent hours sifting through the case files already.

"Well Jim?, what's it to be"? encouraging him with an interesting smile. McGovern sat back in his chair gazing at the ceiling. Gatsby was becoming impatient and leaned forwards. She gave him a lopsided grin. McGovern, trying to process what she'd just said nodded his head, but could think of only one thing. *Beware the smile of the crocodile.*

Stanley Scott had worked with McGovern previously, and had only moved to Teesside two years previously. He was a large man in both body and voice. His swept back hairstyle had remained, as had his goatee beard, only now much whiter. He wore a suit, dark navy, white shirt, tie and a pair of light brown leather shoes. *Never trust a man who wears brown shoes.* Oscar had heard that said many times before. But when it came to Stanley Scott he felt he was right to mistrust him.

Stanley Scott always gave Oscar the impression that he hated the job. He'd always felt that Stan Scott was a copper with a complete lack of drive, a farcical sickness record and absolutely no desire for further promotion. As far as he could see Scott hadn't changed his ways or interview techniques for over twenty years and had always appeared to be cynically counting days to the earliest opportunity he had to take early retirement on the grounds of ill health, whilst retaining his full pension entitlement.

He hadn't been short of the odd controversy either. With many rumours of corruption, bribery and scandal. His links to the underworld and closeness to murdered hardman Don Waterman adding fuel to the fire as to why his transfer to Teeside came so sudden after Waterman was assassinated.

Rumour had it that he was next on the gangland hit list. On a positive note, he and McGovern were friends of similar age, and most importantly knew and trusted each other. Even if in Oscar's eyes the trust would never be mutual.

Felicity Somerton was a different proposition, an unknown, both new and keen to impress. Tyneside CID her first appointment. Yes, she might be a bit raw but had desire and determination that was all too sadly lacking in her other, more experienced and battle hardened colleagues.

Felicity had always wanted to be a detective and had applied for transfer to the CID branch as soon as she had completed her compulsory two years as a uniformed officer. She was accepted and breezed through her further training while a temporary detective constable. She was quick to complete compulsory, national Initial crime Investigators' development programme, which normally took two years. Felicity completed it in less than eighteen months and was now a fully fledged Detective Constable.

She had picture book silvery blonde hair tied in a ponytail right on the top of her head, giving an impression that she was wearing a household Cavalry helmet. Her face small and round with perfectly shaped eyebrows, thin lips and a nose that a celebrity would pay good money for. She gave an impression of being quite confident and keen but that in itself could also make her appear quite vulnerable.

She wore a thin blue and yellow floral knee length dress that clung to her, over the top of which a Silver grey cardigan and matching flat shoes. On her left hand a tiny watch with a small thin white leather strap. She carried, over her shoulder, a large tan coloured handbag.

For the next couple of hours Oscar, Scott and Felicity worked the phones alongside the extra uniformed and clerical staff which had now been drafted into what had now become a double murder investigation.

They all sat at their respective desks. Felicity, intently studying case files. Oscar reading Sara Chang's autopsy report and McGovern and Scott were now rolling back the years swapping humorous stories from their earlier days on the force and more recently.

Stan Scott had half a chicken rogan josh in a plastic container which he was offering around the CID room while telling McGovern a humorous tale of his journey up from Teesside, Chewing his words as if he liked the taste. "So, I get to this service Station on the A19, and I'm bursting for a crap, so I run straight into trap one, drop my strides and sit down, then, I hear a voice from the next cubicle."

"What did it say, the voice"?

"At first the voice just said *Hello.*"

"You didn't answer him, Stan, *did* you"?

"Of course I did, I didn't really have time to think, or expect it, and I just said Hello, back."

"Then what"?

"Well, that's when it started to get a bit weird."

McGovern was all ears, "Weird? what do you mean"?

"The voice just said, so *what are you up to then*"?

"Please tell me you didn't respond Stan did you"?

"Yes, I did, like I said, you wouldn't expect anything like that would you, it caught me napping if you like."

"Caught you crapping, more like, so what did you answer with"?

"I was a little taken aback to say the least, felt a bit nervous, I just told him I was on my way from Middlesbrough to Newcastle for work."

"So was that the end of it then"?

"Christ no, the voice then said, *But what are you doing, NOW*"?

"What did you say then"?

"I told him I was a Police officer and he should mind his own business."

"Ha Ha, fucking Pervert, bet that gave him a shock, did he say anything else"?

Stan Scott swivelled his chair around so he was facing everybody"As a matter of fact he did, he said, *Listen love I'm gonna have to phone you back cause this copper in the next cubicle thinks I'm trying to tap him up!* The bastard was talking to his missus on his fucking mobile phone"!

Scott laughed again breaking off midway into a hacking cough.

The two detectives were rolling about with laughter; Oscar looked at Felicity who just rolled her eyes as if to say, *so this is what we can look forward to then*.

McGovern came over to the desk where Oscar sat, fastening his jacket buttons. Oscar could tell he had a favour to ask.

leaning over he whispered in Oscar's ear "How are you for a bit of babysitting"?

Oscar gave him a sideways glance."You mean Felicity"?

"Yes. I'm having a meeting with Stan, gonna fill him in on the case so far."

"And the meeting is going to be *where* exactly"?

"I thought we'd go somewhere a little more relaxed."

Oscar took a deep breath, "McCaffrey's, by any chance"?

"Possibly, son, good idea, why not join us later. We could have a bit of a new team bonding session."

"What about Gatsby?, She's already snided you about pubs and casinos, are you going to invite her as well"?

McGovern slapped Oscar on the back, and answered somewhat sarcastically "That sounds like a good plan, son doesn't it."

Stan Scott was already standing up and was straightening his tie and as he and McGovern headed out towards the door.

Felicity Somerton had a puzzled look on her face."I can't seem to find records of any interviews with David Leung and Michael Yin."

"That's because they haven't been interviewed, it's quite possible that Michael Yin doesn't even exist."

Felicity thought for a moment, rattled a few keys on her computer and swivelled the monitor around. Settling back in her chair she stretched her arms putting her hands behind her head. "It's just that it says in this report Alex Brennan left the football ground with two men, neither of which were identified, one definitely Chinese could one of these two not have been Leung or Yin"?

"It's a possibility." It was very early days in her CID career, but Oscar was mightily impressed.

"I was just wondering, why they weren't interviewed, that's all."

"Lack of manpower for one, plus, I think we had just been prioritising finding Mick Western, as we know he was seen fighting with Brennan and made threats. He also kidnapped Sara Chang. Your right though, they've both gone under the radar somewhat."

"Mind if I dig around a bit".? She asked without looking, her eyes firmly fixed on her computer screen.

"Be my guest." Said Oscar with a friendly grin.

Felicity, smiled proudly, as if she'd been handed a certificate for first prize.

Her eyes bore into her computer screen as she made some notes and studied information in front of her. Sitting back in her chair she took a swig of her coffee "Say's here, David Leung works at a laundry in the Dragon Gate, I would like to go for a visit, that is, of course if my baby sitter allows me to"?

Oscar could feel his face redden, "Sorry about that, McGovern is a bit of a dinosaur, and I'm sorry you had to hear him speaking like that when you first walked into the office."

Felicity laughed. "I was brought up in a house with four older brothers. Believe me there is nothing I could see or hear that would bother or offend me in the slightest."

Standing up she slipped the strap of her handbag over her shoulder. "Mind if we take my car?, I need the practice driving around the city Centre, it'll also help me find my bearings."

Walter Chang's Launderette was situated at the far end of the Dragon Gate, just behind Stowell Street.

Both Oscar and Felicity were glad to get out of the office and breathe some fresh air.

The two detectives had taken Felicity's car, a mustard yellow fiat 500. She slowed down, looking for a parking place, and found one, directly outside which Oscar felt would be too tight. She stopped in front of the space, preparing to reverse into it. She manoeuvred her vehicle with ease. "That's the good thing about having such a small car." She smiled.

The laundrette was crammed and cluttered, noisy and humid. It had several washing machines in a row along the right hand side. On the left hand side were the driers.

There was a desk in the middle of the room flanked by a rectangle of chairs. At the rear of the room there was a double swing door, which led to a larger room where the ironing, dry cleaning and collection and delivery service was based.

The laundry was a locally run business owned by Walter Chang and the majority of the workers were from the Chinese community. Felicity had been quick to point out according to case notes, it was here that David Leung had, and possibly still worked.

An elderly Chinese lady sat at a desk, she had a curly afro style mop of grey hair, not unlike McGovern. She was smartly dressed in black blouse and trousers with a grey uniform waistcoat. She looked at the two detectives over the top of her large tortoise shell glasses. You could tell from her persona that she ran the place with military precision and Walter Chang wouldn't know what he would do without her.

Oscar let Felicity lead. This was, after all, her idea. She took out her warrant card, she could feel her stomach churning with excitement "Hi, I'm Detective Constable Somerton, and this is Detective sergeant Smiles. We would like to ask you a few questions about David Leung."

Oscar feared the worst, they'd probably have more chance getting a better conversation out of an answer machine. But, he was pleasantly surprised.

The old woman looked pleased and keen to help. Thankfully she spoke almost perfect English "Oh yes, washy. He should be out the back sorting some deliveries, just go through," pointing to some double doors.

The two detectives made their way through the double swing doors and into a hub of activity. The room was even hotter than the main room, with the smell of sweat competing against the smell of washing powder and fabric conditioner.

Several workers were all busy doing various tasks, ironing, folding and packing clean laundry into large boxes which were due to be loaded onto a truck that had pulled up to the large open garage door to the rear.

Felicity shouted out "David, David Leung, Tyneside CID, we have a few___"

That's all she could get out before a young Chinese man; probably David Leung made a run for it. Oscar set off after him, feeling his feet pounding through the hard stone factory floor, but Leung was away quicker than Usain Bolt.

Willing his legs to move even quicker, Oscar ran until his muscles throbbed and his lungs ached.

He recognised him as the young man who had attacked him with the meat cleaver, but by the time he had reached the garage doors Leung was nowhere to be seen. He headed back panting, his face flushed.

Arriving a few seconds later Felicity's breathing was a little more laboured following her unexpected sprint. "If he had nothing to hide, why's he running"?

"If it's who I think it is, no wonder he's running"!

The two detectives headed back through the laundry, they passed the old woman, Oscar took out a business card from his waistcoat pocket and handed it to her. "If Washy *does* come back, could you give me a call please"?

The woman nodded but didn't meet his eyes. Oscar knew she wouldn't ever call him.

As Felicity drove back to the station, Oscar watched her as she carefully negotiated her way through the busy city centre traffic, he saw in her eyes the same freshness and enthusiasm that he once, and, occasionally still did.

"So why did you want to become a detective then, Felicity"?

Felicity checked her blind spot as she overtook a stationary bus, and carefully moved back into the left, once safe. "Because being a detective is a good job. You get to travel, meet interesting people and do things that uniformed officers would never dream of. You also get to put away criminals who do the most horrible things imaginable and you get to deal with the most evil people alive."

Oscar laughed, "This isn't a job interview you know."

Felicity smiled "What about you then"? She lost her patience with a driver in front, blared her horn and swung wide to overtake before the lights.

"My Dad was a DCI. When he died I decided I wanted to become a detective, and finish the work he started if you like."

"So you'd never thought about it before"? She checked her mirror and slowed down to allow a woman with a pram to negotiate the zebra crossing.

"No, I was going to be a solicitor, did all my degrees, my training the lot, something changed in me when my parents died."

"What!, you mean they both died at the same time"?

"Yes, in a crash on the A69, a drunk driver hit them head on, it was just over ten years ago. November twenty ninth."

"Sorry to hear that, It must have been so difficult, don't know how I'd have coped with that."

There were a few moments of awkward silence, Felicity searched his face, trying to guess what was going on in his mind, being careful not to take her eyes off the road too much. she decided to lighten the mood, get back to the initial subject of conversation "Do you enjoy the job"?

Oscar smiled a huge broad smile" I love the job, when I first became a detective, I worked on general minor things. I investigated burglaries, robberies and car thefts, harassment, abusive phone calls, things like that. I worked lots of exciting cases, but mostly dead-end cases. I solved a lot of crimes, helping to recover thousands of pounds worth of stolen goods. I have arrested a lot of petty criminals, following the cases in the court."

Felicity nodded with interest "What's the worst part of your job then"?

"The worst part?.. erm...I like it all really; McGovern hates the bureaucracy that goes with the job. You'll find we do lots of paperwork, and complete detailed reports on every phase of an investigation."

"I don't think I'd mind the paperwork too much, I'm well known for being a paperwork monkey."

"Felicity, as a detective, you'll have the best seat to the greatest show on earth. You'll see every kind of criminal. I have seen upper class millionaires and third generation benefit recipients in the same light like no one else can, but, there is a big price."

Felicity's frown deepened "What do you mean big price"?

"Well Detectives rarely punch out the dot like factory workers. We eat, sleep and even dream about the case. Cases are like a box full of snakes, you can't make head nor tail of them. You'll have to leave parties, dinners, school functions and cinema trips to go to work. You'll sacrifice years of time to the job. You'll get some abuse too, sometimes physical. You could be shot or even attacked with a meat cleaver."

"Thanks for that, Oscar, I think". Her narrowing eyes glinting under her perfectly shaped eyebrows.

"No problem."

Back in the incident room there was a strange atmosphere. The team feeling overworked and out of sorts. They had all been instantly put under pressure from Ann Gatsby to get through the files as fast as possible, and although she had insisted on extra clerical staff being shipped in the strain was beginning to tell, as each hour appeared to bring more questions than answers. The team were getting frustrated that they were still no closer to finding any leads as to the whereabouts of Mick Western.

Felicity had a photograph of David Leung. It was definitely the man who had caused the incident at the Chinese restaurant. Placing his photo on the evidence board, she looked intensely at the numerous tit bits of information and cuttings of what appeared to be ever increasing data.

Oscar was pleasantly surprised when his mobile began to ring, he answered. It was a familiar voice."Lee, where you been ? McGovern's been going spare."

"I've been trying to ring him but his phone keeps going to voicemail."

"He's, er, in a meeting."

There was a slight pause.

"He's on the drink in McCaffrey's again isn't he"?

"Good guess. He's catching up with an old friend; we've had a couple of new officers assigned to the case and a new DCI Ann Gat____"

Lee interrupted, his voice becoming a little more agitated. "Yes, I heard. Tell McGovern he needs to keep his phone on. I'll phone him tonight, there's been some developments, under no circumstances must he phone me, got it."

"Developments? like what"?

"Can't say at the moment, I need to run something past him before I decide what to do next."

Oscar had a sudden thought. "While you're on, can I run a name past you"?

"Go on then, but you need to be quick."

"David Leung. Have you heard of him, or even come across him. He did a runner today when we went to question him."

Felicity looked up from her desk. Oscar had a frustrated look on his face; Daniel Lee's phone had gone dead. Felicity was curious. "What's up? Who was that then"?

"Oh nothing really, just Lee."

"Well it can't be nothing because your brows have knit together a bit like this", she said doing an impression of a grumpy person.

Oscar smiled "That was Daniel Lee; the undercover. He hadn't checked in with McGovern for a few days. He sounded okay at first but got a bit agitated and his phone's just gone dead."

"Try ringing him back then."

"I can't. He gave strict instructions. We have to wait till he phones McGovern back."

Sounds of raucous laughter were coming from down the corridor, McGovern and Scott had returned from their 'meeting', obviously quite a few drinks the worse for wear and were still reminiscing about funny cases they've been on.

McGovern entered the room first, struggling to remove his jacket "Yes, I remember. He got quite aggressive and mouthy and we decided to arrest him, and take him in, and he tried to punch you so I got the cuffs out and then realised, fuck, he's only got one arm."

"Yes, that was a good one Jim; he was swinging his arm like a windmill the handcuffs had themselves become an offensive weapon and all that was going through my mind was how the fuck, do you cuff a man with one arm"?

"We managed to put him into the car and fastened the other cuff to the car door handle, but for a few moments I thought he was going to get away."

McGovern then recalled another incident when he'd spotted a known villain in a Tyneside pub. He knew that the lad had been fitted with an electronic tag and should have been at home on a curfew.

Remember when I phoned to shop that little toe rag Lee Cardull, and I was told by G4S that according to the monitoring equipment at the hostel he was staying at he was still in his room but I told them he couldn't be as I was standing right behind him, in a pub. They wouldn't believe me so I arrested him, took him to the station and sure enough the tag was not on his leg".

"Where was it then, had he forcibly taken it off"?

"No, you can't do that without setting off an alarm, they are very sensitive."

"So what had he done then"?

"It came to pass that Mr Lee Cardull had a false leg which those stupid bastards tagged, and all he had to do when he fancied breaking his curfew was take it off and replace it with his spare one, you couldn't make it up."

"Good meeting then"? Oscar did his best not to sound too sarcastic.

McGovern slumped on his chair and puffed out his cheeks, he pointed at Felicity and then towards the coffee machine outside. "Do me a favour pet, could you go get me a black coffee, please love, plenty sugar in it, thanks."

Oscar wasn't impressed. "She is a detective sir, not your PA."

Felicity didn't mind although she despised being called Pet. "I might as well get us all a drink. We need to see where we are with the case."

Oscar had again been flicking through Sara Chang's autopsy report, he closed it. "Is Scott up to speed, with the case so far then sir."

"More or less, son, yes, in fact he's already had his feelers out. He's heard that little Smack rat Johnny Murray has been roaming around North Tyneside acting the big man, telling everyone who'll listen that he's Mick Western's business partner."

"Johnny Murray? A Business partner"?

"That's what Scott's heard; uniforms are bringing Murray in as we speak. He was easy to find, been mouthing off in nearly every pub. We'll see if he knows anything about where his apparent *boss* has disappeared to."

McGovern got up from his seat and walked over to the murder board where he saw a picture of David Leung. He instantly recognised him as the young man who had pulled a knife on him outside the Snap Dragon Casino, and remembered him from the incident in the restaurant. But he tried to sound surprised.

"Who's this then"?

"That's David Leung. He was one of the two workers we were trying to contact from the football ground. He was also the young lad that caused the scene at the restaurant. Felicity and I went to speak to him today; he took one look and ran off."

McGovern had suddenly become very interested in the latest edition to the murder board. "We got an address for him"?

"No sir, but he works at Walter Chang's launderette, back of Stowell Street, do you remember him"?

McGovern lied. "Maybe son, his face *is* familiar, I've just thought of something. I've just got to pop out for a bit. I Won't be long."

Oscar suddenly recalled the phone call, Lee's message, but it was too late McGovern had left the office. He tried to phone him, but it was still switched off. *Never mind. I'd text him but he never bloody reads them. Hopefully he will realise his phone is off, wonder where he was going in such a hurry? Still he should be back soon, I'll tell him then...*

Stan Scott returned from the toilet entering the room at the same time that Felicity had returned with the drinks. "Where's McGovern? Uniforms have got Johnny Murray downstairs."

"He's had to pop out for a bit."

"Where"?

Oscar gestured vaguely with his hands "Dunno, didn't say."

"Gonna be long"?

Oscar didn't say anything he just held his arms out and shrugged his shoulders.

Felicity was quick to offer her services. "I'll interview him with you, just till McGovern gets back. If it's OK with you sir"?

Scott looked behind him, thinking Crammond had entered the room, only to become aware that Felicity was addressing *him,* as sir.

He smiled "you don't need to call me sir. Sir is for those teachers in the academy or Crammond, Richard Branson and Bobby Robson, (God rest his soul). You can call me Stan, pet."

Felicity had an answer for Scott, "OK, but I'm not your pet either, don't you dare ever call me pet, my name is Felicity."

Oscar laughed at her response, and expression of sheer nothing on Stan Scott's face. "That's you in your place Stan."

Stan Scott laughed and nodded.

Johnny Murray sat in the interview room. He always gave the impression that he wasn't the brightest bulb on the Christmas tree but that was mostly an act, especially for Police.

He was hunched up and straight away Felicity could sense his negative body language. His hair was short but unkempt. He had a wispy beard, a hooked nose and his little piercing eyes appeared to be too close together.

Under the fluorescent lighting his pasty face looked almost white. As pale as a Scotsman's arse. He wore a black body warmer on top of a scruffy grey T shirt, holey faded jeans and scuffed black pumps. He looked ten years older than he was and that was on a good day.

As the Officers entered the room he became more animated and stood up. Felicity followed Scott through the door as she smiled at him. Scott shouted instructions, as felicity's quick smile faded.

"Sit down you little shit." Scott's voice was harsh and aggressive, Felicity could see the anger in his stiff shoulders and the set of his back. It was hardly the textbook beginning to an interview Felicity had recalled from her training.

She was surprised at how small Johnny Murray was, his young face ravaged and aged by drug abuse.

Murray was annoyed that he'd been brought in; and he immediately tried to push Scott's buttons "Are you going to arrest me then, or what?, or do I just bung you a few quid Stan to look the other way, just like the old times eh, or so i've been told," Scott found his smugness was infuriating.

The chairs and table went flying as Stan Scott sprang forward, squaring up to the now not so cocky youngster, ready for all the world to take a swing at the cheeky little bastard there and then and to hell with the consequences.

Felicity quickly calmed the situation. Both men sat down as Scott regained a little composure.

"Unfortunately being a disgusting piece of scum is not against the law."

"Then why am I here then"? Murray wiped away some snot with his hand and rubbed it on the underside of the table.

Felicity attempted to restore order. "Thank you for coming in Mr Murray. I am Detective Constable Somerton, and this, hmm...gentleman, to my left is Detective Sergeant Scott, would you like a drink, a tea, a coffee, water perhaps, We would just like to interview you, that's all."

Johnny Murray appeared to relax a bit and even found time for some sarcasm."Thank you very much but I can't remember applying for any job here, love, let alone filling out the application form."

Scott was on it in a flash. "That's because you probably can't even fucking write, but, then again you do have a job already, don't you"?

Murray attempted a false blank stare "What job"?

"The job that half of fucking Tyneside knows about."

"And that job is.."?

"Stop playing games son, I'm that far...", Stan Scott opened his right finger and thumb about half an inch.. "...away from really losing my patience with you, you've told too many people, you're working for Mick Western."

Johnny Murray began to stammer in a bit of panic, he shook his head "No, no, that's not a job, it's a favour. As far as I understand you get paid for doing a job, he is just a friend."

Stan Scott Stared into his eyes, and laughed sarcastically " A Friend ! You wouldn't know what a friend was if one fell out of a tree and hit you on the fucking head."

Felicity again attempted to regain control of the situation. "So what is it you're doing for Mr Western then."

Johnny smiled, her eyes were so bright they made his ache. The good cop, bad cop routine appeared to be working, and he was sure Felicity fancied him. Her smile sang out to him like a frost in summer. "Just some collecting from his customers...."

Again Scott interrupted him putting it rather more strongly, he was getting tired of the game playing and stood up "Customers, fucking victims, more like."

Felicity held up her hand, "sorry Mr Murray, please continue."

"You know just collecting a few quid here, a few quid there; he told me he needed someone to do this for him as he was planning something big."

"Did he say what it was he was planning"? Scott butted in as impatient as ever.

Johnny didn't speak. He just sat with his head bowed and shook it, gulping himself silent.

Scott pointed in the direction of Johnny's ear. "You know, one time, when you started a new job, on your first day, you got an induction pack and a name badge. Is that what Western hands out to his new staff"?

Again, Johnny sat silently, his head felt big and aching, his nose and eyes stuffed with tears.

Felicity stopped making notes; she lifted her head from her notebook and locked eyes with him."Has he been in touch, lately Mr Murray"?

"Who"?

Scott thumped the arms of his chair. "Prince Fucking William, who do you think"?

Johnny ignored the sarcasm. Felicity reworded her question. "When did you last have any contact with Mick Western, Johnny"?

"Dunno, a few days, maybe a week."

The incident room was waiting eagerly for an update. McGovern had returned with a large carrier bag, inside of which was his lunch. Beef chow mein, crispy noodles, prawn crackers, and chips.

Might have known it would be food, Oscar thought.

"Where's the new signings'?

"Downstairs, interviewing Johnny Murray."

"Oh well, can't let my lunch go cold now, can we." McGovern began scoffing the food, which had to be said had quite a nice aroma.

As Buster appeared from under the desk, McGovern spoke with his mouthful "Oh no you don't, you greedy little twat, go on piss off over there,"gesturing with his foot and pushing the little dog away. Buster growled and flopped down underneath Oscar's chair, with a deep sigh.

"Lee's been trying to phone you sir."

McGovern began to shuffle papers making more room on his desk for his take away cartons.

"Are so the bastard has surfaced eh, what did he have to say then"?

"He wants you to keep your phone on, he's gonna phone you tonight, I think he appeared to be onto something, didn't say what it was. He wanted to run it past you first."

McGovern settled back in his chair "Better turn me fucking phone back on then hadn't I."

"Might be a good idea sir."

Felicity and Scott were soon back upstairs in the incident room.

"How did it go with the Rat Boy then"? McGovern's almost inaudible question, his mouth still full of food,

Scott sighed like a long suffering teacher "Say's he's not seen him, or heard from him in a week", stealing a chip from McGovern's lunch, as McGovern tried to pull his carton away to stop him, glaring.

"And you believe him"?

Scott studied the chip before popping it into his mouth, "No real reason not to."

McGovern sounding frustrated drew himself up in his chair "So where is he then? What's his game? And why did he kidnap and murder Sara Chang"?

Oscar had found something of interest as he thumbed through the latest forensic report. "The DNA results on the semen that was found on Sara Chang are back sir and, the person she had sex with hours before she died, wasn't Mick Western."

Stan Scott sat back down in his chair. "So does that mean she left Mick Western, and was with somebody else, who then killed her"?

"All it tells us is that Sara Chang had sex with somebody an hour or so before she was taken to the timber yard, and that person wasn't Mick Western."

Felicity added a couple of names to the mystery. "Could it have been Leung, or this so called Michael Yin or what about her husband Walter, could have been one of them"?

McGovern was less optimistic. He frowned rubbing his bearded chin "All it tells us is that Sara Chang is a slag who would fuck a table leg if she felt could benefit her. Knowing her reputation, it could have been any one of a number of blokes, and the least possible option would have been her husband! that's not really a surprise is it."

Oscar continued to flick through the report while sipping his coffee. He carefully placed his drink on the desk beside him. "We're still waiting to see if we have a match for that DNA, should know by the morning."

McGovern was less confident about the time scale, and sounded mighty frustrated. He drew a deep breath and stood up. "Christmas is coming, everything slows down, even the forensics. We'll be lucky if we get the match this side of the New Year."

He'd taken some catching, and boy could that young lad run. But he needed to be silenced. He could have spoilt everything. He knew far too much, he had chances to prove himself but had failed miserably and he was never going to make it any higher in the syndicate.

In some strange distorted way he was glad that running him over hadn't actually killed him; he needed him to be alive, until he needed to get rid.

He remembered how he'd enjoyed watching him breathing erratically, trying not to cry. It had taken plenty of effort dragging him through the narrow gap of those trees, the crusty bark scraping his shoulders. Through his knees he had felt the intense cold of the mud. How he'd stumbled to his feet glancing nervously about. It took a while to dig that hole and he'd even had to use the shovel to keep him quiet. Useless bastards who couldn't be trusted to keep stum didn't get buried like normal people, they got put into the ground, alone and alive.

He smiled as he recalled the moist earth spattering on his face, his eyes twitching open like globes of marble, then closing, How his mouth gaped, his throat shrank when he began to choke on the yielding earth and the scream he couldn't release as the darkness finally lay under the soil.

He recalled how he calmly walked back to his car and drove off, how the landscape kept drawing his gaze, hedges and tree trunks fluttered by. The relative dimness had felt like lotion on his skin. His heart pounded as silence clung to his ears and the blackness clung to his eyes. This had dragged him into the dark but he still needed to be dragged a little further "*Nearly done now, just one more to go.*"

CHAPTER SIXTEEN

Oscar had dropped his grandad off at his house with Buster and was off to the airport to collect his sister's family.

The flight from Canada was due soon, hoping the traffic wouldn't be too bad he headed off the busy central motorway and drove towards the airport.

With just three days to go until Christmas day he'd treble checked a list that his sister, Gemma had sent him. The food, wine and items were now bought, and he was looking forward to his few days off away from the case.

Although he never fully switched off from work, he always liked to keep an ear to the ground. As well as seeing his sister, niece and nephew, he was looking forward to seeing his brother in law Don. Knowing that Canada had an extensive Chinese community and that Don had experience with Triad gangs in the past, he was looking forward to picking his brains, and maybe giving him a good hiding at the local snooker club for good measure too.

After he had parked his car he made his way to the arrival area. He looked around at how many people were there. The airport was a village in itself. An extended and refurbished departure terminal had been opened. The refurbishment comprised a large extension which included new shops, cafes and new waiting seats. Millions of passengers used the Airport, which was located near Woolsington, five miles north-west of the city centre. It was the tenth busiest airport in the United Kingdom.

The airport was busy, with numerous flights coming in and out and having searched so hard his eyes began to ache Oscar soon spotted Gemma's bright blonde hair, and it wasn't long before his family were heading his way.

Oscar hugged his sister and picked up her case, as there were hugs and kisses for his niece and nephew, a firm handshake and man hug for Don, ending with the customary tap on each other's backs.

At twenty nine years old Gemma was a bit younger than him. The kids were so excited and voices were so transatlantic, Gemma too had picked up a bit of an accent but still mainly spoke in her soft Geordie twang. Taking out some lip balm, and a small mirror out of her handbag Gemma rubbed it onto her lips with her index finger."How's Grandad doing"?

Oscar answered as he started to drive them towards his home. "He's doing fine, still as protective as always, he's hyped about seeing you all, he's spent a small fortune."

They soon reached the house. Traffic hadn't been too bad and as they pulled up outside the front door. Gemma could see the curtains twitching and the face of her Grandfather at the window. He'd been standing there for quite a while.

In a few seconds the front door was opened and Buster shot down the path immediately jumping up and licking the faces of the two children. There were hugs and kisses all round from Grandad, even for Oscar, which he felt a bit strange under the circumstances, he'd only been away a couple of hours, but never mind.

As the old coal fire blasted out the heat the outside cold was shut out and the family took their seats in the lounge. Together for Christmas.

Gemma gave her brother a wide grin. "So, how's things in Police land then.?"

Oscar gave a deep sigh, "Bit of a complicated case at the moment, not getting very far, think it's got some Triad involvement, but much more to it and that".

"Oh, I see," Gemma's eyes glowed "Maybe you should speak to Don, about the Triad's, he's had a lot of experience in the last few years, and you never know, maybe give you some insight."

Oscar's eyebrows squeezed together, "You're supposed to be over here on holiday, man."

Gemma, however knew her brother well, and with their father also having been a detective she knew that they were never really, truly off duty, as was her husband Don. "Let's just say I understand a lot about the job's the men in my life have to do."

It had been a long trip and it wasn't long before both children, and Grandad were sleeping on the sofa, Oscar took a sip from his cup of tea, and gestured over towards them with his head "I was going to suggest we all go out for a meal, but I guess that's scuppered my plans."

Gemma patted her brother on the knee, she too looked quite tired. "Why don't you and Don go down to that snooker club of yours, have a few drinks, I've got lots I could be doing here, unpacking and stuff and want to chat to Grandad, when he eventually wakes up that is. Maybe he can give me a catch up on what's been happening on the soaps, go on, do you both good."

Don nodded in agreement. "Well, brother in law looks like this here pool player is gonna show you snooker boy how's it's done."

"We'll see son, table's a fair bit bigger mind, and the pockets are a lot tighter."

They both got up, just as Grandad began to waken from his nap.

Getting up from her chair Gemma walked over towards the sofa where Grandad and the kids were sitting, "let's get them two off to bed, eh, Grandad, then you can open that bottle of Bailey's."

The snooker club was quite an old building, and there was always a smoky haze around shaded lights that hung over each table. Nicotine stained walls were still evident as was the always quiet atmosphere which was occasionally only disturbed by the clanking of snooker balls and the occasional bit of echoed distant laughter.

Oscar often called in, quite often on his own; he did a lot of deep thinking and solved many cases through thoughts and ideas while hitting balls around the green baize table. It not only relaxed him but cleared his mind, made him look at things differently.

Oscar broke off cueing well as always, the white cue ball clipping the edge of the triangle of red's and arriving safely at the baulk end of the table about an inch from the top cushion.

Don nodded, "Good shot sunshine, left me nothing to go at."

Although they were both off duty their respective careers weren't one's in which you could totally switch off.

Don played a bad shot, scattered a few red's, Oscar potted a red, perfect on the black, potted it and without taking his eye off the shot potted another red as he spoke. "So, Don, tell me about Triads then, I hear you have quite a problem in Canada"?

Oscar played another safety shot back up to the top of the table; Don was snookered behind the brown ball.

Don looked at the table, and shook his head. "Where you have a large population of Chinese community it's almost certain that you will have the triads. Canada has three quarters of a million Chinese people, approximately half a million in Toronto alone, and just less than that in Vancouver, when you compare a city like London, just over a hundred thousand you can see I know what I'm talking about. Each group has what they call a Dragon Head, the leader, several Red Poles or enforcers , an administrator, who is called the White fan and possibly hundreds or even thousands of lesser members called Blue lanterns or forty niners. In Canada we set up the guns and gangs unit at the Toronto Police Service, this was a specialised command detective unit that is responsible for handling Triads. It used to be called the Asian Gang Unit of the Metro Toronto Police, you may have heard of it." Don missed the reds and left one over the pocket, Oscar potted it with ease and nodded his head, "Vaguely."

Oscar carried on his break while Don continued. "Anyway this unit was responsible for dealing with all triad related matters, but the larger unit was created to deal with the broader array of ethnic gangs in the city. At a national level the Mounties organised crime branch are responsible for investigating all gang related activities, including Triads. The Canada Border Services Agency, my unit, works alongside the mounties to detain and remove non circulated triad members, those in the country who are illegal and try to deport them back to their native country of origin. The Organised crime and Law enforcement act was created to deal with organised crime and gave us a tool for Police in Canada to handle organised criminal activities. This act enhanced the general role of the criminal code of Canada, with amendments to deal with organised crime, in dealing with Triad criminal activities."

Oscar scored a break of forty four, played another safety shot and Don was again snookered, this time behind the green ball. "So, what about the UK and Europe? What do you know about Triad activity this side of the Atlantic"?

Don smashed the cue ball as hard as he could, red balls were hit and flew all over the table, one dropped into the left middle pocket, he went for the pink and missed. "The Gan-Yin are the largest Triad group operating in Britain, mainly based in Manchester, they have affiliated groups in several UK Cities, and so I wouldn't be at all surprised if getting a foothold in Newcastle wasn't within their plans."

Oscar was off and running again. He potted a long red down the left hand cushion and got perfect position on the black ball. "So where do they get their members? how do they recruit"?

Don sat down, and took a sip from his pint of larger, "Many members are recruited in the traditional way, many are business men, who join with the organisation for their own protection or as full participants in their criminal activities, although they abide by the territorial urban districts of other Triad organisations, often centred around Chinese cultural clubs and businesses."

Oscar missed any easy red, "That would explain Walter Chang's involvement, so why target Football matches"?

Don potted the red ball that Oscar has just missed, followed by the pink ball and another red, " Football matches, and in particular, English Premier league has a huge following in the far east, just look at how many English teams go there for end of season and pre season tours. I suppose you know how betting works over there, don't you"?

Oscar chalked the tip of his cue. "Yes, I understand that once half time comes, as far as Asian gambling rules go the result stands, making it an obvious choice to end games prematurely."

"Yes, and that's what makes football such a big target, it's a very popular game, Football, floodlight failure is their number one choice of disruption."

Don played a safety shot but left an easy red for Oscar "One of my colleagues did explain a bit about that, so, paying somebody to permanently cut off the floodlights at a certain score could be worth a lot of money."

Oscar missed, Don slammed in an easy red ball and turned to Oscar "That, my dear brother in law is an absolute certainty."

The two finished their game, of which Oscar won, of course and after another couple of frames the two decided to call it a day.

"Is that Irish bar far from here"? Don asked remembering some great nights they had had in McCaffrey's a couple of years ago.

"Yeah, it's not far; we'd need to take a taxi though."

"That's great, Gemma won't mind, let's just go for one."

"Okay, there's a taxi rank, just around this corner."

Walking around a dimly lit corner they waited in a small queue for the next available taxi, the city was still quite busy and despite the time eleven thirty there were still plenty of bars and clubs open for business.

With it being so close to Christmas there were still a lot of work and Office party's roaming the streets, there was the occasional police siren, but thankfully the mood in the city centre appeared to be reasonably calm.

CHAPTER SEVENTEEN

The taxi got to McCaffrey's in no time and as soon as they got through the door Oscar spotted the familiar face of McGovern sitting on his own, looking the worse for drink.

"You okay sir"? McGovern nodded his head unconvincingly.

"Any news, on the case"?

McGovern took a long slug from his glass, and then placed it onto the table in front of him. "You can never switch off, can you son?, well, if you must know Walter Chang's been in to give a DNA sample, wasn't him either. Like we knew it wouldn't be. Sara Chang had sex with someone else hours before she died. Who?, there are possibly hundreds of possibilities, maybe even thousands, might be an idea to put out an appeal on crimewatch for anyone who's ever fucked her come in for a DNA test."

Oscar introduced his brother in law Don; McGovern was his usual falsely pleasant but unimpressed self.

"Never mind though eh, it's nearly Christmas. Sit down lad's what you's drinking"?

Oscar and Don both asked for pints of Guinness, McGovern pointed to the barman and then his two companions, in what appeared to be some hypnotic way and the barman somehow seemed to understand what he wanted. The drinks appeared moments later.

As they took their seats Oscar lowered his voice and leaned in towards McGovern. "I thought you were going to your youngest daughters for Christmas sir"?

McGovern wiped the froth from his top lip, took a rather discoloured handkerchief out of his pocket and blew his nose. "Change of plans son, change of plans."

McGovern didn't choose to divulge any more so Oscar took it as bad news.

"So where are you going for Christmas Day then, sir"?

McGovern took another large gulp from his pint of Guinness and as he was the worse for wear almost missed the table putting it back down. "Think I'll just have a quiet one, got a frozen microwave turkey dinner for one and two bottles of Bells Whiskey, that'll do me fine."

Don's brow wrinkled as he had an idea. "Why doesn't he come to us? We've got plenty of food, plenty of space, no one should be alone at Christmas."

McGovern was overjoyed, and before Oscar could confirm or reject his provisional offer, McGovern accepted. "Really, that would be great, thank you, thank you son, that's very kind of you."

Oscar was quietly horrified, although he agreed nobody should be alone at Christmas, McGovern was hardly his first choice he'd have for a house guest, he'd probably be a close second to that old TV character Rab C Nesbit, maybe McGovern was related to Rab C

Nesbit, who knows. Anyway it was too late for that; He had been invited and accepted.

Oscar offered to pick him up on Christmas Eve night, tomorrow in fact. As another game of snooker beckoned.

Christmas Eve night had always been a night for special memories. Gemma, such a good cook, just like her mother meant the aroma coming from the kitchen took Oscar back to his childhood years. Redolence of turkey cooking, mince pies and the hum of laughter and conversation.

Once again his home a family home, filled with joy and love. Even having McGovern there appeared to be the right thing to do, Christmas Eve, after all, peace on earth and goodwill to all men, even McGovern.

Oscar's phone started to ring. It was Kim Deehan. "Hi Oscar, sorry to bother you, but, just wondering do you still want those tickets for Liverpool on Boxing Day, it's just I hadn't heard from you."

Oscar felt a flush creep across his cheeks, moving swiftly into another room. "Of course, yes, sorry, as long as it's no trouble". he sat down on the edge of a large sofa. "You got any plans for tomorrow then"? "Yes, I'm at my parents house, my two brothers and their families are also here, you"?

"Oh, I'm here at home, got a house full, my sister's cooking in the kitchen, her kids are tucked up in bed and my Grandad, brother in law and McGovern are having a competition to see who can drink the most without falling asleep."

"Inspector McGovern? He's there as well"?

"Yeah, he's going to be on his own and it is Christmas after all."

"Well Oscar Smiles aren't you such a nice man."

He didn't have the heart to tell her it was his brother in law Don's idea, he just responded with a false laugh.

Kim Continued "If you get to the ground for two O'clock, main reception Milburn stand, just ask for me when you get there, I'm looking forward to seeing you all."

"Yes, it will be nice, Gemma is really looking forward to it, especially the chance she might meet Darren Harrison, he's her favourite player."

Oscar sensed some hostility at the mere mention of Darren Harrison and he was right.

"He's an arsehole, but a very good player, when he wants to be that is, trouble with him is he knows it as well. He is everything that's wrong with professional footballers these days. He, like many footballers, has only three interests away from football, fast cars, designer clothes and which one of them has the largest dick"!

"Oh well, not my type of person either," Oscar somewhat taken aback at Kim's negativity towards Newcastle United's star player and felt there may have been some history between them and a little concerned that he shared no less than two of Harrison's so called interests, "so not you're type then eh"?

"I never date footballers. Well, not any more."

Oscar decided not to discuss it any further but felt by her response that his initial thoughts had been spot on. Tempted to ask her about her ideal man, he let the opportunity pass.

Kim hinted at bringing their conversation to an end "I better not keep you from your family much longer, and my mum needs some help preparing for tomorrow anyway. I hope you all have a nice day tomorrow. See you on Boxing Day."

"Yes, see you there."

Kim stood for a moment tapping her mobile phone against her chin and smiled

Oscar didn't really want the conversation to end but lacked confidence with women.

He'd previously had some bad experiences with girlfriends. Being quite shy around women, his good nature had often been taken advantage of and he'd been quite hurt in the past, especially his last girlfriend he'd had, a girl he'd almost married in fact.

But Oscar *was* married. Married to the job, but enough of feeling sorry for himself, it was Christmas Eve and he owed it to his houseguests to be a perfect proprietor.

Putting his phone back into his pocket Oscar headed back to the kitchen to break the good news that he knew was sure to go down well.

McGovern sitting with a big smile on his face. He'd obviously also had some good news "There's been a change of plan, son. My eldest daughter, Susan, from Carlisle, rang me when she found out that Lorraine was unable to have me for Christmas. She's picking me up early tomorrow morning, only drawback is Edith will be there."

"Edith? was she your first or second ex-wife"?

"First, and what should have been bloody last, Susan's mother. Never seen her for five or six years."

"Should be interesting, sir."

McGovern tried his best to squeeze out a smile that was thinner than a prisoner's roll up, "Be a lot more than interesting son, mark my words. One cunt of a woman, that one."

Oscar walked over to the TV and turned it off. Buster lay in between McGovern and Grandad looking quite content. Buster didn't normally like, or should it be more like tolerate McGovern too much. *Obviously the season of goodwill*, Oscar thought, he gave a smile and headed off to bed.

Susan arrived for McGovern a lot earlier than expected, and had obviously not been drinking last night, as she appeared as fresh as a daisy. She was quite short and obviously McGovern's daughter. In fact a double of her father, that is apart from the unkempt curly hair, creased clothes and bushy beard. Oscar wondered if seeing her father worse for drink in her early years and the resulting divorce of her parents had anything to do with her not having had a drink. After all, if you'd seen your father drunk more than sober maybe that would have an effect on any child. Then again maybe she was just sensible.

As always Christmas day came and went in a flash.

CHAPTER EIGHTEEN

It was easier to travel by metro to St James' Park on Boxing Day. The train was packed to the rafters. Don Carrington had a valid point. "In Canada they'd put extra public transport on especially when there are 52,000 people all trying to get to the same place for the same time."

Oscar nodded in agreement, "That would be too easy though wouldn't it." He hated being so close to strangers and the metro train was full, and hot, with a smell of sweat, stale booze and cheap Christmas aftershave.

There were a lot of football fan's on the train, all dressed in black and white shirts, and also plenty of shoppers bound for Eldon Square and the boxing day sales. At every station more people would get on than get off, including the customary woman with a double buggy, who was she? Was it the same person? Why did she always insist on bringing a double buggy out when any sensible person knew the match was on.?, and why did she always only stay on for only one stop.?

The next station, monument station, was the busiest one and deep in the centre of Newcastle City Centre, just one more stop from the football ground.

Luckily Gemma had managed to wedge herself through a tiny gap and had found a seat. Oscar and Don however were not so lucky. They were standing squashed together crushed, with a number of others with nothing to hang onto. With his hands trapped in his pockets, Oscar just hoped for a smooth ride as any sudden braking would surely propel him violently forwards and backwards.

The Metro train pulled in at Monument, the signal for some movement. Due to a number of people getting on, and off the inevitable happened. Somebody, by accident, pressed the emergency brake button. The Metro train was not going to move.

Oscar looked out to see an official looking delegation heading down the platform, all of which were in uniform, including the driver, a metro inspector, and two Police constables.

As the delegation reached each carriage, doors would open and for a few seconds they would stand and interrogate, looking in at the crushed company of stripe clad people uncomfortably huddled together.

A drunk, middle aged man wearing a green paper Christmas cracker hat had kept everybody entertained with his wise cracks. This was an opportunity too good to miss, as his loud voiced boomed out, "This is like a scene from Schindlers fucking list." There was a thunder of laughter.

The delegation reached their carriage. A small weedy peaked capped Metro Inspector, a Nazi with an icy stare was in his element and full of his own importance as he fumbled with his clipboard. For once he had a captive audience of people who *had* to listen to him, clearing his throat before an important announcement

"Somebody has pressed the emergency brake. There's a five hundred pound fine and this train isn't going anywhere until the culprit owns up to it."

The drunken comedian saw this as another chance and wasn't going to let it go. He free'd his arm from the tangle of bodies, put it up in the air and shouted in a loud and booming voice "*I am* Spartacus."! Gales of laughter erupted from the train carriage, somebody, then taking his lead shouted out too "No, *I am* Spartacus."! The shouts were now coming from all down the train as various carriages full of mostly football supporters all joining in. The best, and most funniest a young child stepping out of the sliding doors at the bottom of the train to squeal in a high pitched voice "I am Spartacus."!

The Metro Inspector's face was red with a mixture of anger and embarrassment. The driver and two uniformed constables were doing their best not to laugh, and failing miserably. Oscar managed to grab Gemma by the hand and along with Don squeezed themselves out and headed for an escalator. Many others followed leaving the driver and the Metro Inspector to contemplate their next move.

CHAPTER NINETEEN

St James Park was an imposing site as you approached it. Towering over the City. The Cathedral on the Hill.

Gemma was as excited as when she went to her first ever game. For Don, it *was* his first ever visit to the famous St James' Park. Oscar was, however somewhat underwhelmed. Much as he wanted Newcastle United to be successful, and kind of supported them, well, followed their results to be exact; he wasn't really a football fan. He was more looking forward to, or at least hoping to see Kim.

They headed up past a statue of Sir Bobby Robson and towards the Milburn stand.

Once inside Oscar approached reception. Something he'd done previously during the first few days of the case, what seemed like sometime ago now.

The same receptionist smiled and seemed to recognise him.

"Oscar Smiles to pick up some tickets from Kim Deehan."

The young receptionist didn't speak but smiled and made a phone call. "She'll be a few moments."

Kim came down the stairs, wearing her usual suit with knee length skirt and a name badge. She held out her hand and Oscar shook it gently, as he made the introductions.

"Kim, this is my sister Gemma and her husband Don." Kim shook each hand in turn. She always gave a very good first impression,

"There you go, Oscar." Kim handed some tickets over, "I'm sorry but I have to work, I promise I'll try and catch up with you all at half time, I hope you all enjoy it," and with that she turned back back up the marble staircase.

Gemma was impressed, "She's nice, and I think she likes you."

Oscar's face reddened a little, "How do you know that"?

"I'm a woman, aren't I; you should ask her out, I'm sure she'd say yes."

"Gerraway man." Oscar doubted he'd be so lucky.

Their Platinum club seats were situated within the main Milburn stand in St James Park, which offered excellent football hospitality and were allocated in an executive section near to the eighteen yard line and offered an excellent view of the pitch.

The game was a bit of an anti climax. Half time came and the score remained goal less at 0-0. Although Gemma appeared to be loving it.

Oscar, Gemma and Don made their way down the concrete staircase and back into the platinum club bar, they found a table and sat down. They were quickly joined by Kim Deehan who sat next to Gemma. A waitress who sounded Eastern European took their drink orders and brought them over in a couple of minutes. Kim took a sip from a glass of Britvic orange.

"So, Oscar tells me you're all over here for the Christmas."

"Yes, and new year, we always go to McCaffrey's on New Year's Eve, you should come, I'm sure my brother would be pleased to see you there."

Kim just smiled "Oscar tells me you're a professional footballer."

Gemma picked at a loose thread on the cotton tablecloth "Semi professional. We don't make a great deal of money in Canada, but we get more than the ladies do over here, but nowhere near the male Premier League players get in this country, what's the average wage for a first teamer here"?

"I don't really deal much with that sort of thing and don't know exactly but someone like Darren Harrison, for example, he's our top earner, he's probably on about £95,000 a week, basic"!

Gemma appeared somewhat misty eyed at the very mention of his name "Darren's my favourite player, Oscar doesn't like him though, thinks he's a stereotypical arsehole footballer."

I wonder where he got that opinion from, Kim thought.

Gemma was very excited "I see he's on the bench today. I really hope he gets on, I was looking forward to seeing him play."

As Gemma drained half her glass and leaned back. Kim explained the reasons he wasn't, as far as she understood, "I don't know the full story but it's got something to do with him breaking a club curfew. The manager would have left him out all together but the transfer window is looming and his agent said there were a few clubs interested and he wanted assurances he would be getting regular football. He is a fans favourite and we do unfortunately have to keep him happy. This club has learnt its lesson about selling star players, no matter what baggage they carry."

"Well, we could do with him in the second half, I'm sure he'd have put some of those chances away."

"Don't fret Gemma. He *will* be on at some point." Kimberly leaned past her and whispered "Word has it the medical staff are trying their best to sober him up as we speak"! they both laughed.

Gemma gave her a stay on her face whatever she was saying smile "So tell me, Kim, how do you know my brother"?

Kim was self aware enough to know that her feelings for Oscar were getting stronger rather than fading. She sensed Gemma had picked up on the signs but decided to answer with a straight bat "Oh just through a current case he's working on, one of my staff here was murdered and the Police think he was up to no good or got in with some crime syndicate who were trying to fix the results of matches."

"Interesting stuff, did you know the worker well, the one who was murdered"?

"Yes, Alex, that was his name. He worked here for quite some time, lovely family man, he's a miss around the place, anyway talking of being a miss around the place I need to get back to work, it was lovely to meet you, and I hope you enjoy the rest of the game."

Kim bid farewell to the group and immediately began talking with the guests at the next table. She was, indeed, the ultimate professional. Although deep down she was desperate to tell Oscar how she felt about him when she was with him.

Walking back over away from the bar, Don squeezed between tables, pushing his way past the crowded bar area sipping from his pint so that it wouldn't slop over. He'd been talking to a fan who had been trying to explain the offside rule to him. Catching Oscar's gaze he pointed at the glass he was carrying. Oscar lifted his hand and shook his head mouthing "No thanks." After all it was almost time for the second half and woe betide anyone caught drinking alcohol in sight of the playing area.

Oscar had always thought that this was a stupid rule. Football was probably the only sport where this silly rule applied. Imagine, he thought if they tried to bring the rule in at a darts match! What did the powers that be expect to happen that suddenly if people were allowed to drink sitting in seats watching the match that they would somehow all be metamorphosed into eighties football hooligans. Surely there was more danger in forcing somebody trying to drink two or three pints during the ten minute half time period, but then again what would he know!

The party made their way back to their seats just as Liverpool were starting the second half, with Newcastle attacking their favourite Gallowgate End. As Oscar looked around the Platinum Club he caught sight of Walter Chang sitting in an executive box. Walter recognised Oscar and raised what looked like a glass of red wine in his direction, *obviously money talks, one rule for one, and he seems to have gotten over his wife's murder quickly*, Oscar thought.

The second half was much more exciting than the first with both teams attacking and looking for a win that would bring Champions League football that little step closer. Just passed the hour mark with the scores still level at 0-0, the crowd went wild as golden boy Darren Harrison was about to enter the fray.

Ten minutes later Newcastle were attacking and a deep cross from the left was headed against a post and guess who was on hand to smash the ball into the empty net. None other than Mr Darren Harrison. Running to a Jubilant Gallowgate end he stood still in front of them, head slightly bowed, his arms outstretched in his usual goal celebration mimicking the Christ the redeemer statue in Rio. Darren Harrison the latest number nine, Geordie football hero, maverick, worshipped by the fans, loathed by the club hierarchy and loved by the press, but not always for the right reasons.

And, that was that, full time, all went home happy, and Darren Harrison's value to the club just got that little bit higher.

Oscar, Gemma and Don headed off out of the ground and down through the Dragon Gate into the cool darkness. As they walked towards the taxi rank the music and atmosphere of McCaffrey's bar was too tempting to resist. Don pointed to the door "One won't harm"? Catching Gemma's eye Oscar was rewarded with a grimacing smile of agreed sympathy.

It was the day after Boxing Day the twenty seventh of December and Oscar's first day back at work following the Christmas festivities. He parked his car in his usual spot, Buster jumping out as they headed into the Station.

As usual Oscar headed up the staircase, counting to himself as he went. *Thirteen, unlucky for some.*

He was greeted, with a solemn nod by DCI Ann Gatsby.

"Good morning ma'am, do you know where DI McGovern is"?

"Oh, DS Smiles, I've been trying to ring you."

Oscar nervously tapped both his trouser pockets, he'd left his phone in the car again. "Sorry ma'am must have been driving so obviously couldn't answer it."

"Yes, well that's good to hear, wouldn't want to be breaking the law now, would we."

"No, ma'am we wouldn't."

"Could you pop into Chief Superintendent Crammonds office for a second, please"?

Gatsby led the way. They walked the short trip through the CID offices; Oscar could tell something was up.

The incident room fell silent as everyone appeared to turn and stare. Many of the Officers looked up and were reluctant to speak. Only Felicity Somerton and Stan Scott even attempted to offer him any kind of eye contact.

Once in the Office Chief Superintendent Crammond was already sitting behind his desk a surly faced Gatsby sat down to his right.

"Close the door, lad and come and sit down."

This wasn't going to be good news, he thought.

Taking a deep breath to calm the rapid beating of his heart, Oscar had always found Crammond to have an assured coldness about him and that sometimes bothered him.

The office was big, the biggest in the station. His desk was the largest too. On it was the usual stationary items and a couple of family photographs

Oscar did what had been requested as Crammond removed his spectacles and sat back in his plush leather chair, wiping his hand across his face.

Crammond gave Oscar a serious look as he glanced up a second time Oscar could almost feel his pain, as Crammond clasped his hands together and leant forward. "There was a body found up the top end of the Dene, near to Heaton Park, a young Chinese fellow, dumped in a shallow grave, multiple stab wounds, the suspected murder weapon has also been found nearby, he was discovered by a young girl walking her dog, a Labradoodle or some other ridiculous breed, not the best of things for a young girl to see, a dead body."

Oscar felt quite relieved. "Is McGovern already there? You must think it's connected to the case is it"?

Crammond took a deep breath then exhaled deeply. Ann Gatsby took up the story "No Oscar, McGovern's not there, he's down stairs in the interview room, you see the knife that was found at the scene had his fingerprints all over it, there's DNA evidence and there's witness statements implicating him as a suspect."

CHAPTER TWENTY

"Has he been charged with anything yet"? Oscar rubbed the back of his neck as he waited anxiously for an answer.

Crammond's voice was harsh, Oscar knew this was going to be difficult. "No not yet, although the CPS are chomping at the bit, but as it's one of our own we're going to give it the full term before charging him. You can see him if you want, this is a real mess. The force has spent a generation tolerating and turning a blind eye to officers like McGovern and his methods, he may well have gone too far, he's crossed the line, this time."

Leaving Crammond's office sheepishly Oscar headed down to the bowels of the Police station, down to the interview rooms allocated for suspects next to the holding cells as always counting each step in his head as he went. Luckily *the usual thirteen.*

Oscar walked the short corridor and could hear the all too familiar sound of McGovern coughing his guts up.

McGovern sat, staring at the wall; seeing him sitting there in the empty, soulless room the seriousness was beginning to hit home.

McGovern was smoking a cigarette and had a polystyrene cup of light brown liquid in front of him masquerading as coffee, which no doubt tasted like piss. He scarcely glanced up over his coffee as the door fully opened but managed a slight smile when he saw that Oscar had come to see him. "Thank fuck for that, you got to help me get out of this, they won't let me leave the station, the way things are looking they trying to arrest me for this. I hardly touched that Chinese kid, I bet Gatsby's doing fucking somersaults up there." He took a sip of his piss flavoured coffee swallowing deeply.

Staring straight at McGovern, Oscar urged him with his eyes to answer his question. "So you know him, then, the victim? And how come your prints are all over the knife?, and they say they have DNA too!, if you did it in self defence then why not just come clean sir."

"Look, son, please don't you start imagining motives where there are none, Christ it's bad enough with Gatsby, Crammond and the CPS. If you're asking if I killed the kid then I definitely didn't have the pleasure. The last time I saw that kid was the night we went to see Chang, in the Casino, it all happened later, after you'd left. It was an attempted mugging, this Chinese kid pulled the knife on *me* outside the SnapDragon, I overpowered him took the knife off him, and he ran away, that's it, worst I did was scare him with the knife I'd took off him, that was all there was to it, never seen him since."

Oscar thought he saw a shiftiness in McGovern's eyes that he'd never dared to acknowledge before. but nodded sympathetically.

The air seemed to have been sucked from the room and his tongue was dry. Oscar sensed the emotion in his voice. He knew deep down he was telling the truth. "Well sir, looks like you've been set up, but by who ?, and I've only got a few days to try and prove it wasn't you before the CPS will be pushing for you to be charged. So, after the young guy ran off what happened next."

Oscar held his gaze but McGovern, at first, said nothing, he just pulled deeply on his cigarette and blew out a large cloud of smoke while scoring lines on a polystyrene cup with his thumbnail while using it as a makeshift ashtray.

"Lee came running over and stopped me chasing after him, he made me see sense, I'd had a lot to drink so the whole thing is still a little fuzzy, I remember walking towards a taxi rank and I'm sure I threw the knife away, I think, into the gutter."

Oscar locked eyes with him, he needed to get his colleague out of this as soon as he could, but needed to be sure he was innocent. This case was just getting more complicated by the day. He also knew that maybe Lee could help put McGovern in the clear, but knew an undercover cop was almost impossible to find.

"I'm going to see Crammond, sir, I'm gonna go check out the crime scene, see what evidence they have. It's early days, but I'll get you out of this."

McGovern stabbed his cigarette out on a saucer

"I know you will son."

"Leave it with me sir; I'll do what I can."

Heading back up to Crammond's office, Oscar's footsteps were loud as he thumped heavily up the flight of stairs to the main body of the station, *thirteen*.

Several officers he knew well and had worked with on several cases dropped their eyes when they saw him coming as he passed without pleasantries. He knew and understood how awkward they must be feeling. He knew that they weren't deliberately trying to make him feel bad but he didn't care anyway.

He went into the toilets splashing water on his face as he looked at himself in the mirror. Walking over to the office of George Crammond he knocked on the door.

"Come in."

The door was slightly ajar, he peered in. Crammond was on the phone and broke off from the conversation he was having. Gatsby sat opposite him and she gestured for him to come in.

Oscar walked over to a vacant chair and sat down without being invited to "He didn't do it sir, you believe that don't you, he's being set up." Oscar felt his chest stiffen with anger. But the facts did little to support his gut feeling. He sensed Crammond and more so Gatsby had it in for McGovern.

Crammond looked over the top of his expensive designer glasses. "Whether or not DI McGovern is capable of murder is, alas, not the issue. There is some damning evidence against him. His fingerprints on the knife and a cigarette butt with McGovern's DNA on it."

Ann Gatsby had a question for him "The young Chinese lad has now been identified as nineteen year old David Leung, is that name familiar"?

"Yes, yes, he was one of the two football ground workers I hadn't been able to contact."

Crammond's tone of voice was getting lower, "It gets worse. There's several witnesses who were in and around the SnapDragon Casino say that they saw a man matching McGovern's description fighting with the victim and that the older man left the scene carrying a knife."

"Yes, McGovern told me all about that, but Lee can confirm that McGovern left and headed in the opposite direction, when the young lad ran off, He didn't tell me his name though, it's just that... ".Oscar stopped mid sentence. He'd remembered the day that he and Felicity had gone to interview David Leung days later, and how McGovern had seen his mug shot on the evidence board and quickly left the station to supposedly pick up some lunch, *surely could it have been McGovern after all, no, of course not*, he thought.

Gatsby sensed Oscar was hiding the truth from them. "Something to tell us Detective Sergeant"?

Shaking his head Oscar knew he needed reassurances from McGovern. He needed him to be honest with him.

Crammond wasn't a fool either, he felt something was up but hid it well. "Okay then Smiles, ask DC Lee to come in and confirm this and hopefully he can help us wrap this whole mess all up."

"Slight problem sir..... Lee's working undercover...., haven't got a clue where I can find him, got to be careful we don't blow his cover."

DCI Gatsby appeared sceptical "Well without his evidence, McGovern's Goose looks cooked; the evidence and the facts can't lie. McGovern admits to fighting with the victim, his prints are on the knife, the stab wounds match that knife, the victim was buried less than a mile from McGovern's home, the DNA on the cigarette, and oh yes, witnesses say the older white man appeared to be the worse for drink. Sometimes people don't act rationally or lawfully when there drunk and we all know what McGovern can be like when he's had a drink, loose lip, and fists."

But Oscar was in a determined mood "Can I go check out the crime scene, get a feel for it, have a word with the forensics there, McGovern wouldn't murder anyone, I still think it looks like he's being set up." *Although he now had a few doubts.*

"Well DS Smiles colleague or not you've only got just over forty eight hours after that McGovern may have to be charged."

TWENTY ONE

Oscar got up from his chair, pulled at his tie and headed out of the office, stopping at his desk he called Lee's number twice and hung up when his answer phone clicked in.

Felicity Somerton wanted to talk but Oscar was on a mission, as he walked past her, she gave him a glum smile.

Eventually getting to Daniel Lee's voicemail for a third time, Oscar, against his better judgement, decided to leave a message. "It's Oscar. Could you ring me as soon as you can, McGovern needs you to speak up for him; he's in big trouble, cheers."

Oscar headed back down to the interview room where McGovern, for want of a better word, was being held. Oscar's face was close and flushed with anger. He needed answers from McGovern.Walking past Stan Scott who was sitting on the stairs having a quick cigarette, who seeing Oscar's anger was building quickly followed him towards the room. Oscar ferociously stormed through the door, McGovern jumped as the door flew open.

"David Leung, you recognised him on the evidence board, didn't you, but you didn't say anything, did you sir? I need you to be honest with me, I trusted you, but I've got to know the truth."

McGovern, for once appeared a little sheepish. "Yes son, I did recognise him as the bloke who tried to mug me outside the casino, and now I remember, yes it was him in the restaurant too, but I didn't want anyone to know about it, it was nothing really, but should have been reported, and then Crammond would want to know why I was there?, if I was drunk?, blah, blah, blah."

"You should have told *ME* sir, were supposed to be partners, do you honestly think I would have told Crammond"?

"Of course not son, Lee only found out because he was there, I wasn't planning on telling anyone. It wouldn't look good would it, a drunken Police inspector brawling with a young Chinese youth outside a Casino in the early hours; I've had enough trouble man."

"Yes, well now that young Chinese lad is dead, and unless we can find some alibi or proof to put you in the clear, you're in big trouble."

Oscar still needed answers, "So, where did you go? that day, suddenly like that. You saw the picture of David Leung and you shot out of the office quicker than a rat up a drainpipe."

McGovern sighed deeply. He was paranoid about anything in his story appearing suspect. "I *did* think about going to see him, especially as I now knew where to find him, finish what we started, so to speak, unofficially, if you like but then I came to my senses and decided to get myself something to eat instead, that's the truth son, I didn't do it, I should have reported the initial incident but didn't fancy the paperwork or having to explain myself to Crammond. How was I to know the lad was going to end up murdered."

"OK sir, I'll do what I can, you coming with me Stan"?

Scott nodded towards McGovern and grinned "I can't Ann Gatsby wants' someone here with Jim all the time."

"You mean like a suicide watch"?

"Fuck off. " McGovern yelled, at least he could still had his sense of humour, and that was the reassurance Oscar needed to know he was being totally honest, and despite making some bad decisions still an innocent man.

Shouting for Buster Oscar left the building for the car park and headed over to the car, yanked the door open with Buster jumping across into his customary position in the passenger seat. Trying to keep his focus; Oscar needed to find that vital clue. He kept telling himself that no matter what the outcome of all this was the world would still carry on, the sun would still come up and the case, and others, would still need to be solved and although he was deeply troubled, surely McGovern WAS innocent, but what if he couldn't prove it. He tried to push the unthinkable thought from his head. He was beginning to realise how much the tension of the day had exhausted him.

Once at the top end of the Dene the white forensic van was parked up. Gatsby had sent in all the big guns.

Scene of Crime Officers and the murder team were alongside Forensic officers who were still going over the crime scene bit by bit, inch by inch, taking samples and collecting evidence. The body has been removed. As always Forensic Officer Peter Devon was the first person Oscar Spotted.

Turning to Buster who sat as usual in the passenger seat. He patted him on the head, "You stay here, good boy, don't want to upset nice Mr Devon again do we."

Peter Devon, appearing pleased to see him, he smiled as he approached, the gravel crunching under his feet "Oh, young smiles, I won't ask where McGovern is, I've heard all about it."

Oscar stuffed his hands into his trouser pockets as he began to scan the crime scene. "What have we got so far then Peter?, any positive news for McGovern"?

Peter Devon walked towards his range Rover that was caked in mud, ducking underneath the tape that cordoned off the murder scene he opened the boot and took a file from which he began to read his scribbled notes and tapping his clipboard with his pen "Well, I don't know what you've been told, so i'll start at the beginning. Body of a young Oriental gentleman late teens to early twenties found in a shallow grave." Peter peeped over the top of his specks gestured with his head. "Just over there, cause of death not yet confirmed but multiple stab wounds, large heavy impact bruising to back of legs, possibly by car, some damage to a front bumper would confirm this, should we find the vehicle, there's a couple of nice shovel prints on his head too, poor chap, eyes were like saucers, and so full of pain, time of death, bit hard to say we'll know more in the morning after we've sliced and diced up the old corpse, so to speak. There was a shovel found in the bushes, no prints, a cigarette butt with McGovern's DNA buried in with the body, a knife found with McGovern's prints, some footprints, size ten, adult, and car tyre tracks that we're waiting to hear back about."

Oscar sensed a possible vital loophole. "You say size ten foot prints"?

Peter Devon nodded.

"McGovern has small feet, maybe size seven at largest, and there were no more footprints at all"?

Peter looked at his file unwisely licking his latex gloved finger and thumbed through a couple of pages. "No, one set of footprints, adult size ten, drag marks nearby suggest the owner of the size ten dragged the body to where the shallow grave was found."

"And what about the knife"? Oscar stood with his hands still stuffed in his pockets.

Again Peter Devon checked his notes, "That was found beside the shovel in the long grass to the right there, prints on the knife but not on the shovel."

Oscar was intrigued, "So why would someone wipe the shovel of prints and then leave them on the knife"?

Devon twisted his mouth into an awkward smile and tilted his head, "Perhaps the victim was killed dumped in the boot and the assailant then wore gloves to bury them, murderer's make mistakes, that is how we catch them, look at the cigarette butt, suppose there's an argument it could have been planted but then again errors happen, and especially when you're behaving somewhat irrationally, I thought you would fully understand that."

"Mmm, yes, I know that, but given his physical condition do you honestly believe McGovern is fit enough to dig a hole big enough to bury someone?, and knowing him as you do, do you honestly believe McGovern is capable of this"?

Peter shook his head, "Unfortunately it's not about what I believe, my job is to collect the evidence, if you're asking me if I think McGovern did it, i'm afraid that's your job to prove he didn't. I've worked with him for a long time and personally I don't think McGovern could have done this, but that's not enough for you, I'm sorry."

"Any news on the vehicle?, make?, model?, colour"?

"With regard to the vehicle I will know more when I get back to the lab, is there anything else you need to know, son" ?

Oscar kept his hands into his pockets, trying to keep them warm in the cold. "Probably, yeah, just trying to get my head round it all, but can't really think at the moment. Are you getting plaster casts made of the shoe prints and car tyre tracks"?

"As we speak, someone should be out in the next half hour, or so i've been promised."

"Thanks Peter."

Just as Oscar got back into his car he picked up his ringing mobile phone, it was Ann Gatsby "We've had a report of a carjacking a few nights back the taxi driver has been waiting here quite some time, can you get back here and speak to him, DC Somerton will assist you, it could be connected, taxi driver remembers a Chinese man being bundled into the boot."

"Okay ma'am on my way back now."

Driving as fast and as legally as the twisting road would allow, Oscar was back at the station in no time, Buster flying out of the passenger seat as the two of them headed up the thirteen lucky stairs back to the incident room.

A small plump shaven headed man sat in the reception area with a freshly bruised face and far too many tattoos wearing blue jeans and a dark grey coloured short sleeved T-shirt.

The desk sergeant pointing him out to Oscar

"That's the taxi driver Crammond wants you to interview."

"Okay, thanks."

TWENTY TWO

Shaking hands, Oscar felt sorry for the small man who was looking rather shell shocked and had obvious signs of being in a fight, a fight he had definitely lost. His face was shiny and he stank of body odour.

"Sorry to have kept you waiting for so long, I'm Detective sergeant Oscar Smiles, and you are"?

"Clive Robson."

Quickly joined by Felicity Somerton, they led the taxi driver to an empty interview room. The room had the usual two chrome framed chairs either side of a teak-veneered desk. Oscar dragged out two chairs from under the table, causing their legs to scrape against the floor, as he offered the man a seat.

Felicity Somerton spoke in her usual calm friendly voice, "Can I get you tea, coffee, water, something to drink"?

"No I'm fine, love."

Picking up her pen Felicity began writing down some details, her pen moved in slow careful thrusts as Oscar began the interview.

"Okay Mr Robson, I understand you wish to report a carjacking that took place when, exactly"?

"Two nights ago. Christmas night, I just got out of Hospital this morning, got a couple of cracked ribs and three teeth missing."

Sitting opposite the taxi driver, Oscar leant forward in his chair and picked up a spare pen that was lying on the table in front of him, he studied the yellow bic before putting the cap back on it.

"Right, Clive, if you could just tell me what happened then."

Clasping his hands together, Clive began his story, his dirty bitten fingernails were still covered in a little dry blood, the plastic Hospital identity bracelet still attached to his wrist and his bare arms bared the evidence of the bruised, slightly yellowing needle mark where he'd had a drip attached.

His blood shot eyes widened as he looked from Oscar to Felicity and back, he was hardly able to look at them, as the pain restricted his movement. "Monday night, Christmas night, late on after midnight this Chinese bloke flags me down, I know I'm not supposed to pick up like that but I'd not had too good a night so I thought I'd take the chance. I stopped and wound the window down and he just hits me full in the face, pulls the door open, drags me out and starts kicking and punching me. I thought it was a mugging at first, then I thought he was going to kill me, he seemed to be enjoying it, a fucking nutter he was, but it was the car he was after."

Oscar leant forward concentration on his hawk-like face "What type of car is it"?

"A red Ford Focus, I've.... em... given the registration details to the young girl there," pointing at Felicity, who nodded in silent agreement.

Oscar continued, "Okay then so, this bloke, what did he look like"?

Closing his eyes as if in deep thought Clive Robson pinched the bridge of his nose "He was definitely oriental, about six foot tall, quite athletic, stocky, very handy with his fists, *and* feet for that matter, he thought he'd knocked me out but I saw trying to put someone in the boot before he drove off."

"Did you see who it was, being put in the boot"?

He swallowed and then shook his head "No, but he sounded like they knew each other and he was screaming in Chinese and then went quiet, the other man struggled free and he managed to run off but then the one who attacked me took off after him in my taxi."

Felicity took the pen from her mouth and continued to make a few more notes, as Oscar asked, "What direction did they drive off"?

Clive swallowed hard and took a sharp intake of breath as he held his ribs, "Out towards the outskirts of town, towards the Dene, It looked like he may have knocked him down with the car further up the road, then put him in the boot."

Inching further forward in her chair Felicity had a final question, "Were any names mentioned, anything that could give us a clue as to his identity"?

Clive gave a long sigh and looked at her "Sorry, no, the only thing I heard was them speaking to each other in Chinese."

Sitting back in his chair Oscar tapped the arm of his chair with his fingers. Clive Robson had given them very little with regard to identifying the attacker and the interview, Oscar felt had run its course. "Thanks, you've been very helpful, should you remember anything else , no matter how small or insignificant you think it may be please call me and if we hear anything about your car, or need to speak to you again we'll let you know."

Getting up from the table Oscar walked the taxi driver down the corridor towards the lift, as Felicity stayed in the interview room to finish her notes.

Ann Gatsby was still in her office, taking a call and signalled for Oscar to come in and wait. She hung up the phone, leaning forward she lowered her voice.

"We've had results back from the lab, possible make and model."

"Wild guess, I'd say a Ford Focus car maam"?

"Very good Oscar, so we seem to have identified the car-jacked taxi car then"?

"Looks like it, maam. Any more from the forensic report or autopsy"?

"Well, nothing other than we knew earlier but it's been promised for first thing in the morning, there's nothing like an Officer in trouble to quicken up proceedings."

"I know ma'am. McGovern does still have a lot of respect here, despite his methods, and manners."

"Did you find out anything new from the crime scene then"?

"Still early days, and we're still waiting for the autopsy report, but, some good news, for McGovern anyway. Devon reckons the murderer wore size ten shoes, and McGovern can't be any more than a seven."

Thinking for a second Ann Gatsby rubbed her forehead. "Well, I suppose it's a start, but we'll know more in the morning. I need you in early, first thing, that okay"?

"No problem ma'am."

TWENTY THREE

Oscar hadn't slept too well, knowing McGovern was now, probably in a holding cell, swinging himself out of bed, he forced his sticky eyes open and threw off the humid duvet. He stumbled blinking as he walked to the window. He felt that this was going to be an important morning with regard to the case.

In the bathroom he shaved, cutting himself twice because the light over the mirror stung his red rimmed eyes. Surely now the evidence would be there to put McGovern in the clear. His mobile began to ring, it was DC Daniel Lee.

"What's the stupid bugger done now"?

"Lee, thank the lord, not a lot, just about to be charged as a murder suspect, that's all, he's been in the station overnight."

Lee cleared his throat and spoke with a bubbly tone "So what do you need from me then"?

Oscar's eyes widened "The incident outside the SnapDragon, when McGovern was seen fighting with that young Chinese kid, well, it turns out that was David Leung and he's now turned up dead, in a shallow grave."

Lee's voice soared "Fucking Hell! And McGovern is in the frame then"?

Oscar swallowed rapidly and nodded his head,"Yeah, but if you could ring Ann Gatsby and let her know what you saw, could help a lot."

"Who,"? Lee's voice had an uncertain tone.

"Oh Yes, you haven't met her yet, she's the new DCI. We've also got a couple of extra officers Stan Scott, an old stager and felicity Somerton young and new to the job."

"Okay, I'll do that now."

Before Oscar could ask if he'd found anything out with regard to Mick Western or Walter Chang the line went dead. *Obviously busy*, Oscar thought. *But at least McGovern will be pleased that he can confirm his story and that he's checked in.*

Gatsby had called a briefing, and was looking tired, as they all were. Once back in the incident room Oscar met up with Scott and Felicity and as they compared their recent notes from the interview, Gatsby appearing at the door waved them into her office. "Just to keep you up-dated, we've received some more forensic evidence. Devon reckons the time of death was at least two days ago."

Oscar smiled as his face upturned. "McGovern has an alibi for then."

Gatsby locked her cold eyes on him, "Really,? you sure"?

Taking a deep breath Oscar willed Gatsby not to doubt him "As sure as I'll ever be. He came over to my house on Christmas Eve and stayed the night."

Gatsby lifted a single eyebrow, "And for Christmas day"?

Oscar felt a warmth gradually spreading through his body, "His daughter, Susan, picked him up, took him to Carlisle, she brought him back on boxing night."

Gatsby sat in deep thought for a few seconds and spoke with a soured expression on her face "Well if the timeline was correct it couldn't be him, and the tyre tracks are confirmed as being from a vehicle matched to the one stolen on Christmas night."

Oscar sat up straight and alert, his voice light and bubbly, "The taxi driver, ma'am he was car-jacked by a Chinese man, he saw..., well, *heard* another Chinese man trying to avoid being bundled into the boot."

Oscar nodded vigorously smiling, as Gatsby began to sum up the facts in her monotone voice, "So, inspector McGovern has size seven feet, the attacker was Chinese, and size ten feet, and the Chinese man he eventually put in the boot of the car was very much alive when he was taken away. This happened two or three nights ago and McGovern has an alibi for then, oh, and DC Lee has just confirmed, in the last hour, McGovern's side of the story about some incident outside a Casino, something I had to remind him that should have been reported. We know McGovern's prints were on the knife and we now know why and as for the cigarette butt, well, that's obviously a plant to try and frame him."

Gatsby stood and paced around the room, she had made it well known that she didn't like McGovern or his methods but she let out a huge sigh and flopped back into her chair, "Okay, you can give him the good news; he's free to go, but who would go to all that trouble"?

Felicity raised her perfectly shaped eyebrows and offered Gatsby a questioning gaze,"Mick Western, possibly"?

Stan Scott's smile appeared to tighten,"He still hasn't turned up yet, has he"?

"No,"Gatsby scrubbed her hand over her tension filled face, "It's a bit unusual, no reports of him at all, he could be lying low, after all he's well aware that he's the prime suspect in the Sara Chang murder, but he'll turn up, possibly when we least expect him to.

Felicity Somerton's mobile phone began to ring, number unknown. She excused herself from the room and walked into the corridor answering it.

"Felicity,? This is Daniel, Daniel Lee. Is anyone around?, Are you in the incident room? McGovern?, Oscar?, Stan Scott. I need some help."

Felicity looked around furtively but didn't want to disturb the meeting. "I'm in the station but we're all busy with Gatsby, I can get someone to call you back"?

Lee's voice became shaky as he began to mumble, "No, it's OK, no time, maybe you can help"?

It was the big break Felicity had hoped for, her first case and now a chance to assist an undercover operation, her pulse increased as her voice softened. "What do you need me to do"?

TWENTY FOUR

New Years Eve was here. The Smiles house had what you could call a quiet time. In just three days Gemma and her family would be flying back to Canada. What had happened with McGovern had meant that Oscar hadn't spent as much time with them as he'd wanted to and felt he needed to make the most of the next few days. It would be the usual few drinks in McCaffrey's and home for their own personal family New Year celebrations.

Kim Deehan was getting ready for what she hoped would be a New Years Eve to remember. Preparing for a big night out was supposed to be fun, hair and nails had been primped and polished but Kim was getting a tad frustrated, as things were becoming a little intense. *Remember It's not a date Kimbo, but a girl had to look her best at all times didn't she.*

She hadn't spent as much time in front of a mirror since her early teens worrying about acne. She'd spent an age getting ready, changing her clothes and had bought new shoes. Picking up a hair brush she yanked it briskly through her hair.

Fumbling in her make up bag she found some concealer, meticulously applying it as she sent a text to her best friend "*I don't know what to wear.*"

A message came back through on her iphone and she picked it up from her dressing room table. Plugging it into its speaker she put some music on, the music was so good she began to wonder if she should go out at all or just stay in with her friend when she *eventually* arrived.

He might not even be there after all. Kim looked at the paleness of her freshly shaved legs, *do I need fake tan? And are my calves too offensive to display in public?*

The doorbell rang. The evening air felt cold against her cheeks as she opened it. There stood her best friend Donna, only an hour or so late and dressed all casual, Kim super smart. Another outfit changed beckoned.

Twisting around in front of the mirror, Kim's arms tied in knots trying to reach for her zip.

"Need a hand Kimbo"? Donna said while lifting two large bottles of Blue wicked from her Morrison's bag for life and pouring out two pint sized plastic cups full, handing one to Kim. "I hope this detective of yours is going to be there tonight."

Kim had always tried to keep relationships at arms length, especially since the huge mistake that had been footballer Darren Harrison, she shook her head and wished she'd never mentioned Oscar to her friend. "It's not the bee all and end all of the night, you know."

"Wouldn't know it from where I'm standing, you've done your hair different."

Kim laughed at her own thoughts and smiled at Donna's

"Well he *is* cute."

The taxi flashed its headlights and Felicity, glanced at her watch and headed over, her eyes straining to see beyond the beams.

Lee sat on the back seat, strangely wearing shades, gold chain and a tight plain back vest. He bit his lip as he looked at her, his expression stern."Get in, I'll explain everything."

Felicity climbed in beside him, her heart raced, this was what she'd become a detective for.

Lee took her hand and squeezed it to let her know she shouldn't worry "I'm onto something big, huge in fact, it all makes sense I just need some proof and hopefully you can do that for me."

Felicity couldn't help but notice how good his body was through his tight fitting vest, well defined, firm pecs, biceps and taut stomach. Her eyes glowed wider "Anything to help, what do I need to do"?

Through the thin material of her trousers she could feel the warmth of his leg against hers as Lee sat forward in his chair he whispered quietly so the taxi driver couldn't hear. His eyes twinkled. "There's this meeting, well more like a party at a hotel and I need you to go there and mingle. Be my eyes and ears. There's a bloke meeting us outside, don't be alarmed but I think you may recognise him. You're new so he won't know who you are but he'll trust my judgement.

He'll watch out for you so you'll be fine, I hear he can look after himself."

Felicity chewed on a fingernail, her palms were beginning to sweat. "Is this safe?, are you coming in too"?

Lee shook his head, his handsome features frowned and he said with a straight face "unfortunately no, it's too risky. If i'm recognised that's the case fucked, if you play this right we get them all, the monkey the organ grinder the whole fucking zoo."

Lee saw a weakness in her eyes "Look, are you sure you can do this?, I don't want you going in there and meeting these people if you're scared or not up for it, you should be OK but it could be dangerous and if you blow it, the whole case is fucked, and so am I."

"No, I'm fine, I'll be OK, just a little nervous, I guess."

The heat in the car was such that the windows were misting over. Was it his sweat she could smell or hers?.

The taxi sped through the busy City streets past Eldon Square that had earlier, despite the weather been a mass of hippies and weirdo's, Goths with partly shaved heads tattoos and pierced faces.But not now, it was all quiet, dark and still and the hotel was now in sight. "There he is',' Lee's face split into a grin.

Rubbing a circle on the steam covered window with her fist Felicity felt her heart hurl itself into her mouth as none other than Mick Western stood outside the door of the hotel. He stood leaning against the wall, shifting his considerable frame every now and then from one foot to another.

Lee gently patted her on the thigh and gave her leg an enthusiastic squeeze. He wasn't bad looking when he smiled, a cheeky naughty smile. As he leaned closer along the back seat, she felt the warmth of his arm when he moved against hers, his eyes flickered towards her face "Yes, I told you this was massive, don't worry, just mingle I'll pick you up here in about an hour."

Felicity nodded, checked her watch and took a deep breath "OK, let's do this."

"You sure,"? she watched as he stifled another smile. She nodded unconvincingly.

"Just be careful," hissed Lee as he signalled to the driver and the taxi pulled into the side of the road. The tyres squealed as it pulled up outside the hotel.

A lorry flew past, so fast it made the taxi vibrate as Felicity blinked her eyes and pushed one hand up through the side of her hair. Climbing out of the car she pulled her shoulders back, trying to make her posture more confident as she felt herself stiffen. Could it be the fear or the excitement that was making her shiver and not the cold frosty night?. In her mind things had become a little more sinister and full of dangerous possibilities. *Just have confidence in yourself girl.*

Western was standing in front of a shop window looking at his reflection in the darkened glass. Felicity turned and looked back at Lee, who nodded from the car gesturing her forward with his hand.

Western approached and guiding her with one of his large hands at the small of her back took Felicity inside the hotel. The little smile she flashed at Lee told she felt nervous as they went inside.

Seeing she was biting her lip, Western gently touched her mouth with his thumb. "Don't do that," he said softly "You'll ruin those lovely lips of yours." She met his gaze directly. His eyes were so dark they looked like the ends of expired matches. She could sense the evil behind them and the sound of his voice made Felicity's blood run stone cold, she felt anxious and out of control. Not knowing but only thinking about what might happen gave her a very uneasy feeling. She felt her stomach turn but it was too late to back out now.

TWENTY FIVE

Kim Deehan yelled out in horror as she became aware that the adhesive she was using to attach her false eye lashes had glued her right eye shut.

Donna headed quickly towards the kitchen, her voice bubbly and animated,"Don't worry Kimbo; I'll fetch some water," returning seconds later with a small bowl of warm water and some cotton buds, Donna gently bathed the eye until it opened. Checking her face in her small makeup mirror, Kim's smoky eye look now ruined, as one of her eyes was now bloodshot and watery.

Taking a shiny red lipstick from her small hand bag, Donna held it out to her "Here, try this, see what it looks like on you."

Kim reluctantly took the lipstick and gave her friend a sarcastic stare "You mean it'll match my right eye."

"No, no, it's a new one that cost a bomb, go on try it."Donna enthusiastically nodded her head and made a show of rubbing her lips with her fingers.

Kim put it on and quickly decided that it wasn't going to be a good idea, or was trying to wipe it off with some toilet roll. "Shit, look at the mess it's made, you got any face wipes, I'll have to do the whole lot again."

Donna handed Kim some face wipes from her TARDIS like tiny handbag and Kim began the facial make up process all over again, while noticing that

Donna was sitting back in her chair with one hand over her eyes, frantically typing on her mobile phone.

"What are you doing Donna"? Donna responded without looking up "I'm deleting social media friends and followers I haven't seen or contacted since last year. I do it every new years eve."

Kim nodded her approval "A Facebook cull, eh, I think I'll do the same."

Donna noticed that Kim was singing away but didn't recognise the song "What's this we're listening to"?

Kim rubbed her hand against her heart "It's George Ezra, you must have heard of him, you know Shotgun"?

"Off course, I've heard of that one, just not heard any of these others before."

Kim smiled broadly, "This album's my favourite."

Standing up, Donna began to dance around the floor "I prefer Cascada or a bit of house before I go out."

Kim rolled her eyes, "Each to their own Donna, my dear."

Looking out of the window Donna checked her watch. "You nearly good to go, I'll phone for a taxi."

Kim wrinkled her nose like there was a bad smell in the room, "On New Year's Eve, you'll be lucky, I've already booked one for eight thirty, what times is it now"?

Donna took another sip from her pint of blue wicked, and her eyes dulled as she checked her watch, "It's ten past nine."

Kim took a deep breath and let out a long, deep sigh, "Oh well, we better start walking then, at least that rain stopped."

By the time the Smiles family had arrived at McCaffrey's bar the New Year party was already in full swing. The bar, as always, was crowded. New Years eve at McCaffreys, Christmas decorations, and scented candles that smelt so good cinnamon, heather and hollyhocks.

There was a particularly noisy table, with a few middle aged men cheering as a young woman was taking part in and apparently losing a drinking contest. Recognising the girl, Oscar was shocked to discover it was Felicity Somerton. There were no other girls or women visible at the table, just her and three older men.

Gemma and Don were lucky enough to be in the right place as a man and woman vacated a nearby table, so the three of them sat down. Getting up and walking over to the busy bar, Don had offered to get the first round in. Gemma watched her brother's interest in the noisy table. Her expression hard. "Why don't you go over and join them, don't let us stop you."

Oscar shifted uneasily in his chair, "No Gem, it's not like that, the girl, she's a colleague, a detective constable, I didn't think she drank *that* much and I don't recognise any of the men at her table either."

Gemma glanced around looking for Don, "Do you think you better go over and check she's alright"?

Oscar's eyes remained fixed on Felicity, "Not for the moment, I'll just keep an eye on things. I wonder where all her friends have gone"? Gemma looked around in the hope of seeing a group of girls coming back from the bar, "Maybe to the loo or getting drinks."

But Oscar's gaze was locked on the men,"That's why I better wait."

Don returned with the drinks, three pints of Guinness. "There you go," handing Oscar his drink, but Oscar wasn't taking any notice. His detective intuition was telling him that things weren't right at the other table. His inner instinct was tingling again.

Several minutes passed and it became apparent that Felicity was on her own with what were now, five men. Getting up from his seat Oscar headed over. Felicity's eyes were glazed, she looked like some intoxicated Zombie reincarnation of herself but she still recognised him, "Oscar."

Felicity staggered up and put her arms around his neck as Oscar tried to stop her from falling, he also failed to dodge the persistent attempt at a drunken kiss that Felicity launched at him before falling back into her seat. Oscar had seen enough.

"I'm going to take you home; looks like you've had more than enough Fliss."

One of the men, a large man with a Eastern European accent had other ideas "Leave her be, who are you anyway? her fucking father, the lady is having a good time, and were paying for her drinks, so why don't you fuck off back over there and leave us alone."

Feeling the hostility, Oscar knew that these men were not friends or indeed people that Felicity knew. She would be in danger if he left her.

Another man even larger and also Eastern European stood up and pulled Felicity to him, who by this time had attempted to stand back up, stumbled and fell onto the floor of the bar, two of the other men in the group got to their feet, the atmosphere had changed. Thinking quickly. Oscar pulled his Police ID badge from his pocket and held it up.

He stared into the eyes of the larger man and could see pure hatred. "Now then gentlemen, Let's not make this any more difficult than it has to be eh, I'm going to escort this nice young lady back home where she belongs and in case you were wondering she too is a Police officer. Now has anybody got any problem with that"? There was silence, as luckily one by one the men left the bar. The predators would have to look elsewhere this evening for another unfortunate victim.

Don came running over and helped pick Felicity off the floor. She looked OK, but had been drinking far too much that evening, even just standing up was a major issue for her. Gemma and Oscar helped her towards the ladies loo. Oscar standing outside while Gemma accompanied her in.

As Oscar watched to see if the group of men returned he heard the sound of Felicity retching her guts up coming from behind the toilet door. She had collapsed again. Gemma having to give them a shout to assist getting Felicity onto her feet.

Gemma gave Oscar a pained gaze "It's just gone eleven Oscar; we'll finish our drinks and head back home, where are you going to take her"?

Oscar's expression was pensive, "We've got plenty of space, I'll just take her back there, make sure she's OK, and maybe phone her mum in the morning, you two stay and see the new year in."

Gemma lightly stroked her brother's forearm "You sure,? OK, see you later on."

Oscar helped Felicity out of the pub, she again tried to kiss him as they waited in the queue for a taxi, the next car was theirs.

Kim and Donna had called in at a few pubs on their way into town. The buses had stopped, as had the metro service, and all the taxis were already waiting in the busy City Centre for the New Year revellers. They'd had to walk and already Donna was carrying her shoes, and complaining like a seven year old child, "We nearly there yet?, Why did I wear these bloody things", she hissed "I could barely walk in them."

Kim responded with an ugly twist of her mouth, "Yes, we are for Goodness sake, McCaffrey's is just round this next corner."

The two girls walked around the corner just in time for Kim to see Oscar helping this young attractive blonde girl into a taxi before getting in beside her. The girl placed her head on Oscar's shoulder as the taxi pulled away.

As Kim's shoulders drooped and the colour drained from her face, Donna could tell that the man in the taxi was the person all the effort and trouble had been for. "Never mind girl, plenty more fish in the New Years Eve Sea. She's a lot younger than you mind, and blonde"!

Kim leaned against a bonnet of a parked car she closed her eyes, blinking back tears and gritted her teeth she growled almost screaming "And what fucking difference does that make, blonde"?

Donna could sense more than a little steel in her voice, her obvious anger and disappointment. Donna gave her a big hug and sighed heavily. "His loss babes. I don't know, come here," and grabbing Kim's arm she linked her despondent friend, as the two women turned round and headed away from McCaffrey's to find a better pub, maybe even a nightclub. They would still try to salvage what was left of New Years Eve.

She must have been fifteen years younger and ten times prettier than her, what hope is there for the rest of us, and I thought he was so different. Damn that Oscar Smiles.

TWENTY SIX

It had been a long week, Christmas and New Year had come and gone and Ann Gatsby was feeling ragged when she got to work. The team could see the pressure was coming down on her for some time now without any major breakthrough. Oscar had taken Gemma and her family to the airport and waved them off back to Canada.

Getting to the Office for eight O'clock he'd been busily working at his computer for some time, to the background soundtrack of McGovern's heavy breathing and cursing.

The desks were littered with rows of empty coffee cups and everyone had been instructed to gather in the incident room for a briefing.

By the time she'd finished summing up the work or lack of it in the last few days Ann Gatsby was in a foul mood. How long before Crammond paid another visit, monitoring the progress on their case or lack of it.

Felicity Somerton was sitting in her corner desk, her eyes like piss holes in the snow, red from crying. She screwed up her face, then rubbed her nose with the cuff of her jumper. Oscar gave her a tentative smile, her eyes were sunken and her skin looked like tissue paper. "You need to go home, take the rest of the day off and stop beating yourself up about the other night."

She could barely remember how she even got back home. It had all been a blur. She covered her face with her hands and started to sob, she spoke quietly and hesitantly "I can't remember much about the other night. I'm sure I must have been drugged. I've let everyone down, especially Lee, God only knows where he is, or what's happened to him, I feel he is in grave danger now and all because of me."

Trying to console his young college, Oscar reached over and took her hand, resting his fingers over hers on the desk "Look, go home take the rest of the day off. If he turns up I promise I'll let you know. Lee knows the score he's probably in hiding. I'm sure he'll be OK, can you still not remember anything about that night"?

Felicity looked at Oscar with sad eyes, the tears welling inside her as she shook her head and covered her face with her hands. The only thing she did remember about that night was her predatory lunge at Oscar at the taxi rank. What a tit she'd made of herself. "I can't go home, we've too much to do."

Leaning forward and keeping his voice low, Oscar forced her to shut up and listen to him. He suggested again that she went home and this time she didn't argue ."Do you want me to ring your mum"?

She knew it would do her good to return home and go straight to bed. Her legs were leaden and she was feeling depressed and tired out, but tell her mum,? "Christ no, the less she knows about the sordid thing the better, I'll get a cab, go home, get some rest and be back tomorrow." Picking up her coat and bag Felicity headed out the door.

McGovern was less sympathetic, "What's the matter with her then"?

"She's OK, just under a lot of stress at the moment."

McGovern puffed out his cheeks "Ah well, were all under stress son, it's just how you deal with it, and she's got to learn about the importance of asking for back up, nobody's a one man band: could have been a fucking disaster that, and might still be. We work as a team here. She has to think about being a team player."

Oscar looked up, raising his eyebrows, "Like you always do eh"?

"Me!, good God, what do you take me for"? McGovern laughed, and shook his head.

As the day wore on Oscar pulled a hand through his hair while continuing to check the screen on his computer, he appeared unable to keep still as his senses heightened. "Just found something interesting on the internet, sir?", turning his monitor towards McGovern.

McGovern was his usual sarcastic self, as he yawned and scratched his balls "If it's that bird from Thailand shooting ping pong balls out of her fanny, I've already seen it"!

Oscar wrinkled his nose in disgust "No, sir. Twelve years ago there were several similar crimes across Europe, in seven European countries. At first it was thought there was a serial killer operating across Europe until there were three murders on the same day in different countries, there were also some football match fixing issues then as well, particularly in Italy, which again were linked to a Hong Kong based crime syndicate. The murders however were never linked and most of them remain unsolved. Twelve years and then it starts all over again, do you not think that's a bit odd sir"?

McGovern got up from his chair, stood up straight, stretched his arms up into the air and farted loudly. "There could be a link son, I'll mention it to Gatsby, keep looking I think I need to go and drop the bairns off at the pool."

"You gotta do what sir"?

McGovern, holding his backside left the office, walking slowly towards the men's toilet "And it needs to be soon as I think Robbie wants to leave Take That again, and quickly," Oscar closed his eyes to try and push the image and thought as far from his head as possible, as McGovern shouted from the bottom of the corridor "Keep checking, let me know when you have something concrete," farting again, "Oops, I'm sure I might."

Continuing to look back at previous similar murders across Europe Oscar found more cases from twelve years ago, connected to the Chinese community. Oscar was sure, there had to be a link. *"So what's so significant about twelve years ago and now, why twelve? A strange number, it's got to mean something."*

A young uniformed PC rapped on the door and popped his head round into the office. "Is McGovern in"? Oscar tried to be diplomatic, "He's in the... erm little boy's room."

"Well his Chinese take away was delivered down stairs, Beef Chow mein; I've brought it up for him, where shall I put it"? The young constable scoured the room, looking for an empty space.

"Just leave it on his desk," Oscar's attention drawn to a brightly coloured item in the bag that was definitely not part of McGovern's meal, "What's that"?

The young PC put McGovern's takeaway down on the desk as requested and handed Oscar the brightly coloured item. It was a calendar, a Chinese calendar. It had written on it to 'prepare for the year of the Dragon.' Looking at the twelve signs of the Chinese zodiac Oscar thought to himself *so if we are preparing for the year of the Dragon, twelve years ago we were also doing the same then.*

Getting up from his seat Oscar walked over to the increasingly cluttered Murder evidence board and picking up a red marker pen he wrote on the only space he could find *'the year of the Dragon.'* Walking back to his desk, he sat down, placed the pen on the table, leant forward on his elbows and held his head in his hands. He was beginning to get the mother of all headaches.

McGovern returned to the office, stifled a yawn, and spoke with a frown. "Fucking upstairs neighbour's had a burst pipe, flooded my flat, I'm gonna have to go and sort it out."

Oscar shouted after his colleague "Your take away tea has arrived, sir,"! and held out the brown paper bag for McGovern to grab, as he quickly came back in and then back out of the office frantically stabbing numbers into his mobile phone and shouting from the corridor "Thanks' son, keep me posted on any developments, and if there are any updates, make sure you tell me before her, there's a good lad."

Oscar didn't have the time or indeed the energy to chase after McGovern with his Year of the Dragon theory, or indeed seek out Gatsby or Crammond. His headache was getting worse, all this thinking, concentrating and supposing. He was feeling like he'd been hit over the head with a mallet. It was after six and he had been in the office and staring at a computer screen off and on for almost ten hours, without a break, anything to eat or even a cup of tea, so involved and determined he was to crack this case.

Getting up from his desk he walked over to the murder evidence board again staring at the photos of the three victims. He began to think *Alex Brennan, Sara Chang, David Leung, what's the connection? where's Mick Western fit into all of this? and why was the year of the dragon so significant.* In his thoughts there were far too many questions than answers. They seemed no nearer to catching whichever sadistic bastard was responsible.

Walking over to McGovern's desk, and checking his phone messages, there were none from Lee. *Was he onto something,* he thought, *then again, maybe not, and was he OK?.*

Deciding to call it a day. Oscar stood up and stretched his arms above his head. His headache wasn't getting any better and he felt as though he wasn't really getting anywhere. His head ached from monitoring call after call. He needed a break, some clue, a tiny morsel of evidence that could be the answer.

He had to drive past McGovern's place on the way home. McGovern's flat had always been surprisingly tidy on the few occasions that Oscar had called in which probably had little to do with McGovern and more to do with the woman from up the road whom he'd employed to come in one afternoon a week and keep the place clean, hoover and dust.

Driving down the street Oscar could see two burly workmen types removing a sofa from McGovern's flat. There was a mound of items piling up in the garden, some of which were personal items that had been ruined by the flooding.

McGovern was standing in the garden, cigarette in one hand and scratching his bollocks with the other. Catching sight of Oscar as he drove past, McGovern waved, a wave that Oscar felt obliged him to stop. Yes he was maddening, sarcastic, confrontational, and could be a pain in the arse but Oscar, sometimes, couldn't help but feel sorry for him.

Parking his car on the opposite side of the road Oscar got out and turned his head up to the sky, feeling the misty rain on his face as he walked the short distance along the tree lined street.

As he got closer to McGovern's flat he could hear the dulcet Glaswegian tones of abuse being aimed at the unfortunate workmen as they carried a China cabinet out of the front door. "Hey, be careful with that, it's a family heirloom, belonged to my dear old Granny, poor old cunt, never the same again after she fell down the stairs."

Oscar raised his eyebrows, smiled, and gave McGovern a questioning gaze. "Anything I can do sir"?

"No, son, it's all under control, the flat needs a total re-decoration. Most of my electrical stuff will have to be binned, telly, microwave, toaster the lot."

Oscar thought, *Telly, microwave, toaster, that's McGovern's life really, take away those three items alone and he's fucked.*

McGovern was re-telling the story to another workmen, as he squeezed past some furniture that had been dragged into the passageway "Aye, old Connie upstairs had a burst pipe; she'd been staying at her son's over the Christmas, came back this morning and found the place soaked."

Oscar squeezed McGoverns shoulder, causing him to stop talking and turn towards him. "Are you sure there's nothing I could help you with sir"?

McGovern flicked the end of his cigarette butt into an overgrown unkempt flower bed and placed both hands firmly in his pockets. "No, thanks all the same son, just waiting for a removal firm to take away all the furniture and stuff that's not fucked to a storage unit on the Trading Estate, then it's just a case of letting the place dry out, bit of paint, some new carpets and that should be about that, looking at how things have panned out, it could have been a fucking lot worse."

"We'll sir, It's good to see you taking the old positive attitude, and you know where to find me should you need anything."

McGovern clasped his hands to his chest "You really mean that son, Anything"?

Oscar nodded, holding up three fingers "Scouts honour."

McGovern winked and smiled, "Thanks son, I appreciate that."

Turning and heading back towards his car Oscar began to feel a bit guilty leaving McGovern and all his worldly goods piled up in the garden, but he had offered him his help and assistance and McGovern had said things were in hand.

Driving the short journey back to his Jesmond home Oscar parked outside his front door, rubbing his hand back over his forehead and then bringing his head forward all the way until it was resting on the steering wheel. He sat for a few moments, contemplating the day's events, the case so far, this headache wasn't getting any better either, maybe a nice strong cup of sugary tea, a couple of paracetamol, and an early night would do the trick.

Entering his house through the large heavy wooden door he removed his shoes and headed down the passageway towards the kitchen. Buster was there to meet him, wagging his tail as usual, pleased to see his master home.

Filling the kettle he switched it on. Turning on his CD player, the Eva Cassidy CD, which was his mother's favourite, was still inside. Gemma had been listening to it a few nights back. His mum's favourite song, Fields of gold, was on repeat. It always reminded both him and Gemma of their mum, she loved that song. The kettle had boiled and Oscar filled his favourite mug with the steaming water, placed a tea bag in the mug and added a little milk, and four sugars. Opening a kitchen draw he took out some paracetamol tablets and popped them into his mouth with a quick swig of hot tea.

Walking through to the lounge he settled into the large comfortable sofa, lifting his feet and trying not to spill his cup of tea as he melted into the furniture, Buster jumping up beside him and curling up into a ball, twisting his head first to lick his hand.

Oscar took another large sip of his sugary tea as he tried to relax. He listened to the music. He was glad that track was playing. He hated the quiet emptiness of the house, and missed his family and in particular his mother, why them, why did they have to die, why. He always felt over emotional when he'd spent time with Gemma and the Christmas and new year were now over, with tears in his eyes he closed them and lay down on the sofa, trying not to disturb Buster.

That song made him remember how it used to be, how happy he was and if he closed his eyes, for a second or two he could hear his mum singing along in the kitchen. He wished he could lie down and never get up, the case as far from his thoughts as the moon. Things were itching at the edges of his mind, demanding attention, memories he was unwilling to scratch. Tension and lack of sleep had finally caught up with him.

'You can tell the sun in his jealous sky when we walked in fields of gold.'

The sofa had never felt so comfortable . He felt himself relax: he was close to smiling. Within a few moments he was on the verge of sleeping, the end of a busy, stressful, and not very constructive day. He lay there listening to the song accompanied by the sound of rain on the window pane.

*****

A few miles away he sat in his living room, high on cocaine and pleased with his last few weeks' work.

Lighting a cigarette he tossed the spent match into an ashtray. He'd enjoyed himself. He sat and watched the crudely made sex tapes of him and the blonde. He watched himself holding her head down and smiling as the mop of blonde hair rhythmically moved up and down, remembering the irresistible feeling he had to climax into her smooth hot wet mouth that took him to the edge of ecstasy. Shame it would never happen again with her. She could have made him a fortune. But he hadn't needed to see her eyes to know she had been lying to him. But no time for that. He had somebody to get rid of, someone had to burn in Hell.

****

Oscar woke suddenly, the combination of Buster's barking and the hammering on his front door was enough to have woken the dead. He gazed at the old Grandfather Clock; it was only twenty past nine.

TWENTY SEVEN

As Oscar stormed along his passageway towards the incessant banging on his front door he noticed his mobile phone was vibrating in his pocket and the person he could see through the frosted glass looked familiar. It was the portly figure of McGovern, soaked by the rain and patting his pockets for his lighter.

"Do you never answer that fucking phone of yours? It's a waste of time you having one"!

"Sorry sir, what do you want."

McGovern pointed at the suitcase he was carrying. "You did say if I needed anything, I knew where I could find you, it'll only be for a few days, and I've tried everybody else." McGovern pushed past Oscar and headed down the passageway and into the living room.

"I suppose you better come in then, make yourself at home, why don't you."Oscar shouted down the passageway "And take those shoes off."

McGovern was lying full stretch on the sofa when Oscar got back to the lounge. He'd taken his shoes off and one of his big toes were sticking through a rather dirty looking very off white coloured sock, and what was that smell ? "Sorry son, it must have been that beef chow mein, always gives me wind".

It was going to be a long night.

******

The smell of petrol was nauseating, his eyes stinging from the fumes. It woke him, but he couldn't move, feeling like he was waking from a prolonged sleep, his eyes moved quickly, then widened in the expanding darkness. He understood why he was doing this to him. But what exactly had he found out, who had double crossed him? He was supposed to have worked out a deal, Who was he? He was initially just a guy he'd been introduced to, met in a pub, a businessman. What had he drugged him with? questions he would never find answers to as he tried one last time to lift his arms but gave in, head down and accepted his comeuppance with a nod.

Inside the car it was getting hotter, the air getting less and less, the windows beginning to take on a coating of mist. The fire surrounded him so fast he didn't know what was happening until it was too late.

The dark figure left the scene calmly. Even from outside the car the smell of burning flesh was overpowering, the flames leaping up and through the windows. He laughed low in his throat "*I really enjoyed that. The stupid fucker deserved it.*"

****

Oscar wasn't sure of the exact reason behind it but he'd slept through his alarm and was annoyed at himself for running late. He'd woke with such a start that the drop out of sleep had felt like a fall into an abandoned pit shaft.

His hair spiked on his head and his eyes still full of sleep. His neck stiff from sleeping hunched up.

It was gone nine thirty and McGovern had already left. The house looked like a bomb site and he'd only been staying there one night. He went into the living room, sat on his sofa and stared at the mess, the house no longer felt much like his. Crumbs on benches and dishes unwashed in the kitchen sink, in the lounge cushions on the floor and the TV remote control in the wrong place.

Seeing McGovern's mess and clothes strewn all over his house made him even more amazed at the cheek of the man. Oscar hated mess, especially someone else's mess. His bathroom looked like someone had been bathing a horse in it, water on the floor and even, suspect small curly hairs in the sink, and not his either. The real shocker though was the once perfectly clean beige towel with the very suspicious looking brown stain on it. *"The dirty bastard's been wiping his arse on my towel, I'm gonna kill him."*

The spare room where McGovern had been sleeping was horrifying. The stench of damp, dirty socks and takeaways intermixed with the foulness of primeval farts and stale beer, and he hadn't even noticed the cigarette burns on the carpet.

Oscar was less shocked at the thought of McGovern actually having had a shower, and although wanting to have it out with McGovern over his filthy living habits, he couldn't leave the house without cleaning it throughout first.

Entering his kitchen picked up a pair of yellow marigold gloves from the cupboard under the sink, and got to work paying special attention to his beloved bathroom. It took him a while but he couldn't leave the house untidy.

Still angry when he climbed into his car, but before he headed for the showdown with McGovern at the station he jumped back out and went back into the house. He'd forgotten, in his rage and needed to do his usual checks. *Oven off, TV, off, windows closed and lights off. Always good to check.*

McGovern had only been there for one night but he *had* to go. The annoying way he used his fingernails to tweak one or two nasal hairs away that were always poking out of his nose and the way he would just drop them on the floor. How he'd had to witness McGovern picking the last of the chicken from his sweet and sour takeaway out of the foil container with his fingers then watch as he poured the remainder of the sauce into his mouth, and belched loudly. The man was a fucking animal, and not just that. Surely on his salary McGovern could afford at least one decent suit that would fit him. The very thought of that man in his house for a second longer sent a shiver down his spine.

****

Deciding to walk the short distance from his rented City centre flat to the station. Stan Scott's face pressed on into the wind bleaching his skin as he swallowed down the fresh air. His five o Clock shadow dark, his tie loose and his cigarette stuck firmly in the side of his mouth which he did well to keep from blowing away.

The City was slowly beginning to wake up to the sights and sounds as people made their way to work. The hum of a milk float and the grumble of the first bus.

A loud rattle of shop front shutters being pulled up startled him, as a council workman was idling along clearing up discarded paper, bottles and cans with a long litter picking implement and due to the stiff breeze,he struggled to control a large black plastic bin liner that he was attempting to put the rubbish inside. They nodded as they passed each other, as a solitary pigeon pecked at the ground, hoping to pick up any crumbs that had dropped from the take away cartons the council workman had overlooked.

He watched a taxi, with only one working headlight pass him along a deserted bus lane. Just as he got to the bottom of the street it indicated left and turned. When the taxi stopped outside a cafe, he was pleasantly surprised when a familiar face got out, someone he'd like to have a chat with, a person who might just know where Mick Western was. His former informant, Sammy Greenwood.

He stubbed out his cigarette and immediately took another from the packet, deciding to slide it back instead of lighting it as he followed Sammy Greenwood into the cafe.

TWENTY EIGHT

The cafe was a bit more down market than the more famous coffee houses in the City, a bit shabby, with its zinc topped counter and bare floorboards but the coffee was cheaper, fresh and strong. Although it was early there were still a stream of people collecting a takeaway latte on their way to work.

Inside a young mum with a tired face was dipping her baby's dummy into a cup of sweet tea, two old men read the racing post, one of which was gumming his way through a slice of toast. There were a couple of night shift workers having bacon sandwiches and cups of tea before they headed off home, and a thin faced student type with a chunk of tough curly hair, making his coffee last.

Sammy Greenwood sat at the back of the cafe. His table against the back wall, in a maze of plastic cubicles. He sat, shoulders hunched up as he held his mug of coffee in fingerless black gloves. His scraggly hair could just be seen underneath a large blue bobble hat, thick stubble on his chin, wearing a brown body warmer off white sandshoes and dirty blue jeans, which had all seen better days.

Scott shoehorned himself along into the tight plastic seated booth opposite him. "Long time no see Sammy, good to see you. You still look like shit by the way."

Sammy rolled his eyes and lifted his head back. His first intention was to leave but he had just paid for his coffee and had nothing to hide. Turning his head away trying to hide the evidence on his face that he'd had some kind of altercation, but Scott had already spotted it.

"Been in a bit of bother have we"?

Sammy looked straight ahead and didn't attempt to make any eye contact "You should see the other fella."

"Mick Western, by any chance"?

Sammy's eyes scanned the room; he didn't want to be seen sharing a drink with a copper. "What's it to you anyway"?

"So, when did he do that to you then"?

Shrugging his shoulders, Sammy drew on his cigarette deeply and stared at his hands."Didn't say he had, I didn't mention any names."

"What about Johnny Murray then? Was it him"?

Raising his voice Sammy forced a laugh "Johnny Murray! You're having a fucking laugh Stanley, come on, stop being a wanker for five minutes and give yourself a day off will you."

"So it *was* Western then"?

Looking him straight in the eyes Sammy's fingers fumbled in his pockets for another cigarette. "Like I said, I didn't mention any names."

"When did you last see Mick Western then, Sammy"?

Sammy sipped his coffee, wincing at the strength and for a moment closed his eyes, "Not seen *him* for a couple of weeks, bit before Christmas in fact."

"Any idea how we can find him"?

Giving a hint of a smile Sammy looked down at his coffee "Have you tried looking in the yellow pages under L for lunatics"?

Scott turned away relaxing in his chair "And Johnny Murray"?

"The day after I saw Western."

Stan Scott looked out of the window, those pigeons were still going about their business "So what did you and Western talk about then"?

"He told me that he was taking over the debt that Johnny Murray owed me. I thought he was going to pay the debt off but instead he gave me these (pointing to one of many painful looking bruises). He then told me that Murray was going to be collecting for him from now on and to leave him alone."

"Did he say why"? Stan Scott probed deeper.

"He just told me he was onto something big, a new business opportunity, something along those lines; he didn't say what it was, though."

Scott shrugged his shoulders, "I wouldn't expect you to tell me if he had Sammy."

Sammy leaned in closer, smiling a playful grin "What do you want Western for then? Has he been a naughty boy"?

Scott didn't say anything he just sat back in his chair. A waitress came over to him and he ordered a coffee, with milk, sugar and biscuits. Returning in minutes with a tray on which the said articles lay.

Scott carefully tore off the tops of the milk cartons and poured them into his cup. Ripping open the three sugar bags he tipped the contents into his cup and stirred vigorously with the plastic spoon. Leaning forward he pointed a finger at the younger man's face. "Let's just say we'd like to speak to him."

"Help you with your enquiries ehh,"? smirked Sammy.

"Something like that."

Picking up a discarded empty sugar sachet Sammy rolled it into a ball between his fingers as his eyes narrowed "You lot don't have a clue do you"?

"What do you mean"? Scott's watchfulness heightened.

"You know, you lot, the Police, the law, you think you're in charge don't you, but you're not."

"So who is in charge then? Western"?

Looking at the dregs of his coffee, Sammy drank it, laughed and placed his empty cup down in the middle of the table. "No, not him. Things are changing Stanley, and not necessarily for the worse."

Stan Scott gazed at him with focus dipping a biscuit into his coffee "What do you mean, not for the worse"?

Sammy laughed his thoughts from his mind. That breezy confidence had been replaced by a guarded sullenness. He shook his head and smiled as he gazed out of the window. "You really don't have a clue do you? They have ways and methods of pressuring people most of your lot would only dream about."

Stan Scott scribbled his phone number onto an empty sugar packet. He squeezed himself out of the booth and stood up. He bent forward placing a supportive hand on Sammy's shoulder. Sammy's smile had troubled him, made him think he was trying to tell him a secret he was too stupid to understand. "Enlighten me then, who?...., look if anything happens you think I should know about, give me a call, will you?, you may need a favour from me one day."

Sammy gave him a resigned glance that made him smile uncertainly, leaning forward in his chair he put his hand on his stubbly chin. He picked up the piece of paper that Scott had given him, studied it, rolled it up in a ball and flicked it away

"Those days are gone Stanley. All I want in life now is to make a living, pay my way and have enough left over for two weeks in the sun, if I'm lucky a couple of times a year."

Scott sat back down and nodded his head "Isn't that what we all want"?

"No Stanley, not everyone."

"Who then?, tell me, he pressed."

"Them."

Darkness filled Scott's eyes as he felt as if his mind had gone out. "Who's them"?

Sammy spoke quietly. "Them Triads."

It didn't take long before Oscar was at the station and heading up the stairs with Buster not far behind, as usual counting as he went. He had been hoping to drop him off at his Grandad's house but for once he wasn't at home.

McGovern was sitting at his desk reading the local paper.

Oscar approached him with a pensive expression, "I need a word sir."

"I'm all ears son, fire away, you looked shagged out by the way."

"You living at my place. It's not going to work, you're gonna have to find somewhere else sir."

McGovern sighed, looking past him towards the window "OK son, I did say it was only for a short while, I'll be gone by the end of the week, I promise."

Oscar shook his head "Ah, ah, no, I'm sorry sir, it's got to be today, you see it's your habits and hygiene, they're driving me insane."

McGovern's mouth fell open "Habit's and hygiene! What do you mean, I have my standards. I clean up after myself. I had a shower this morning and I even cleaned the bog with the brush afterwards, and it fucking stank so much that I even opened the window."

Oscar crossed his arms across his chest "Standards wow, great, let's hope you don't Judge everyone else by your own standards eh. Least you would if you had any."

The stress of the last few days was beginning to tell, Oscar did not hold back as he continued "Yeah, and left the toilet brush full of you know what, putting back in its holder and about the shower, there was water all over the floor, dubious looking hairs somehow in the sink and you wiped your backside on my towel."

"No son, I dried it on your towel."

"No you didn't you wiped your arse on it."

"I dried my arse."

"GENTLEMEN"! A sour faced Ann Gatsby entered the room holding her hands over her ears, "Please, I can't stand it. You two are like a bickering old married couple. What you two get up to in your personal life is up to you but while you're here I expect you to act like professionals."

Oscar rubbed his nose, "Sorry ma'am we will sort this in our own time." McGovern just grunted some inaudible response.

As the days wore on Oscar grew more impatient with McGovern. It was never going to work. The two of them sharing a house. The arguments became as regular as McGovern's bowel movements, and it was going to be better for both of them if McGovern could find somewhere else. It had only been a few days but that was more than enough for Oscar.

A solution wasn't too far away though. McGovern needed to be close to his own property and had been informed that his place would be ready for him to move into by the end of the week. There was a place and it seemed perfect. Grandad Alfie's.

He had a spare room, would enjoy the company and wasn't as house proud as his grandson, plus he had a cleaner come in twice a week.

Oscar got quite a shock when, during his morning walk with Buster, he called in on his grandfather and found McGovern sitting with his feet up watching the TV, his grandfather in the kitchen making his guest some toast. Oscar's eyebrows squished together. "So when was this all sorted out then"?

McGovern explained "We'll you didn't fucking want me did you, and it was his idea, before you start, I did explain to him that you wouldn't like it but at least you've got rid of me now."

Grandad Alfie came into the room, sat on his favourite chair and patted on the arm of the sofa for Oscar to sit down. "I went to the club and I saw Jim sitting there. We chatted and he told me that he was moving out of your place and needed somewhere till Friday. I offered straight away and he initially said no thinking you would think he was taking advantage, but I insisted."

"Well as long as he doesn't expect the five star treatment."

McGovern remained quiet, for a change, but Oscar could see that the two of them appeared to get on well, after all his Grandad had much more in common with McGovern and enjoyed the company.

As Grandad Alfie sat on the edge of his chair, his eyes glowed . "And Jim is bringing us both some Cod and chips for our tea, isn't that right son," McGovern nodded.

"Well, as long as you're happy with the arrangement, I suppose it's okay with me."
"What time are you heading to the station sir"?

McGovern checked his watch, "Probably set off about nine, gonna be a long day."

"Yes sir, it is, I'm heading there now, I'll see you there shortly then"?

Oscar got into his car and drove the short distance back towards the station. Newcastle had changed so much in a short space of time. Large industrial estates and business parks were a common site built on land where the old ship yards and factory sites once stood proud. One thing that had also changed was the volume of traffic, bus lanes had made it even more difficult to get in and out of the town centre quickly.

Oscar sat in yet another traffic jam, *how much time must he have spent sitting motionless in his car over the years*; it would have been quite frightening if he actually tried to work this out. He flicked a switch on his car door and opened the window; he could hear the familiar sounds of the city, the blaring horns, the car engines and the occasional siren from an emergency vehicle. The short journey took him no less than an infuriating and stressful forty five minutes.

All the familiar faces were still there in the Police Station. The place hadn't changed in years. The dry heat of his car had made him thirsty, his throat the need for moisture.

He decided against his usual cup of sugary tea and opted for a drink from the water cooler. He lifted several clear plastic cups from the cup dispenser and took one from the bottom, carefully placing the cups back in the rack. He always did this ever since he saw someone take a drink out of a cup and place it back at the top of the line of cups in the dispenser, Not McGovern either, for once, *dirty unhygienic bastard*.

As he walked towards his office desk Ann Gatsby nodded a good morning as he passed him in the corridor. Placing his water carefully on what for him was quite a messy workplace, he spent a while writing up reports and then went through the case files once again.

Crammond entered the incident room, in full uniform, including cap, twitching his arms to adjust his cuffs."We've a press briefing in an hour, is McGovern not here yet"?

"No, sir," Oscar felt that's all his superintendent needed to know for the moment.

"Shame, I was hoping to have a chat with you all before I speak to the press, any updates or leads we're following, that sort of thing."

Oscar took a sip from his water, he already felt he would need to escape the room that had quickly grown hot and stifling. "It's pretty much as it was sir, I'm afraid."

Crammond crossed his arms as he carefully prepared his press briefing plan of attack. "I don't want to give too much away anyway. You know what the press are like. If they don't get enough information they normally either exaggerate what you tell them or in some cases even make stuff up."

"Well sir, rather you than me."

Crammond gave a slight false laugh, closed his eyes and rubbed his forehead "Well if McGovern can drag himself in before ten thirty get him to call me."

"Will do sir."

Crammond looked at the floor checking his polished shoes before looking over the murder evidence board to check his notes he'd written on a small A5 size notebook were up to date. There was a lot of information on there, interview transcripts, reports from door to door enquiries, medical and pathology, forensics, and scene of crimes. A montage of photos and documents relating to the case, most attached with blu-tac or drawing pins. He wanted to make sure he gave the press, not only the facts but the right sort of information.

Calling over to Ann Gatsby they both headed towards his office to compare notes before the press briefing.

They hadn't been long out of the incident room when Oscars mobile began to ring. He saw from the caller display it was McGovern. Standing up, he checked his watch, as he walked over to look out of the window "Where are you sir,? Crammond's been asking for you, and Gatsby's going crazy."

McGovern sighed dejectedly. "I'm at the Hospital son, the RVI, it's your Grandad, I'm sorry son but they think he may have had another heart attack."

Oscar squeezed his eyes tight shut as he tried to swallow down his worry. He wondered what the silence reminded him of. In a few short seconds everything seemed to be changing for the worse.

As he drove to the Hospital he thought he didn't know what he wanted to know anymore. He was afraid to know in some ways. He felt he had become vulnerable again and on the brink of another living nightmare.

TWENTY NINE

From broken bones in the Emergency
Department, to tropical fevers in the infectious diseases
unit; from brain conditions to problems with
your child's immune system, they provided a full range
of modern healthcare services at the Royal Victoria
Infirmary.

As usual there was nowhere to park, except the
multi-storey. Oscar drove his car round and round the
tight helter skelter like turns of the winding road from
floor to floor. Each level fuller than the last. Eventually
finding a space but he wouldn't have won any pladits
for the straightness of his parking.

Heading to the entrance down several flights of
concrete stairs,counting them , as usual, the
exaggerated sounds of other equally frustrated
motorists' car engines amplified by the enclosed space.

It was quite busy as he entered the Hospital and
headed for the main reception area. In what seemed an
age he got near to the front of a very large queue. Oscar
waited in line as his heart beat faster.

A middle aged woman with shoulder length black
hair, stud earrings and pearl necklace sat behind the
large desk.

"My Grandfather was brought in earlier, Alfred
Smiles"?

She tapped frantically and checked her computer
screen "One moment sir....Oh Yes Mr Alfred Smiles,

he's in the Cardiology ward, just head down the main corridor turn left at the shop and follow the signs."

"So it *was* a heart attack then"?

"I'm sorry sir"' the woman hesitated slightly "You'll have to see the staff at the ward for that information; if you head to cardiology they will have all the information for you."

The Cardiology department, at the RVI prided itself on their Comprehensive range of facilities and advanced technology, their comprehensive range of cardiology clinical services and facilities including a Coronary Care Unit and catheter laboratories, as well as pacemaker and rehabilitation services, in addition to the usual inpatient wards and outpatient clinics.

His Grandfather was definitely, to coin a phrase, in the right place.

Walking down what seemed endless corridors in what was a very large busy Hospital, Oscar followed the signs as directed by the receptionist.

There were lots of different types of people walking past him from kids in wheelchairs to old people in their dressing gowns heading outside to brave the elements for a dose of nicotine. Reaching the Cardiology ward he spotted a young female Doctor.

The junior doctor on the ward who should have gone off duty at eight am was still there because her colleague who should have taken over was detained at another Hospital. Oscar approached her grabbing her attention with a cough and polite "Excuse me."

She didn't look very old at all, just into her twenties he thought. She was quite tall and slim, and had her hair tied back quite tightly in a ponytail, her face young, quite fresh, and free of makeup. You would never have guessed she'd been working for almost sixteen hours. She responded with a professional smile.

"Yes, can I help you"?

"My Grandfather Alfred Smiles is on this ward somewhere, he was brought in earlier this morning, suspected of a heart attack, could you give me any more information please"?

"Alfred Smiles"? she paused for a few seconds and checked her clipboard in front of her turning a couple of pages as she spoke, "Yes, he's over in bay three, end bed by the window."

"Was it a heart attack"?

"Possibly, we're still not sure, could have been an angina attack, but we're still doing tests and waiting for results to come back."

"What do you think caused it"?

"Well, it could have been a number of things. Your Grandfather's medical history has just muddied the waters a bit but, usually, if it was angina, one or more of your coronary arteries is usually narrowed. This causes a reduced blood supply to a part, or parts, of your heart muscle, if he had a lot going on, sometimes, change, stress, excitement, all these things could have contributed."

"Yeah, well he has had a few busy weeks, what with Christmas, seeing the family fly back to Canada and, of course, his new lodger."

"Oh yes, your father is with him at the moment, he said he'd moved back in with him."

Oscar frowned before clearing his throat. "Father, oh no, he's not my father. He's my erm....partner."

The young female Doctor's neck and face began to redden slightly "Oh sorry I just..."

"No, no not that type of partner, Oscars cheeks burnt with embarrassment, work colleague, he's my boss; I'm a Police Officer CID, heaven forbid."

The young female doctor giggled out a laugh, "Oh well there both over there, anyway."

Oscar had one more question before he headed for the bay that his Grandfather was in "So what happens now, then"?

"It's still early days and we still need to get a blood test to check for anaemia, thyroid problems, kidney problems, a high glucose level, and a high cholesterol level, as these may be linked with angina. Then we'll do another ECG, after that it's just a case of sorting the right medication, if he needs any that is then plenty of rest. Hopefully he should be home in a couple of days, or sooner, he'll need to speak to Mr Ingram he's coming to see him soon, hopefully within the next half hour. Oscar sighed, he was worried, needing to know, and he might still have to wait at least another half an hour."

He willed himself not to turn his head and look at the clock "Thanks."

As he approached the bay he could see McGovern was sitting on the edge of the bed. His grandfather was wired up to the ECG Machine and a glucose drip was in place. A nurse was present checking his blood pressure.

"How are you feeling"?

"Me, son, I'm fine, no thanks to this gentleman sitting here". He pointed to McGovern. "Think I'd still be laying there now had it not been for him being there, perhaps him living at my place was a good thing after all."

The nurse wound his left arm in the black Velcro-tipped cloth, slipped on the gauge and pumped, watching the dial and then let the air hiss out.

Oscar was philosophical, "Every cloud and all that, I suppose."

Getting to his feet McGovern looked at his watch impatiently "Anyway son, now that you're here I'll head off back to the station, Gatsby's has already called me, we've got a meeting, going through the case so far, where we go next, any leads, etc, that's err...." he pointed to his grandfather lying in the bed, "...Everything is okay with old Alfie here."

Grandad Alfie hated fussing "I'll be fine man, probably be sent home tomorrow, anyway, it's nowt this, made of cast iron me man."

The nurse gave a rueful smile as she completed his checks and filled in his charts "That's much better Mr

Smiles, your blood pressure and temperature was quite high when you first came in but they're almost back to normal now."

Inwardly Oscar sighed with relief, as the nurse left the bay to check on another patient, "Actually Grandad they said you might be in for a couple of days, they're gonna do some more blood tests and stuff, give you a good MOT if you like."

Grandad Alfie's shoulders drooped, "But I feel OK now son, but I suppose what with my history they don't want to take any chances, do they" ?

Oscar often worried as to how his grandad coped on his own."No they don't. Look, do you think you should move into my house."

Grandad Alfie placed a hand on his chest "Look son, I know you're concerned but everything I need is just round the corner from me. If I was to move into your place you'd need to drive me everywhere."

Oscar sighed, "Just felt it would be safer, you know, as you said, if McGovern hadn't been there, could have been quite serious." Just like the last time.

Oscar recalled his Grandfather's first heart attack. It had happened two months earlier. He recalled the fear, the uncertainty, the feeling of helplessness.

CHAPTER THIRTY

At long last Mr Ingram was on his rounds. Rudolf Ingram was the head consultant at both the RVI and the Freeman Hospitals. He *was* the man when it came to Cardiology.

His grandfather's heart problems began soon after the accident resulting in the unexpected death of Oscar's parents, some ten years earlier.

He'd had a triple bye-pass a year later, but this was the first heart attack he'd had since his operation. Oscar had special reasons to be concerned, he loved his Grandfather and didn't know what he would do, or how he would cope, should the worst happen.

Rudolf Ingram looked a bit like an old style school teacher. He was quite tall, in his late forties and wore a tweed jacket, brown flannel trousers and brown shoes. He had these tiny spectacles on the end of his nose which he peered over the top of when he spoke. It had been Mr Ingram who had performed the triple bye-pass surgery on his grandfather all those years ago, and he knew his circumstances and indeed the length of time that had gone by since the last incident.

He approached the bed in his usual confident manner, "Now then Alfred, it's been a while since I saw you looking like this. You're results show that indeed you've had a heart attack, but thankfully, this time, only a minor one, nothing like you're last one, but, nevertheless we'll keep you in for a couple of days and hopefully when you're medication is reviewed we can let you go home, now have you any questions"?

Grandad Alfie shook his head.

Oscar's expression was downcast. He couldn't think of anything specific to ask Mr Ingram, although there were probably a million things going through his head that he *wanted* to ask.

"OK then gentlemen,I know you want to go home as soon as you can, so, all being well, Alfred, you might be able to go home in the morning, no promises mind, we'll have to see how you go, we'll keep a check on you overnight but you have to start and take things a little easier, and make a few better healthier lifestyle choices."

"OK Mr Ingram, I will," lied Grandad Alfie. *Some hope of that* thought Oscar.

The consultant left them both sitting in the private room on the side ward; Grandad Alfie had felt his grandson had done enough. "You should go home son, I'll ring you in the morning, tell you what time I'm getting released" ?

"It's discharged Grandad, prisoners get released."

"Well it's like a bloody prison in here, no booze, and no fags."

"Sorry to say Grandad but I think you've smoked your last fag, you heard what Mr Ingram said."

Alfie shook his head in defiance "He didn't say I had to stop smoking."

"Not as such he didn't, no, but what do you think he meant about healthier lifestyle choices then"?

"Take more exercise and eat more salad, I dunno son, it's the drink and the fag's that keep me going, I enjoy them, give them both up and I might as well be dead man already I'm seventy eight years old, and been OK so far."

Oscar raised his eyebrows "Yeah, apart from the two heart attacks and the triple bye-pass surgery."

But his Grandad was in a defiant mood, "Look son, I know you care about me and would do anything for me, but no matter what happens, no matter what you do for me it isn't going to bring them back now is it"?

"It isn't Grandad, no, you're right and I'm sorry, it's your life and your choice. I just don't want to lose you that's all. After all you're the only family I have left, over here as we all only get together at Christmas now."

Grandad Alfie touched his grandson affectionately on the arm, "And I'm going to be around for a few Christmas's yet, but I promise you I'll cut down the fag's and try to take things a bit easier, now get yourself home, I'll see you tomorrow."

Oscar hugged his Grandad, and, as requested headed home. Tomorrow was another day and, thankfully, his Grandad appeared to be on the mend, and who knows maybe there would be some new evidence that would finally crack this sodden case.

THIRTY ONE

Oscar had wanted to get to the station early. He went through his usual checks, before leaving and went back and checked the front door was locked, *always good to check*.

The weather outside was pretty severe. Not only was it dark and cold but the tempestuous rain had now begun to fall.

Getting into his car Oscar turned the ignition but nothing happened, he tried again as the engine spluttered. *Bollocks*, he thought. He tried once more, nothing. He would have to take the dreaded Metro, with all those people and germs, all the way into the City centre.

Oscar got out of the car and headed towards the nearest metro station, it was still quite dark, freezing cold and to make matters worse the rain was now torrential.

He walked quickly as he hadn't time, or even thought about a coat, walking quicker to stave off the growing chill. A paperboy cycled along the high street, whistling and taking his hands off the handlebars to comb the rain through his hair and by the time he reached the Metro Station Oscar was soaked through and had just missed a train, as it pulled out of the station. *Bollocks*, he cursed again.

He noticed from the digital information board, that the next train was due in twelve minutes. He picked up the free Metro Newspaper as the main headline had caught his eye.

Multiple Murders, the hunt continues. Street lights were lighting up the dusk but it was too dark to read the small print so he made his way to the centre of the station where there was a fluorescent lighted canopy which would not only shelter him from the rain but also enable him to read the paper.

An older man, in work clothes had, eventually, bought his ticket, cursing and swearing to himself as his pound coins dropped through the ticket machine without recognising payment. He too had just missed the previous train. He looked just as cold and wet and nodded a good morning as he walked passed whistling one direction's that's what makes you beautiful ironically through his half dozen remaining teeth.

The man removed his haversack, wiped down the droplets of rain from his coat, and opened his bag. Taking out his spectacles case he carefully opened it, took out his glasses, put them on and sitting down opened up his free newspaper. He had just started to read it when, in an instant, the lights all went out, leaving the station in almost total darkness. Oscar checked his watch. It was seven thirty.

In the darkness of the metro station the deployed sarcasm of the older man cut through the rain in his voice. "You know what son, I bet some cunt sat in a nice warm office with the fucking kettle on has just pushed a button, without giving us poor bastards, who actually *have* to work for a living, a second thought."

Oscar just nodded his agreement. He didn't have the energy to explain that the lighting system was probably on a timer that hadn't been changed since the end of British summer time, when the clocks had since gone back an hour. He did find it quite amusing though, to think that there just might be *some cunt* sitting in a nice warm office, hot cup of coffee in hand playing God with the peasants.

The train seemed to be taking an age; it had been a long twelve minutes. Oscar braved the elements and poked his head through the foggy drizzle from the shelter of the canopy and could just about see the distant lights of the oncoming metro train.

When it pulled into the station, the train was quite empty as people sat in a symmetric pattern in the blocks of four seats, each person sitting facing forward in the window seat, maximising their personal space and adhering to a strict social distancing policy. Oscar sat, directly facing the window, on a three person seated chair, between two carriages.

The gentle sway of the metro train was almost hypnotic. No one spoke. Oscar looked at the people on the train, each one having their own reason to be out in this terrible weather.

As the train drew nearer to the city centre the carriage began to fill up with more tired looking sullen passengers, their minds slowly coming to terms with what challenges lay before them in their working day.

At each station, more of the same would get on, and off. A silver haired, mahogany skinned couple complete with suitcases on the way to the airport for a winter break, builders in overalls, cement encrusted boots and high visibility orange backed donkey jackets, each with varied carrier bag lunches. Several smartly dressed young women with good legs, dark hair and small leather handbags who never took their heads away from their mobile phones. Office workers, bankers in suits and ties and unfortunate care workers in nurses tunics on their way to no doubt, do some unsavoury personal care task for minimum wage. There were university graduates with their Vodafone ID and polo shirts and the customary array of early morning hard faced female cleaners who's armpit aroma had an unpleasant smell of stale meat pies.

Despite his metro journey Oscar still managed to get into the Police Station reasonably early and was waiting for McGovern, who just made it before the Chief Super arrived with his trademark scowl on his stress filled face.

Crammond had news that would send a shiver down their spines. His demeanor was all sad and serious, "There's been another body found, and I'm afraid to say it appears to be that of DC Daniel Lee."

Turning to Ann Gatsby, Crammond cleared his throat before continuing. "I want you to assemble your whole team, ten minutes in the incident room."

THIRTY TWO

McGovern and Oscar sat down at their respective desks, half heartedly leafing through files from the past few week's evidence and briefing Gatsby on how some recent interviews had gone.

They were quickly joined by Felicity Somerton, taking the opportunity of a few moments away from making her usual neat and copious notes, who after pouring a coffee for herself sat looking up at the ceiling as she wound a strand of hair around her finger.

Stan Scott was a little later, and had news of his own, the previous coffee morning meeting with Sammy Greenwood, but that would have to be for another time.

Scott closed the door behind him and sat in the last vacant chair in the cramped and stuffy incident room.

George Crammond stood hands in pockets; he spoke in a calm and clear tone. "The fire service was called to put out a car fire last night just after midnight, back of Grainger Street. When they got there, there appeared to be somebody in the driver's seat, they tried in vain but the fire had taken hold by then, it kept them back, too intense and by the time they had put it out the person in the front was dead and had been burned beyond recognition. We're still waiting for confirmation but we're pretty sure it's Daniel Lee, he's been off the radar for a few days, with no contact, the victim has a similar body size and shape, and his badge was in the car. A mobile phone had been stuffed in his mouth.

Remarkably the sim card appears to be okay and that's being checked out now, I'm sorry to be the bearer of such bad news." Crammond turned and closed the office door as he left the room. The stunned detectives all sat in silence for a few seconds.

McGovern was in a sombre mood, there was nothing more distressing than the murder of a fellow Police officer, especially one which he had worked so closely with. He sipped his coffee, it was stale and he pulled a face. Oscar was still wide eyed with shock. He had a thought about why the phone had been placed in his mouth. His heart sank, clutching his hand to his chest "That's a message, his cover *was* blown, it was *me*, when I called him, God, he said not to, said it could blow his cover. What have I done"?

Felicity was also inconsolable. "No. It was all my fault, those men I was with they must have found out that Lee was undercover and I was a Police plant."

McGovern tired his best to console his younger colleagues, "No, it's neither of your faults, I called him a few times as well you know, Lee knew the risks he was an experienced undercover copper, it might have been nothing to do with either of you." McGovern got up from his chair, his knees creaked as he walked over to where Oscar stood and Patted him on the back.

Oscar and Felicity both felt like that member of a firing squad who wasn't sure if their gun had fired the deadly round.

Ann Gatsby, popped her head back into the incident room, she had a request for McGovern "Jim, could you give Manchester CID a call, just to let them know about Daniel Lee, you know how it works, the men he worked with are usually the last to know, especially in undercover cases."

McGovern just nodded somberly.

Oscar's chin dipped to his chest as his posture slumped, he remained quiet and nodded his head in agreement.

McGovern tapped out the number on the telephone keypad, it began to ring, he switched the phone to his other ear and picked up his pen, as he waited for the call to be answered. After a few seconds somebody picked up. McGovern didn't wait for the pleasantries of the hello. "This is DI Jim McGovern from Tyneside CID; I need to speak to a senior officer with regard to a DC Daniel Lee"?

After a few moments McGovern was put through to a senior officer.

"Hello Inspector McGovern, I am DCI Matt Taylor, Lee's supervising officer, how can I help you"?

McGovern took a deep breath "I've got some bad news for you. Unfortunately it appears his cremated body has been discovered in a burnt out car in the early hours of the morning up here in Newcastle, I'm sorry, I know this must be a shock for you."

The voice on the other end of the phone had an uncertain tone. "Daniel Lee? can't be"?

McGovern continued... "Yeah, he was undercover, working closely with a suspected Triad gang, looks like he'd been rumbled, the evidence at the scene certainly points that way."

There was a short pause from the other end of the line "We'll Inspector I'm afraid you are very much mistaken. DC Daniel Lee's body was pulled out of the Manchester ship canal some six weeks ago, I don't know who's body you have up there but it certainly isn't his."

McGovern's stomach clenched Now it was his turn to be confused, his voice getting higher with disbelief. "I don't understand that, you sure"?

"Yes, Daniel Lee was indeed undercover, but working in Manchester, not Newcastle. he drowned in the canal, we believe murdered, have you had the autopsy report yet? As it can't be Daniel Lee."

"No, no we haven't but because the body was so badly burnt..." McGovern turned in mid sentence and looked over towards Oscar." I'm told that we had to wait for a forensic anthropologist and they take time, the body matched his size, and body shape, and we found his phone and badge in his car. We assumed the autopsy would just be a formality."

"We'll, you have got yourselves a John Doe up there in Newcastle, if I can be of any further assistance please let me know."

"Thanks Matt, and sorry for the confusion."

McGovern replaced the receiver, trying to stay calm, but his bulging eyes gave away his shock.
"Well I'll be buggered."

Oscar stopped what he was doing and spun his swivel chair around in the direction of McGovern, his pen wedged firmly between his teeth. "What wrong sir?, how did they take it"?

McGovern sat back in his chair and put his hands behind his head exposing his pale, fat, hairy stomach. An action that made both Felicity Somerton and Stanley Scott stop whatever they were doing and stare. "We better get Gatsby and Crammond in here. The body in the burnt out car isn't Daniel Lee, It's not him, he was murdered six weeks ago, in Manchester, his body was fished out of a canal."

Oscar's jaw dropped, as a sudden coldness hit him to the core. "Well if it's not Lee, who is it"?

McGovern had a far bigger concern, "Exactly, and If Daniel Lee died six weeks ago, who the fuck has been working with us for the last month"?

THIRTY THREE

Oscar had been to visit his Grandad. The two mile drive back through the busy outskirts of the City Centre took the usual forty five minutes.

It was almost lunch time when he arrived back at the station. McGovern sat cursing at his computer screen.

Oscar was relieved that his Grandfather appeared to be on the mend, it could have been much worse and the incident had made him think more deeply how people deal with grief, bereavement and family emergencies. His thoughts went out to Walter Chang.

"Think I'll go and visit Walter Chang, sir, it's been a while since we heard from him, see how he's coping."

McGovern was his usual unsympathetic self "That's what family liaison is for son, let them deal with all that shite, we've got enough on our plates."

Oscar's eyes narrowed,"It's just what's been happening with my Grandad, puts all this sort of thing into perspective of how important family is, just wonder how he's coping with it all."

McGovern gave a half hearted shrug, "We'll if you must go on then, you could probably do with a bit of time away anyway, with what's just happened, how is the old twat doing anyway"?

"He's doing OK for now, I'll tell him you were erm... Asking after him."

"You do that son."

Oscar decided to walk to the Dragon Gate, it was quite cold but dry and the New Year sales were well underway. Newcastle City Centre was a busy place. People in a hurry, people taking their time, the coffee shops were bursting at the seams and there were people everywhere, making it impossible to walk quickly. The streets were so full of people looking for a bargain that he had to slalom past person after person like a downhill skier on the piste. *Where do they get all the money from?*.

As he turned and headed towards the Dragon Gate the crowds began to subside, walking under and through the large Chinese arch, the streets were a lot quieter although still busy.

The sight of crooked Chinese lanterns descending into a gathering mist made him feel nostalgic and peaceful. Chinese New Year preparations were in full swing, restaurants were being decked out in colourful banners and bunting, as some children excitedly ran across the street waving toy dragons and flags.

Passing one of the cafes he spotted Walter sitting outside playing what looked like chess with a much older mandarin Chinese gentleman who resembled a cross between fu man choo, and Wishy Washy from the Aladdin pantomime.

The man looked about ninety years old, had a long grey ponytail, even longer wispy goatee beard and wore a small skull cap. Spotting Oscar Walter beckoned him over.

Oscar was somewhat surprised at Chang's upbeat persona, bearing in mind what he had been through.

"Good day to you, Detective Smiles, and isn't this a fine crisp afternoon."

"Nice to see you're on the up, Mr Chang."

"Please, detective, call me Walter, yes, I'm doing fine. I've been told all about Sara and what she and that Western got up to, behind my back, I had a lucky escape really, she got what was coming and the money I lost in ransom was a drop in the Ocean as to how much a divorce would have cost me."

"I suppose it was, if you put it like that, a lucky escape," *or even a pretty good motive for murder he thought with his detectives head on*, "So what's this game your playing? and who's your friend"?

Walter Chang pointed to his colleague "This is Jimmy, he owns this café and he is the best XiangQi player this side of the Great Wall, and I mean the Chinese one, not Hadrian's one down the road."

Oscar gazed at them with focus as he raised his eyebrows "So what is XiangQi then, looks a bit like chess"?

"That my boy is exactly like Chinese chess."

Old Jimmy who had remained quiet, loosened his frown of concentration and appeared pleased at having a captive audience interested in what he had to say. He suddenly spoke up, making Oscar jump.

"The game dates back to the Warring States period; to the first century BC. It was one of Lord Mengchang of Qi's interests. Emperor Wu of Northern Zhou wrote a book in AD 569 called Xiang Jing. It is believed to have described the rules of an astronomically themed game called xiangqi. The name means constellation game, and sometimes the xiangqi board's river is called the heavenly river, which may mean the Milky Way. The end of the game, as you know it, check-mate, we call the gathering of the seven stars."

"Can you show me how to play"?

Walter removed his glasses and wiped his hand across his brow. "Sure we can, pull up a chair, new players are always welcome."

As Oscar sat for a while he watched the old master at work, his brain ticking over picking up the moves and rules as he watched and began to try and learn what it was all about. He switched his gaze from board to player, watching, learning.

As the game progressed Oscar began to realise the importance of the end game, the gathering of the seven stars. He knew and fully understood that the Gan-Yin syndicate were a traditional group, could it be a coincidence that there were seven countries in Europe all experiencing similar crimes.

He needed to check this out; he made his excuses and headed for the seat of all knowledge the City library, where he was to make some interesting discoveries

*****

Something was afoot as Crammond, following a big pow wow with the top brass, was in on the morning briefing. It was depressing because no matter how much work they were all doing they seemed to be making little progress.

All weekend leave was cancelled as Ann Gatsby had taken drastic steps to try and drive things forward.

George Crammond sat in the incident room, he checked his watch, he wasn't happy with McGovern's usual bad time-keeping, neither was Ann Gatsby. It wasn't too long before McGovern arrived, the coldness outside making the broken veins on his nose more noticeable, still wearing the same clothes as the previous day and looking like he'd slept in them again.

He made himself a strong black coffee with sugar and sat down. Oscar could still smell the stale alcohol on his breath and was sure Crammond and Gatsby would do likewise

DCI Ann Gatsby began the briefing and had a news update, "Ladies and Gentlemen, You will all be pleased to know that Mr Mick Western has turned up, he *has* at last, been found." Gatsby's mood was strangely sombre, somewhat even frustrating as she continued "But we have a huge problem."

THIRTY FOUR

Oscar's eyes widened, "A problem? Has he got a good alibi?, Is he in the holding cells down stairs, ma'am"?

Ann Gatsby expression was grave "No, Detective Sergeant he's on the pathologists slab, it was Mick Western's body in that burnt out car, not the person we believed to be Detective Lee, The car was also the very same car, the red Ford Focus, that was car-jacked in ChinaTown, and the car used to carry David Leung's body to the Dene."

Oscar looked at Gatsby with a furrowed brow and he had a relevant if not obvious question, "So where is the fake Daniel Lee then and why would somebody kill Western and want to try and make us think it was Lee"?

Gatsby had no concrete answers "I don't know, maybe to buy themselves some time"?

Crammond shook his head, they were getting nowhere. "Has anyone got any idea what's going on here?, any leads?, Come on!, somebody must have something"?

Oscar sat back, took a sip of his now tepid tea and explained that he'd spent most of yesterday afternoon in the library researching ancient Chinese history and customs and especially this ancient emperor Gan-Yin of whom the triad syndicate idolised and followed.

Crammond gave Gatsby a bright eyed look, as McGovern rolled his eyes to the ceiling.

Oscar stood and began to pace around as he spoke "The Emperor Gan-Yin sent some of his best trusted Generals to all parts of Europe, not to conquer but to look and learn, that's how I think they differ slightly from the Triad group, the general who went to Italy was impressed with how the Roman Empire was being built."

McGovern gazed out of the window and yawned noisily as Oscar's long winded explanation and the warm office were starting to take its toll. "Go on then, get to the point, son, we ain't got all day."

Gatsby gave McGovern a look that could have turned him to stone "Your not helping matters Jim," as the two of them exchanged dirty looks and further inaudible unpleasantries.

Crammond quickly hushed everyone up "Go on Detective Sergeant continue please."

Oscar continued. "The Emperor also gave the following somewhat fanciful description of Roman customs and natural products undoubtedly based on what he was told by sailors in Persian Gulf ports: How their kings are not permanent. They select and appoint the most worthy man. If there are unexpected calamities in the kingdom, such as frequent extraordinary winds or rains, he is unceremoniously rejected and replaced."

McGovern was now reading the health and safety information poster on the wall, he'd read it twice, his coffee was cold, tasted like piss and he'd forgotten to put sugar in it.

Ann Gatsby like Crammond was also hoping that the young detective would soon get to the point but unlike McGovern was a little more diplomatic. "Thanks for the history lesson but is this leading us anywhere? Has this got any relevance to the case Oscar? I'm struggling to find a link."

Oscar held up both his hands "Okay ma'am, nearly there, I promise, in ancient China, Taoist scholars and mystics developed a profound understanding of life based on minute observation of nature. Along with the law of Yin and Yang, the ancient Taoists observed a pattern of expression in nature that they interpreted as and named, the Five Elements or Five Phases. These elements, or energies, were described as Wood, Fire, Earth, Metal and Water and were understood to be the prime energetic building blocks from which all material substance in the phenomenal world is composed. The Elements are representations of the transformation that occurs in the world around us; they are metaphors for describing how things interact and relate with each other."

Crammond was enjoying the communal energy the young detective brought to the room but also was beginning to wonder what the connection was.

Oscar headed towards the murder evidence board. "Everything was made up of some combination of these elements: people, companies, games, plants, music, art and so on. All can be examined and understood from the perspective of the Five Elements. Don't you see"? Oscar's eyes began to sparkle and gleam his gestures becoming more animated.

They could all see he was onto something. A buzz of excitement was beginning to build in the incident room. Oscar pointed at each photo on the evidence murder board in turn. "Look at the deaths involved in this case already, there's five in total, and each one could be connected to each of the five elements, as I've just described."

McGovern scratched his head, as he summarised what Oscar had just said. "Right, the facts are these, Alex Brennan was killed with a blade."

Oscar nodded "Yes, a metal blade,"Oscar's eyes shined, locked on the source of relief, at last they were starting to get it.

Crammond nodded intensely."Sara Chang was crushed to death by the wooden Pallets at the DIY Store."

Oscar again nodded, "Yes, killed by wood."

McGovern stood up as he now surveyed the murder evidence board with a new found confidence." David Leung's cause of death was the amount of soil in his lungs, he was buried alive suffocated by the earth."

McGovern puffed out his chest, he got it and he was on a roll "And We've just found out that Mick Western was burned to death in the car."

Oscar turned to the room with a radiant smile,"Yes, yes, keep going sir, Just one more."

Ann Gatsby joined in "And the real DC Daniel Lee drowned in the water of the Manchester Ship Canal."

George Crammond grin could not be contained "You're spot on Oscar, once again."

Oscar continued. "I also visited Walter Chang yesterday and he was playing this ancient Chinese chess game with an old master. I found out that the typical end to this game, what we call checkmate, they call the gathering of the seven stars, don't you get it, this whole case, it's a competition, a game. I believe this Triad group has sent seven members to Europe to take part in some kind of competition."

Crammond sat forward, "Are you sure of this"?

"That's what I believe sir, yes."

Gatsby spoke while stirring her coffee "Well, if all five elements have been completed, what next then"? Oscar's brow furrowed as he gave a curt nod "That is what we still need to find out."

THIRTY FIVE

Mick Western's charred body lay draped in a green cover on an aluminium bench in the Morgue. Forensic officer Peter Devon had the report from the anthropologist, and was reading out the report to the four detectives.

Felicity Somerton was looking, a particular off shade of green, as Oscar swallowed excessively while taking quick random glances at Western's body and then back to focus on Peter Devon.

As for McGovern and Scott, nothing appeared to faze them; they had seen it all before, and worse.

Peter Devon began, "The tests prove that the body had a large amount of opium based substance in his blood, more than likely heroin. Cause of death was incineration, the body didn't appear to move at all during the fire, this tells us that it was the amount of heroin in his system had somewhat incapacitated him. The mobile telephone found in his mouth *was* that belonging to Daniel Lee, as was the remains of the warrant card. The sim was remarkably OK and the only numbers either dialled or received were that of the incident room, DC Somerton, DI McGovern and DS Smiles, unusually there were no text messages."

Oscar took a step forward, "It's not that unusual for someone working undercover not to use texts though, is it"?

Peter Devon cocked his head to one side "Probably not, but I'm no expert on undercover work so I stand to be corrected."

Felicity had her hands over her eyes, as Peter Devon moved to one side giving her full view.

McGovern's brow wrinkled "What about time of death?"

Devon checked his clipboard and turned over a few pages. "He died in the fire, so shortly after midnight."

As the detectives headed back up the stairs to the incident room. McGovern could hardly speak; and was puffing and panting, and sounded like someone on the verge of an asthma attack, "The only thing we need to find out now...... is, who ?..... Daniel Lee really was, and..... where is he now"?

Back in the incident room McGovern issued his instructions to Scott and Felicity and headed over towards Oscar, who had news.

"I've just emailed Don, my brother in law. He explained that he told me that he's heard from a very good source that there definitely *are* seven Red Poles operating in Europe. He's promised to get some information to me as soon as he can."

McGovern was somewhat dismissive "So what *source* does this brother in law have then? Where does he work again, oh yes, an airport somewhere in Canada, a lot of fucking use that's gonna be, Marvin the fucking Mounty, no doubt."

"No sir, the FBI."

McGovern gave a false cough to clear his throat, "Fair enough, can't argue with that then, good work son, and erm... tell Don, hello from me, will you, the next time you contact him."

"Will do sir, in fact I'm expecting something from him in the next few minutes."

THIRTY SIX

Felicity and Stan Scott waited outside a plush apartment block on Newcastle's trendy Quayside. Finishing his cigarette, Scott dropped it on the ground, extinguished it with the ball of his foot, and gave a heavy sigh. "McGovern's idea and he wants *us* not *him* to check Lee's flat, see if he's alright."

Felicity was more positive. "Well at least it beats sitting in the office, it's lovely down here, I bet the apartments are a bit pricey though."

Stan Scott, gave a slow steady tut and again impatiently pressed the intercom button. He remarked in a voice that carried across the street.

"He's not in. There's nobody in there. We going back or what"?

Felicity checked her watch. "The landlord should be here any minute, we'd better wait. McGovern wants us to check inside."

Oscar sat at his desk awaiting the email from his brother in law Don Carrington. Don had used all his contacts, and favours, in his role with the Canadian Border Services Agency.

He had managed to put together a list of the suspected seven stars. The list wasn't necessarily correct, but it was the best he could do.

Oscar watched as the number one popped up in his email inbox. "It's here sir, the email I've been waiting for, one of these mug shots could well be the person responsible for all these murders, it could be one of these who is active in our City."

McGovern dragged his chair over from his desk as the two detectives looked excitedly at the screen, as each file was downloaded and the faces appeared.

The first photo download. McGovern wasn't impressed, "Well isn't he an ugly fucker."

Oscar turned and looked at his DI, and raised his eyebrows "Say's George Clooney sitting next to me."

McGovern got out of his chair and went over to his desk to get his spectacles, "Okay, son, point taken, who's that then"?

Oscar began to read the information. "This is Sun Jian Ming, 34 years old originally from Singapore, he is a suspected Red Pole with connections to the Gan-Yin, he is wanted for suspected extortion, racketeering and murder."

"Sun Jian Minger, more like, don't recognise him, and believe me who wouldn't remember that face, a face only a mother could love, who's the next one"?

"Just waiting for the photo to download, sir, here he is, He's called Rong Yujie, six foot tall, from Hong Kong; he's wanted for, drug dealing and people trafficking."

McGovern gave a deeply weighted sigh "This sounds more like an Jeremy Kyle version of an episode of fucking blind date, please spare me the very bad Cilla Black impression"!

"As if sir.".

The two detectives studied the face on the screen; again, he was not instantly recognisable.

"Right sir, here's the next one, Hu Chao, five foot six."

McGovern gave him a double take as he moved in for a closer look, seriously invading Oscar's personal space and just an inch or so from Oscars face, shouting "Five foot fucking six is this the seven stars or the seven fucking dwarfs, who's next Dopey?, poor sod, any shorter he'd be under fucking ground."

"Shush, man sir, why so loud, and why do you always have to shout right in my ear, Oscar had willed McGovern to shut up so he could think and concentrate. "He sounds a right piece of work this Chao, known for extreme violence and torture, money laundering and illegal money lending."

"Definitely a small man with a chip on his shoulder, or should I say a bean shoot"!

Oscar shook his head at another one of McGovern's corny wise cracks as the next file began to download. "Right sir, prepare to see Mr Lu Yu, 34, Originates from Thailand."

McGovern couldn't stop himself, "Well, we've already mentioned Cllla Black, we might as well have fucking Lulu as well, look son, I'm grateful for your brother in laws help but really, this is taking an age, and you must admit, a bit of a waste of time, how many more of these mug shots to go."

"There's just three more, Zhang Han, Xu Yan and Kong Hao."

McGovern's demeanor changed as he instantly became interested in the last name. "I've heard that name somewhere before, didn't Lee, well, the fake Lee mention him"?

"Yes, he did sir, he was the one he said he was going to give evidence against."

McGovern now complete with spectacles moved closer again to the screen, in an unhurried and relaxed movement, his voice slower, low and more controlled, "So, what's the info on this Kong Hao then, let's see the fucker"?

"He's got quite a rap sheet, Say's here, he's a suspected senior member of the Gan-Yin Triad group, a Red Pole, who is head of the militant arm of the clan, he is considered to be the worthy successor and a lieutenant and the enforcer of the clan rules. He began by taking control of a small drug operation, using his good looks and charm to target upper class women, and teenage girls, making them addicted to Heroin, so that he could exploit them and force them into prostitution to support their addictions, from the profits he laundered money into larger drug operations and would invest further in the entertainment industry, pubs, clubs, boxing, martial arts clubs, casinos and the pornography industry, using the poor girls as actresses in his disgusting movies. He's known as no nonsense and has been suspected of several rapes, brutal murders, specialising in torture using excessive force against anyone who gets in his way. Problem is so far he's managed to get away with everything as nobody will give evidence against him. He was arrested and charged a while back but was sprung on his way to court for trial, and hasn't really been seen since, although he has always been on the radar of Interpol and other agencies, including the FBI."

The two detectives gazed at the screen, waiting for the photo to appear, slowly the picture began to form in front of their eyes, they were both dumbfounded when the photograph fully downloaded.

McGovern's mouth fell wide open, as he shouted in a disbelieving voice. "It's Lee, the clever bastard."

It was all beginning to make sense to McGovern, "When Leung tried to mug me; He knew that Leung would talk if he was ever caught and as he could recognise and identify him, he had become a liability, he had to be killed."

Oscar also had some answers, "And when Leung ran from me and Felicity, he must have told Lee that we were after him, and when I spoke to Lee I mentioned Leung's name, that's why he killed him, Hoa just couldn't take that chance, and made his next victim choice an easy one."

Oscar shook his head, as he continued, "And he knew fine well we would blame ourselves for blowing his cover and getting him killed, he planned it well, putting Western's body in that car, leaving his phone and Lee's badge in there and then torching it."

Although shocked, McGovern could not hide his satisfaction of a job well done. "So that's all five murders that he's the prime suspect for, and now we have a name, and a face."

Oscar had figured something else out. "It's the year of the Dragon, he's got to be heading back to Hong Kong for the gathering of the seven stars."

McGovern sat silent in deep thought, rubbing his bearded chin as his mind raced searching his brain to make sense of it all.

Oscar now knew he was right "We now know that Hao *is* the Red Pole who was operating in England as part of the Gan-Yin's competition to elect a new Dragon Head."

"Okay, yes, I understand that, go on then son."

"To see if he would be a worthy leader. We know that he committed all five murders by using the five Chinese elements."

"Yeah, we discussed this yesterday; I understand that, I'm not stupid son, So, if you're correct. Hao's mission, to call it a better word, has now been completed; he just needs to make it back to Hong Kong for the Chinese New Year."

"Yes, sir, the year of the Dragon, for the end game, the gathering of the seven stars."

"And when exactly is this Chinese year of the Dragon, son"?

"Five days sir, so we haven't got long, where's Scott and Felicity"?

McGovern hair lifted on the back of his neck, as he suddenly felt the sensation of being dragged through his own arse backwards "Oh them, yeah, shit, I've sent them to check out the flat that Lee, or as we now know him Kong Hoa was renting."

Oscar's face turned ashen. "We better let them know, stop them. It could be dangerous, he could be in there, they don't have a clue what they could be walking into, and we now know what he's capable of."

McGovern got up and raced over to Gatsby's office. "Better still, I'll speak to Gatsby get the OK to send in the armed response unit, and I better warn them we have officers present we want a result here not Sergeant Barney Stallone and his trigger happy bunch of expendables charging in for a gun fight at the OK fucking corral."

THIRTY SEVEN

Felicity Somerton and Stan Scott were still standing at the main door of the block of executive flats waiting for the landlord to arrive and neither were really surprised when Walter Chang turned up.

Stan Scott rolled his eyes to the sky "Might have known it would be you Walter," shaking his limp clammy hand.

Chang's lips pressed together in a tight grimace as he was quick to distance himself from the tenant. "I had no idea who was living here, honestly, the rent was paid upfront for two months, and I never heard from the tenant and didn't even know who he was."

Stan Scott stared at him miserably then looked away as Walter fished the key from his pocket with his bony hands and turned the lock.

Just as Walter was about to open the front door of the apartment, there was a shout as his face seemed to shrivel.

"ARMED POLICE, NOBODY MOVE"! At first Stan Scott thought that this was some kind of joke that was of course, until several armed officers in full battle dress rushed in and passed them all carrying MP5SFA3 semi automatic weapons. His smile quickly dimmed.

Each room in turn was carefully and methodically checked by the firearms officers then, and only when they were sure nobody was home, were the two detectives and Walter Chang, allowed to enter.

They walked along the long passageway with an extremely high ceiling. The floor was intricately patterned with marble and the furniture was gold and ornate.

Felicity Somerton was well impressed."Not bad," she said sarcastically. She, along with Stan Scott could only dream of being able to afford something of this grandeu "It's a lot more upmarket from my humble dwelling, with my wickes wallpaper and Eastenders. A girl could get lost just going to the bathroom. Do you own any of the other apartments in this block, Mr Chang"?

Chang shook his head; he stopped to pick up some takeaway leaflets that had been dropped on the floor. "No, just this one, couldn't afford any more."

Stan Scott was equally impressed, glancing around, craning his head, trying to take it all in."So what was the rent for this place then"?

"Fifteen hundred pounds, per calendar month."

"This isn't homes under the fucking hammer you know Walter, so how did Lee afford to pay that much"?

Chang just shook his head and remained silent. Felicity Somerton looked out of one of the large windows at the end of the passageway. "I think it's fairly likely that it wasn't him who paid it, you said it was paid two months in advance"?

Chang nodded his head, "Yes, the money came from the same Hong Kong based bank that the money for Alex Brennan came from. The lady I spoke to said it was for a Doctor who was having a two month placement at the RVI."

Stan Scott had other concerns "And you didn't think to mention this earlier, Walter"?

"Well, erm, no, sorry."

"Just slipped your mind eh."

The place didn't look lived in, but was mightily impressive. It was luxurious living of the highest possible nature. Complete with a bespoke glass spiral staircase, contemporary furnishings throughout and magnificent panoramic views all within the most exquisite of this quayside penthouse. It was a most impressive and luxuriously appointed Duplex Penthouse apartment which was superbly located.

The search of the apartment continued, they went to work, but found nothing. Scott taking the bedrooms and kitchen, Felicity the living room and bathroom. The property was a spacious apartment, with floor to ceiling full-height windows to the North West aspect across the River Tyne and Newcastle City, with glazed doors leading out to a balcony, combined with a stylish kitchen with window overlooking The Sage music venue.

The kitchen like everything else in the apartment was unnecessarily large. Stan Scott looked in the fridge, and what a fridge, an enormous American style brushed steel one with two doors, nothing inside, not even a can or bottle of beer.

On the first level were three double bedrooms, one with an en-suite, and one with a balcony, along with a second bathroom. There were no toiletries, towels or even toilet paper.

Stan Scott had checked all the wardrobes and drawers, slowly and carefully, room by room each containing nothing at all. There was no sign that anyone had *ever* been living there, no personal items, nothing. Whoever had been there had gone, and wasn't coming back. Stan Scott's phone was ringing; he'd had three missed calls, all from McGovern. He had a voice message. He listened to the message and sighed, lifting one eyebrow.

"Daniel Lee's real name is Kong Hoa, he's the Red Pole, don't, under any circumstances, go into the flat, until the armed response unit get there, he could still be in there."

"Now he tells us, I better give him a ring." McGovern answered immediately

"Jim, the place was empty; looks doubtful anyone *ever* lived there; it's totally clean. He's packed his stuff and fucked off."

"Can you two get back here as soon as you can, we need to contact the airport security, Hoa will be trying to get out of the country."

THIRTY EIGHT

Back in the incident room there was a buzz of excitement and adrenaline. Things were moving fast.

Ann Gatsby walked in, her heart was pounding. "We've got to act quickly; Kong Hoa could be on a plane as we speak. We need to get the airport security on board, get the fire arms units over there, if he's heading out of the country we've got to get him stopped, he turned to the other officers, you three start checking the passenger bookings, call in any spare officers we've got. Check the next few flights to Hong Kong."

Oscar for once was a little concerned at the size of the task, "It's not gonna be easy maam, it's Chinese New Year in a few days, you got any idea how many Chinese people will be heading out the country"?

"Get that mug shot, of Kong Hoa circulated." Ann Gatsby had the bit between her teeth. "We're gonna catch this bastard before he gets out of the country. We're pretty sure he'll have a fake passport, we know he's got money. I'll contact some people in the know, see if they can fast track us to some flight manifests, and check on foreign travel."

Gatsby and McGovern went into the office of George Crammond as Oscar received the email lists from the airport with the passenger names for the next few flights to Hong Kong. McGovern was back in the office after a few moments and was busy fastening his coat. "Any luck son"?

"No sir, but just as we thought, there's a lot of Chinese people heading out to Hong Kong, the airport has said there's extra flights on. It's gonna be like looking for a needle in a haystack."

"More like a fucking noodle in a haystack, Ha Ha." McGovern was well pleased with his cheesy attempt at a pun.

"To be fair sir, until we know what name he's using it's going to be like looking for a needle in a stack of needles, now what alias is he going to use"?

McGovern scratched his bearded chin, "I suppose it would be too easy if he went by Kong Hao or Daniel Lee."

"Yes sir, there's a few Daniel Lee's on some of the flights but as you say he aint gonna use that name, he isn't that stupid, but we should still check them out just in case."

"Well, get the uniforms onto that, we've got enough to do."

Felicity offered an opinion.

"What about Michael Yin"?

McGovern stopped in his tracks "Why is that name familiar"?

Felicity opened her note book to check her facts,

"He was the one employee at the football club that we couldn't track down, false address, false paperwork, that might be the name he's using, but there's a lot of

Michael Yin's heading out of Newcastle airport to Hong Kong, at least thirty on these lists, if he was going to use a false name, it may as well be a popular one."

"Well, get them all checked out, what we've got to hope is that he hasn't left the country already, get airport security to check the CCTV."

"Will do sir."

McGovern left for the airport as Oscar, Felicity and Stan Scott continued to check lists and enlisted the help of a couple of Detective constables that Gatsby and Crammond had pulled from other lesser cases to assist. Oscar passed on the information needed and left to join McGovern at the airport.

Oscar drove through the heavy traffic and his mind went over and over the case. He wasn't convinced Kong Hao would be on *any* of the flights, *surely he would know that once we were onto him the airport would be on lock down.* He was pleased that the case appeared to be coming to a conclusion. Due to the joint efforts of him and other forces across Europe all but three of the supposed seven stars had been apprehended. Kong Hao and the other two operating in Holland and Italy.

Oscar's car came to a stop in a long traffic jam. He looked to his right. The outside lane was also blocked. He looked at some billboards on the side of the road. He read the catchy slogan.

DFDS ferries gateway to Holland, Europe and the world. Oscar had a hunch, *Wait a minute; he's not leaving by plane, he's leaving the country the traditional way by ferry boat.* He pulled over to the side of the road and got out his mobile and phoned McGovern.

THIRTY NINE

Newcastle airport was busy most times, but, due to Chinese New Year it was busier and more disorganized than usual.

In no time at all extra armed Police wandered around the groups of hundreds of people in the departure lounges, uniformed officers and interpreters spoke with passengers showing them photo's of Kong Hao, no planes would be leaving for Hong Kong today.

If Kong Hao hadn't fled the country by now he wasn't going anywhere today, but with Chinese New Year in a few days, lots of disgruntled people queued to complain at various information desks, in a word it was chaotic and how anybody had hoped to spot Kong Hao was any bodies guess.

McGovern pushed through a large group of Chinese people as his phone rang he could barely hear it. He answered it. "Sorry son, can't hear what you're saying, it's like fucking pearl harbour in here"!

Oscar quickly corrected his Inspector "Pearl Harbour was Japanese sir, not Chinese, well, actually it was in the South Pacific____"

McGovern Interrupted but something about the poor signal made him sound like he was standing in a deep hole "You nearly here? We could do with a pair of extra eyes and especially someone who knows what Hao looks like."

A middle aged Chinese man spoke in a raised voice at a poor airport worker who couldn't understand a word he was saying.

McGovern put his finger in his other ear and scrunched up his face trying to listen to what Oscar was telling him "Never mind that son, where are you, Hoa's not getting out of this airport, it's in lock down."

Oscar did his best to be heard "I think he will try to get out of the country by sea sir."
McGovern's face tightened. "You what, *sea*, what's your thinking behind that"?

"The Gan-Yin are a traditional syndicate. They pride themselves on using traditional methods. The Emperor who sent his generals to Europe sent them *BY SEA*. I'm sure he's going back via the ferry, that's the rules, that's the game. He *has* to get back to Hong Kong by sea or at least out of England that way."

McGovern gave a deep weighted sigh, "That's a massive call son, you sure"?

"It's got to be by sea, it's part of the game. He knows the airports would be the first place we'd lock down anyway. I think he's heading for Holland to meet up with the other two of the remaining seven stars and they will travel together from Italy."

McGovern spoke while nodding his head, he'd never doubted Oscar's judgement in the past and it wasn't time to start now. "Okay son, I'll need to speak to Gatsby. We better still have a presence here just in case, you're wrong." *But then again you're never wrong are you.*

McGovern ended the call and put his phone into his pocket. He knew what was left of his career was on the line if Oscar had got this wrong and he'd backed his judgement. But the buck wouldn't just stop with him. All he had to do now was convince Ann Gatsby and Chief Superintendent Crammond.

Gatsby and McGovern stood in front of Chief Superintendent George Crammond as he leaned back in his chair.

McGovern got the impression that he was being hung out to dry.

"Now let me get this straight, We have every available officer looking for this Kong Hao fellow at the airport and now you want me to put the ferry port in lock down too?. Just how many people do you think I can free up to do this, and I suppose this is all your idea Jim, and just because a young detective has a feeling, no evidence or sightings, just a whim."

McGovern gave a disbelieving double take when Ann Gatsby spoke up. "No sir, this is my call, we need to do this. I have spoken to my team and we ALL believe this is the best thing to do. I've spoken to DS Smiles and I agree with both him and DI McGovern. You asked me to come here and lead this team and I have every faith in them."

Crammond sat in deep thought as Gatsby looked at McGovern who nodded his head in agreement.

Crammond leaned forward staring at them both intently. "Well, we have to get this so well organised they'll not scream at the cost." He picked up the phone and began to dial the ferry port "Oh well, what the Hell, but Ann, this is on you if it all goes tits up, we must come away with something that will prove it was worth it."

"Thank you sir." They both nodded in agreement.

CHAPTER FORTY

Kong Hao made his way through the many passengers at the ferry terminal. He bought himself a black coffee and sat in a large lounge looking around, pleased with himself, his trail almost complete.

Need to keep my nerve, play it cool, if they get any clue I'm here the armed response unit will be round so fast they'll melt the tarmac on the road.

He got up from his chair and made his way through the security checks, he handed his fake passport over. He didn't blink as much as an eyelid as the security offer scrutinized his ID

"Thank you Mr Yin, have a good trip."

"Thank you."

He had enjoyed being Michael Yin but had enjoyed being Daniel lee much more. Pity he'd had to kill Sara Chang she would have made him a lot of money and boy was she up for it.

He smiled when he thought of her ample buttocks swaying, her wide moist mouth and her bright red lips. He became aroused at the memories of the agony and suffering he'd put her through for his own sexual delight.

And what about young Felicity?. It was amazing what a girl would do for you with the right mix of Rohypnol and vodka, and, if Mick Western hadn't got so greedy and kept his fucking mouth shut she would now be starting her new career in some seedy old brothel somewhere south of Bucharest. She did give him a fantastic blow job, just a shame she couldn't remember it. But he'd always have the crudely made videos to remind him of their time together.

The boarding was almost complete, the ferry left in an hour. As Hao was on board ship he was unaware of the growing Police presence around the Terminal, he too was unaware that his journey home was about to become a little more complicated than he had anticipated.

Oscar's car raced to the Ferry terminal car Park, following several speeding patrol cars. The scene was already somewhat disorderly as the Police were just beginning to try to evacuate the immediate area around the terminal.

There were lots of discontented passengers. Nobody else would be allowed onto the ferry and the huge job of evacuating the ship had begun.

A tannoy announcement made Hao's stomach churn.

"Could all passengers please disembark from the ferry in an orderly fashion, please make your way to the exits; please don't be alarmed, we will hopefully sort this problem out soon, sorry for your inconvenience."

Hao felt had only one option, to hide on the ship, and mingle with the other passengers. Once the Police were sure he wasn't there and had let the passengers back on board he was as good as gone.

But Kong Hao was a man under pressure and he was about to make a mistake that would confirm to the Police that he *was* onboard the ferry.

The terminal building was slowly but surely filling to capacity, but as no movement onboard it became very full. Several passengers asked what was happening. Why aren't they boarding? and when boarding would commence , but no information was available.

Oscar flashed his badge and made his way past the police cordon, through the crowds and the chaos, onto the deck of the large ship, the Princess.

Built in the nineteen eighties the impressive ship had recently been renovated bringing it fully up-to-date. With room for over a thousand passengers this large cruise ferry offered a great mix of restaurants, shops, a casino, bars - and much more.

The ship, to his untrained eye, appeared to be an old one that has been obviously refitted, Oscar noticed that it had plenty of eating options, a buffet-style restaurant, an a la carte called Blue Riband, a steakhouse, a cafe/cake shop that also serves snacks and bar food, fish and chips, *McGovern would love it on here!,* he thought, as well as a compass bar, roof bar, casino, evening entertainment, shop and a children's play area. Plenty of options and more importantly, plenty of places to hide.

Finding Hao was not going to be either quick or easy on this huge floating village, and the biggest problem they had at the moment was evacuating the ship.

Deck five was very crowded. The passengers waited for more direction from the intercom, and the crew, before coming down to disembark. Many disgruntled passengers with no room to go to with their luggage were obviously frustrated that their mini break to Amsterdam was on temporary hold, and looked to take out their anger on anyone in a uniform.

There was always going to be a few drunken parties of lads on mini breaks and stag do's and also groups of hen parties too, these made the job that bit more difficult but the police and cruise staff were doing a good job at keeping things good humoured as the evacuation continued.

A small mixed race Chinese girl was playing hide and seek with her mother, the sound of her chortled laughter and bright shiny smile was captivating.

Deck five of the ship had large pillars and thick carpet, ideal terrain for a game of hide and seek.

The girl would creep up behind her mother and shout 'Boo' as her mothers fake shock would send her into further hysterics. As Oscar smiled at the sound of her deep uncontrollable laughter, he tried to keep his focus as he looked around. Kong Hoa was on this ship somewhere, he was sure, and the sooner the ship could be evacuated the sooner the search could intensify.

As the little girl's game continued, Oscar's attention was distracted by a scuffle. Two men from rival stag parties being pulled apart while they remonstrated with each other.

The commotion was interrupted by the little Chinese girl's cries "Mommy, where are you?, Mommy"? her sad, pale face and dark hair made her seem even more fragile as the tears welled up in her eyes.

Her mother was nowhere to be seen. Her mother had disappeared. Kong Hao needed an insurance policy and Kong Hao now had a hostage.

FORTY ONE

As news of the pending evacuation spread, press reporters, TV and radio crews began to arrive just as vultures would when spotting a dying animal, or as McGovern would put it flies gathering around shit.

As he waited for Gatsby to arrive McGovern was aware that he did not want to cause any unnecessary panic especially as there were still several hundred people to be evacuated from the ship.

Releasing a statement to the press that there was a fugitive suspected of several murders hiding on the vessel would have been excellent box office, and great for the reporters, however, wouldn't have made the evacuation process any easier. That would be Crammond or Ann Gatsby's job anyway, *thank fuck*.

Although Ann Gatsby was in overall charge of the investigation Chief Superintendent George Crammond was in constant contact. This after all, was a very high profile case involving five murders.

Crammond informed Gatsby that the armed response unit was on standby and parked up half a mile away. He was concerned, like McGovern, that the sight of Police officers with firearms would cause a great deal of panic; they had to clear the area of the general public first.

Oscar approached McGovern with news "I think he may have taken a hostage, Chinese woman, she's disappeared, a young child she had with her is currently with a female PC. It's too early to tell but she was there one minute and gone the next, they've put out various tannoy announcements but as yet, nothing."

With everybody heading the other way, Kong Hao led the woman along the increasingly sparse corridor that smelt of metal polish, carpet cleaner and un-emptied ashtrays.

His hand jerked up, he knew if he'd tried to cover her mouth she would struggle, his voice had a menacing tone, "Just do as I say and everything will be fine." The frightened woman didn't speak, she just nodded her head. Hoa looked through the large porthole window. He could see the increasing number of Police cars and the ferry evacuation was in full swing.

They walked through some double doors and into a restaurant area of the ship. Spotting the kitchen area Hoa went through the staff only door, dragging the woman with him.

Inside he found meals in the process of being prepared, it was all a little eerie and Marie Celeste like. There was no sign of anyone.

Hoa scoured the area, thinking of his next move. He began opening drawers; he hit the jackpot almost straight away. The knife draw. An abundance of different sized knives with different coloured handles. He picked up a large six inch bladed knife with a red handle, and looked at the chart on the wall in front of him.

Turning to the woman, he smirked, "Red handle, for red meat, got to have the right knife now, haven't we"? The woman remained silent as Hoa moved behind her and grabbed her by the hair pulling her head back towards him as he put the large knife to her throat. "You *are* going to be a good girl, aren't you?, none of this shouting or screaming shit." Again the girl just nodded.

Hoa removed the knife from her throat leaving a small red mark against her skin, where the blade had rested heavily and grabbed her by her wrist tightly causing her to wince as he led her further, deeper into the ship's cabin areas.

What exactly he planned to do, he wasn't sure. He had to find a place to hide out as he walked along the passageways trying cabin doors, each one locked until he eventually found an open door. He took the woman inside and locked it.

The security man was quite pleased with his work as he reported back to McGovern.

"That's almost it sir, most of the passengers are off the Ferry, we've checked the names."

McGovern nodded but remained solem, "Sorry son but most is not good enough, we need them *all* off. I don't want anybody else at risk."

The passengers were now being escorted away from the terminal area and into the large car park, as uniformed officers began to cordon off the area.

Many passengers stayed but most headed the short trip up the road to the Royal Quays shopping outlet for much needed refreshments, coffee's tea, or indeed something a bit stronger.

McGovern was looking around for Oscar and tutted loudly when he saw him assisting an elderly lady with a rather heavy looking suitcase.

McGovern took out a cigarette, lit it, and walked over towards him. "That's very honourable of you but, there are uniforms and Ferry staff to do that sort of thing."

"Sorry sir, just thought I'd help things along a bit, we got a plan yet"?

McGovern took a large drag from his cigarette and let the smoke out slowly, "Crammond wants the armed response and dog team in ASAP, he wants things brought to a head."

"Anything we can do"?

McGovern shook his head, "Not really Gatsby's thinking of putting an appeal out to Hoa, give him the chance to give himself up."

Oscar nodded, "Well, I don't think this is gonna end well somehow."

"Me too son, but she's adamant, we've got to give him the chance to come quietly. I suppose she's right though, the last thing we want is a fucking bloodbath."

The security officer came back over to where McGovern and Oscar stood, he had news. "Everyone booked on board is now accounted for except Michael Yin and the missing woman, 30 year old Lizzie Sutherland."

"Sutherland, "? McGovern gave the security man a dazed look. "I thought she was Chinese."

"She could be married sir, to an Englishman."

"Or Scotsman," McGovern quickly pointing out the Celtic sounding surname.

A large BMW X5 Police car, pulled up just outside the Police cordon. McGovern nodded his head towards it while dropping his cigarette and putting it out with his heel.

Chief Superintendent George Crammond and DCI Ann Gatsby stepped out of the back seats, Crammond in full uniform. McGovern rolled his eyes, hardly ecstatic at what he saw as certain glory hunting interference. "Wouldn't be a fucking show without punch and Judy would it."

Crammond walked quickly towards them, "The press want answers, I've arranged to speak to them in half an hour. There's some rumours of a terrorist attack flooding social media so we need to make a statement, what's the latest here."

McGovern gave a sigh and began updating them. "Hoa's on board, he's going by the name of Michael Yin, and has a hostage, a woman, 30 years old called

Lizzie Sutherland. The boat has been evacuated, and as far as we know there are only those two on board now."

Crammond nodded slowly and turned towards Ann Gatsby,"Are the armed response team and the dog unit in position yet"?

"No sir, there on standby, I think we should give Hoa the chance to give himself up first."

"Yes, Ann, that's a good idea, I have to agree with you."

Now *There' a fucking first,* McGovern thought.

Oscar had gone back to the gangway of the Ferry, it was deserted.

A Police helicopter hovered in the sky above him. He looked at the river; four small Police launches from the Tyneside Police's marine unit circled the starboard side of the large ship, the putt-putt sound of their small motors, overwhelmed by the noise of rotating helicopter blades in the sky.

A long loud continuous beep from the Ferry PA system rang out, signaling an important safety announcement, it was loud enough to ensure everyone who was on the ship would take note. But only two people were on board, and the message was only for one of them.

"This is Detective Chief Inspector Ann Gatsby. Kong Hoa, we know you can hear this message, and we know you have a hostage with you. Release the girl and give yourself up. There's no-where for you to go. The Ferry is surrounded, please; don't let anybody else get hurt. I will give you thirty minutes to give yourself up. I assure you will not be harmed if you comply with this request."

Couldn't say she wasn't giving him a chance, Oscar thought.

Lizzie Sutherland sat on the cabin bed, her hands bound with thick wraps of cling film. She was small, quite petite and had long straight shoulder length black hair. She wore a knee length white skirt, pink blouse and matching flip flops. She at last found the courage to speak "Are you going to kill me"?

Kong Hoa gave her a lopsided smile "No, I'm not going to kill you."

"Why"? she asked hesitantly.

"Like the Chief Inspector said, enough people have been hurt, I'm trapped, and killing you wouldn't help my situation, would it"?

"Well, are you going to let me go then"? her lips were stiffening, trembling.

"Not yet, what's your name anyway"?

"It's Lizzie, Lizzie Sutherland."

"Sutherland, now that's a good old traditional Chinese surname isn't it"?

"I'm married to a local man, a doctor."

Hoa gave a disgusted snort. "Chinese people should stick to our own kind. I don't agree with these mixed marriages we Chinese are a proud nation. We should be at the forefront of world politics; we should be ruling the world. People like you and that Walter Chang and your love for westerners, makes me sick."

Lizzie bit her lip as tears welled in her eyes. Hoa was heartless. She could tell this man didn't feel an ounce of compassion for her. She could see the anger growing in Hoa's crazed eyes as he bared his teeth in his growling mouth, the veins on his temple and neck standing out. He took out the knife, lifted it up and banged it against the cabin wall, causing a loud metallic clang.

Hoa did not accept women were equals. His feelings for women, and what he knew about them could have been written on the back of a toilet door, and usually were. In fact he felt they should all be kept in a cage and only let out when men wanted to fuck or be fed and he wasn't feeling hungry. She could read horror in his eyes, it was her own.

He raised his sharp chin and gazed down at her. He found her pleasing to the eye. The way her skirt clutched at her hips aroused him.

"You know a girl with your looks could make a lot of money back in Hong Kong."

She gave him a nervous smile.

"For me, that is," her face turned sad.

"Bet you've never even had a Yellow dick inside you either have you"?

Lizzie remained quiet, but feared the worst, just as Sara Chang had. Her mouth was dry, her head felt doughy as her skull throbbed.

Hoa continued, "I've probably got about twenty minutes before the cavalry come after me, just twenty more minutes of freedom, and twenty minutes before you'll never see me again. I know I'm not going to get away."

Hoa stood up and began to undo his trousers. "You might as well have your first bit of fun with a Chinese man, who knows, you might even enjoy it."

Lizzie Sutherland felt a horror growing inside her that she had never felt before. She felt the breath leave her body, fear took hold as Hoa approached her. The fury and dismay in her eyes was replaced with something else-fear.

To Hoa rape wasn't a crime. It was just another weapon to be used to annihilate or break someone and this time it was to be the unfortunate Lizzy Sutherland.

FORTY TWO

McGovern was pacing around the terminal area.

"I don't like it, I knew he wouldn't give himself up. We should have gone straight in, I told her, don't give the bastard a chance."

The armed response unit was prepared and waiting for the call to action. The dog section was ready too, four German Shepherd dogs barking in anticipated excitement.

"I didn't think that this was going to end well either." Oscar checked his watch, there was five minutes to go. "I've got an idea sir, that woman Lizzie Sutherland. She must have a mobile phone; maybe we could ring her, speak to Hoa, and see what he wants."

McGovern nodded but his tight expression told he wasn't so sure. "I suppose it's worth a go, might buy us a bit more time but I doubt it."

Oscar approached the front Desk of the security officer who was the only member of staff still in the terminal area. "The missing woman? Lizzie Sutherland, does she have a mobile number on record"?

The security man checked the computer and there was. He wrote the number down for Oscar, who dialled the number and placed the phone to his ear as he made his way back over to where McGovern was standing.

A faint trembling voice answered. "Hello."

"Lizzie"?

"Yes, that's me."

"Is he with you? Kong Koa? Is he there"?

"No, he's gone."

"Are you okay"?

There was a pause. "He raped me"!

Oscar was lost for words, but he knew they needed to get to her as soon as they could. "Do you know where you are"?

There was another pause. "Hold on I'll just check." Oscar could hear Lizzie moving around the cabin. then her trembling voice came back on the phone. "Cabin thirty six on the fifth deck."

"Lock the door, we're coming to get you."

Once the news that the hostage had been safely locked in the cabin, Gatsby gave the signal for the armed response unit to take over proceedings.

There were five Armed Response units at the scene; each with three officers in police uniform who ensured the fastest response. Each member of the crew had specific functions whilst responding to calls. The operator was responsible for the many communications and extracting the maximum amount of information prior to their arrival. The observer had a plan of the ship and provided the other firearms officers with all the information they needed for a full search of the vessel.

Oscar couldn't count how many firearms officers boarded the ship, must have been at least twenty.

Crammond arrived at the scene. "I see he hasn't given himself up then, never mind, we tried our best to end this peacefully."

McGovern and Oscar followed behind the armed officers. Hoa could be anywhere; they had to keep their wits about them. Slowly but surely the firearms officers made their way along deck five, heading for cabin thirty six, checking every nook and cranny as they went.

Crammond was wearing a headset and was in direct contact with Gatsby and the lead firearms officer. Each cabin was methodically checked, and double checked. Only when the armed officers were sure that an area was secure they would shout out a loud "Clear,"and let the detectives proceed.

It was taking an age, but they needed to be thorough. No passengers could be allowed back onto the ferry with Hoa still at large. Imagine the public panic and outcry should he manage to get away.

At last they reached the cabin where Lizzie Sutherland was. "Armed Police, open the door." There was no response.

Oscar decided to give it a try. "Lizzie, this is Detective sergeant Oscar Smiles, we spoke on the phone, you're safe now, could you open the door, please, if you can."

They heard a slight shuffling noise and then a click, as the door slowly opened. The armed Police raced in first scaring the already traumatised woman who screamed out loudly.

McGovern wasn't impressed. "Stupid Bastards, take it easy man, the woman's been through enough."

Lizzie sat on the bed in her bra and panties. She clasped her knees and bent forward. her eyes were reddened with tears and her face bared the bruises of a roughing up. Her back was covered in bite marks. Her skin was pale, her eyes had lost their sparkle.

Oscar approached her to hand her a dressing gown that was hanging on the back of the door, she turned away from him and screamed. He took out his phone and dialled a number. "Could you get a couple of female uniforms up here please as soon as you can thank you"?

Oscar tried to reassure Lizzie that her ordeal was over. Hoa had killed five people in some warped, perverted way she had been the lucky one. *Although try telling that to her now.*

The female officers arrived in no time at all, with Felicity Somerton a few seconds later, Felicity helped Lizzie into the dressing gown, produced a tissue and dabbed her eyes, which filled with tears and her hand grasped Felicity's even more tighter, as another uniformed officer picked her discarded clothes from the floor.

Lizzie was still trembling and her eyes were red rimmed from weeping. She was biting her lower lip as tears welled up and as she wiped her face with the back of her hand the tears trickled back down her cheeks as

Felicity put her arm around her and led her out of the cabin and along the narrow corridor.

Oscar and McGovern now stood alone in the cabin, as the armed response unit continued to search the lower decks of the Ferry.

McGovern's throat was parched "Not much we can do now son, better let the experts do their thing, Fancy a drink? Crammond's press conference should be on the TV Soon."

"Only if you're paying and it comes via a boiling kettle."

"Spoil sport."

They headed off the boat and into the deserted terminal area, the TV was on and the coffee machine was working. Oscar brought the drinks over to the table where McGovern was sitting.

Sky news were live from the North Shields ferry terminal, McGovern pointed to the screen, and to a reporter with a familiar face. "Must be the biggest news story they've had for a while. It wouldn't be a major incident without Kay fucking Burley, you know, that gobby bird off the telly."

Sure enough Sky news had sent the big guns up from London.

McGovern took a lazy sip from his strong bitter coffee and his face grimaced "This coffee's fucking horrible. They're probably hoping it's a terrorist attack."

"Don't be daft sir, who would hope for a terrorist attack"?

McGovern pointed towards the TV, "Those bastards out there, the press, Sky news, BBC, they like nothing better man."

Oscar sat beside McGovern, and took a guarded sip of his tea, not quite as bad as McGovern's coffee, but hardly anything to write home about.

The press conference was about to start. Some uniformed officers joined them in the large empty terminal area as they all crowded around the nearest table to the fairly large screen on the wall, the sound was on, but thankfully, so were the subtitles.

Crammond and DCI Gatsby appeared on screen to a few boos and catcalls, mostly from McGovern. "Wehhey it's the fucking Krankies!"

Crammond kept it brief and to the point in what turned out to be a text book press conference. "Following a hunch from investigating officers, armed Police officers were deployed to the North Shields Ferry terminal earlier today. As we speak, highly trained firearms officers are currently searching the King Seaways Ferry. We believe a fugitive is on board who is a suspect in on-going murder enquires. We are not looking for anybody else in connection with these crimes. The area has been secured, the ship has been evacuated and we feel there is no immediate danger to public safety. It is very unlikely that this man, Kong Hoa.....", Crammond held up an A4 size photograph, and was almost blinded in a blaze of camera flash bulbs from the dozens of cameras in the makeshift press room "....It is highly unlikely that he would be able to get off the boat, however, we believe him to be armed, extremely dangerous, and he shouldn't be approached by the public, any questions please"?

"Kay Burley, sky news. Does he have any hostages? as; earlier reports stated he had taken a young woman."

Crammond looked to Ann Gatsby who took a sip of water before gathering her thoughts "We don't believe that there are any hostages left on the ship. No."

Kay Burley continued, "Can you confirm there was a hostage and that she is now safe and well"?

Crammond answered this one "A thirty year old woman was taken from the ferry approximately thirty minutes ago by our officers."

"Was she injured, was she harmed"?

Again Crammond answered "She is currently being assessed by a medical team; we believe her *physical* injuries to be minor."

Although he hated him, McGovern was impressed, "You gotta hand it to the old bastard, they're not gonna get any change out of him are they....."

"Shush man, sir," Oscar interrupted him and held up his hand.

Back on the TV screen Crammond pointed to an older grey haired reporter near the back of the room.

"Colin Briggs, BBC. Is this man the main suspect in the murders of Alex Brennan, Sara Chang, David

Leung, Mick Western and Detective Constable Daniel Lee"?

Crammond thought deeply for a second or two as if to ensure the names quoted were all familiar to him. He conferred silently with Ann Gatsby before answering. He nodded, "We believe so, yes."

"Do you have any motive, as yet, how are these murders connected"?

Ann Gatsby took this question "We believe the murders are connected, yes, but it's all part of an ongoing investigation, and I'm not obliged to give out any theories on motive as yet."

A young female reporter raised her hand, Crammond spotted her."The young lady in green, second row."

"Thank you, Sophie Richmond ITN. There are rumours that these murders are related to some kind of turf war involving a Triad syndicate and that some Police Officers are going to be implicated in corruption allegations; can you throw any light on this"?

Ann Gatsby was about to answer but Crammond took the lead, shaking his head and holding up his arm "No, No, I can categorically rule out any wrongdoing from Police officers, this is also no turf war. The man we are looking to apprehend is believed to be a member of a Triad group, yes, who are operating, not just in Newcastle but all over the country, but there 's no truth in any corruption stories."

"Is there any truth in the internet rumours, that the wanted man was once a Police Officer"?

Again Crammond took another sip of water and wiped his top lip before answering, "The man we are looking for *Is not* and has *never* been a Police officer, however there were reports circulating that he may or may not have been impersonating a Police officer at some time previously."

Sophie continued. "There have been reports of similar crimes all across Europe involving members of this Triad group, surely these are connected"?

That was an easy one that Crammond let Gatsby answer. "We believe so, yes." Crammond stood up from his chair "There will be another update as soon as we have any news, but as for now, please, ladies and gentlemen, no further questions."

Oscar was also impressed, "Well, sir, they certainly know how to handle the press, just as well it wasn't you up there eh"?

McGovern gave Oscar a playful slap on the back of his head. "Cheeky bastard."

FORTY THREE

The initial search of the Ferry had produced nothing. Not a sign of Hoa anywhere. The next stage was to send in the dogs. If he was still on board then there was no way they would miss him.

The dog's had waited a while and were raring to go. Oscar thought about Buster as he saw the dogs let off their leashes on each of the five separate decks, closely followed by their handlers and the new shift of firearm officers.

The police dogs always provided a vital supporting role in the reduction of crime. They tracked Kong Hoa from deck to deck, the firearms unit, searched cabin by cabin, inch by inch, the net was closing and fast.

Oscar had considered becoming a dog handler. But alas it wouldn't be for Buster. The Police looked for dogs that were energetic, focused and toy-orientated. They needed dogs that would be able to focus on the same task for a long time. That's where Buster would have probably fallen well short.

Not all dogs had the skills and personality to become a police dog. The dogs saw their work as a game, that's Buster alright, but the handler needed to be able to direct them and teach them how they want it and Buster was never going to be reliable like that. *Wonder how he was, the little feller, better call his granddad and ask.*

Oscar walked outside the Terminal building. He could see the Police cordon some two hundred yards away. There seemed to be more press, and TV cameras than bystanders. Oscar took his mobile phone out of his pocket and phoned his Grandfather. He answered with his usual comment

"Hello, Alfred Smiles speaking."

"Grandad, you okay, how's things going"?

"Things are good son, Buster's just had some chicken for his dinner, hey, I'm watching the news, and it's live from the North Shields ferry. You not caught that bugger yet"?

"No, not yet, but the net is closing, the dog's have gone in."

"Ah well if they only had Buster there you'd have him banged up by now, hey see if you can get in shot, give me a wave Oscar, go on."

"Grandad, it's not transfer deadline day you know, anyway, I'm sure there's no shortage of little chavs pulling faces and behaving like performing chimps for the TV Cameras."

"Yes, there is, young Kyle from down the street, I've seen him and Steven and Brenda's youngest Callum, he's been riding his bike round and round on that bloody mobile phone of his, it's compulsive viewing this, it's better than the soaps"!

Oscar didn't really know who his Grandad was talking about, and was sure that Steven and Brenda's youngest son he knew of would probably be about twenty four years old!

"Any way granddad, I better get back to McGovern; do you want anything bringing in"?

The line went quiet for a moment, and then, "Tin of beans and some toilet rolls," Oscar laughed at the somewhat nutty combination.

"Okay, I'll get some on my way home."

Oscar joined McGovern just inside the Police cordon, everything was eerily quiet and then, the sound of shouting and barking dogs broke the tense silence.

"ARMED POLICE PUT YOUR HANDS UP"! As Kong Hao reached inside his jacket for his knife, the order was given. He was hurled back under a hail of bullets, and swayed like a well twatted boxer, before falling backwards with only the water to break his fall.

Moments later the Tyneside Police Marine unit were fishing a body of a Chinese man out of the River Tyne and that person was definitely dead. Three gunshot wounds to the head and one to the neck. Dead long before he hit the water.

The body was lifted out of the river and into a small Police launch craft; and put into a black body bag.

Oscar walked over to the edge of the jetty next to the ship where Felicity Somerton and Stan Scott were standing.

McGovern was some yards away polluting the environment smoking his customary cigarette as Ann Gatsby approached him "Well Jim I would like to thank you for your efforts in helping to solve this case. I know we haven't always seen eye to eye but I have enjoyed working with you and wanted to be the first to tell you that Crammond has asked me to stay on for a bit longer."

McGovern smiled at her for probably the first time ever. "You did well Ann, really well. You didn't have to trust that lad's instinct but you did, putting your neck on the line like that and believe me, I respect you for that. It means a lot, you've said yes, I take it"?

Ann Gatsby gave a prim smile, she still disliked him intensely but as a team they had all worked well together and they had got the result.

Gatsby looked over towards Oscar, Felicity and Stan Scott in the distance. They were laughing and chatting. She knew that she would have a fantastic team under her "I've asked for some time to think it over. I'm proud of you all. You *have* a great team here, all the knowhow and experience of you and Stan, little Felicity beavering away, she's good, and as for Oscar Smiles, he's a bit weird but boy, what a detective he is. As we might be going to have to all get along I need you to start by remembering to call me ma'am in front of the team and not Ann please, if you could be so kind, but well done again."

"Thank you_Ma'am, " he said, disliking the woman's attitude, *she couldn't do it could she, it had to be a backhanded compliment, never mind.* but for the first time ever he respected her as a boss and more importantly as a woman.

The marine unit had reached the jetty and the body was being lifted ashore.

McGovern and Gatsby joined the rest of the team. McGovern needed to be sure. As impatient as always he had the usual edge to his voice. "Go on then, Einstein, open it up."

They all waited with baited breath as a young marine officer struggled to open the body bag, his hands trembling as he tried to get a decent grip, and then drew the zip fastening sharply down.

Kong Hao lay lifeless, his skin pale and mottled, his once hateful eyes now somehow appeared to be at peace, it *was* over.

It wouldn't be long before the Terminal would be back to normal. In a few hours time you'd have never known an incident had ever taken place. The TV Cameras would be gone and today's news that was headlines in the newspapers local, tabloid and broadsheets would become tomorrow's fish and Chip wrappers.

FORTY FOUR

Oscar and McGovern sat in the busy and buoyant McCaffrey's bar mulling over the successful case that they had just cracked.

McGovern took a crumpled tissue out of his pocket, blew his nose, and took a large gulp of his well earned pint of Guinness. "So, the betting scams were just a front to some kind of competition then, a bit like a triad X Factor in a way"! they both laughed.

McGovern handed Oscar a shot glass full of whiskey "Drink this, you've earned it."

Oscar downed it in one, cringing. The fire in his throat felt surprisingly good. He put the shot glass to one side taking a sip from his pint as McGovern took another swig of his Guinness, and wiped the froth from his top lip."

Oscar leaned in closely, "I suppose you're pleased Ann Gatsby's here now. Saves you having to write out the big report for Crammond. I can do our stuff if you want, tie up the loose ends, that is unless you've already done it"? Oscar wasn't hopeful that McGovern had.

"Would you, son that would be so kind of you, besides it'll help you, give you the experience for when you become an inspector."

"Not for a while yet sir, I'm quite happy just being your bitch"!

They laughed and took another gulp of their drinks and they were joined by Felicity Somerton.

Stanley Scott was weaving his way through the crowds towards them, holding aloft two overflowing pint pots. Scott keenly shared some news he'd received as he sat at the table and rubbed his wet fingers dry with a napkin, "Just spoken to Gatsby, she's definitely staying on and she wants me back in Newcastle permanently like, as part of her team so this is a double celebration, this round's on me."

Scott took their orders and headed back towards the bar. Oscar noticed that Felicity Somerton looked quite tired and drawn, "Well Fliss, how does it feel to get your first case solved then"?

Felicity smiled, "I hope they all are not going to be as intense and draining as this one was, it was some case to be my first, my emotions are all over the place."

Oscar stared into her tired eyes,"It certainly was, I can think of few things in this life that matter as much as emotions, you did well though, holding them together and McGovern would probably never admit it, but you did very well. It was you who put the name of Michael Yin back in the frame and that was the name Hoa was using."

Stan Scott returned with the tray of drinks, he almost tipped it up as he tried to find room on the small round table "So what about the rest of the so called seven stars then? What happened to them"?

Oscar told them what he'd managed to find out "Well only one of them made it back. They were all top Red Poles, they had been picked from a pool of thousands. They were the most fierce and deadly members in the Gan-Yin, each one wanted to be the boss. The gathering was supposed to be them all making it back to Hong Kong for an election, the end game if you like, but as I said only one made it, as far as we know anyway. They had to prove themselves as being worthy leaders."

Stan Scott took a large gulp of his Guinness "So we know who their new Dragon Head will be then"?

"Yes, the Red Pole who was based in Italy, forgetting his name, I think it was that ugly one, you know, sir, the one with the face only his mother could love."

McGovern, for once could remember his name "Ah yes, Sun Jian Minger, that's his name, he probably would never have made it without the help of the Tacconi family who run Naples, Sicily and most of southern Italy."

"I'm impressed sir that you almost remembered his name correctly."

"I'm not just a pretty face you know"! McGovern placed his drink on an already stained beer mat.

"Have to agree there sir."

McGovern knew all about the Tacconi family, "So he got help from the old mafiosa ehh?, they got him off the mainland to Sicily and then on to a boat. I'm sure they think he could be a useful contact but they don't realise that very soon it will be the Gan-Yin running Naples and not the Tacconi family."

Oscar raised his glass, "Anyway, Gong hey Fat Choy."

"What, you going mad son"?

Oscar placed his elbows on the table and leaned in towards McGovern. "Gong hey Fat Choy," its happy New Year in Chinese, and tomorrow is Chinese New Year"!

The four detectives all raised their glasses, not unlike the musketeer's swords as Stan Scott gave the toast "All for one and sod the rest."

McGovern, Slugging at his beer, finished his pint with a final glug and loud belch and spotted someone entering the bar. "Hey look over there, it's that bird from the Football Club, and she's waving at you."

Oscar looked across to the entrance of the bar. Kim Deehan had just walked through the door and was heading over towards them. She saw Oscar and instantly her face brightened.

She smiled as she approached their table. She was a woman who knew what she wanted and this time had gone all out to get it. "I was just sitting in my apartment with a bottle of wine for company watching the news and saw that congratulations are in order. Half a bottle later I decide to phone you to tell you well done and your Grandfather answers and tells me your down here, So, after I finished the other half I felt it might be a good idea to come down and congratulate you in person, after all I'm sick and tired of waiting for you to ring me and ask me for a drink, thought I would just take the bull by the horns and come and find you."

McGovern lazily rose from his chair, belched loudly, farted and had a stretch " Well, not wanting to play the Gooseberry, I think I'll head off and get something to eat, Felicity, Stan, you can join me if you want, my treat."

He hadn't seen Ann Gatsby come into the pub. "No Jim, it will be *my* treat for my new team."

Kim Deehan offered some advice "There's an excellent Chinese restaurant just around the corner, they do takeaway as well."

McGovern held up both his hands, "No offence Pet, but I think we'll go for an Indian's."

McGovern had, for once, made them all laugh with his excellent pun. Stan Scott threw back his head and poured the remainder of his drink down his grateful throat. He rose to his feet as McGovern, Felicity and Ann Gatsby bid farewell to Oscar and Kim and headed towards the exit, and then through the doors into the ice cold Tyneside Street.

Oscar turned to Kim "Drink"?

"Wow wee Detective Smiles, I thought you were never going to ask, I'll have what you're drinking."

Kim finger combed her hair away from her eyes, Her drink arrived, Oscar smiled as he handed it over.

Taking a tiny sip from her drink which seemed to barely touch her lips Kim let the silence hang between them for a few seconds before speaking, "Are you sure you don't want to go with your work colleagues"?

"No, to be honest I'm sick of the sight of them, I'd much rather be here with you."

Kim smiled, "Well, This is a special occasion, I'm glad I came." clinking her glass against his,

"*Special Occasion*"? Oscar appeared somewhat puzzled.

"We'll, this *is* our first proper date isn't it."

"I suppose it is, so, where do we go from here then"? Kim winked in an alcohol induced forwardness "Well, my apartment on the Quayside is only five minutes away in a cab; I've got a nice warm fire, comfortable surroundings and another bottle of wine."

Oscar's face reddened slightly, but the thought excited him. A little flustered he awkwardly began to babble on about what he knew with regard to where Kim's flat was and the new housing developments on the Quayside. "I remember reading at the time about the estate regeneration fund that would allow property developers and builders to provide wonderful new homes for existing residents and radically improve the quality of housing in many neglected communities."

Kim Deehan put her elbows on the table and placed her chin on her hands as she stared into his eyes while fluttering her eyelashes at him, he tried to ignore her. He mumbled on shyer than ever. She rather liked him that way even less confident of himself than she had imagined.

He stammered as he continued, "Th Th They wanted to create welcoming neighbourhoods in which people aspire to live all across the North east. I'm told many of the old buildings dated back to the fifties and some even pre-war and it was high time that they received a new lease of life. The developers applied for the funding and got building. The Quayside was no exception. They look very nice from the outside, however I hear there a lot more spacious than expected as you'd expect them to be rather small as a lot of these new apartment types that are being built so quickly by developers____",

Kim interrupted; she put down her glass that she'd stopped short of her lips, she moved forward, quickly grabbed him by the lapels of his waist coat, pulled him towards her and kissed him full on the lips making him grin broadly as he at last shut up with his nervous babbling.

Oscar, at last relaxed as Kim placed her head on his shoulder. "What are you doing tomorrow then Oscar Smiles"?

"Nothing much, we've been given the rest of the week off, I was thinking of going with Buster down to the beach."

"Buster? Who's Buster"?

"Oh You'll find out soon enough, do you want to come with us"?

"Sure, that sounds great; I'll phone the Football club in the morning, no home game this week so it's going to be pretty quiet."

"So that's another date then"?

"Suppose it is, if you say so."

"So, Kim, what's your address? Where do I pick you up from then, tomorrow"?

"We'll. Once we've finished our drinks, I'll show you."

The two sat for a short while, and finished their drinks. The music at McCaffrey's was getting louder, the pub was filling up, and the live band began to play their final set.

Oscar looked out of the window. He saw lots of people wandering from pub to pub, heading for night clubs, taxi ranks and kebab shops, some headed towards the Dragon Gate area. Through the darkness he could see the large Chinese arch. The Chinese community were getting ready for the year of the Dragon, and for the Gan-Yin in Hong Kong, they were getting ready to crown their new Dragon Head, but thanks to the efforts of the Tyneside CID department it was never going to be Kong Hoa.

Kim finished her drink and pushed her glass to the centre of the table. "Better go and phone that taxi".

As Oscar stared into Kim's eyes he had only one thing on his mind. *Better not forget his Grandads tin of beans and the packet of toilet rolls.*

If you've enjoyed reading this book, please leave a review on Amazon. I read every review and they help new readers discover my books.

Andrew James Graham

Contact the author

Website

https://www.amazon.co.uk/Andrew-James-Graham/e/B08Q4D3RZY/ref=dp_byline_cont_pop_ebooks_1

Twitter- @AndrewGrahamJa1

Facebook- facebook.com/andrewjames.graham.94

Cover photo kindly provided by www.langshotphotography.com

Printed in Great Britain
by Amazon

85165183R00242